# BLOODWORK

## A DARK ROM-COM

## MELISSA DEMIREL

Black Rose Writing | Texas

ISBN: 978-1-68513-375-7
LIBRARY OF CONGRESS CONTROL NUMBER: 2023945320
PUBLISHED BY BLACK ROSE WRITING
www.blackrosewriting.com

Printed in the United States of America
Suggested Retail Price (SRP) $21.95

Cover art and design by Matthew Demirel

*Bloodwork* is printed in Garamond Premier Pro

*As a planet-friendly publisher, Black Rose Writing does its best to eliminate unnecessary waste to reduce paper usage and energy costs, while never compromising the reading experience. As a result, the final word count vs. page count may not meet common expectations.

For my mother, Helen.
Thank you for teaching me about honesty, friendship, respect,
the beauty of optimism, the power of love in every single one of its forms,
and for showing me the importance of keeping promises.

# BLOODWORK

# CHAPTER ONE

# THE NIGHT

*It's a fucking sin to have to kill people all by yourself. The weight, the pressure of the cleanup that inevitably interferes with the high afterwards. Everyone likes eating; no one likes washing the dishes.*

Unless you *do* like washing the dishes. In which case, you're probably sick in the head. Sicker even than me.

Eating surrounded by people you care about, people who care about you in return—it's a special thing. Even washing the dishes with such people could be just as special.

I liked doing both all by myself. And then I was just *okay* with doing both all by myself. Till...well, recently.

*I know, I know:*

*Then just don't kill people in the first place, you fucking idiot. Isn't that a sin all on its own, anyway?*

That's what other people would most likely say—if I ever talked to them for longer than half an hour, if I even told them about my separate and secret nightlife, if they cared enough the way I could, the way I might if they let me or inspired me to.

But I'd like to at least have half of all the fun in the world if I can't have it all completely. I don't *have* to kill anybody, but I enjoy it so much, it might as well be a sort of nightly task driven by my small acid soul, if I even have what other people would call a "soul." I consider killing bad, annoying, idiotic people to be only half a sin. Just the good one-half.

Nothing is really a sin when you don't have religion, anyway. Just about everything tastes a little sweeter when all you believe in is yourself. Still, I like those words, the way they sound when solitude dares to consume me in a bad way instead of the occasional good way, and the way they taste when I say them to some god-fearing, me-fearing asshole. The words: Sin. Soul. Blood sacrifice—the thing that no real god except for the killer requires.

But, after some time, that sweetness can get...sour. Lonely. And killing people *alone*? For a people-person, it can make the nice night so much darker. For a people-person who kills people? A loner, an introvert who, deep down, wishes to summon an old outgoing energy from a previous life, who wishes to socialize, if only the right person would let him? It can make this kind of lifestyle maddening, sometimes, amidst all the magnificence.

*Sometimes. Only sometimes, for some time now. Lately...*

Lately, the loneliness has been gnawing at me like a rabid dog that just won't let me go. Lately, I've been craving something other than the sight of spilt blood. At the beginning of all this, even the smallest thing got my blood pumping, got me excited, made me feel elevated, encouraged, eager to continue a streak or two or three till, eventually, a few years passed by and the night turned into my only true friend. But, now, these days, it feels like something is missing in this solitary life of mine. A humanity in me that I used to have and now miss.

I used to speak to people so naturally, like it was the easiest thing, barely an endeavor and more of an electricity that just surged out of me whenever I wanted. But time passed. I saw other people as they were, assumed the worst in them, and...even when I wasn't assuming the worst in them, they revealed their worst selves to me, anyway, like they thought I deserved to see it or like they weren't doing any thinking to begin with.

People became pawns, passionless and so full of poison it felt contagious. It *was* contagious. Blame it on whatever you want: lack of childhood discipline, untapped trauma, untamed tempers, technology, so on and so forth. People became dead as they lived.

Thinking that I'm doing them a favor when I choose them helps if I ever happen to feel *off* about my own little hobby, if I ever hesitate or feel just a little too *human*. Human, the way human beings have forgotten to feel today, it seems. The only time I feel off is when I see the potential crawl out of someone's eyes right as they show me who they really are. It's an awful moment for the person trying to penetrate my bubble, but I can pick it out every time, the coming disappointment. It's like foreshadowing. It's the moment I start debating how I'll end them.

So, over the years, before I did what I do best these days, the more I became exposed to the truth of humanity, the less excited I felt to meet people, to call upon strangers, to invite them into my life. I stopped being so...talkative. Outgoing. I erased that side of me in order to see most of the world for what it was: an empty grave, waiting to be filled.

Off my rose-colored glasses came, off my sunglasses, off the smile on my face. The night approached me with the truth, and I absorbed reality with an open mind and open arms, death in one hand and life in the other.

People suck, and that's the gist of things. That's what I learned the hard way, by stepping out from under my reclusive rock when I was just a teenager. Well into my twenties, failed relationship after failed friendship and so on, I discovered that socializing and partying and having a nice conversation is all fun until people do what *they* do best: betray, disobey, treat you like prey.

So, yes, I put an end to all the socializing and partying and having a nice conversation every now and then. I started to give rude, cruel people a taste of their own medicine. I tried, and I'm still trying, and it feels better than being betrayed, disobeyed, treated like prey—feels better than letting the world step on you without any consequences.

And I guess it all really started with one key betrayal quite some time ago:

My girlfriend cheated on me when I was in my early twenties—dead ex-girlfriend now, of course. She was my first kill, my first taste of what a bitch most people are at their core and how good it feels to get rid of such moronic monsters. The dumbass she cheated on me with was my second. After that, I knew I needed to lie low and generally live a "hit and run"—"*kill* and run"—kind of life in order to survive and simply be happy.

I *used* to be a people-person. The sickest part is, deep down, I am *still* a people-person. I still want what I want, and it goes beyond seeing stupid people die; it goes beyond looking down with knowing at their little, irrelevant, frightened faces as I finish them off. What I honestly, truly want, more than anything, is to have company. But I *can't* have company because I can't seem to come across anyone who is actually deserving of that company.

It's a sad cycle that I feel locked within. In the moment, when the kill is being performed, or the minutes earlier as I think out how to take this particular life, it never really feels like a cycle.

But it's like alcohol, I suppose. Only when you're drinking are you truly at peace, without a care or a thought in the world. It's the time you spend pouring the evening's first glass, and the time you spend waking up and trying to piece your messy night of mistakes together, when you realize that it is a cycle you've both intentionally and accidentally drowned yourself in.

It's an almost addictive cycle that you adore and can't get enough of and have now become accustomed to, and, of course, it isn't without its cons. *Especially as of late.*

Because I always end up alone, so alone. *Too* alone.

And everyone always, expectedly, ends up a disappointment. Begging for that sweet touch of the knife.

*Like little Lucy here.*

The tiniest reflective sparkle from the streetlight nearby bounces off the blood covering the right side of her face where I've bashed her head in with the empty bottle of whiskey she stupidly brought along on our little walk. She probably thought we were walking to some nearby city motel room where she could drunkenly fuck my sober brains out, like the one I'm currently inhabiting.

But I'm not interested in mindless sex, especially not *drunk* mindless sex whether I'm the one who's drunk or not—in this case, I would've been the abuser who took advantage of some alcohol-absorbing lady, which would've been more morally wrong than murdering her. Besides, I always make sure to have a clear head when I know I just might have a night of blood ahead of me.

I haven't been interested in people in that way for quite some time. I've been celibate, I guess you could say. Not because of religion or anything—which, again, I'm not into, anyway—but because I feel better when I'm making myself feel good and because people, these days, aren't good for much, least of all successfully pleasuring others' bodies or even their souls, because that requires a genuine selflessness that has been sucked out of most of them, *so many* of them, over the years.

Poor Lucy just had no idea about who she was trying to seduce. Lucy annoyed the wrong man this evening.

Lucy was actually somewhat nice at the bar a few blocks away. *At first.* Before her mouth apparently found a will of its own. I guess she just saw that I was alone, sitting on one of the stools like more of a sock puppet than a person, with an empty glass in my hand and a just-as-empty soul and empty stools next to me, one at my right and one at my left, and emptiness surrounding me like an echo of all my inner screeching, solitude-soaked sufferings.

There are times when I would like to *stay* alone within any kind of environment I initially find myself in, times when I would prefer the ache of loneliness over the attack of disappointment. And, as soon as a disappointment is either too drunk or too alone to fight me back, I'd follow them out and into a more private space and the night would bear witness to the end of that person's miserable life.

These people are typically a waste of space. I can see it in their behavior, the way they interact with me or anyone else nearby. They're the kind of people who get a kick out of pissing other people off. Sadists, sociopaths, psychopaths. I'm no better, but at least I'm making sure they don't bother anyone else, and the only person who gets to bother these suckers is me.

Lucy, loud and livid Lucy who was already lifeless even when she was under the bar lights and breathing, started talking to me. Pretty randomly. Quite unfortunate for her. If she hadn't blabbered so much, so meaninglessly, so maniacally, someone else would've definitely taken her place on this night. I wasn't *expecting* to kill her tonight, though I suppose I rarely ever expect to kill anyone before the night has officially started.

Maybe she'd been stood up; that could be part of why she decided to approach me. Maybe she just thought I was attractive enough. Maybe she, too, was lonely, though in more superficial ways than I was, a sad comparison. I'm still not too sure what her deal was, nor do I care much.

But, anyway, she just started talking. And once she started, she couldn't stop. And once she couldn't stop, I started thinking about cutting her throat. And once I started thinking about that, I couldn't stop. And, so, since I couldn't stop, I had to start thinking of ways to turn my deafening little dreams into my relentless reality for the night.

It's a shame you never really know who you're speaking with, who you're involving yourself with, till it's too late. That goes both ways, for both the predator and the prey.

"Hey, there," she squeaked, a little too happy at that hour, a little too chirpy for my taste. "You alone tonight?" She propped herself up on the barstool next to mine. She wasn't acting subtle at all. Which I wasn't a big fan of. I enjoy a secret or two from another person, a silence that reveals so little and yet so much, like a sinkhole.

I nodded. Tapped and tapped the edge of my glass with a suddenly very restless and animated and anxious finger. "Yeah."

"Oh. Well, same here. I'm Lucy."

She waited for me to tell her my name. I sighed and told her the truth. I'd lie, sometimes, just for fun, but it's not like anyone I ever met and inevitably grew tired of was ever going to be capable of doing anything with the very-real information I could give them. And so, I gave Lucy some of that useless, very-real information: "Hi, Lucy. I'm Timothy."

"Timothy." She nodded, took my name in with a great weight upon her lips and within her mouth, as if it was supposed to be the name of her future husband. "Want to...maybe not be so alone together? I mean, you don't...mind if I sit right here next to you, right?"

I shook my head. I did mind, but then she, in her slightly already-buzzed state, started saying nice things to me. That's what I mean when I say that she was "somewhat nice" at first. It got to me a little, I guess, being sweet-talked by an objectively good-looking young woman like that. I'm stupid for letting it, but I wouldn't be human if I didn't. It's all just fake, though. That I knew, deep down. None of it was real. None of it *is* real. She didn't really mean anything she was telling me. It was all just to benefit her in the end, sexually or however else she wanted to win. We all just want to win in this game we call life, in these levels we call passing years with the days peeling away like dry glue, the present plastered on us like dry blood, the future unpredictable and unprecedented and as unforgivable as the power I hold in my hands next to every idiot I come across.

"Forgive me for maybe being a little too honest here, or speaking out of place, but…it really doesn't make much sense to me, how a nice-looking guy like you ends up alone at this time of night." *Because I want to be. Until the night swallows me whole and the moon watches and winks.* Still, I couldn't help but grin just a bit at her empty words.

But, of course, it didn't last, those surface-level niceties, the "nice enough"-ness. Because, before long, she was showing her true colors and my imagination ran free like melting ice—as it always did whenever the darkness outside and the darkness within me grew till it suffocated me. And then I was coming up with ways to carry out the side effect of simply being irritated.

Her third empty glass came slamming down on the long, wooden bar table. "And this town," she slurred. "Ugh, just—oh, fuck this place, y'know? I keep tellin' my girlfriends, let's leave this town, this city, let's just…even this bar, this bar that just—just keeps expecting sad people to…occupy it and…cry in it and…" She gave me a look then. A mischievous and mindless look which sealed her fate for the night. "And, you and me, huh? What about you and me? Why don't we just—just…why don't we just fuckin'— why don't we just leave this bar, right now?"

Of course, I agreed. Followed her out into the nothingness. The sweet, still night. She kept slurring, whiskey bottle swaying loosely in her hand, and she kept stumbling over her own two feet in the loosely lighted, lonesome streets. Her words were the usual complaints that came out of most drunken fools disheartened with the reality of their lives, the kind of reality that destroyed their dreams of what it all might be like—living.

So, I relieved them of their lifeless living. Tonight, I relieved lackluster Lucy.

Maybe she started thinking just a bit more than the alcohol was letting her—which was barely—when she turned around and maybe caught me putting my gloves on in the dark and maybe even caught a crimson glint in my eye subtly lit with cruel intent. Because an awkward smile curled upon her crooked, fading face and, as I led her back into a tight dead-ended alley, she asked me, "Oh, now, you're not gonna hurt me now that we're all alone, are you?"

"No, I'm not," I told her. "I promise."

And then I lunged forward, grabbed the bottle from her hand, smashed it against her face a few adrenaline-pumping times, and watched her go cold—not in an instant but in a drawn-out minute as smooth as a drying river or an emptying sink—and felt hot as a newly lit match as everything she knew ended with me.

This endlessly repetitive roller coaster I've put myself on and strapped myself in only to find the itty-bitty itch of emotional pain in the midst of my pursuit of peace, my search for shared power—this loop, this *trap*, of my own making makes me yearn for something lost, something that would feel much more real and much more beautiful than causing even the cruelest deaths once in a blue bloodmoon. And tonight, the moon above is more than teasing, like a glowing and smiling beast with sharp shiny teeth. I don't want out, don't want the blood on my hands to fade. I want an addition, something new, something to pile upon the foundation of my already hard-earned tranquility.

I want what I can't have, the same way everyone else does when they feel stuck, when the smallest voice of ungratefulness whispers into even the most seemingly content ear. I want what I *shouldn't* have.

Killers aren't supposed to crave company, right? No, not really, least of all at night when they prefer to kill whatever company they could've had, could've kept. The cons of the people I am misfortunate enough to meet keep outweighing their pros—the cons consume these creatures of cursed company like cracks in the concrete. They all end up way too flawed for me to let go. Also, killers aren't supposed to bite down hard on that most human side of them just to give the inhuman side what it wants, what it needs. Most psychopaths I read about or know of aren't supposed to have a human side, period.

And blood, all this *blood*. Blood from mouths that aren't worthy of speaking, blood from limbs that aren't deserving of an embrace. An *embrace*.

I haven't really hugged anyone in years. A hug would be nice, but one that isn't fake or just skin-deep—one that doesn't come from a two-faced person, or someone whose job it is to give you a blowjob or a hug, or from a sex doll or artificial intelligence that only mirrors real movement and emotion like a shameless shallowness, a shadow where the shine of the moon should be. Something warm, something that is woven deep into the fine layers of muscle and tissue and bone and sits with you long after that person has said goodbye, something that wavers and wanes in your mind and that you think of when you least expect it. Something *true*. Honest.

*It's not a sin to kill people or to kill people alone. Not really. It's a sin to* be alone.

Me, I always end up dreaming, begging the night for that sweet touch of the post-kill high.

But if I wasn't alone, if I had someone to at the very least help me clean up after myself, someone who wasn't so awful of a person, someone who didn't deserve to die, someone who honestly liked me as a person and who liked doing this as much as I did...then the high wouldn't be so short-lived. Having someone by my side would surely benefit me in more ways than one.

I look at the moon, take in the night. The night, still my only true friend with which the heat of the high is shared.

Sometimes, like tonight, when this loneliness of mine is still lapping at my lips like a sandpaper kiss, I wonder, desperately, if there's anyone out there, *anyone at all*, who thinks of the night in at least almost the same way I do.

Yeah, nothing is really a sin when you don't believe in religion, anyway. And, yeah, just about everything tastes a little sweeter when all you believe in is yourself. I just can't help but wish there was more. Maybe I've been loving this too long for it to last the way I thought it would, the way I wanted it to. I just wish I could taste something else, too. Company. I'd have something, someone, more to believe in. It wouldn't just be *me* anymore.

But I have to remind myself. This is just a dream. Out of my reach, so darkly distant. A fantasy. In the real world, not every Clyde gets his Bonnie. Hannibal doesn't find his Clarice, or his Will. Out here, the villain ought to stop wishing for someone capable of being just as vile to fly into his life like some chaos-seeking hero. In the real world, the monster is isolated and must stay that way in order to keep playing the monster, keep playing the role it loves being in. Monsters don't get partners.

And, besides, don't partners usually do some betraying, too? Engage in some kind of sabotage? Which, in turn, becomes self-sabotage, in one way or another. Partners are too much to take care of, so hard to keep in check, right? Wouldn't having someone here also threaten to destroy me the exact same way it would claim to complete me? Even the most supposedly trustworthy ones could turn on you and are just as worthy of suspicion if they're committing countless crimes just like you all the time, whenever they want, whenever they can.

*Yeah. Fuck that.*

I leave Lucy in the dark, leave her tucked away neatly in just another place that it'll take people days or weeks to find her. I'll be long gone by then, a ghost without a trail, in another town, another city, with another identity. Some new area that people will drunkenly complain about again and again and again in some other old, stained, filthy, passively populated bar. People who don't want to know me and then suddenly people who do want to know me who I, unfortunately, regret getting to know.

*Yeah. So, I'm just alright on my own. All on my own. I'm okay. I'm fine. I promise.*

# CHAPTER TWO

# PARTNER WANTED

It doesn't matter what you do. You could be a painter, a chef, a teacher, an athlete, a scientist, a motivational speaker, a stripper, a thief. A serial killer. Eventually, the routine gets to you. It *will* get to you. Just wait and watch and see the moon wink.

*Something* about the routine gets to you and impacts you in ways you never thought possible. If you stay serene with the routine and if it suffices, if it suffocates all the sadness inside you even after years, then you should consider yourself to be quite lucky. Grateful, normal, glittering gold without the green of greed.

But if you're like me, restless and reddened under the moonlight, something about even the most perfected and blazing passions will start to bother you after a while, like a blossom melting under rain and tears and sweat and a storm of teeth and fears.

*I am not alright. Fine. Okay.* This could be something close to a mid-life crisis. Call it a quarter-and-a-half-life crisis. Maybe I'll start putting up posters in every new town, just to see what happens. And crazy people are everywhere, those who want to get rid of the routine hiding amongst the normals who relish in it. But when you're crazy yourself, you can't be too careful. I wouldn't want to find myself paired with someone who just so happens to out-crazy my crazy.

Maybe I'll even "get with the times" and create a social media account and start posting something like: "HELP WANTED."

*No, no, no, wait. Not "help." It should sound more...inclusive. Intimate. Like I'm looking for my other half. Which, in a way, I am.*

"PARTNER WANTED. Thirty-two-year-old lonely nomad serial killer seeking partner in crime. Doesn't want to kill alone anymore. Meeting spot: local bar at 8:00 PM next Tuesday. Every Tuesday and Thursday night until I find the perfect partner. We'll act normal, have a few drinks and snacks, and then go out and stalk and slice into a few unsuspecting fools." That's what the paper posters would say, too.

But, with my luck, the fool will probably be my partner, not our prey. And so, the fool will inevitably end up being my partner-turned-prey.

But what if I did? What if, just once, I did something incredibly silly? Incredibly, desperately, human. What if I put up a poster, or what if I made a social media account—later to be deleted, of course, both the post or blog and the account—and what if I made my desires known, the way everyone else does these days, out and about on the streets or online? Maybe someone will read my words, take them seriously, take *me* seriously—they'll be looking for a good time out in the dark and they'll simply be insane enough to give me a chance.

I wonder whether I'll be insane enough to give *them* a chance.

People are wild enough to blab about every single one of their icky and icy intentions, shameless enough to make sure the whole world knows it's them who needs: a date or just a good fuck or some drugs or a therapy session, maybe three, related to their mommy issues or a Pilates instructor. So why can't I just do it? Why shouldn't I?

Maybe not online, actually—not with a public account, welcoming access from anyone and everyone from anywhere and everywhere. But maybe with just one poster, one old-fashioned poster taped to a pole or maybe the wall or door of a building around here, and not a few posters, just to mitigate any potential risks. Just one.

I can. I should. I will. Why not? At least it'll be one little interesting change in this nightly habit. This rude and red and radiant routine of mine that I have simply required more and more from for quite some time.

I am losing my mind. And to say that about a mind that society would regard as already lost...

*Well. If I'm going to really lose my mind or go even crazier...I guess it's best to do it the right way, which is to do it all the way through. Lose it* all the way through.

• • •

Watching the printer bleed out my one most persistent pursuit in an already peaceful but painfully lonesome life with the beauty of death every night—on the one hand, it makes me a little anxious and sweaty, but on the other, I feel like a child that's about to buy a brand-new toy. Well, maybe not really like a child that's about to buy a brand-new toy—that sounds a bit superficial and possessive, and if I had the perfect partner, I don't think I'd ever view them in such a surface-level, skin-deep, empty way. Really, I feel oddly optimistic, maybe even a little delusional. All in all, I feel stupid but steady and excited.

I've never felt this way before.

Well, actually, I sort of *have*—during my first several kills over my first few years of no longer trusting people even though I still so badly wanted to. I *want* to see the good in people, the things that let me see myself in them and let them see themselves in me and the things that can let us all be good pals and maybe even more than that with time—but people have never let me, and people have never given me time, and so I haven't been able to give them much time, either, let them go on living as the assholes they are. During my first several kills, I felt the rush, and even to this day, I still do. But, again, that rush just hasn't been the same.

The last time I felt this way without feeling so lonely and sad and grumpy before and after the high of the moment, the blood being spilt, without these current thoughts of "What if I wasn't so lonely anymore?" and "Maybe I'll find the one"—that was a while ago, maybe a year or two.

I feel almost...filled to the brim with nostalgia, now that this feeling has returned and isn't going away and is driving me towards a possibility of newness. What a beautiful brim, what a fresh and fruitful feeling. I feel *good*. And even if no one suitable contacts me, if no one contacts me at all, and I end up ultimately feeling nothing but disappointment in the end, well, at least I tried, right?

I pay for the paper that I printed with that polite everyday exchange of "I'm good, thanks, and how are you?" that completely contrasts the words on the page—the cashier is dead-eyed and doesn't seem to care enough about his job or the world around him to notice or believe the words I've written, and maybe he thinks it's for a movie or experimental project or maybe he just doesn't give a shit, which, honestly, conjures just a teardrop-shaped kiss of doubt in me, doubt that I'll discover what I need, who I deserve. And, even so, I can't help but leave the local printing and copying store with, I dare say, the smallest skip in my step.

*I'm* the fool here. Not my potential partner, not my prey. Me, the primary predator.

And, still, I go on. I pass the time, use as little as possible of my dead family's money—*I didn't kill them, I promise*—to grab some lunch at a nearby hotdog stand. And while I munch on the bland ketchup-covered meat and buns, wishing it at least had garlic aioli or sprinkles of pickled garlic relish on top or a side of garlic-cheese fries, I think about what my ideal partner would be like, staring blankly out into nothing, not seeing all the individuals who pass the street or drive on by.

Whoever this person is, the most important thing would be for us to be blissfully like-minded, extremely similar in belief and banter and brain, similar to the point of solid sameness. Stereotypically, it'd probably be a man like me, or at least someone who defines themselves as a man or manly—statistically, men are more likely than women to kill others and much more likely than women to be serial killers. But it just doesn't even matter, whoever they see themselves as, however they view themselves.

Because I'm not looking for someone to hold and cherish for the rest of my life—though that would be nice, too, and I certainly wouldn't complain if that's what I happened to get besides a fellow killer. I'm not looking for someone who'd be by my side at *all* times, but just at night—though, again, if that's what I ended up having, I wouldn't mind. I'm not looking for a significant other or future spouse or someone who could be my best friend or found family or brother from another mother or sister from another mister or whatever else kind of close relationship or friendship it is that normal people look for.

I'm looking for a partner in crime, and whatever relationship or friendship stems from that would probably be okay with me, as long as however we feel about each other is returned on both sides and as long as we're right for each other and as long as we make sense together and as long as we get along just fine while we're killing.

As I finish my lunch, I start thinking about the printed paper-sized poster that sits rolled up in my backpack along with tools sharp enough to kill, knives of different makes and sizes and all—but no guns, nothing with recognizable or traceable bullets and nothing that'd make noises louder than human screams, noises loud enough to attract attention. I think about where I should put the poster up.

It has to be a place where the ideal partner might stop by, might catch a glimpse of my summons. Where do most psychopaths prowl, both during the day and at night?

Me, I frequent local bars, specifically at night, but a bar is too risky since *any* kind of unpredictable crazy can be found there. The bars I choose are specifically those underrated or badly rated ones on Yelp that barely anyone goes to unless they're simply strange enough to do so. If someone's going to find me, they'll meet me at such an almost-abandoned bar, where we can quietly be ourselves before making the night ours, but a bar won't be the place I call out for them. No, I have to summon them from someplace else— the poster has to be hung someplace else.

I realize now that my dream partner has to be someone with a steady job, a stable income. Someone who fits in with society in ways that it's always been hard for me to do. This is where we'll differ, but our differences will benefit us both. I can hide in their shadow. In a way, I can *be* their shadow as much as they become mine, as much as we amicably allow each other to be. To simply *be*.

I have no job—I can't have one because of what I do and because of the background checks and because of all my moving around—and all the money that the family had left that I now have left will honestly probably last me for approximately only a few more years. I might be dead or arrested by then, anyway.

And I'm now understanding that I feel so alone that I don't even feel too fazed when thinking about my own death—I've taken so many lives, anyway, brought upon so much death on my own, even if I felt, every time, that it was deserved and justified—or when thinking about a life prison sentence—maybe I'd even make a friend or two in prison unlike out here in the world, though that might be hard, too, making a proper selection in between all the chaos in jail.

But *since* I have no job and *since* I can't afford to take care of a whole other person besides myself, my partner will have to be someone who is independent. Maybe I probably shouldn't be too picky, but when you kill people to feel joy but also because you believe that idiots and assholes simply shouldn't get to live, maybe being picky is exactly what is necessary. If I am going to go hunting with someone, they've *got* to be perfect in my eyes, shining like the moon, maybe even shining like the sharp sun even when it is dark out.

So, I need to put the poster up someplace where there's...well, work. Thriving careers.

What kinds of careers do psychopaths tend to have?

I look it up on the Internet, typing and scrolling on my smartphone, and I'm quickly met with this list:

CEOs. Lawyers. Media hosts on the radio or on the television. Doctors, specifically surgeons. Salespeople. People of authority. Cops. Journalists. And on and on. Nothing I've ever had to do a day in my privileged, little, private but pitiful, peaceful but poisonous life.

Some of the most genuine, kindest people pursue these careers. And among them, hide the demons, trying their hardest to blend in so seamlessly with the angels.

So, what about psychopaths who might tend to get a kick out of actually killing others with their bare hands?

My mind immediately jumps to lawyers. They know they law—they'd know just as well how to avoid it, how to take advantage of it. The same thing could be said about cops, sheriffs, all those sly, seasoned police officers.

And doctors. Specifically surgeons. They always get their hands dirty, don't they? Their gloved hands are always soaked with someone else's blood. One wrong move, one wrong snip, and they could take someone's life either accidentally or intentionally, with or without the help or knowledge or acknowledgment of the surrounding nurses. They'd know enough about human anatomy to do just as much harm, instead of lending help, outside of the hospital environment, too.

I've heard so many stories about cops and police officers and lawyers and doctors who commit crimes during work or outside of it just because they feel like they can, just because they're under the impression that they're so powerful that they can get away with just about anything—until the world catches up to them and they find that they can't. Because they're simply still human. Simply just too human.

The media calls these stories "real-life horror stories." I find them fascinating. The stories, and the sickly smart minds behind them.

I wish I could study one of these so-called "corrupt criminals," observe these cocky geniuses who eventually get in over their heads. I wish I could have a cup of coffee and a conversation with someone like that, pluck them out of their everyday lives, their daily jobs, and dangle them in front of me, in between my two fingers, and ask them if there is anything about the two of us that makes us close to one and the same, if I think I am worthy enough to be like them and if they think they are worthy enough to see themselves as similar to me, if we are worthy enough to let our inner beasts loose at night together.

But lawyers and cops and surgeons...their ego eventually evolves into a problem so potent that it echoes throughout everything they do like the stench of a rotting egg. Their hubris results in hell. Hells of their own making, so much more drastically destructive than the lonesome cycle I have created for myself.

Their habits are self-centered. There is nothing about the protection of the world in what they do, even if they seem to serve the best interests of society during their own running routines. They do not locate and lunge after assholes. They treat kind people and cruel people as if they are the same—and even though I am a cynic myself, it is clear, with all my loneliness and with this printed paper in my backpack and with my unyielding yearning for company, that I still know kind eyes, rose-colored eyes and caring eyes and eyes that mind their own business, when I see them. But these proud authoritative figures—they go after everyone and anyone alike and they think they can get away with more and more and more until they simply and suddenly no longer can.

Can I stop that from happening? I can't change a person, can't get them to deviate from their personality or from their set path like some therapist that isn't even getting paid. Can they stop themselves from going too far? Can I take this risk just to feel a little less empty and can I share control with someone else, someone I'd have to get to know first? Can they grow to be humble about what they do, the way I've always tried to be? For I feel that I am simply a mountain lion hiding amongst mice that could very well suddenly, against all my judgment and observation of behavior, turn out to be as monstrous as me, murderers disguised as the meek and the mindless.

I have always done what I feel like I have to do, and I have enjoyed it. But I'm not making sculptures from bodies and I'm not keeping any trophies from my kills—I'd hate to always have to carry pieces of dead idiots and smart-mouths around with me. I'm not overly joyful or ecstatic about the deaths I cause, except for when that death is about to take place or is taking place or has just, seconds ago, taken place.

I simply take in the momentary high as it is happening, as I am making it happen, and I revel at the power I've presented to no one and nothing other than the night and the moon. And then, I leave and go back to the other things that I deemed normal and that the public would also deem normal, things that fall under the umbrella of living and only include enjoying dipping fries into garlic sauce and having a cheap, red, refreshing, berry-flavored cocktail every now and then, without letting addiction become a part of the equation.

And *that* is the key, *always* the key: like an addict, I *have* trapped myself in my own cycle of killing and having to be lonely as a cold consequence of that, and I do love it—the killing, not the consequence—but, unlike an addict, when I do not encounter some rat worth killing, I do not go looking for one. I do not make it a nightly task unless it really has to be one. Rather, the rats happen to come looking for me, and they sign their own death warrant when they do.

And that is why I'm still here, taking the night for my own whenever I find that it is necessary. Because I do not exceed my stay. My grasp does not exceed my reach. I do not make a spectacle out of killing any more than those short few seconds and minutes allow.

It would be a dream to encounter some kind of psychopathic, secretly murderous lawyer or police officer or doctor who *isn't* clouded by their pride. Someone to collect the idiots and other ill-intended people with, and someone who'd leave genuine jewels of the earth alone, people who truly don't deserve it, like the homeless, cancer patients, the elderly. It seems like a stretch. An impossibility. But I have to try, even with all the risks and the potential disappointment. I have to feel better about my life, feel fulfilled, feel like only one half of a whole with that other half at arm's length.

I have to try, and I *do* have to go looking for a friend, a *real* friend.

Putting up my poster will be the first step.

•　•　•

I'm standing in front of the local law firm building closest to the hotdog stand I was just at. I've been somewhere in Chicago for the past few days, though the towns and cities and states always blur when life is just being lived and the night and the moon just wait and wane behind the clouds and waver, the only things to warm me up when another's arms and hands and understanding and support cannot do so.

I'm standing in front of the local law firm building in broad daylight, and everything feels wrong.

I have to sit on a nearby bench to collect my thoughts and digest my emotions.

The passing, flickering people running up and down the several steps, walking in and out of the building—the quick-paced people hit me as sharp and blaring as a heat wave while they constantly move till they're out of sight. They all look so busy, so hurried, *so fucking hurried*, so focused with their buttoned shirts tucked neatly into their pants, their black or beige or white or gray or cloud blazers matching their black or beige or white or gray or cloud trousers and shiny leather shoes.

There aren't many of them, these seemingly hardcore workers, just a few every now and then as the minutes fly by, but the way they come and go and come and go makes me sweat even though I'm sitting down and staring and even though I've got nothing on my mind except slaughter, nothing really concerning like having to defend an abuser or having to prove puny little minds of powerless points or...empty promises. If I was in there, handcuffed, I'd, as usual, break every vow that leaves my mouth.

I don't think I can trust someone who can turn around and pin all of hell on me with just a few words and just a few pieces of evidence if they wanted, if only to boost their careers, if only to be promoted from associate to partner in these firms.

I cannot trust a lawyer. Someone who'd be so meticulous, manipulative, calculated. Careful, which I'd admire, but careful to the point of it being a curse, to the point of annoyance. Especially if some, if not most, of our killings are going to be spontaneous. At least, that's how I'd want it to be. Affected and inspired only by rudeness and cruelty.

If my partner ends up having some longtime vendetta against someone else, something like that might be easy to trace. A passion fueled by that sort of personal fallout could lead to my partner's downfall if they follow the aftermath of that fallout long enough—and it could lead to my downfall, too. I'd get captured. But maybe, then, upon capture, I'd, again, find a better source of company behind bars. Or maybe I'd simply die.

I *cannot* have a lawyer for a partner. Not anyone whose entire career revolves around the law, anyone who is in that very specific position of power or taking authoritative action, anyone who particularly protects others from getting fucked over whether those people deserve it or not, while also fucking other people over, also whether they deserve it or not.

I am, after all, a serial killer with *standards*.

I immediately stand from the bench.

*Okay. So, no lawyers. No one with a gun or a deep and intimate knowledge of the law that could lead me away from the beauty of the night and the moon.*

So...who else? What kind of psychopath could I trust? Who would be alright with getting blood on their hands without giving me paranoia, without making me feel all kinds of petty or passive about my passion or, overall, pointless and powerless?

Someone who already gets blood on their hands on probably a daily basis—and without seeming to intend to do any actual harm, at least, according to the world. According to those who bite their nails and tremble and cry out in waiting rooms. Waiting for an answer. *Any* answer. The way I, too, would wait for the rest of my little life.

I have to get to the closest local hospital.

· · ·

The moon is ready to come out and so am I. People in scrubs start entering the hospital, getting ready for their night shifts. Victims enter with coughs or a limp in their leg. One in a wheelchair, someone else being carried in a man's arms. I watch from afar, from across the hospital parking lot, like the shadow I've always been. Seeking another shadow now, someone to hide in the dark with.

My fingers fidget with the tight strap of my backpack over my right shoulder as I move casually towards a utility pole behind the parking lot.

Since I do not believe in anything other than humane power and the honey-sweet, small hope that has sewn itself into me, I cannot pray. I can only wish. Dream. Believe that there is someone out there as sick and strange as me.

The backpack falls off my shoulder. I set it down on the ground and then look at the utility pole as if within it there hides the tiniest temple of some make-believe deity that listens to and serves serial killers. I stare and I wish. Dream. Believe. Look back at the quiet hospital building. Look back at the untouched pole.

I kneel before the pole like a faithful servant. I have always been faithless, but I now see that, against my better judgment, I would follow faith till my end if it would mean having a friend. An honest friend. All I want. All I've ever wanted. *A friend.*

I unzip my backpack. Take the poster out. The white of the paper shines so wickedly under the parking lot lights and the distant streetlights—and under the moonlight. So pretty, sometimes so pearl-white and other times like the cream-colored underbelly of a seashell. Sometimes, when the night sky has no moon, I mourn, just a little, and I feel a little darker inside. As I let my fingers roam across the printed poster, I think about how nice it would be to no longer mourn this lack of natural light when a partner with, hopefully, just as much light in their step and in their eyes and in their mind and in their heart could fill up the dark with me.

I reach into the backpack again and pull out some scotch tape, rip out about five pieces, one after another, and place the pieces on my left fingertips. I rise with the paper in my gentle, careful grasp, as if this poster is gold itself, one lost and lonely psychopath's advertised American Dream.

I place my special gold leaf, my summons, my innermost desires, my search, my simultaneous selflessness and selfishness, upon the utility pole, and take a deep breath as I start placing four of the pieces of tape on the four lengthy sides of the paper, before placing the fifth piece of tape in the right-hand corner for good measure. I'm not shaking, but my breath keeps coming out quite shakily, and as I kneel back down, I decide to rip out three more pieces of tape, and when I stand back up, I place those three pieces in the remaining three corners of the poster. Again, for good measure. I need this call to stick. For as long as I need to complete my little treasure hunt.

It's only then that I can take a small step back and stare at what I've written, try to take the words in, not as if I'm the creator but as if I'm just a passing stranger:

## PARTNER WANTED

Thirty-two-year-old lonely nomad serial killer seeking partner in crime.
Doesn't want to kill alone anymore.
Meeting spot: local bar at 8:00 PM next Tuesday.
I'll be the dark-haired guy sitting alone on one of the stools.
Every Tuesday and Thursday night until I find the perfect partner.
We'll act normal, have a few drinks and snacks, and then go out and stalk and slice into a few unsuspecting fools.

According to Waze, the nearest bar to the hospital is about a mile away. That's the "local bar" I'll be at. If whoever is reading this is smart, they'll figure that out and that's where they'll meet me. If they're not smart enough to figure it out, then I don't want them as my partner, anyway.

A doctor, I really might be able to trust. A doctor with some free time on their hands, a doctor who doesn't have to go off saving other people's lives—some, by chance, very worthless lives—during every waking second of their own. Maybe a doctor important enough to take some time off every now and then, more than a local hospital would allow but just enough for us to bond over blood.

It's obvious that a hospital is the kind of place where so many authoritative figures might find themselves, including police officers escorting injured criminals who'll be handcuffed while getting stitches. People who might see my poster and get very suspicious, people who *aren't* looking for a partner like me.

But I'm tired. So tired. At this point, I'd do anything, go anywhere, to find company, to find a friend. I'll leave my poster up here for the next three weeks. But, after three weeks, if I'm not dead or arrested by then, I'll move someplace else, to another city, another state, and select a new spot for my poster. Select a new space of surrender, a new stain for the revelation of the true nature of my plight.

• • •

I walk alone into the small motel room I'll simply have to keep staying at till I get out of this city. I walk alone and I sit alone and I sleep alone and I wake up alone and pass a day or two or three alone and I am always all alone. And, although the world would whisper in my ear that I've got no one to blame for that but myself, I'd argue that the world is actually the one to blame, at least until I see how the first Tuesday goes. And, until Tuesday, I've promised myself *no killing.*

That promise, of course, as it is with most or arguably even all of my promises, quickly goes out the window.

It's Monday, a few days now since I put up my poster, and my excitement is eating at me in much the same way that my loneliness did and still very much does. Both my excitement and my loneliness give me no rest, no residue from the momentary highs of weeks and kills before, no relaxation, no relief. No power. There will be no peace until tomorrow night.

I find myself at the bar at night once again.

Even before promising myself that I wouldn't kill at least before Tuesday, I also promised myself that I wouldn't be at the bar before Tuesday, either—that I wouldn't somehow find the inescapable *need* to be at the bar before Tuesday night.

And here I am. On Monday night. At the local bar just a mile away from the hospital. Just a mile away from my precious paper poster. Just a mile away from the curious eyes of my potential future partner. They could be reading it *right now*. They could be thinking about tomorrow night just like I am right now.

My fingers keep twirling, spinning the empty glass of a mixed-berry cocktail in front of me, and my leg keeps bouncing up and down and up and down on the leg of the stool I'm on. Fuck, I'm nervous. I'm *eager*. Could this emptiness of mine finally leave me? For the rest of my life, maybe? Could the excitement replace the loneliness for all time, until my time on this planet is over? Will I find a fulfilled destiny and a dream come true, just once, instead of nothing more than disappointment and deserved deaths?

I close my eyes. Pretend that the bartender behind the bar isn't there, pretend that the pool of six or seven other people in the bar aren't there, pretend that the poor music choices in the bar aren't bombarding my ears, pretend...that I'm in another place entirely.

I pretend that I'm...at the utility pole my poster is pasted to. I'm right by it. I'm leaning on the pole, waiting like an invisible spirit. There's nothing but the voice of the wind and the slight background noise of hospital-related commotion, sirens and doors sliding open, people rushing themselves or others inside. I wait and watch and the moon winks but, tonight, I'm winking back, a different kind of wickedness wrapped around both of my heavy lungs.

I pretend that someone stops by, that the poster has caught their eye. All I see is their non-specific silhouette, and all I can do is hope that they are perfect. Perfect for me, that we'll be perfect for each other if they decide to meet me tomorrow night. Whoever they are, I'd love to see the world from behind their strange sight. I'd love to absorb my own words with whatever emotion or thought they're having as they read and think and reread and rethink. Fear, confusion, disgust. Fascination. Question upon question. Devoured by interest.

When I open my eyes, the dream is dead and the dead bar returns to me and I have to wait for the death of tonight in order to, possibly, start living a whole life tomorrow, if my dream-made-real appears at all.

The bar smells like cheap smoke and stale snacks, cheap bourbon and cheaper, sweaty bodies, all spoiled with a stench. It looks cheap, too, with the appearance of something that only an amateur architect and interior designer could come up with, the atmosphere dry and without any personality—or, at least, without the personality of even the mere husk of a human being like someone whose shell is even emptier than mine, something ugly on the verge of minimalism while somehow feeling much too crowded at the same time with all its random framed photographs of horses and working men and sexualized women.

The worst bars are the ones that the worst people can be expected to come to, and even if they have a penny in their pocket, you can never be too sure about what their soul is worth. And since I'm looking for someone as soulless as me, I pick these terrible bars like underrated and underestimated gems, small and stiff but secretly superb, exactly what the damned could inhabit without feeling much irritation. It's a good thing for me and that perfect partner I dream of and all our future victims, and a not-so-good thing for all the breathing obstacles between us.

I'm staring into my empty glass, my throat dry as I think of my dream—and that's when I hear it, a voice, raspy and oh-so-ready. "Hey, I, uh…are you the…guy with the…guy with the poster, the poster…by the hospital…'bout a mile away…?"

The voice is male. This person sounds a bit drunk, a little *too* ready for my taste, and this is already wrong, because my perfect partner is not supposed to be asking me if I'm the guy with the poster by the hospital about a mile away, but rather whether I'm the dark-haired guy sitting alone, just like the poster says.

"'Cause *I'm* the guy who's...y'know, lookin' for *that* guy."

And why is this guy here on Monday night instead of Tuesday? The same thing could be asked of me, sure, but I'm the one who came up with the whole damn thing, the one who's doing the interviewing, not the interviewee. How'd he even know I'd be here tonight? Has he been following me?

*No, no, no, I don't like that. I don't like that at all.*

All I can do while I panic inside and while my fingers fiddle with my empty glass is give the stranger the smallest and most expressionless of nods. I barely have to turn to look at him, he's so close to me while he stands.

"I just...well, I just..."

This is the first chance he's ever gotten to let his own inner killer loose. The first chance anyone's ever given him. And it doesn't even matter, because he's already failed, so it'll be his last chance, too.

"I just thought, y'know—"

"You didn't think," I tell him, my voice monotone. "You weren't thinking. You're still not thinking. The poster said every *Tuesday* and *Thursday* night. Monday isn't Tuesday or Thursday, is it?"

He's dressed down so much he looks like the kind of person who doesn't even have a place to stay. His shirt's all shriveled up, and his hair is sticking up, and his eyes are red, and he's got the most awkward smile I've ever seen. Maybe he's even wearing a wire, and maybe the police or a few pranksters are using him to catch me, to get to me, and I don't even care.

Whatever the reason, his smile isn't real. Whatever he wants with me, *it isn't real*; whether he's wearing a wire or not, he just wants a good, interesting night, not something as honest as the company I am looking for and won't find in him.

"Yeah, well...you're here, ain't you?" I don't give him an answer. I won't give him anything he wants. Because he isn't who, what, I want. I stare at him with one of those cold-blooded, frustrated stares. I don't like him, and maybe he's awake enough to catch on now, because he says, "Hey, look, you're not gonna get mad at me or, uh, well, *hurt* me for comin' here now, are you?"

"No, I'm not," I tell him, questionably calm, having already made up my mind. "I promise."

And then, when we're outside and alone, I break both the promise I've made to myself and the promise I've made to the stranger. The knife I pull out from my backpack tears into his flesh all over—no wire, only his last whimpers. Nobody comes for me. No sirens, no handcuffs.

Only the looming whisper of my continued loneliness, and yet...

I feel better about Tuesday now. I sleep alone once more, but I feel better about potentially being able to do other things near the aura of someone else. Someone worthy. I feel like I am much more capable of only killing on Tuesday and Thursday nights if I come across stupid and stubborn and suffocating people, people who are the opposite of the kind of person I'd share my most secret self with. I'll spend the other days of the week, and my weekends, keeping to myself, keeping my head down, keeping my mouth shut, trying to live like a normal person who won't be having heart palpitations whenever Tuesday or Thursday comes around.

And Tuesday comes around, and I'm screaming, hoping, hoping, *hoping*. Crossing my fingers. Acting and *believing* like a blind idiot.

*Find me. Please find me.*

But no one shows up. It's Tuesday night, and no one comes. No one at all, not even a shimmer or shadow.

And yet, I can't stop believing. I *won't*, not after all this time, all these years of biting down on my wish, all these lonely, lifeless nights, lives ending, the light in my victims' eyes fading, their laughs fading. But my cravings? My belief, my wish? *Never* fading. Only growing.

I'll just have to wait to see what happens on Thursday, and then the next few Tuesdays and Thursdays. I'll hold on just a little longer for someone to step in and save my life. Save me.

It feels like weeks before Thursday night arrives.

And, when it does, I feel it again, feel it like a fool in love with nothing more than sheer possibility: the feeling of a flower in bloom, awakening in the day and, against all odds, looking forward to the cover of night.

I go into the bar early, at seven, and the next hour feels like the most drawn-out, slowest hour of my entire life, the same way time has felt since just Tuesday, excruciatingly prolonged. The aching I feel, and have felt, makes me feel awake, alive, adamant, almost angry, like an animal that's been locked in a cage too long and must now experience a wildness that can only be brought out amongst other wild animals, alongside another of its species, another of its kind.

I take in Thursday night with all the belief and bravery I can muster, though my eyes are slowly turning as dead-eyed as the cashier's from the printing and copying store.

And then, there comes a tap on my shoulder. The tap is light, and yet, I can't help but interpret it as an annoying invasion of my privacy and space. I guess I asked for this, with those desperate words on the poster and all.

*No. I didn't ask for it. Not* this.

Nothing as specific as a stranger's finger on my shoulder. Tapping me like they believe, so deeply and so naively, that I'm the kind of person who wouldn't cut off that fingertip later for popping my bubble.

"Hey." Now I have to turn around, because, against my expectations, it's a woman's voice, sultry and low, very feminine, the voice of a rose instead of the thorns I know I need.

The woman radiates red. Her lips are bold red, her hair is dyed wine red, her short dress is a seductive burgundy, and her eyes—they glow a molten, golden brown, the kind that absorbs all the red she's wearing, the kind that sinks deep into you, stares inside your soul and states without a spoken word that the owner of these bold eyes will swallow you whole when you least want her to.

"Are you the lonely guy with the dark hair?" She stands a little too close to me. I gulp, not because her beauty affects me—I'm careful not to let it affect me the way it'd affect a normal lonely man—but because I am already disappointed, and I am already close to certain that she is not here to be what I need her, what I need my actual partner, to be. I sigh, feeling sorry for her, and for myself.

All I say is: "Yeah, I am."

"Okay, great, 'cause...well, I'm...I'm looking for someone who could...help me." She sounds a little too confident in me, a total stranger *and* untrustworthy serial killer, already. I notice that she has a big, dark red purse with her, attached to the hand that wasn't on me, the hand that wasn't used to approach me so innocently and yet with such intensity.

I pause and frown at her. "*Help* you?"

She bites down on her lip, and at that, I have to turn back to my empty glass. "It's just...there's someone that I...think would be perfect for...for us, tonight." She sounds nervous, and from the corner of my eye, I know those white, smooth teeth of hers are still tugging at her red bottom lip, and, in a moment of weakness, I imagine how it'd feel for her to bite down on mine. And when she leans in and whispers near my ear, she suddenly no longer sounds so nervous: "Someone for us to kill together. Someone I know, someone bad."

I exhale, lean away from her, rub the bridge of my nose, close my eyes, my eyebrows coming together aggressively. I grit my teeth and wait for the bartender to disappear from sight behind the bar and I try not to raise my voice as I attempt to, kindly, explain to the eager woman: "I won't take on a partner that has any desired personal kills. Any...any kills that are premeditated for more than, say, just an hour or two, anything...*easy* to trace. And if you've got some sort of present or previous connection with this person you want to kill, then that makes it easy for the authorities to trace the kill back to you. Killing anyone close makes you an immediate suspect."

I try not to look at her as I say what I need to say, what she needs to swallow. I look down at my empty glass while quickly, in a low voice, running through my expectations, guidelines that should be followed by whoever I allow into this part of my life:

"And you can't have anything holding you down or holding you back like that, especially if you want to stay in one place. For a partner, I'd be willing to stay in one place instead of moving around like I often do— especially if my partner is someone who works and pays their taxes, which is what I prefer. So, no personal kills. I guess I...should've written all that on the poster, but then...it wouldn't be much of a poster anymore, would it?

It'd be a thirty-page letter. And no one's going to stop and read a bunch of stapled pages pasted to a pole."

I wait for her to absorb my warning. But all she can manage is a curt scoff and an unkind: "Yeah. You should've written all that on the poster."

I sigh at her response, and then, she puts a hand on my shoulder. Another invasion. Not a fingertip, not a finger, but her hand, her entire hand, soft and warm and intrusive, meaning to persuade me, her palm flat against the curve of my muscles. She has long fingers, I now realize, and very long fingernails with a dark glaze of nail polish, long vein-red fingernails that subtly dig into the collar of my shirt.

"Look," she starts, "just give me this one kill. This one night. And then—"

I pull away from her. "And then, what? No more personal kills?" I shake my head. "Yeah. Sure. That's what you'll say once or twice, and then a few times after that, and then *every* time after that—to me, and to yourself. *Look*," I mock her, removing her hand from my shoulder and placing my hand on her bare shoulder, so pale that the red of the strapless dress stands out against her skin like a puddle of blood. "You'll *find* more personal kills, that I know, or—oh, *they'll* magically find *you*." I scoff at her. "Someone flirted with you for too long, someone"—I gesture to the wall of the bar, where the bartender stood only minutes ago—"poured you the wrong drink. Someone *looked* at you funny."

She scoffs right back at me. She thinks this is a game, poor girl. "You think you know me, do you? From just a few words? An introduction? From just one simple request?"

"The request is nowhere near simple."

"But it is!" she insists. "Hell, *I'll* do it, and all you have to do is watch and then help me clean up." *I've always wanted someone to help me clean up. But, still...*

"It's *not* simple. And, you're right, I don't know you that well. But I do know *people*." I look at the empty, clear bottom of my glass, wishing it were a portal to another place that I could just jump through, vanish inside. "And you're a person."

"Okay, well. I'm not most people."

I roll my eyes, feel the smallest smile playing at the corner of my lips like a traitor. "C'mon, that's what *everybody* says. It's too cliché. Sit down and have a drink and maybe you'll come up with something more original."

She hops onto the stool next to me. "Are you paying?"

I chuckle, once. She's a little funny, I'll admit. But I hold back any more laughing, any more of an effect she could have on me, like a sneeze I'm not allowed to let out in the middle of some important politician's speech. I hold back and try to control myself, my emotions. I grit my teeth again as I say, "No. I'm not paying. But I *will* be paying the price—as will you—if you obsess over some personal vendetta. One that doesn't, and *shouldn't*, involve me. I'm not a hitman. No personal kills. Period. Oh, and, some advice?" She crosses her arms. "Don't take my refusal *personally*."

I stand up to leave her, the silly little dreamer that she is, stand up to leave the bar, but she stops me. She puts her hand on my chest, and it lingers there, searching for my quickening heartbeat. She stands, too, softly, slowly, gracefully, and her hopeless eyes stare into mine. "Please sit back down," she whispers, her voice poisoned with pain, her pleading eyes widening. *"Please."* I try to pry her hand away from my chest, but then she says: "I'll pay you."

"You'll pay me?" My hand freezes on hers. Seconds ago, she was asking me if I'd pay for her drink. Me, a nomad without any ties, without any place or person to really call home, for now. Someone with just enough cash to survive, to live day-by-day till the inheritance money evaporates, not to mention the cash and change I take from the bodies I leave behind. Now, she's telling me that she'll pay me.

She nods, whispers fervently: "Yes. Yes, yes, I'll pay you."

I consider this. "How much?"

"Enough."

I remove my hand from hers and simply repeat myself: "How much?"

"A thousand dollars."

I sit back down on the stool. People like money as much as they like eating. They hate *not* getting money as much as they hate washing the dishes. Normal people and I have a few things in common—breathing, pissing, eating, masturbating—and this is one of them. Now, I need to make sure

I've heard this woman correctly, make sure she's not fucking with me: "You've got…a thousand dollars with you?"

She nods. "Cash." She gestures to her big red purse. "Ten hundred-dollar bills in my wallet." She's an idiot for telling me this. She is, generally, an idiot. I already know I will not be taking on an idiot as a partner.

I wonder, for just a second, whether she is simply a very intelligent woman *pretending* to be an idiot, to get under my skin, to get to me, to play me, and perhaps this consideration is what, only in part, prompts me to nod back and to reply to her carefully: "Okay. So, I'll do this…just tonight…and you'll pay me."

"You'll help me kill him. And you'll help me clean up. And I'll pay you. And then we'll be partners. Or not. Whatever. Deal?"

I have no choice now but to agree with her. Completely. "Okay. Deal. I'll help you kill him, I promise. But…well, what can you tell me? About our…potential victim?"

She sits back down on her stool, too. "He tried to assault me. Although, he did…manage to…*actually* sexually assault one of my friends."

"One of your friends?"

She looks down, uncomfortable, recalling a sad reality, a harsh truth. "My best friend."

"And he *tried* to assault you?"

She looks back up at me, her eyes bold, bitter like caramel coffee. "I drew a pocket knife on him. Got away."

"You fought back?" Will she fight against me if, or rather *when*, I decide, either with my own knife in hand or not, that she's not the one for me?

"Made him bleed, but…not enough."

"Okay. A guy who…assaults."

"Actually, we don't need to sugarcoat it like that." She's almost hissing, revenge ripe in between her ready teeth. "We'll call him what he is. What he really is. He's a rapist."

"A rapist. I was just gonna say that he…already sounds exactly like the kind of person I'd hunt at night, anyway." I look her down, and my eyes trail down her thighs, down her long legs, down to her high heels. "You're gonna need a new pair of shoes if you plan on hurting him tonight. Hurting him successfully."

"I know." She taps her big purse, a bigger smile in her twinkling, starlit, dilated pupils. "I came prepared."

*So did I. As usual.*

She grips the straps of her purse, and I grip the straps of my backpack, and, now, we rise from our bar stools together. Walk out into the night. Together.

•   •   •

We don't take a cab and we don't call an Uber or a Lyft for a ride or anything, nothing anyone can use to track where we were or where we'd gone or how we think—ultimately, who we are. We don't, and we won't, use any credit cards, no cash—none of the cash she plans on giving to me— and we don't interact with any other person who could see our faces elsewhere and recognize us—say, in a lineup, in a police station.

She puts her sneakers on, stashes her red high heels in her purse, and we start to walk. It's a ten-minute walk away, or so she says. I guess I chose a good bar, someplace close to the area our victim inhabits. "It's fate," she tells me with a smile, and I follow her into the dark. We don't talk much on our way there. I just keep picturing blood spilling out of her throat or her arms or legs—or her eyes going frozen like those carved onto a statue's face.

We stop at the foot of a townhouse. We hide in the shadows, near the corner of the building, and she peeks around the corner, tapping the wall of the building with her hand. "This is his place. The first door, right around this corner. He always stays in at night. We'll have to make some noise to draw him out."

She's been stalking him, planning a way to get back at him, to ruin, end, his life. She's been waiting for someone like me to come into her world and give her what she wants. She hasn't wanted to do this alone. I can understand that, relate to it. But the company of someone else means nothing if they don't fit who you are, if you don't match, if you're not perfect for each other.

Such a shame, that she thinks I might be perfect for her, whereas I know better. A grain of pity pollutes me once more.

She turns to me, then, and, seemingly out of nowhere, she asks: "Hey, what's your name, by the way?"

"Timothy."

"I'm Angie."

"Hello, Angie." *It's "fate" for me to end you tonight, Angie.*

"Hi, Timothy." She blushes, which isn't a very good sign at all.

"Angie...I'd recommend knocking on his door. We don't have to...'make noise to draw him out.' We can just be...drawn in, instead. You can...act like you want to talk to him. Act innocent, and let yourself inside. Find a way to let me in, maybe through a backyard door, or something. And you'll have to...do something, anything you can, to lure him to...well, either the backyard, or the bathroom, specifically the bathtub...someplace it'll be easy to clean up the mess we'll inevitably make."

"Oh, wow, you've...really got this all figured out, huh? You've just...thought about all of it and...everything."

"I've been doing this for a few years. It's not hard for me to think of something on the spot."

She smiles, impressed with me. I *am* affecting her. It makes me a little sad, since I know how tonight will end. It also makes me sad how obvious it is, that she's been using her body and her pretty face to get me to agree with her, and how pathetic it is, and how pathetic it makes me feel to ultimately be agreeing with her, at least to some degree and only on the surface. At some point, soon, I'll agree with the voice in my head, my own deeper drives and motivations, and it will all be over for her. "Improvise," she muses, "and still get away with it. Still make sure there's no...blood trailing behind you."

"Right."

She gives me a grin. Such a hopeful, genuinely happy grin. It's embarrassing and it tugs at my chest ever so slightly, even though I swore to myself that I wouldn't let it, let *her*. "Well, just as long as *I'm* still trailing behind you, right?"

"Right. Promise."

She turns away from me, still smiling, ready to turn the corner and approach the doorstep of the monster who lives inside.

But I've already pulled my gloves out of my pockets and shoved them on, and my gloved hands are already around her neck from behind, and before she can even decipher what is happening, she's gone, even without me having to pull out my knife from my backpack.

"I'm sorry," I whisper to her dead body as I lay it on the ground, behind bushes right up against the wall of the rapist's townhome. "But I did warn you. I said no personal kills. And you didn't listen. You didn't understand. And I need a partner who can understand."

I then reach into her purse and try to find her wallet, and find my fingers rustling against something sharp—a knife—and her high heels, until I finally get to a medium-sized piece of leather. I grab hold of it, take it out—it's her wallet, and I open it up. And I pull out...a single hundred-dollar bill.

I sigh, chuckle a bit, and click my tongue, staring at Angie's dead, frozen face. "A thousand dollars, huh? Ten hundred-dollar bills. Yep." I sigh and shove the single hundred-dollar bill into the front pocket of my jeans.

But I can't leave the scene the way I usually do. I can't just stuff the body someplace else and hope for the best and run away. It's not that simple this time. This time, I have to stay in the same place, but for more than one reason.

The monster inside this shapeless townhouse with cracking paint on its walls and nearly shattered windows still lives—he still breathes. It's nothing personal on my end—but who would I be if I let this monster live? I'd be a monster who simply watches an arguably even worse monster. This assaulter, *rapist*, waits and stares and winks and doesn't waste any energy or breath on the truly wild and the terrifyingly wicked. I wouldn't be myself, wouldn't be the monster I trained myself to be all these years alone, if I slept comfortably tonight knowing that a rapist still roamed free near the areas I've currently decided to prowl.

I give Angie's lifeless face a nod. I move my gloved fingers and pull her eyelids over her motionless eyeballs. "For you. And for your best friend." And then I make my way to the doorstep of the rapist.

And after I ring his old and rusty doorbell—I have to press it hard, press deep *into* it with my finger for it to make any noise—and when he, the monster, opens the door, looking quite confused, I hold on tightly to the backpack straps over my shoulders and tell him, before he has time to ask me who I am or let any other phrase or word leave his mistake-shaped mouth:

"Hi. I know Angie. Or *knew* her. Anyway, I made her two promises tonight. I've decided it'll be good if I only break one of them."

• • •

When I'm done with him and I've laid his breathless body in his backyard and I've cleaned up after myself—sighing and panting as the workout of erasing evidence takes its usual toll—I try to leave the scene, both the devil-like man and the *almost* angelic Angie, with my head held up high. But my head has been hanging low and again it hangs tonight, hangs heavy like heartbreak.

Because, once more, I leave a scene of mine alone and I leave the stunning and empty scene feeling sick and just as empty inside.

And there's a chill in the air, the kind I dislike. It's the kind of chill that the all-mocking, all-mourning, all-mothering moon seems to send down. It's the kind of chill that suddenly makes me feel like I have to watch my back, something I've never really felt the need to do before.

It's the kind of chill that makes me feel like something other than the moon is watching me.

*Someone. Watching me close. Like a promise.*

# CHAPTER THREE

# NUMB NIGHTS

I *have* to find someone like me. *Truly* like me. Someone who considers themselves to be a human-shaped god, and, at the same time, someone who can embody the kind of humility that is simply human enough to understand. A pride just polite enough to tolerate. To be human is to care, even if it's about all the morally wrong things in the eyes of so much of humanity. The passion of a person, the bones of a human being, and yet, the power to carry out that passion, the boldness to do bad things to those who look down instead of up.

But the days, the drawn-out and daunting days, come and go and come and go.

*Friday.*

And I am a man hearing people speak all around me without listening to them.

*Saturday.*

I am a man watching people come and go and come and go without seeing them.

*Sunday.*

I am a godless man making a wish, not upon a deity or a star, but upon the watcher in the sky, asking for mercy from the merciless moon.

*Monday...*

I am a mundane moment, searching for a miracle so sweet and serene that it might as well be immortal compared to the multiple stretched-out moments I seek.

*Tuesday.*

A mistake, searching for meaning.

And worse mistakes come and go, come and meet me and die.

I am met with a slew of odd characters, all of them fascinating in the worst ways, none of them the kind of character I could appreciate.

Tuesday night, I'm on the same stool from last week. Tuesday night, some guy with long hair who smells like weed approaches me, asking me if I'm "the man." Obviously, I'll need a partner who can help me accomplish my work sober. Sober company is worthwhile. I lead the high guy out into the darkness, and he passes away, floating, resting on clouds, his eyes rolling into the back of his head. Tuesday night, once again, I find myself ending the day alone.

*Wednesday.*

Is it too late? Will these next few Tuesdays and Thursdays be the same? Will I die without telling a single soul that I am grateful for their existence? Will a soul ever tell me that they feel the same way about me?

*Thursday.*

I glimpse someone at the window of the bar. A boy—no, a young man, at least from what I can tell from the corner of my eye as I try not to make it obvious that I can see him from where I am inside. He's staring into the bar, this quiet and tasteless bar with no distinctive or tempting qualities. He looks odd. He keeps looking back, away from the window and out into the rain, and his mouth is moving, indicating that he's talking to people that are with him, people I cannot see from my spot on the bar stool. It's just an odd look, and there's that chilling sensation again, and it prompts me to go hide in the bathroom.

I wait and I hope that they'll leave the bar after being unable to find what they're looking for, which, most likely, is me.

But then I hear footsteps, *multiple* footsteps that seem to shuffle—one after the other—right behind the door of the bar's public bathroom, a door that would swing right away, right now, and with such ease, if someone were to enter. I hear hushed talking:

"Yo, you think he went in here?"

"I don't know, man, but I don't think this is a good idea anymore."

Two people are outside—and then there's a third: "C'mon, you don't think he'll do groupies?"

"I think he wants to work alone, man. *Mano-a-mano.* Two people, dealing with each other, in a bad way, a good way, whatever. He wants *a* partner. *Uno.*"

"This shouldn't be a prank, dude. Guy—well, *killer* lookin' for a *fella* killer shouldn't be pranked on."

"C'mon, I'm pretty sure he *just* went in here. Let's just check it out, and—well, check *him* out, too, yeah?"

Hushed talking, three people and all their hushed talking slowly making their way closer to the bathroom. They're still debating. They're not ready to open the door yet, and they shouldn't be.

I don't know what kind of damage I'd cause if they did come inside—if *any* damage at all—but I'd be more than determined to try to take them all on, something I've never done before—trying to kill a few people at the same time—and I'm too stubborn to change the location of my bar because of a fight or a few deaths or injuries, so I need to leave. Now. Find a way out of this shithole. *Now.*

I'm not going to wait around to find out what their decision is. It'd be too late for me, and too late for them, by then. And, if I succeed, there'd be too many bodies, two more than my usual count, and if I don't succeed, I'd die without pride. If I ever die, it has to be as I am, with pride. *Just enough pride to tolerate.*

I walk to the bathroom window. I slide it open, and, one hand holding onto my backpack, the other propping my body up, I manage to hop out, with as much subtlety as I can muster. I don't wonder whether they can hear me as I slide the window shut behind me. They are now the past, unless they're silly enough to carry whatever "prank" they've thought up with them into the future, *my* future.

I disappear into the darkness, reminding myself that I do not work with groups of people—that's too risky, too many minds to understand, too many mouths to oversee and listen to, *too much*—and I do not have enough room in my mind for mockery, not without the thought or inevitable aftermath of murder.

*Friday.*

Invisible.

*Saturday.*

I feel invisible. I don't want to be. Not anymore.

*Sunday.*

Though, I don't want to be *visible*, either, like some kind of attention-seeking killer who thinks their work belongs in a gallery. My work doesn't belong in a gallery.

*Monday.*

My work is simply something to be shared with one other person. And that is the person who will make me feel visible. Because the world won't matter, at least, not as much. But they will, this dream person. Only *we* will, to each other. The both of us. The two of us. It sounds so cliché, but it will be us against the rest of the world, in a way, under the night sky and under the moon when it's out—and isn't that the kind of thing everyone wants, anyway, deep down?

*Tuesday.*

Nighttime.

I'm not *at* the bar tonight. I'm *inside*, but I'm not sitting on the bar stool I've labeled as temporarily mine—my spot—or *any* bar stool, for that matter.

I hide in plain sight, as always. And, still, I am currently hiding, really hiding, in the shadows. I am in the small lounge area of the barroom, leaning back against the black leather seats, sitting at one of the booths, toying with an empty glass on a little table, staring at nothing and nobody across from me, an empty lounge seat I wish would be filled by now with my partner already.

The hood of my black sweater is pulled up over my head, covering my dark, messy hair. I need to conceal myself as much as I can tonight. The assholes from Tuesday might come back, and I'd like very much to ignore them. And, maybe, I can do a better job of observing any potential partners from my new spot for now.

Sure enough, though, the assholes from before are the ones who return.

They're quite stupid, *very* stupid—they enter the bar with such carelessness, and the three of them walk separately, stand in their own little fake bubbles mere feet away from one another, as if they are not part of the same group.

*Nice try.*

I keep my head down, mind my own business, and wait for them to leave.

They don't leave just yet, though.

I can hear them. They're closer together now. They've given up on acting like they don't belong to each other, all three members of this friend group of idiots—it makes me jealous, for a second, that even idiots and assholes have others to call "the one" in their small social lives.

"Where do you think he's at? No one's here."

"Is that him?"

Even if it is truly *me* they've noticed—amongst the very few other people inhabiting this lounge space—they probably don't like what they see: this creepy-looking guy, all alone, hood up, empty glass but no intention of leaving this bar that might as well go bankrupt soon. Because, then, they leave. I hear the entrance door of the bar swing open, and when I peek up through my long eyelashes, I do not see them standing there anymore. *They've really left.*

I wait a bit more, but no one else shows up, and I'm too tired to wait any longer, so I start heading to the motel room I currently call my home.

I'm too tired to even consider going after all those assholes from earlier during different times, going after them when they're alone, individually, going after them when we can be alone and I can show them what happens when they take risks with someone who takes risks and uses riveting blades to rip into wrists as a hobby.

*Wednesday.*

I'm too tired to do much of anything. I'm tired because I'm impatient and I haven't found someone who can help me feel alive, who can *awaken* me. I'm starting to think I won't find my perfect partner at all. Someone to really feel comfortable with—someone to really feel for.

The worst part is, I've gotten close to feeling *something* before. Empathy, care, even sympathy. Back when heartbreak was the thing that led me to my first few kills, and then occasionally, and then, most recently, I felt the tiniest of something for Angie, before reminding myself of what she was, what her inability to understand or listen to me could, and would, mean. And I'd only like to feel that way with someone who I am *sure* is the one.

For some, "the one" is the person you'll say your "I do's" to at the end of a wedding aisle. For others, "the one" is the career you love, the home you own, the child you parent and take care of and raise and mold into an adult. "The one" is a significant part of your life, whoever or whatever they are. "The one" changes everything for you—*could* change everything for you. For me, "the one" really is a fellow knife, fellow killer. Those assholes were right. They put it bluntly, inappropriately, in such an unromantic way, and yet, they were right.

*Thursday.*

The night has ended. Soon, it will be tomorrow morning. Still dark out.

My potential partner-turned-prey of the night was a man who seemed to be getting a little ahead of himself—and too much, at that. He approached me in the bar—I finally felt well enough to sit back down on one of the bar stools tonight—with too much of a spring in his step, too much of a greedy glint in his wicked eye, too much smoothness in his overly confident voice. Too much, *too much*.

Now, I have left him behind, left him in some alley, behind large, plastic, black trash bags to hide the smell of decay. I made sure to place him, hide him, with such care, and the smell of garbage is still wafting up from my...

Hands. *My bare hands.*

I've never forgotten to wear gloves before. *Never.*

I really am tired. My hands start to tremble. My bare hands.

I think of my fingertips all over the body, the dead man's clothes, the plastic, black trash bags, everywhere. I think of my identity, exposed. My crimes, laid bare.

I wouldn't mind getting arrested. I really wouldn't. Perhaps my friend really is behind bars right now.

But I can at least prevent my current lifestyle from being taken away from me. I can go back to the scene. I can fix things. I don't have to stop living my life *now*. There's still time. There's still hope, out here in the world—there has to be, otherwise I might as well be dead, kill myself or let my prey become my predator for just one night. I'm still an optimistic idiot, deep down—even if a poisonous pessimism has been taking me over more and more each day, with each failed partnership on these past few Tuesday and Thursday nights.

I start to run back. Start running fast. I run towards where I left tonight's body with my stupid bare fucking hands.

I spot the trash bags, laid up against the wall. I hid the body in between the trash bags and the alley wall of some random apartment building.

I keep looking around as I approach the trash bags, like someone is going to come out from the shadows and kill me or kidnap me or imprison me.

I move the trash bags...

The body isn't there.

*The body isn't there.*

The body isn't where I left it, where I *know* I left it.

I try not to panic, though, inside, I *am* panicking, panting, shaking, wondering who could've possibly moved a whole body, a heavy man's body, in such a short amount of time, only several minutes since I left it here.

I run from the scene, and I take with me the sense that I am being watched.

*Friday.*

Where did the body go?

*Saturday.*

The question haunts me.

*Sunday.*

All day, every day, it follows me around even with the most minute movement, follows my mind and peels me away from every other miniscule thought, every melody, every manufactured fragment of magnificence or mayhem.

*Monday.*

I know where I left it, and it was not there when I went back, and the chill follows me along with the question, and so does that feeling of literally being followed—the night promise, a dark and distant promise I do not know what to make of, a chill splattered across my skin like so many tiny drops of blood, goosebumps and that continued ominous yet simply fascinating feeling of being watched, the way I'd watch, being stalked the way I, the predator, would stalk.

*Tuesday.*

This is the last week. If nothing comes of my efforts this week, I'll take my poster and I'll move elsewhere, spend my later Tuesday and Thursday nights at some other local bar.

There's been news, over the past few days, in papers and on screens, of people disappearing, bodies going missing, no culprit caught, and I'm sure that the authorities have been catching on to the area they ought to watch out for if they're going to investigate and search for the killer—the area circling the local bar and the local hospital.

It doesn't matter to me. Again, finding someone, *anyone*, is my priority.

I'm at the bar, anyway. Sitting on my stool, anyway. I'm listening to "Put Your Head On My Shoulder" by Paul Anka blare from the speakers in the bar, wondering what it would be like for someone to put their head on my shoulder, or even for me to put my head on theirs, dreaming, only dreaming, *always dreaming.* Listening to the sad, new, pouring rain outside. If those assholes return, I don't care what happens to me anymore, and I especially don't care what happens to them.

And if a person, or *people*, other than those assholes show up, then what? What would happen? What would I do? What would *they* do?

It's great timing for me to be thinking about that, because, then, from the corner of my eye, I see it—not a person, not even an object of any kind, nothing to grasp or gasp at...

I see light through the cloudy rain consistently pouring down. Red and blue light. Red, flashing, and then blue, flashing.

The silent, flickering spark of sirens.

There are *sirens* right outside. The *police* are right outside.

They're here for me. I know they are. They must be. Who else? They've found me. They've found their local mystery killer. Were they the ones who moved my previous body, or someone who was helping them track me down, perhaps?

A middle-aged-looking man steps in through the door, completely drenched—a police officer, dressed in uniform, with a flashlight in one hand and a gun in the other. Two more men make their way into the bar while a small squad of others wait outside near their cars, with the red and blue siren lights still echoing through the glass of the bar and reflecting off just about everything inside.

"Hands up!" the middle-aged-looking police officer bellows at me, the brown mustache upon his angry mouth twitching just a bit. "Yeah, you're the guy, ain't ya? The 'lonely guy with the dark hair' just sittin' all by yourself in this little, unoccupied bar. You're him. Hands up. I won't ask again."

I put my hands up. I don't have a fight here. I *can't* fight. I guess this is where it was supposed to end all along: my lifestyle, my nights. But this isn't necessarily where my search has to end, not unless they throw me into solitary confinement once they get me behind bars. Not unless they give me an immediate death sentence and I'm killed so soon.

"Yeah, it's him," says another police officer behind the middle-aged one everyone else seems to be following. This other police officer then pulls something out of his pocket, a white piece of paper that he starts to unfold, and I know that it's all over, and they've got me. They saw my poster. They tracked me down. Maybe they're what's been causing the chill all over me for the past several nights. *They've* been watching me. "It's him, alright. It is, isn't it?"

"It is," I answer him, leaving my hands in the air, surrendering, completely surrendering myself to them and to the system, to whatever they want to do with me or to me and whatever is meant to happen to me after all these years of empty roaming, euphoric red, empty roaming again. "I'm 'the guy.'" I nod at the white paper, my courageous call, in the second police officer's hands. "That's the poster I put up by the local hospital. I'm who you're looking for."

The first police officer scoffs, starts lowering his gun and flashlight. "Giving up that easy, huh? What, are you that desperate for friends?" And then he reads me my rights.

I keep my eyes down. I know I must seem pathetic to them. A killer, and a very lonely one, too. How stupid, how strange, how silly and contradictory. How unfair, both to me and to the victims I've, according to them, senselessly killed, but, according to me, have murdered with such meaning. I don't care. I *am* that desperate for somebody, *anybody*. Even a prison guard, at this point. Hell, maybe even one of these guys.

Maybe the drive to the station or prison or wherever the fuck they're supposed to take me will be a long one and they'll have no choice but to *be human* and to start some sort of "innocent" conversation with me. Maybe that conversation will include them criticizing all the cruelty I've caused, but would that even bother me, so long as we're simply having some kind, *any* kind, of conversation?

Maybe I'll turn the conversation around in the police car, during this hypothetical long drive, and maybe I'll even get them to like me, just a bit, the way the dumbest people even come to like the most damned demons. Maybe we'll *bond*.

Once he finishes reading me my rights, he says, "Well, alright, then. He *is* that desperate for friends. Friends just as fucked, huh?" The second police officer, who looks younger, pulls out a pair of handcuffs and walks over to me. He takes my arms. "Well, alright, then," the middle-aged one says again, mumbling in such a nonchalant tone that I find it almost offensive, though I can't find anything too offensive at this point since none of this matters. "You'll find plenty o' friends like that in jail." *I sure hope so.* He pulls my hands behind my back. "Easy-peasy." I feel the cuffs locking onto my wrists. "Walk forward, *guy*."

I do as I'm told. I *listen*. Obey. And, once we're all out of the bar—me and the few police officers at my back and in front of me—I keep my eyes down, unable to look anyone who's waiting outside in the eye, not other officers or nearby curious citizens. I stare at the rain splashing on the ground at my feet. I can hear murmurs, even chuckles, comments, scoffs, ripples of confusion and questions amid the strong, hard sound of the rain.

I'm shoved into a police car. Everything happens like the locking of a door. Sharp, straight, harsh, started and finished in an instant. I'm in the back seat of the police car and I can see the sirens of a second police car right in front of this one. I can hear the doors of that police car opening, closing, hard. The door of the one I'm in opens, too—the first police officer with the flashlight gets in and, at the command of his fingers, the engine makes a low growl as it comes to life. A steel fence, a strongly reinforced divider, separates where I sit in the back from where he sits in the front. His friend, the second police officer who spoke to me in the bar, gets into the passenger seat.

They don't say anything to each other, or to me. Were all their words inside all for show? I guess they *can't* say anything, and I guess *I* can't, either. I've taken many lives—too many, across state border after state border, too many for one lifetime. I'm real, and this isn't a joke, and I will have no choice but to answer now, and soon again, for what the police officers and all these citizens outside these doors and what most people regard as sin after sin after sin, rather than deserved death after dense debt after depthless breath.

The car jolts forward, after the car that I can slightly see moving up ahead—and we're off.

About five minutes pass us by. Buildings pass, the rain persists, and my thoughts are as numb as the rest of me. I want what I want, and it is that simple, and if I can't find it while I'm trapped in my cycle, then maybe I will find it trapped elsewhere, in the legal system's cycle.

That's when the first police officer, the one who's driving, finally makes a comment, and a snide one, too: "What's that saying? That people who're headed to hell look for someone to take with 'em, too? So that, at least, they won't be alone when they get there? Is that what you're hopin' to find? A partner in hell?"

This makes the second officer laugh a little.

But I can't even smile. I can't even tell the police officer how right he is.

*It's not a joke. It's real. And I'm real. And my dream is real.*

*And my dream will be real as long as I am alive.*

I can feel tears forming in my eyes as I look outside the police car window. I stare at the rain. And, still, I do not dare pray. I can't even hope right now—I will continue to think about my dream, and to let it weigh heavy on whatever kind of sick and sad and selfish heart I have, when I've been thrown in my box. I can't even find the moon, can't even see it—there is no visible moon tonight. Only clouds up above, and only the roar of the restless rain.

The car jolts again—but not forward this time. It simply halts, stops in its place.

I see that the police car in front of us has stopped moving, too, right in the middle of the empty street, its blinding red taillights frozen and piercing through the fog and rain.

The driving police officer speaks into something—a walkie-talkie. "Is everything alright over there? Why're we stopping?"

There's a beep and then a response from one of the officers in the front car: "We think we...saw something. *See* something."

"Well, what?"

No response.

A strong smashing sound erupts from the other car, which jolts a little. It's hard to say whether this smashing sound impacts the car as a whole or just its windows, which I can barely see shattering.

"Hey, is everyone okay over there?" the policeman in the driver's seat asks the walkie-talkie.

Still no response.

And then—screaming. The police officers in the front car start screaming.

Their screams are muffled inside the car, blocked by the pouring rain. They're all screaming—two or three police officers. And, while they're screaming, I can hear them saying things. The words, I can barely make out, but I know they're calling for help. And, while they're shouting for help, the car is jolting again, shaking, rocking from side to side, and the screaming gets even louder from inside. I can barely make out something that...looks and sounds like...some kind of whizzing through the fog-covered storm...

The two police officers sitting in front of me can't say a word. They're too shocked, all their bravery shattered like the glass from the front car. They're too confused to even speak.

And then the driver is picking up his gun from inside the car, and so is the police officer in the passenger seat. They both look ahead, look around, their breathing heavier now, a tension between them, a tension so thick it feels like the fog from outside is making its way inside.

The screaming from the vehicle ahead dies out, completely comes to a stop just like the front car itself did, and then the police officer in the passenger seat finally manages to say something. "What is it?" he whispers to the police officer in the driver's seat. "What happened?"

The driver doesn't answer. The surreal silence outside slides inside like a snake, sneaky and strange and suffocating in its slowness and how it stalls all around us.

Even with their bullet-filled guns in hand, it is clear that the officers no longer feel safe in their little cop car. If they, with their guns instead of knives and with their authority instead of anonymity, do not feel safe, then I suppose I shouldn't feel safe, either.

I would very much prefer not to die like this—or to die in *any* way tonight, really. I'm not sure what happened to those police officers up front, whether this is a prank on their end, something they're pulling just to poke some fun at the police officers I'm unfortunately stuck with or even at me— but if the screaming and then the sudden lack of screaming means that they are dead, then I'd very much like to not die in whatever way they have.

I cannot emphasize just how much I want to die with pride when my time comes, exactly as I am, with either a knife at some loser's neck, or with a knife at mine, by my own hand or at the hands of someone, loser or not, who I've allowed to end my life. I won't be dying with pride if the simple jolting of some car, and whatever caused the jolting, is the thing that kills me. Something happened to the officers up front, and the fact that the two police officers with me don't know what happened, either, is honestly making me quite nervous.

The driver moves his hand to his door. He unlocks it.

The police officer in the passenger seat whispers, "Hey, what are you doing?" But the whisper is so feverish it sounds like an agonized wheeze. "Don't go out there, man, this shit feels like some kinda sick trap. Hey-hey-hey—"

But it's too late.

The one in the passenger seat is right—the lack of motion and the lack of noise means that, whatever's out there, it's waiting. Watching. *Waiting and watching, like a promise.* It wants us to leave this car.

And the driver's doing exactly what is expected of him. The driver's leaving. He's leaving the car. He's opening his unlocked door, and...he's out.

"Hey, get back in here right now, you fuckin' moron," the second police officer hisses at him from inside.

But his friend, his colleague, isn't listening. Instead, the guy aims his gun out in front of him, and I can barely see him blindly pointing the gun all around him, not sure where the threat is.

For perhaps the first time in my life, I feel like nothing more than a bystander in the dark—a *threatened* bystander. I am in no condition, especially with my hands cuffed behind my back, to protect myself from both these remaining police officers and whatever is still out there. I am not a threat.

*I am prey.*

And then there's that whizzing outside again, a blank and bright flash— it comes and goes in just the blink of an eye and it causes a gut-wrenching groan from the police officer, who falls to his knees with the shape of his fragile and flailing silhouette more ominous than the mere darkness of the moonless night.

The second police officer shifts in his seat at the terrifying noise, the sound of excruciating pain. Obviously beyond frightened, he anxiously holds his gun up, glances over at me, uncertain, and then he looks back at the open door, right next to which his co-worker has fallen on his knees.

I don't know what my expression is like or how I seem. I'm not sure if the police officer would interpret my current state as calm or cold, but all I know is that I, too, feel lost and confused, completely unsure of what's going on, which is never a good feeling. I gulp and try to breathe evenly—

And then, there's another flash—and there's a blinking noise. It's the sound of the open door unlocking. No...it's the sound of...*my* door unlocking, through one of the pressed buttons of the open car door.

In just a flash, my door is unlocked through the click of the open driver door.

*I'm free.*

The second my door unlocks, the second police officer's eyes pierce into mine, the second startlingly stressing, both on his end and mine, our eyes wide, this breathless second wicked and warm like the whisper of a coming war—

In that second, I start scooting my butt to the side, the left, towards the inside of my closed door, making sure that my fingers, though restrained in movement and power because of the cuffs tying my wrists together, can feel their way to the car door handle. And, in that same instant, the police officer jumps out of the car through his passenger door, and he scrambles to get around the car, to get to me, to stop me from freeing myself of his watch.

At that moment, the both of us don't care about getting killed. We don't care about what'll happen to us, so long as we simply escape each other—or, in the police officer's case, so long as he simply catches me and gets me to a holding room or an actual cell, if we don't die first, either at the other's hands or because of whatever out there silenced all the other police officers.

What I *am* sure of is that this is another trap just to lure me, and him, out of the car—and I don't care about that, either. Not now. I just have to get out of this damn car, get away from the red and blue sirens—at least while I still can and while the eerie echo of the flash outside has allowed me to, even if that ghostly unlocking of my door is scarily suspicious.

I manage to find the door handle—my fingers try to fold around it, and then I hear the popping sound of the handle being squeezed towards my back, and I push against the door and it opens and I stumble out of the car and into the wild rain.

But the police officer is already stumbling around the police car and towards me—his gun is aimed at me and he stands a few small feet away from me.

"You're not going anywhere," he pants, his breath cloudy in the fog. "Stay where you are."

But I can't do that. I need to flee this scene, as I always flee every scene, and it would be a good idea for him to do that right now, too, and for us to go our separate ways. Why doesn't he understand that? He's just trying to do his job, it's clear from the terror in his big eyes, but his colleagues are all gone.

*Gone.*

I turn, then, towards where the other police car is, just several feet ahead, very close to the one I was just in.

And there they are, through the fog: all the other police officers, including the driver who made the very bad decision to leave the car—a decision that I and his still-alive co-worker are making right now.

They are all on the street, splayed out under the hard rain. Rain that splatters off their dead bodies. Blood covers their skin, sinks into their clothes along with the rain, and creates puddles of red, too, along with the rain, underneath and around them. They've all bled out—three police officers from the car ahead and the driver of the car I was in. They've all been struck with such significance that I can't make out where on their bodies the blood is coming from, exactly, can't see any open wounds under all this fog and rain.

It really does look like something out of a battle, albeit a very one-sided one and, therefore, not a battle at all—a *murder*, so many of them at once, so like the ones I've committed and yet so unlike anything I'd even ever dare to do. It looks like they've been attacked not even by a mere human being such as myself, but, rather, like they've been mauled by some sort of animal, like a rampant coyote or an enraged bear.

And, yet, there were no animal noises before, and there are none now, nothing to indicate exactly *what the fuck happened to them.*

The *whizzing* seemed to perform this power play with such poisonous, borderline perfect calm.

"What the...fuck...?" The second police officer starts trembling with his gun in his hand.

But the gun is no longer aimed at me.

The gun is pointed at the dead bodies, and the second police officer is clearly in a state of shock. The people he's worked with, probably every single day, are all dead, and he can't help but wonder whether he'll be joining them. I can't help but wonder, too, and the thought grates against the inside of my head like a blade against ice. I guess I ought to take advantage of the man's currently unstable state of mind now.

I sprint forward and lunge into him—I hear his gun go off once, and then twice, but I don't feel anything at all, no scratches from any bullets or actual wounds, which I take to be a very good thing as I straddle him to the floor with power from my skin-tight and muscled legs, mainly my knees, and my slightly muscular shoulders as I use them to pin him down.

But he pushes me off with his strong arms and hands—and now I'm falling to the ground, close to the police car behind me. I grunt, but I'm quick to get back up—but so is he, with his gun in hand.

"Stay right there," he warns me.

But I take a step forward—and he shoots, though intentionally missing, just to frighten me and make sure I listen to him. But I don't listen. I can't. I have to leave. I'm not dying tonight, not like this, not without my pride, not without engaging in what I'm passionate about. A gun in his hand while my hands are still cuffed behind me—it's just not a fair fight, and there is no pride here.

I take another step forward, and he shoots again, missing me again.

He redirects his aim when I step forward again, unorthodox with my confidence, unafraid and as cold as the night. There's that chill in the air, in between all the rain that has the two of us soaked and all the fog that it's hard to see through, and, for some reason, that chill drives me forward, makes me feel less pathetic, even with my lack of complete pride.

He aims right at me.

My foot moves on, and the other foot follows, and he yells out, "Don't move!" This police officer, and all the other officers, are probably good cops, and good men, too. They do not want to kill when they find it unnecessary, and, in my own sick way, neither do I.

I don't think that the man in front of me is rude or vile or disgusting. I'd like to think that he took up this job because he wanted to save the world from bad people—we're not so different, in that way. And if I murder a police officer tonight and live, that'll send the whole station, a whole department, everyone, after me. I'll be hunted. The "PARTNER WANTED" poster I placed on the pole at the hospital parking lot, now in the hands of dead authorities, will be replaced by a poster of my face put up by more authoritative and very alive authorities, only the word "WANTED" big and bold and bitter.

But if he doesn't give me any other choice, I will kill him. If the thing out here with us, hiding in the shadows, doesn't kill him first—right before killing me.

*Where is it?*

"Don't take another step," the police officer demands.

But I do. I have to. I wouldn't be human if I didn't. I wouldn't be human if it wasn't in my nature to test my chances, to try. The way I have been every Tuesday and Thursday night at the bar.

And when I do step forward, he shoots. Right at me. I'm not given enough time to move. This is it. This is how I die, or how I get put behind bars, injured in a hospital and still cuffed before being moved to yet another prison, yet another trap of my own making.

I'm too proud to kill myself, so I can't do that, but letting someone else take my pain away from me, take my loneliness away from me for good—that, I can do. Just so long as I let it happen or at least die defending myself. These past several Tuesday and Thursday nights—no, these past *weekly* nights, *all* of them...have been so *numb*. *I* have been so inescapably numb.

What I'm looking for—a partner, no, a *friend*—isn't real. What I'm looking for—care, trust, love in one form or another. What I'm looking for...doesn't exist.

And I don't think I can exist without it. I can't exist while it, too, doesn't exist.

*He shoots. Right at me.*

*And I can't move.*

No—I *don't* move.

There it is, the flash of the beast again—the blinking movement whizzes between the police officer and I.

I don't feel anything. The bullet didn't hit me. The bullet hasn't fallen to the ground like a heavy raindrop. The bullet is gone.

The police officer is frozen, staring at me as if I'm some kind of demon or ghoul. But I'm staring down at myself, too, completely taken aback because I'm alright and uninjured even though the man was, and still is, aiming *right at me*.

I take another step forward, testing my limits once more, now that I'm unhurt. And the man shoots again, testing himself, too, testing me, testing...

The blinking flash, the ominous blur—it whizzes between the two of us again, faster than we can see or comprehend. I flinch, take a step back, and I hear the police officer gasp again.

*What the fuck is that thing?*

I step forward again. The police officer shoots again. We're now only a few feet away from each other—but the flashing abnormality comes to interrupt his efforts again, and the bullet he's shot has disappeared again, and I'm not hurt at all, and the subject of our curiosity is so close to the both of us and we're so close to each other that it's like a single, strong gust of wind has just gone by between us, strands of my hair and the light cloth of what I'm wearing moving in that direction with a great heave of air, along with the officer's.

He looks in that direction—it's moved to my left, his right—and so do I.

*Curious. Does the quick thing want to watch us struggle before it ends us by itself?*

Maybe I'll survive, either against the officer or against the whizzing being—something out of alien or ghost stories, just a speed that takes and kills and goes. Whether things go right or wrong or something in between tonight, it doesn't matter. The officer in front of me is still trying to kill me. If I die and he survives the night, he'll report my end to those above him as self-defense, and they will understand, tell him he did a good thing by relieving this fine country of yet another serial killer.

And, still, I step forward. And he shoots again.

This time, the speed is so close to us that I realize, in the second it takes to come and take the bullet with it and go, that the being within which this incomprehensible speed resides is shorter than us two men by about a whole foot, and that its figure takes up enough space between us to be considered the figure of a human being. And the second the speed comes and goes, with a high-pitched whistle-like rustling sound to match its quickness, I lunge forward again, at the police officer.

But, this time, I lunge specifically for his arms as he holds the gun, and when the gun shifts and is being held solely by his left hand, I lean down and, with everything I've got, bite his wrist, and, at the impact, he screams and the gun falls to the puddle-ridden street—it goes off when it hits the ground, but the gun is facing away from the police officer and I.

As the man screams, I move forward, *past* him—and I do something I've seen done and achieved time and time again in movies and shows, something that I hope works out here in the real world. I move my cuffed hands, my stuck arms, up above my head—feeling so many of my bones crack in the process—and then, once I'm back up against the groaning police officer—who I know is still holding on to his bleeding wrist with my flat tooth marks shining upon his wet skin—I move my cuffed hands and my arms back down—

And my cuffs are around his neck.

Without turning around to give him a chance to pull my cuffed hands away from his neck, I lunge forward, towards the wet ground, hearing his groans deepened behind me, and I pull and pull with my bending arms till he falls to the ground, taking me with him, though now, on the wet street, it should be easier for me to win, to survive.

I grit my teeth—still stained with the blood I pulled from his wrist, coppery blood I still taste and spit out in disgust as I continue my efforts—and I tighten my cuffed hands, writhing there on the ground, my entire back drenched from the puddles I'm struggling on, and I pull until the police officer stops squirming. I hear the crack of his neck, and the officer goes completely still behind me on the ground.

Panting, I loosen my cuffed wrists and move my arms back over the man's head, and I slowly start to sit up, staring at the world around me, the seemingly empty buildings, hoping that the fast blink won't come for me now. I turn my head, and inch my way towards the dead police officer, and I use my cuffed wrists to search the officer for keys. I hear jingling, and it's difficult to see with my fingers, but I take my time and I feel my way around until...my fingertips scrap some sort of metal, and there's the jingling noise again.

*The keys.*

No, not *keys*, but *one*. There's just one. One key.

I don't know how long it will take me—a few minutes, maybe several. As it's happening, it feels like forever.

I twist and turn and my fingertips do not dare let go of the metallic tip of the key, till I tighten myself against the body of the police officer at my back and I do not allow any room to be made between my fingers and the key, save for the space needed for me to find the lock of my handcuffs. Even then, when I do feel the smallest of openings, the tiniest of cracks within my cuffs with the tip of the key, it seems to take an even longer amount of time for me to press enough for the key to make its way straight into the keyhole.

The key's in—and then it pops back out. I manage to get the tip of the key back in—and then I slip and the key squeaks out and scratches my skin a bit.

And then, it finally happens: the key sticks, lodges itself perfectly within the keyhole of my handcuffs. Now, I have to turn the key. My fingers are already cramping, and as I twist them even further, gripping the bow with everything I've got, I let out an uncomfortable groan—but the key is stuck, and nothing is happening, and I'm turning the key the wrong way. I exhale, frustrated, the stubborn downpour not making things any easier, and I give out another groan as I attempt to make the same motion to turn the key, but the other way this time.

It works. It clicks. The cuffs go loose around my wrists. I pull them apart. I take my wrists, my hands, my fingers away. No longer restrained by metal.

*Even freer.* Truly *free.*

I bring my hands in front of me and give them a shake of relief, wiggle them a bit, flex my fingers, rub my wrists...

Except that I am not free. I am not free at all.

That thing is still out there. I'm sure that it's still waiting. But if it is, then *why* is it waiting? Why hasn't it killed me yet, like it has everyone else here? Why has it allowed me to free myself at all? Does it want to freak me out some more before ending me?

I stand up cautiously, trying to take in my surroundings—but, through the rain and the fog and all the dead bodies and blood nearby, I can't. I am justifiably terrified. And I need to get the fuck out of here before I end up like the officers.

But I don't think I can. I think I'll end up *exactly* like them.

And I don't even think it matters. I think I'm...alright with that now, which has explained my uncanny calm amidst all this confusion and shock and even terror. Perhaps, I'm free *because* that thing is still out there, close. I'm fine. I'm ready for my life to be taken.

*I promise.*

The chill in the air deepens, and the moon isn't even out to wink at my daunting misfortune or the dream of a miraculous fortune.

Nothing more than a dream. A partner, a friend—nothing more than a dream.

I'm ready to be killed. I'm alone. I'm all alone. And I'll *always* be alone. And there is nothing worse in this world than being alone. *Feeling* alone. So I'm ready.

I close my eyes. I tilt my head up, take in the unstoppable rain. I prepare myself for the unstoppable creature out there. I don't care about what it is, whether or not aliens or ghosts or demons really do exist—all I know, and all I'll bother knowing, is that I'm just ready to fucking go.

*Take me, thing, strange once-in-a-lifetime experience that killed off everyone in just a few mere seconds like some undiscovered wild animal, demon, whatever you are. Just take me.*

But the thing doesn't take me. It doesn't even fucking come for me.

I wait, and there's nothing. No one.

And, when I hear a small growl nearby beyond the fog, and even when it does come, it doesn't come for *me*.

The high-pitched growl gets closer, louder, and just barely through the fog, I see a small crouching figure—and then I see something grab the dead police officer with the broken neck in front of me, and take him away.

Instinctively, almost as if some subconscious and suddenly revealed part of me is *almost* ready to stay alive and survive even against the wishes at the surface of my mind and against all the odds before me—all the continued despair and darkness and desperation and isolation—I start to run away, run all the way back to the motel room I emerge from every morning during my time in this city. But, all the while, nothing follows and the chill at my skin disappears, so I keep wondering whether I'm being punished and why a thing that has killed all these police officers hasn't even bothered to try to kill me and save me from my stubborn loneliness.

· · ·

When I get back to my motel room, I'm filled with fascination, and yet, a tingling fear that maybe the thing has actually followed me to the fucking motel and I'm just going to get attacked in my sleep, without pride, without a knife at my throat or at someone else's, without a fight, without relaxation or release or consent. Unconscious and unrecognized.

So I decide I won't sleep at all.

I start packing my things. Even though I always use a fake identity and strictly cash when I check in and check out of motel or hotel rooms, there have been multiple murders tonight, the murders of important local police officers who had caught onto my previous crimes—multiple murders tonight that I didn't even commit—so I simply have to get going again, move somewhere else again.

I won't go far. I'll still make sure to stay somewhere within a two-mile radius of the local bar—the one I'll go to one last time on Thursday. If my perfect partner doesn't show up on Thursday, I won't just be moving from motel to motel, but I'll get out of Chicago entirely. Or, maybe, if there is a deity out there that maybe I ought to start believing in, I'll get killed, conscious and accepting.

*Wednesday.*

Call me paranoid, always watching my back these nights and especially tonight ever since yesterday's attack, or call me a paradox, but what if I *am* wrong, and there *is* a god, and that's the thing that killed all those officers on Tuesday night, without me even having to lift a finger, the thing that prevented me from being shot to death or taken away from my abnormally normal life even though it was, ironically, exactly what I wanted that specific night? Last night.

News of the incident is spreading from newspaper to radio station to live television news station. The cops haven't arrived to investigate yet—to take a look at the place where this all started, the local bar, and then to follow those officers' trail to the alley-shaped abyss where they all died.

But they will, soon, maybe tonight or tomorrow. They will, and when they do, they'll be looking for me, or someone like me, someone who they think might be me, the person they were last after. Will they notice that all those officers seemed to die in a way that no mere human could honestly cause?

I don't know why I'm at this bar today, on a Wednesday. I keep trying to drink my shock and confusion and fascination away, but I can't. I've survived some kind of animalistic manslaughter, not even baring a single bruise or scar while others bare bloodless bodies on hard, drying streets.

Was this...*god*...trying to show me that I should stay alive, or at least *want* to stay alive for the time being, that my life *is* worth living and that, maybe, I *will* eventually find what I'm looking for? Was there any actual *meaning* behind the attack and the ultimate decision to let me live?

•  •  •

*Thursday. Thursday night. Moonless again. And I—alone again. At the bar again.*

I don't mind that I can feel people looking at me—those who frequent the bar and saw me get arrested, and now see that I am back, totally fine, thinking that maybe they had the wrong guy even though I said I was the right one. Still, my leg keeps bouncing.

And then, someone comes. Someone approaches me. They don't tap my shoulder. This person only speaks, sitting on the unoccupied stool next to mine:

"Thought you might not be here, what with all the stuff that happened nearby." I turn to face the owner of the male voice, maybe even to greet this person. It's a young man, maybe my age. "They ought to close off this place for investigation soon, since it's where all those dead officers were last seen."

He looks...decent enough. Short blonde locks ending just beneath his ears, trimmed facial hair, light playful eyes. He's dressed casually, too. *Decent enough. Could it be? Could he be it?*

"Well, you're the guy, aren't you?" His eyes and his grin are sparkling.

"The guy with the dark hair sitting all alone at the bar. Yeah. That's me."

"Oh, good. Good. Exactly who I'm looking for. I guess *I* just wasn't brave enough—or, say, crazy enough—to put up a poster." This, to my surprise, makes me smile.

He makes me smile.

•  •  •

"So, how long have you been doing this?" the young man asks me as we walk. It's completely dark out now, except for the streetlights and the glow of the occupied rooms of apartments, the shine from stores and restaurants that are still open, cars that pass us by, the drivers on their way to, I imagine, a little less loneliness.

"Quite some time," I tell him. His name is Ollie, if that is his real name—I've given him my real one, only a drop of doubt drifting beneath all the shared darkness I dare to dream of. And this *Ollie* is still decent so far.

As we move forward, the world around us seems to be getting darker and darker, the lights shutting on and off till they settle on shutting off completely, and I start to wonder, if only just a bit, if this man isn't even human, if he is simply man-shaped, and if he is the thing I, and those unfortunate police officers, crossed paths with. I feel myself tense up a bit at the thought—whether it's out of fascination or fear, I don't know. *Both.* But he's too tall. The *thing* was close enough to appear, at the very least, a noticeable whole twelve inches shorter than me.

He gives an intimidated exhale. "That's...impressive. You mean...you've been doing this...*continuously* for 'quite some time,' then?"

I nod. I can't tell if he's excited or nervous, or if he's even *real.* Either way, somehow, against all the odds, he is still managing to continue to make me smile. I don't know if that's a good sign. I'm trying to stay positive on my last Thursday here before I give up, either on my choice of quest or choice of location or both—before I give up on everyone and everything, including myself.

"I'm...ashamed to admit that I am not as...*experienced*. I only have about...oh, between five and seven confirmed kills."

"What were they like?" I wonder aloud.

"The kills?" I can feel him frowning.

"The people, specifically. The people you chose to kill."

"The people?" A serial killer, interested in personalities, in people. It must sound strange to him, but does he only count his victims as nothing more than mere numbers? Does he not get to know them first, to see whether they even deserve to die in the first place?

"Yeah, the *people*," I stress.

"You mean...how did I choose them?" I nod. "Well, I just...choose them," he says, in the most matter-of-fact way. But then he pauses, takes my silence in, and backtracks: "Or, well, actually, I guess *they* choose *me*. They *chose* me." I still can't tell whether he's real. These words—they're exactly the kind I would choose. Has he been following me, studying me?

"But why? How? I mean...when it happened, when you encountered or came across these people, what did you see in them, before you decided to kill them?"

"What was it about them that *made* me want to kill them, you mean?"

All he's been doing is rephrasing my questions, my sentences, and, again, I nod.

"Well." He takes a deep breath. "I chose them the same way I chose you."

We're at a dead end. In an alley. Darkness all around us.

He's lured me here, isolated me, in the same way that I have lured and isolated my victims.

*He makes me smile. Until he doesn't. Everyone makes me smile until they don't.*

"You see, they were all...*bad* people."

"But...that's the kind of people *I* target. I go after bad people," I explain.

He snickers. The sound disgusts me. "No. You go after unsuspecting fools, according to your poster."

"Yeah, and fools are bad." *Usually, in my experience.*

"Not *all* fools are bad. Fools *can* be bad, sure, but...idiots aren't evil. Even if they happen to be evil, they certainly don't *mean* to be, since they're idiots and all."

I take this in. Take in his words. His manipulation. "So you chose me...you chose to meet me...because you wanted to kill me."

"And *you're* an idiot for warming up to me so quickly. See, you *are* an evil idiot. An idiot who means to be evil."

"I guess I should've rephrased: All bad people are fools."

"That's a more...understandable philosophy. Still. It doesn't change anything. I interpret you as a bad person, and therefore, to me, you're a fool. So it doesn't change any of my intentions."

"Your intention to kill me."

"And to make sure I cover up my tracks, of course," he adds.

"Of course." I sigh. Scoff at him. "It really is a shame, y'know. I think we would've actually been pretty great partners. Perfect, almost."

"*Almost.*"

I let my backpack slide down my right shoulder, and unzip it. I take my knife out, and Ollie watches me the whole time, his face eerily unemotional.

He keeps his distance. We'd been walking side by side this whole night, and now, we're a few feet apart from each other. We are more strangers to each other now than we were back at the bar.

"You know, I'd call you a fool, too," I tell him, "except that...you've caught me in...quite a sad mood tonight. And I've been in a sad mood for...quite some time. I thought you were the one. I thought *many* people were the one. The one for me. And now that you're not, and they weren't, now that I see that 'the one' isn't even a real thing"—I drop my knife, let it fall to the ground—"I think I'd rather just...die alone right now, right here, instead of waiting several more depressing decades. I..." I sigh shakily. "I'm really tired. I'm...sick of it all. I'm...sick of all this waiting and hoping and waiting and *waiting* and...I'm just really fucking sick of it."

He chuckles once in disbelief. "So, that's it, then? You're just gonna...let me kill you?"

"I am." I don't make any promises I won't keep. I am exhausted. Enraged. Stuck in a storm-shaped swarm of sorrow and static, simmering blue flame. Encaged.

"You're not even going to try to fight me?"

"No."

To test me, he steps forward...and then, when he's close enough, only about a foot or so away from me now, he lunges and he punches the air right in front of my nose, pretending to try to hit me—but I don't flinch, and I am not fazed by his attempt, and this is the last time that I'll make a fool out of myself by having hope, I promise.

This young man, he thinks he is *me*, that he is doing the world a favor by getting rid of bad people, and he doesn't understand that I am doing the same thing, and that I have many more years of killing under my thumb than he does. *Experience*, he'd called it.

But all he understands is the death against his hands. And *I* understand that. Perhaps this is poetic, for someone very much like me to be the one who ends me—someone who, ironically, doesn't see how alike we are. That's the shamefully imperfect part of this man's plan to take my life and take all my prospects with it.

But no one is perfect, least of all me, so I guess my death can't be perfect, either. And Ollie isn't the strange thing that killed all those officers, and that's alright. Maybe some things really are better off not being understood, not being known—despite my curiosity, I think I'm okay with dying without knowing what the fuck that very unreal thing was. That is how tired and how disappointed with my life I am. A life that *could've* been so very perfect.

*Maybe in dreams...maybe when Ollie succeeds here and I can go to sleep...*

He lunges again, punches the air again—but he hits me this time, and my head flops to the left at the impact. I feel pain roar through my cheek, but it doesn't matter. I can feel the inside of my mouth bleeding, but it doesn't matter. *It doesn't matter, none of it matters.* The blood and the pain are good things, I try to remind myself. It means that it's working, that I *will* die tonight.

"You're *really* not going to try to fight me?" Ollie asks. I can hear the frown in his voice. I don't look up at him as I shake my head. "Hmm. Okay. Fine. Cool. One less...piece of shit in the world, huh? One less...*lonely* piece of shit."

I don't say anything. I keep my empty eyes on the dark ground below us, waiting for the next blow, for the next rush of agony, for more blood, waiting for everything to go dark.

And that's when Ollie really lets loose. And I am already so lifeless inside, so unenergetic, that I don't even let out a groan or a grunt or a whimper or a whine whenever he hits me. I lay silent and still and slathered in sad solitude, blood that keeps swimming from open wounds he's wired into and across my skin with his knuckles, his fingers, his long and sharp fingernails.

He punches the other side of my face, punches me in the chin, the nose, the jaw. I feel pressure at my abdomen area, feel that same solid pressure at the backs of both my knees, one knee giving way after the other, and then that same pressure takes hold across my shoulders, my stomach, my eyelids while I'm on the flat, hard floor. The pressure of his heavy shoes. He's kicking me, too.

I lie there while he beats me up. I feel myself fading. I can capture only the loneliest, saddest, smallest stars of the sky above me whenever Ollie moves ever so slightly to give me a view beyond him and his bloodied fists. I wish I could see the just-as-lonely moon from here, but, even if it has found a way to come out on this initially moonless Thursday night, I can't. I can't see much of anything at all.

Ollie stops, momentarily. I can barely see now. I know my eyes are bruised and swollen. So is the rest of me. Everything hurts so fucking much and I feel like a puppet or some abused doll, and I tell myself over and over again that the whole point is for everything to hurt until there is only a bleak black hole, an immediate darkness swallowing me up, and no hurt left.

I wonder why he's stopping—he needs to beat me up more if he's going to ensure my death. I need, at least, a good concussion, or I need him to snap my neck, or to do something that is simply irreversible, something that leaves me literally breathless.

I turn my head to the side to follow what I can barely make out to be him moving away from me. From my crooked, halfway-closed, blurry eyes, through my droopy blood-soaked eyelashes and under my heavy eyelids, I can see what looks like his silhouette beside my broken and battered body, what looks like...him, picking something up in his hand. The thing shines a little under the lights that echo into the dark alley, and I understand, without having to see clearly, that he is holding my knife. The knife I dropped, to show him that I meant no harm and that I was ready to surrender to whatever he'd do to me, so long as it meant my heart would stop beating before tomorrow morning.

I can see him, and then feel him, coming back over to me...and he gets on top of me again, and then I feel it, my own knife at my neck.

*Do it,* I beg him in my head, unable to speak, too tired to do anything except continue to stay where he has put me, where I have let him put me. *Slice my neck. Please just let it be over.*

Perhaps he registers what my lack of body language and what my lack of actual language is telling him, because, then, he takes the knife away, and he lets it drop to my side, knowing that if I had what it takes to pick the knife up and kill myself on my own terms, I would have already done it. He knows I won't touch the knife. And he knows he won't kill me on my own terms, even though I have given him permission, even though, no matter how he kills me tonight, so long as I am dead, it will be at least partially on my terms.

*And I have always enjoyed half a sin more than no sin at all. The good one-half.* Without religion, I can only begin to call it, not a sin, but a sorrow, as I prepare myself for whatever he wants, whatever he has up his death-bringing sleeve.

I don't back off, don't do anything to try to protect myself. What'll he do, then, if he won't use my own knife against me?

He answers all my inner questions by putting his two hands around my throat.

"No, you need to suffer more," he tells me in a low and powerfully decisive voice, the kind I appreciate especially now, the answer solidified like all my past, and present, seclusion.

*I will not be alone in the future, because I will have no future. Everything ends now. You are doing me a kindness, Ollie. If only you could've saved me, Ollie, some other way, by being the one. But it doesn't matter how much more I suffer, so long as you finish it all, sooner or later on this night. I have suffered my whole life. This last time, these last moments of suffering, I will welcome as a gateway to sanctuary. I do not have religion, cling to my lack of belief in a higher power like a baby clings to a mother's teat, but perhaps the moon and the night, at least, will stay with my soulless body once I completely drift away.*

Certainly, this is a more intimate way for me to die. I accept it. I close my eyes as Ollie's hands squeeze and squeeze at my throat, and I try not to let my body instinctively struggle. It's no use, though, as my breath grows limited. My lungs are fighting, and my hands are rising to try to stop him— I have to relax and bring my hands back down to the ground. Better yet, my hands are now gripping the cloth at my shirt to keep from defending myself, from attacking Ollie back—Ollie, who is freeing me.

I feel all purple and red and blue and dark and I start to see the moon in my head, bright and forgiving and beautiful.

I am dying.

*Thank you, Ollie, stranger, idiot from the bar.*

And then the pressure at my neck is gone. Gone in an instant.

There's a high-pitched whirring noise, and Ollie's hands are off of me, released from around my neck.

There is no one on top of me anymore, and I take in a huge gasp, a huge gulp of fresh night air, and it bothers me to feel my body grow alive and heavy and simultaneously light with the wash of miraculous breath after breath after continuing breath, my heart trying to steady itself out with beat after beat after repetitive beat.

I can hear him screaming behind me, at the dead end of the alley. Ollie is screaming.

The man who is supposed to be killing me right now is letting out noises I was too proud to make tonight as I endured such perfect and passion-driven pain. His screams are blood-curdling, and I have to force myself to sit up so that I can see.

A figure is on top of him. I can see him still trying to lash out with his hands. He is trying to fight back, trying to survive. But he is not being choked to death. He is being...torn. Torn apart. *Dug into*. I can't really see much, but what I *can* see is enough: the figure is...covered in light blue cloth. Light blue...almost light turquoise, blue-green, like my eyes. And then Ollie's screaming stops, and I can only assume that I'm next, but that's okay, because that is exactly what I want.

The noise that the figure made when it took Ollie away clicks in my mind, stays there and rings till I realize that it's the same noise that came from the thing that killed all those police officers the other night. It's the noise of a flash, a blur, a blink, a whiz, the noise of nothing more than the purest and quickest of speeds.

"It's you," I manage to make out, my voice raspy, a cross between a desperate, whistle-like wheeze and a drawn out, blood-gurgling gasp. My curiosity has irreversibly increased now, and, before the entity kills me, too, I must know just one thing. The being turns around at my voice, and, only by its silhouette, I can see that it is a female-shaped creature. "What...are...you?"

The female-shaped creature stands, then, and moves towards me. The last thing I see before I fade are her lovely, lotus-pink lips, still barely pink in one corner and then along the left line of her upper lip, all mostly overshadowed by dark blood, *so much blood*, and the sweetest smile made up of incredibly white teeth, save for two long, pointy, overwhelmingly bloodstained fangs in the front of her otherwise very human mouth. The last thing I hear before I fade is her voice, high-pitched and optimistic, something delightful to hear before I go...finally, an answer to my question—albeit, I realize, too late as I close my eyes for good, not the answer I wanted or expected:

"Your partner, I hope," she says.

# CHAPTER FOUR

# THE NURSE

I hear people as I start to dream. There are flashes, visions, lights, in my dream.

"Shit, what happened?" A female voice, different from the one I last heard.

"He's my friend." There it is. The female creature's voice, light and airy. *The moon, come to life. Made real in my arms. In my arms...in my arms? No. Not in my arms.* I'm being carried. I can hear her voice up above me as she speaks. I'm in her arms—*she* is carrying me. And she is calling me her *friend*. What an intimate word, one to be so immersed in. *Friend.* "He got beat up pretty bad."

Doors open and close, and then there's more light. A room. A hall. The lights up above are changing as I blink, going from the dull golden glow of living rooms or waiting rooms to the bleak white flash of...office or hospital hallways.

And then I understand that I am not dead—after all, I do not believe in an afterlife. I am very much alive, and then it all comes rushing back to me as I struggle to keep myself awake, swaying in the female's hold—her last words, the strange and shocking answer to my question.

*What are you?*

*Your partner, I hope.*

This is not a dream. This is reality.

And I am listening to a very real conversation as I fade in and out of consciousness.

The other female scoffs. Is she a fanged creature, too? Am I being taken to a cult full of aliens or demons that secretly exist amongst human beings? "Okay, your 'friend'—well, what'd you do, make out with him while he was all beat up with all that blood on his face?"

"This *is* his blood—he fell on top of me after he passed out. Look, I gotta go. I'll take care of him. Tell Doc I have a patient to tend to."

"Look, hon, all that blood all over you looks way too much for me to believe that he *only* got beat up, but I like you and I like stayin' out of all the *personal* business a pretty girl like you's got goin' on behind the scenes. So, if you want me to cover for you in there when big boss is roamin' around and shit, it's gonna cost you."

"Okay. But you can't say anything, okay?"

"About your man here?"

"About my *friend* here, yes. No other nurses. No doctors. Just me. This is an emergency, and it's a secret."

"Yeah, I figured. Does your 'friend' not have insurance, or...?"

The creature huffs. "I don't know, I'll ask, but I don't think he does, no. Right now, I guess it's just safer for me to assume that he doesn't."

"What, you don't think anyone else saw you haulin' some beat-up dude in here once it got empty?"

"No one else saw. You're the only one who came rushing. Even if they *did* see something out of the corners of their very busy ER-nurse eyes, you'll tell them to keep their mouth shut, or *I* will. I'm capable of carrying a grown man without getting a hernia, so I'm sure they can all imagine what *else* the 'hospital freak' is capable of. You'll see to it that they keep whatever it is they *think* they saw to themselves."

"Or what, you're gonna beat my ass, too? Turn one of these hospital rooms into a wrestling ring?"

"There's no need for that. You'll be beating yourself up once I tell you that I won't do whatever it is you want me to do right now oh-so-badly. Now, *tell me* what you want."

A pause. "It's gonna sound silly, but—but it'll be easy."

"Really? Okay. 'Silly but easy.' What do you want me to do, pick you up?"

"Look, babe, we all know you're weirdly strong for a small gal because of protein shakes or genetics or, shit, steroids or whatever the fuck your deal is, and, sure, sometime, that'd be pretty fun, I'm not gonna lie—but, no, I'll skip on bein' cradled like an adult child for now. Does your 'friend' here know you were some miracle bodybuilder without a single muscle in another life?"

The creature groans. "Janie, seriously, what do you want from me?"

"Okay, okay. Just...um...okay, *please* put in a good word for me with Stevie C."

"Stevie C.?" She stops walking, and the world around me stops spinning but stays blurred. "So, you want him to pick at *more* than just your brain, huh?" *Oh, great. Female-creature-posing-as-a-normal-human's got dirty jokes. My head hurts too much for jokes.*

"Lynn, I can't help myself, okay? He's so *hot* and *smart*! He *absolutely* did not cheat or buy his way through med school like at least a *few* of the stupid and sexy and spoiled assholes here."

The creature carrying me starts walking again, and the world is swinging again. I am swinging in her arms. "Okay, okay. Look, I don't even know the guy, I mean, I've been here *years* and God forbid anyone other than you interacts with me socially for longer than a full minute...but, for your sake, *if* I do see him, I'll tell him—what do you want me to tell him?"

"I don't know! Be discreet, but just, I don't know, say good shit about me! You'll figure it out."

"'Janie and Stevie.' It's got a nice ring to it. Think I should just say that?"

"Shut up, you know you can do better than that."

The creature adjusts her arms under my back and legs like I weigh nothing. "Sure, sure. He doesn't seem to surround himself with *good* people, though, you know. I mean, he even spends time talking to *Sunny*, and—"

"Well, maybe *I* could be the good he surrounds himself with, and he could learn a thing or two about who he *ought* to be spending time talking to from you and I both. And, you're right, though—it *does* have a nice, poetic ring to it, 'Janie and Stevie.' Okay, look, I'm trustin' you, and I've got to head back now."

"Like we haven't risked getting fired for 'silly but easy' before. Years of nursing school down the drain, all for good ol' 'silly but easy.'"

"Hey, now, *true love*—or even some good sex, at least—is worth it."

"Worth anything and everything?" the creature teases.

"Worth anything and everything."

"Alright, Janie, see you later."

I hear the woman's footsteps start to fade off into the distance. "Have fun patchin' up your...'friend.'"

"Stop saying that!" the creature calls back.

"Saying what?" the other female shouts.

"Stop saying 'friend' like it's a dirty word! He *is* my *friend*!" I like the way she says these things. *He is my friend.* Such assertion, such animalistic intensity. Is she an angel? Am I actually dying?

All I hear is an echoing laugh from the woman, and then there's nothing left in the world except for the creature's repetitive footsteps under me. I see that same light turquoise color—the color of whatever she's wearing.

The next time I manage to open my eyes, only partially and for a few seconds, I can just barely register the fact that the lights above me have changed again, turning dimmer, and...the atmosphere has changed, too, and the air feels a little more closed, a little colder. And the female creature's small hands are no longer carrying me. I'm on a soft surface now. Something that feels very much like a bed.

"You're gonna feel a pinch, and then you'll be fast asleep, and I can patch you up without having to keep you from squirming or screaming. We don't want to draw any attention to ourselves. At least, not any more than we already have. But Janie's a good person—a perfectly trustworthy human, from what I've gathered."

The creature's voice is very human. And, yet, there's an otherworldly quality to it that makes me feel terrifyingly tranquil, so at peace despite all the piercing pain placed on my skin and throughout the insides of my body.

"Look, I'm gonna take care of you—then I'll go say something stupid to Stevie and I'll come back to check on you. You'll be awake by then, and I won't leave your side till you...fully come to your senses."

*Being taken care of*—it doesn't sound so bad. I can't fight anymore. I feel that pinching sensation she warned me about, somewhere on the inside of my left arm, and I can only fade now. I give a small nod of approval and acceptance before I drift off in front of the creature once more.

*Please just help me...help me, and help me feel better, and help me make my dream come true...*

*What are you?*

*Your partner, I hope.*

The words equally haunt me and harmonize with my own wishes in the dark, equally frighten me and fascinate me, just as the creature did on the night all the officers died—were killed.

*What are you?*

*Your partner, I hope.*

*Your partner. I hope. Hope.*

*Partner. Your partner.*

*Yours. Promise.*

•   •   •

When I open my eyes again, I feel the bed beneath me, see the light gray-blue ceiling above that makes me feel like I'm floating atop clouds—it hits me that the ceiling isn't what makes me feel like I'm floating in the sky—and I hear beeping all around me. Steady beeping. It's the sound of my steady heartbeat—it's the sound of an EKG machine. A heart monitor? *Beep. Beep. Beep.*

I've been laid down on a *hospital bed*. I'm hooked up to...fluids? Blood, serum? Also, oxygen? I don't know. But I feel alright now. The female creature isn't here—where is she?

There's music playing softly in front of me. It's a cover of "Put Your Head on My Shoulder." The turned-on TV screen is dull and I can barely make out the name of the artist performing the cover: a band called T. Rexico. The song makes my head hurt a little, makes things blur and reverberate all around me. I groan and reach for the TV remote and turn the TV off, wondering why this soft, sweet song has followed me from the bar and from the night of my almost-arrest, thinking about how the female creature has followed me, too, and why she has.

*Seriously, where is she?*

I sit up, immediately feeling a bit better, and I start ripping out the tips of the things pierced into me, start tearing at clear bandages over needles, start slowly picking the needles out and putting the cotton underbellies of other, not-clear, sandy and white-pearl bandages over the little spots that have been pricked and start to bleed just a bit. I remove my oxygen mask, try to remove everything except for the bandages and stitches all over me...

And then the female creature whizzes through the door, and I flinch at her sudden, speedy entrance.

"Relax, it's just me." I can sort of see her better now, but I still feel like some old man who's lost his prescription glasses. She must be exceptionally pretty, that much I can tell. Dark, short hair. Pale skin. Turquoise...scrubs. She's wearing scrubs. She's a nurse, and so was the other woman she was speaking to earlier, I deduce.

"Okay," I groan. "But—"

"Who am I?"

But she doesn't answer her own question right away, a question that isn't as important to me as the many others I have in mind: *Why are you here? Why do you apparently want to be my partner, or did I mishear that back in the alley, in all my dizziness before I drifted away for good? Did you see my poster? What* are *you? Not "who." But "what."*

Instead, she sighs and starts picking up all the hooked-up needles, and when the answer starts coming, I'm already trying to stop her from putting the needles back in. "I'm—"

I hold my hands up in front of myself as a gesture of wanting to be left alone—wanting the veins in my arms to be left alone. "Look, I'm okay, seriously. Don't...put those things back in me. Please."

"Don't like...your flesh getting pierced?" She smiles—not at me, but at herself, eyes fluttering down, like she's got some inside joke.

"It's not that. I'm just...seriously fine. I feel okay. Good, actually."

"That's not *you*. You're just all—"

"Drugged up? What'd you...do to me?"

"Well, it's not like you lost enough blood to replace. Your blood type's O positive, and we've got bags of that in the blood transfusion lab—um, the 'blood bag room'—but, well, you didn't actually really need any of that. But you did need some—well, you were beat up *pretty* fucking bad. Hence the IV fluids." She gestures to the bag of fluid above me. The one I'm no longer hooked up to.

"Look, I'm *okay*, and I just want—"

"To know who I am and ask me a bunch of other questions. Great, because I've got questions for you, too. But, first, you've seriously gotta keep resting." She reaches over to fluff up my pillow, and she smells like the most glorious of gardens, golden, garnet hiding in the ground, gushing waterfalls. "I'm a nurse first and a vampire second, okay?"

*What the fuck did she just say?* I still do feel a little woozy. My head pounds a bit as she sits by me on the bed. "I'm sorry, you're a...what?"

She shrugs. "A nurse."

"No, the other thing."

"A vampire," she says in a very uncanny matter-of-fact way—the same way she said "A nurse"—that makes me feel like I'm still asleep, dreaming, maybe even actually dead, trapped in my own trippy version of an afterlife or hell, with maybe a-very-real-god mocking me.

"Vampires...don't exist. Like, they're not...real."

I can tell that she's frowning at me. I still can't make out exactly what she looks like, can't make out the details of her face—but her voice is soothing, even as she scoffs and, leaning towards me, says, "Um, I fucking beg to differ."

Confused, I pull myself away from her, press the back of my head deep into my pillow. But she comes towards me, and she's so close to my face I can feel her breath on my mouth, coppery, bloody. And then her normal, human, white teeth—her canine teeth—abruptly elongate and sharpen, going from flat-toothed to fanged in a mere second.

"What the hell did you *think* I was?" she teases me, leaning away from me, retracting her fangs as she speaks. "I mean, you *saw* what I did to all those police officers."

*She's real. She's a vampire, and she's here, and this is real.* I struggle with my words. "Well—r-right, but—well, I don't know, I guess I thought you were...look, I...I confess, I honestly thought you were...maybe some sort of, I don't know, some sort of demon or alien or god or..."

She laughs. "Well, metaphorically, I guess you could say that I am those things. But you didn't think of anything as specific as a *vampire*, did you?"

I shake my head. "I'm still confused. Why did you kill all those officers? And not me? Why did you save me tonight? Why are you helping me right now?" *What are you? Your partner, I hope.*

I gulp. "Well," she starts to answer. "I couldn't let my future partner get *arrested* or *killed*, could I?" Before I can open my mouth to ask her to elaborate, she's already doing it: "I saw your poster. Outside. At the end of the parking lot. I was...on my way to work here. It was time for me to start my night shift, but I...saw your poster and it made me stop, and I...read it, and...well, I got curious. I work five shifts per week from night till the early morning—"

"Okay, but why do you keep calling yourself my *partner*? I mean, you're—I'm sorry, but you're not even *human*. Why are you calling yourself *my* partner?"

"Well, if I'm gonna kill people for the first time in many, many years, then I might as well not do it alone, right?"

It hurts to frown, but I do it, anyway. "What, you can't find another vampire to befriend?"

The smile disappears from her face; that much, I can tell. "I've never met anyone like me. Except for maybe the vampire who turned me—I think it might have been...some guy who wasn't 'some guy.' I never saw him. It happened while I was drunk. Blacked out at a party with my friends and many strangers, celebrating yet another milestone in the journey of becoming a nurse. That night, at the party, at someone's house, a friend of a friend of a friend—that's when he turned me. I don't know why he did it. Maybe he didn't mean to. Maybe he did. I don't know. I stopped caring a very long time ago. Maybe he's dead now, he never really bothered to show up and explain anything or even show me the ropes—even if he did, I might've killed him before he had the chance, because I was *enraged* about my...*situation* during my first few years of...well, being *this*. And those 'friends' I had...all those coworkers from the hospital I used to work at when I was human...well, they're all old now. *Older*. Most of them are middle-aged parents. Some are grandparents already, last time I checked from afar. No longer close to them to know for sure."

She sounds incredibly lonely, and it sends a pang of painful understanding through me. "You don't...have friends anymore?"

"Even if I did, I'd have to keep my distance from them. In my experience, friends are the kind of people you want to *completely* be yourself with—the kind of people you *can* completely be yourself with. And I can't be myself with anyone. This vampire, this...killer at heart. At least, that's what I thought, until..." She looks at me with such longing, it hurts—my absurd ability to relate, so far, to this *thing*, hurts more than any physical agony I've endured tonight.

"Until you saw my poster," I conclude.

She nods in this...almost *shy* way. *A shy vampire.*

It's still hard for me to wrap my head around the fact that she's real, and she's here, and she's speaking to me so...calmly. I fear being eaten, drained— but if she wanted to hurt me, she would've done it already, either by herself or by letting me be arrested by those officers or killed by that most recent waste of a potential partner.

Still, it doesn't make it any easier for me to breathe in and out steadily as I watch her with dry eyes, with vision that is still a bit blurred.

I am moved by her decision not to kill me right here, right now, and mesmerized by the magnetic draw of her voice, and mortified at the thought that such a magical creature could be as manipulative and monstrous as a serial killer like me, in the eyes of society. We're not so different, her peaceful presence implies, not to mention her very odd decision to want to be my partner—and it terrifies me just a tad to think of what might happen if we were simply to piss each other off like two regular people, like two regular *partners*. She could tear my head off my neck, and I could drive a stake into her chest—behind which I'm not even sure is a frozen or a still-beating heart.

"If people knew what I was, they'd freak out, and I'd be hunted," she tells me. I nod slowly, empathizing completely. "I mean, well, yeah, sure, I could just easily kill everyone in the blink of an eye, but I'd never...rest easy. I'd never be able to just...*live*. Being 'alive' might as well be the same as being completely dead—buried somewhere, under the ground. I wouldn't be able to live my life to the fullest. And keeping my identity, my true self, a secret isn't the hard part—it's the..."

"The loneliness that comes with it."

She gives me a small nod again. "I'd be even lonelier than I already am now, if I revealed myself. And that's this...impossible, unimaginable thought that I...don't even want to dwell on. Look, I've been...watching you. Following you, and—"

I try sitting back up through all the lingering pain. "Wait, you've been *watching* me? Stalking me?" I'm smiling sarcastically. I feel...amused. "Okay, great, *so* not creepy. Because *that's* what I want for a partner, a *creep*."

She scoffs at me. "Dude. You're a psychopath, and I saved you, twice now—show some gratitude."

"Sorry, *dude*, but it's a little hard for me, a *psychopath*, to 'show some gratitude.'"

"Okay, I misspoke. You're not a psychopath. You're...a guy who kills people."

"*Bad* people."

"Society would argue that it doesn't make a difference who you kill so long as you kill them. Either way—killing objectively bad people or objectively good people—you're committing a crime."

She's right—I've always thought the same thing, about how society would interpret my actions, though I interpret them differently. Still, I roll my eyes at her. "Whatever." There's a pause, and then my pride drives me to clarify: "By the way, for the record, you didn't save me."

"*Excuse* me?"

"I'd...given up. Twice. I thought that...maybe I'd...make a friend in jail, at least. And then, when I *failed* to get arrested, no thanks to you, there just...wasn't any hope left, and..."

"Yeah, I got that. But I thought you might've recognized *me* as hope."

"A symbol of how great my life can be if I just...hold on a bit longer, persevere with all my dwindling patience? Right, because *that's* what vampires are known for, in mythology. Being symbols of *hope*." Strangely enough, her existence, which is threatening as a whole, doesn't keep me from being sarcastic, annoying, or a general pain in the ass—someone to be pissed off at. And, strangely enough...

She puts her hand on top of mine. Her hand is small and soft and the gesture is sickeningly sweet. "You *don't* need to make friends in jail and you *don't* need to give up on life."

I move my hand away from under hers. "Oh, no, no—I just need to partner up with a vampire that could kill me whenever they want!"

"I'm *not* going to hurt you. Thought the whole 'saving you twice' thing would've given that away. *Saving* you is *exactly* what I did. I'm not going to cause you any pain—I promise."

I squint at her. Has she been following me long enough to know that I don't keep my promises? Is she mocking me?

"Okay, look, I don't *know* what to call you. It doesn't matter. Don't know what a *psychologist* would call you, nor do I give a shit. But I'm a *vampire*. Living—no, living *and* working amongst human beings to secretly get my fill of food. Nutrients. So, *of course* I'm a fucking creep. But *you* can't judge me. You stalk people, too, and not even to, like, eat them or drink from them or whatever it is you wanna call what I do—or whatever it is you wanna call what a vampire *ought* to do."

"Right, I just kill them 'cause I like it. For sport."

"Right, so that's not any better. In fact, I'd argue that it's even worse."

"It's not. It's the same thing. You're just trying to make yourself feel better about the fact that you're not even human."

"Why would I try to make myself feel better about it? I already feel great about it. It's not so bad."

"What, drinking fresh human blood?"

"No, actually, not drinking fresh human blood. All I get is...stale blood from the 'blood bag room.' I mean—not being human. That's generally...not so bad. I mean, sure, my first few years, I was freaking out a little. Actually, a *lot*. But then I got used to it. I watched people die, watched them be born, watched them die again. At the hospitals, I mean—the old one I worked at as a human and the one I work at now as a...secret non-human. Anyway, I...” She sighs. “Look, I’ve never met a serial killer before. I’ve never *talked* to someone who wants to kill as much as I do—though, again, I haven’t done it in a very long time. Killing.”

“Why not?” I wonder aloud. If I, a mere human, can do it on select nights and get away with it for so long, then why can’t she, a walking beast, do it, too? “You mean that you really don’t do what a...vampire ‘ought’ to do? Is *that* what gives you the right to judge me? You’re a vampire who can’t even ‘vampire’ the right way?”

She sighs. “Look, just—just go back to sleep, okay? We can talk more once you’ve gotten some more rest.”

And then I’m already starting to feel inexplicably tired. Sleepy. I’m not sure whether she has any special powers that can get me to be so at peace, but, deep down, I don’t really think that anything like that is the case. It’s strange, to feel so naturally comfortable next to someone—something—so inhuman, especially when I haven’t even felt so comfortable next to other people before. But I know that I won’t die tonight, not under her watch and not under her care—she said so herself that she is a nurse first and a vampire second. I will sleep on this bed, and maybe when I wake up, she’ll still be here, watching over me, thinking of our near future as potential partners, a future I am still unsure of but still very curious about.

She strikes me as undeservedly lonely—or, arguably, deservedly lonely by society’s standards. Either way, I understand that.

And I relax myself on the hospital bed, still afraid and still anxious, but...not alone. Not upset or quite as incomplete as I usually always feel. She won’t hurt me. Even if she hurts me, it won’t matter and I won’t escape the pain nor the death that’ll surely come at the touch of this dangerously strong demon—she’s right; I had given up on everything, on myself, already.

But she’s also right that, in some sick way, she’s been the shadow of hope all along, keeping me from successfully giving up. But for what? So that she could have me, a serial killer, all to herself? So that she could share her thoughts and her presence with another being? Something that I, again, completely understand, and do not blame her for. I’d been doing the same during the past Tuesday and Thursday nights—seeing, stalking, searching. And, now, I have found something so strange and so surreal that I still feel like none of this is really happening to me, like *she* isn't really happening to me. And, at the same time, for the first time in a long time, I have simply found something that could really be worth finding—or, rather, she has found me.

There's so much I'd like to ask her when I get up. Burning questions, and the even bolder burn of her beautiful, magnetic, big, monolid-shaped eyes—eyes so dark they must be as black as the night from which she emerged to save me from my own pessimism, to save me from my own stark stupidity and from other poisonous people's acidic attitudes, stained upon my even starker soul as blood...to save me from myself.

Before I close my eyes, before I drift off in front of her a third time, I catch a peek of an aggressive light shining through the hospital window—it's the moon.

The night wasn't moonless at all. The moon was there, but it just hadn't bothered to show up till later—much like the vampire, the nurse, the vampire nurse.

And the moon is full and so am I.

•　•　•

I don't know how to feel. Because I feel everything. When I wake up, I feel everything, like a newborn baby. I am scared, soothed, startled. I am suffocating, summoned, set free. I am a hundred stars, longing to be near the moon. I am everything—everything but lonely. I feel everything, but I don't feel alone.

I can't pin myself against one feeling. I wake to a wave, a myriad, a constellation. I wake to the vampire nurse, the moon, at my side again. I do not feel terrified of her. And, yet, when I wake, my bottom lip is trembling ever so slightly, and my eyes are twitching as I try to absorb her in her entirety.

"Hey, sleepyhead."

Her voice—still such a dreamy, delicate voice, one that takes me by surprise even though I am fully awake, conscious, and aware now. She greets me like she's known me for years. But she doesn't know me at all. She doesn't know that, should she happen to piss me off, I could...well, what *could* I do, against an annoying vampire? I could try out all the traditional things, ask her if anything would work against her as if it's just out of curiosity—a stake in the chest, exposure to the sun or silver or garlic.

But, for once, I can't focus on whatever it might be about her very human personality that might turn me off. It wouldn't matter what she said, what she did, or how she said or did it—she saved my life, more than once, and even if it was a mistake or a miracle, it makes everything about her seem so...stunningly unusual. Sick and strange in the most splendid of ways.

*As sick as me? As strange as me?*

I wonder for how long she's been this way, for how long she's been alive but not alive—and for how long she's been lonely enough to seek company in someone like me, a serial killer. It might just be for as long as I've been lonely enough to seek company in anyone, desperately, like a vampire disguised as a human, living among them, among us, so discreetly, yet with such definition to her actions and her being that she could, at the very least, be regarded as "weird" or "a freak" or "wrong" or just not a very normal person.

I blink and rub my eyes to really *see* her this time. Not that it would matter what she looks like...because, against every little human and understandably cautious bit of me that's been fighting it, she's already done it: she's already left her mark on me, and I've thought about her in my dreams, and I've dreamt for so long about killing people with some odd miracle by my side, and I've already subconsciously made my decision in my sleep with her eyes frozen upon me with all my flaws and all my unique freakishness, drool at my chin and fresh bruises and drying blood everywhere. So long as she swears, *genuinely promises*, not to drain me of my blood, I'll give her a shot, give things a try with her, the promise of partnership.

She's so pale that if I didn't know she was a vampire, I'd think that she was simply an extremely ill human being, maybe iron-deficient at the very least. Freckles and makeup are the only two things that create the smallest cascades of color across her skin, most notably on her face—both her freckles and a very natural-looking, powdery flush are smoothed out over the bridge of her nose an inch below the space between her dark eyebrows and come under both of her eyes. Her eyes are the darkest I've ever seen, with black, thick, long eyelashes.

She's wiped all the blood off herself, and she's wearing a different set of clothes—pajamas, I think, silky and white-pink—and her hair is wet, sleek and as black as her eyes and chopped shorter, longer towards the front, framing her heart-shaped face.

She looks, and is, absurdly adorable for a blood-draining, skin-tearing thing, and the unrealistic paradox, the contrast, of this makes my throat tighten. I cough and try to awkwardly swallow how immediately smitten I feel before I give her the simple, appropriate response of: "Hello." My face feels wet, like she's taken a wet towel and wiped the blood away before doing all the necessary further cleaning and stitching, but, as I look down, I see my clothes haven't changed, still bloodstained, and I am thankful that she did not undress me without asking me first.

"Your heart's beating awfully fast," she comments playfully, sitting again at my bedside. "You don't like being called 'sleepyhead' or am I just making you nervous?"

The way she's listening to my heart rate makes my heart beat even faster, and I feel like I'm going to pass out again—falling asleep in front of the creature for a fourth time would simply be unacceptable. I try to calm down, but I can't—and then her tiny hand is wrapped around mine, and I start to breathe a little better. She gives my hand a sweet, small squeeze, and my heart rate slowly goes back to normal.

*How is she doing that? Is she superpowered or is she having this effect on me just because she isn't human and I am?*

She is having more than one effect on me, and, instead of freaking out, I only find myself relaxing more, as if it's the most natural thing in the world, to relax beside a demon—for one natural killer to relax beside another.

"I *am* making you nervous," she concludes, almost to herself, her voice lowered.

She sounds a bit ashamed, but I don't say anything to lessen or end her assumption. I can't possibly begin to explain myself, or how she's the cutest killer I've ever laid eyes on, how her voice drips so close to my ears like a fountain of newfound youth drowning caked layers of ash, how my mind still has trouble piecing together the chain of events that have taken place ever since I put up my poster near the...hospital.

The hospital. We were at the hospital she worked at. That's where she took me.

But, now, we're not in that same hospital room anymore, and I'm not on the hospital bed she'd put me down on. She has laid me down on another bed entirely. A softer one, a larger one. We're still in a small room, but this room is different, with dimmer light, and the curtains are drawn, and the walls are still a blinding white like those of the hospital room. And it's then that I notice that the room is very close to being a replica of any hospital room, though it looks more like a mix of a hospital room and the kind of room the elderly live the rest of their lives out in once they find themselves in a retirement home.

We may not even be in the actual hospital anymore.

"I'd like to be called my name," I tell her. "Instead of 'sleepyhead.'"

She smiles at me, her teeth all human, normal, wonderfully white. "And your name is...?" She hasn't followed me around long enough or closely enough to know what it is. That's a relief, somehow. Or maybe she's just pretending not to know—to be polite, for us to be properly introduced.

"Timothy." I take my time sitting up on the bed. "What's yours?"

"Lynnette," she answers.

"Lynnette."

I take in her name as easily as I have taken in the moon whenever it has shown up. She has a name as lovely as herself, as lovely as her gesture to save a serial killer, rescue the kind of asshole who justifies nightly murders and lives without much of a purpose other than to move forward and count the dollars remaining and count the lonely mornings and evenings remaining and count bodies—and she, a vampire who thirsts for blood and for the chaos of a cruelly caused death, has much more purpose than I do, than I ever will or might, being a nurse and all, someone who helps save lives for a living. No human alive would do such a thing. Not even the most abnormal human out there would come to my rescue—those who at least tried ended up failing, ended up a failure. She's come to me, ready to be at my side, ready to be a literal partner in crime—but can she be at my side emotionally, too? Can she understand and support and accompany me mentally as even the vilest partners in crime could?

"Lynnette, where are we?"

"My home. It's a townhouse. It's two stories tall, and...it has a basement, too. For me to sleep in, during the day. I can give you a tour, sometime—some night."

"So you *do* sleep during the day?"

"Oh, like a baby," she laughs. "Just because I'm 'undead' or whatever—that doesn't mean that I don't need my rest. I'm a *nurse*. I watch some of the other nurses falling asleep during their night shifts sometimes—they take pills to stay up and do their job. And I live off blood bags—which aren't exactly as tasty, fresh, or energy-inducing as living people. So, yeah, sometimes, I find myself...begging for the sun to come up, just so that I can..." She shuts her eyes and makes a high-pitched snoring noise, and I chuckle.

"Okay, then. And, Lynnette, how long have you...been like this?"

"A vampire?" I nod. "Thirty years," she answers. "I was turned back when I was twenty-nine. I should look like a fifty-nine-year-old mom—or, I don't know, maybe a young grandma. But I don't."

"Well, people probably ask you—"

"How I 'manage to still look so young for my age,' yes. The people who see me—really, the only people who always see me, like my coworkers, have asked me what my 'secret' is. And I told them it's a mix of genetics and plastic surgery. Some people judge, some people don't. There was once this...patient who made this kind-of-uncomfortable comment about how people of my ethnicity 'age slower' or whatever. Guess I was supposed to fit that stereotype or...well, whatever. I'm sure he 'meant well,' in his mind, but that didn't make things any easier for me. Though, I guess I can really get away with using a stereotype like that to my benefit now. Anyway...well, I guess, in my experience, at least, you get over things a little more quickly when you've seen enough shit to last more than half a normal lifetime—an amount of time that isn't even half of my own special, endless lifetime."

I nod, try to absorb all the information that radiates from her so coolly like moonlight. "You can't read minds?"

"Nope, no superpowers here. The only superpower I've got is...being a total weirdo." *Me, too.* "I wish I could just tell those people that I'm just lucky. I feel like if I'd still been human, I'd be too scared to...get any work done on my face, anyway. I'm okay with putting a needle in someone to get a blood test done—"

She glances at my arm, and I look down, and that's when I realize that there's a bit of cotton, a bandage, stuck to the inside of...not my left arm, where all the other needles were, but the inside of my right arm. *Wait, what the fuck? Did she draw blood from me? While I was unconscious? For what?*

"But, even if I was still human, I still *wouldn't* be okay with someone poking at my face for purely cosmetic and superficial reasons. Just a personal preference." She shrugs again.

"Wait, did you get a blood test—?"

"Yeah, I mean, I had to make things look official, you know, just in case anyone saw me or checked the hospital cameras and asked. But they would've asked about...all the blood, so I'm really glad no one saw—or that no one, at least, got curious enough to come and ask me what the hell I was doing, even if they did happen to see me. Anyway, you should get your blood test results in about several hours or a day."

"How can you be sure no one—?"

"Because I hear and see everything."

"Are you, like...also, a god, or...?"

She rolls her eyes at me. "I can hear and see everything that's...close enough to wherever I am. Say, a few miles away from me, if I'm listening or looking closely enough."

"Okay. So, you've...been like this for...thirty years?"

"I was...quite young when it happened. I'd barely gotten done with my first few years of *actually* being a nurse. I don't really...remember what happened, though, or *how* it even happened, how I was turned, exactly. Like I said, it happened when I was blacked out, super drunk, after I was done partying and celebrating just 'being a nurse' with my friends, my coworkers from the first hospital. When I woke up the next morning, I tried to leave my apartment, but the sun burned me, and for breakfast, I hungered for oats and cereal swimming in a bowl of blood instead of milk."

She sighs, her eyes far away from me now, staring at the curtained windows.

"When I woke up that morning," she continues, "thirty years ago...I wasn't human anymore, and I *did* kill people, for a while, during my first few years as a vampire. And I *liked* it." Her black eyes are eerily empty now, hollow with hunger, wide with wicked intent. "But then I..." Her eyes soften suddenly. "I thought about...my parents. They, uh..." She inhales sharply. "Well, they died a few years ago, and...while they were alive, I had to stay away from them, even more than I usually did. My education and my career had already kept me away from them for quite some time, and then I just had to be kept away from them even more. I already had my own place, an apartment I shared with a few close-friends-slash-colleagues, but...well, I had to move. Move here. I had to go someplace they couldn't reach me, during their last years. And I could only...take up night shifts, at *this* local hospital, after that. Again, five a week."

She speaks with such passion, such *emotion* in her voice. It's clear that she's been bottling up all these words inside her for such a long time, chewing on all these truths and ruminating on her unique reality and simply *waiting* for someone to come along and just *listen*.

I imagine it'd be quite difficult for a paranormal creature to seek out a therapist, one who can chat via email and accept messages that only arrive at interesting intervals during the night, or one who'd understand her perspective *and* be trusted *and* deem *her* trustworthy.

I've been waiting, too—for someone to come along and simply listen—and I wonder whether she could take a breath at some point after she's released all this rawness within her, whether she could listen to me finally ruminate aloud, too. I wonder whether I'd be as brave as she is, to bare my past and present soul to a complete stranger, even if the stranger is one you feel like you've known your whole life, one who completely reflects how you also feel—for now, I highly doubt I'd be capable of such a thing. In this respect, I really am only human. *A shy serial killer.* I wonder what this kill-shy vampire—shattering her shield, and just for me, now—would think of that. Of *me. All* of me, especially the shameless and not-so-shy parts.

"So, I just couldn't see them as often, because they were available to catch up with me during the day, and I...never could be. I was always just so...I *am* always just so...*tired* once the sun comes up. And, as for the close-friends-slash-colleagues, I cut ties with all of them—ghosted them, pretended I didn't care about them anymore. It was just...easier. Once I stopped killing, once I moved here and tried to adjust to living the kind of life my parents would've wanted me to live...it got easier, knowing people without forming severe, deep attachments, socializing, acting normal, doing my job at night while taking 'bathroom breaks' or 'snack breaks' and secretly drinking from the hospital blood bags. It became—"

"A routine. I know. I've had my own nightly routine for a while now, too. Were your parents...also nurses, or...?"

"Yes, they were, both my mom and my dad. They were...incredibly intelligent and incredibly selfless people, my two role models in life, people I knew I'd always look up to, no matter what their flaws were. We never argued much, not even when I was a bratty pre-teen and then an even brattier teen before understanding more about who I wanted to be when I reached college—I honestly wanted to be as generous and loving of a person as they both were. But, when I turned, well, I just couldn't...be that person anymore. I couldn't *be a person.* I killed people because I was thirsty. And my nursing days, my days at the hospital, were simply over—all I wanted was to nurse my need for blood. Till I realized...a little too late, maybe...that my nursing nights, my nights at the hospital, didn't have to be over, too."

"Is this when they passed away, your parents?"

She nods. "I always wanted to follow in their footsteps, ever since I was little." *You're still little, sweet and strange and lovely creature.* "There was...a gap in that desire, of course, once I was turned. All I wanted, then, was to...quench my thirst. It was the only thing I could think about. And when my thirst was quenched and when I wasn't thinking about it, about blood...I was thinking about when I'd grow thirsty again, waiting for that time, planning out when and where and how I'd make my next attack, do it discreetly enough, carefully enough, away from prying eyes or listening ears."

"How did you...stop?"

"I tried to focus on the way my parents raised me to be. On what I was like before I was...bitten. What I wanted before I changed. It took me some time, but...eventually, I got the hang of it: meditation, centering myself long enough for my parents' dreams for me, and for my own very human dreams, to sink in—sink in deeper than the fangs of the vampire who turned me, deeper than the marks I left on my dead victims' bodies. I felt...balanced, then. Like I *could* be human, even while I had these inhuman urges. You know what I mean?"

She looks at me with such desperation, such longing. I am reaching from within for her in quite the same way. Can she tell? Have my eyes given me away the way hers have? "I may not be a vampire—and I may never like to be one, no offense—"

"It's a personal preference."

"Right. Regardless, I know exactly what you mean. So, the not-killing-people thing—that's because you...want to respect your parents' wishes and because you also want to respect who you once were, as a human. Okay. But...*how* is that a thing, now, or how can it *continue* to be a thing when you...well, literally killed *and* ate people to save me?"

She clicks her tongue. "Right. That *was* a little messy. My first time in *years* and everything. But what was I supposed to do, let my future partner get—?"

"You *really* want to be partners?"

She nods quickly, feverishly, assuredly. "I really tried not to kill or hurt anybody. But I saw your poster, got curious, and I...realized that you...only go after people who seem to annoy you or piss you off or are generally unlikeable. People who don't value you or respect what you believe in. People who seem pretty intolerable right off the bat. And it got me thinking—what my parents wanted was for me to be a good person, and to help people, because a nurse never discriminates against who they're treating. Good, bad, it doesn't matter—if you've got a patient, if you're helping prep someone to see a doctor or to get a blood test or whatever it may be, none of your opinions on the personality of the patient can *really* matter in the end. Of course, not unless they're a direct threat to you— which they rarely are, with insults ready at their throats, and cuffs at their wrists and ankles, anyway, where my fangs could be but never are."

She shakes her head, then, trapped briefly in some tasteless memory.

"I mean, listen, I've had some patients who were a *real* pain in the ass. There were times when I *really* had to control every instinct I had to rip their heads off. But I was a nurse, and it's a given that, as someone working in healthcare, you've got to be understanding and patient and kind. So, I just did my job and ignored all the shit-talking, the ignorance, the rudeness, the total disregard for someone else's feelings, hell, the racism. I took it all. But my parents...came here all the way from Japan, struggled for years adapting to life here, so that we, in the long run, could have a better life, so that *I* could have a better life, and they did not raise me *not* to stand up for myself, not to stand up to *bad* people. You and I, we see the world as it *is*: in black and white, desecrated by devils and appreciated by angels, and shaped by the human-silhouetted demons who roam in between—those like you and me. Besides, I figure that if I *do* start killing again—specifically terrible, terrible people, with you—I won't need to stick to blood bags anymore! I've adapted to them, sure, but...nothing beats *super fresh blood*, bursting and dripping and warming you up!"

I open my mouth to respond to her, but she's already talking again. I've never felt such prolonged patience for a person before—this need to say something, but a simultaneous and maybe even stronger need to hear them speak. Hear *her* speak, the sound of her voice alone a breath of fresh air compared to all the other voices I've heard on so many, *too* many, of my numb and noose-like nights.

"I...didn't see this as a second chance, once—at the beginning. I saw it as a curse. But, now, I see it as a blessing. I can do whatever I want, be whoever I want. I can save many more lives than the other nurses, but I can also take many more lives, too—it creates this sort of...balance, I think. Especially if the lives are worth taking, which is why I want *you* to be my partner. Because you're good at picking the bad ones out—the ones who are beyond saving, beyond understanding. And for such a long time now, I've been *needing* something other than hospital blood. Not the sight of it like you. But the taste, the smell. Something that is...alive, out there. Beyond these walls, and the hospital walls. I've just been...waiting to do it, I guess. Needing an excuse."

Now, as she finally takes a breath, I speak. "So, is that what I am? An excuse?" It frightens me, how offended I sound.

"You're an opportunity. Partner. Friend. I'm thinking that we really could...achieve some great...*bloodwork* together."

"Bloodwork." The word, like "friendship," "relationship," "partnership," "bond"—nothing at all like "getting a blood test done"— shines destructive and delicious on my mouth. "And, even though you're a vampire, *you're* not good at picking the bad ones out?"

"I'm old enough to recognize a bad person when I see one. But I don't exactly have the time to do anything about it. To follow them, to make sure I'm right about them. I have a job, one that I can only attend to at night. I don't have the time or energy or strength during the day, or even other nights I'm off, to follow my hunches the way you do. The sun won't let me."

"So that's what you want me to do? To be your eyes during the day? To choose our...kills?" She nods. I frown at her. Is she really that overwhelmed and lonely? Is she as desperate as I am? "Why do you trust me so much? My ability to...choose properly?"

"Because I see you inside me," she says abruptly, and then her eyes widen and I start blushing. She laughs awkwardly—her laugh is contagious, and I can't help but mimic her, an embarrassed giggle escaping me. "Sorry, that came out wrong." She sighs. "I guess I just...I see myself inside you, inside who you are. We're very different, I know that. But...we have a lot in common, too, I think." She waves her hand in the air, a nonchalant but very necessary gesture. "I don't know, I guess it's just...I have hope, too. I don't want to be alone, either. I *especially* don't want to go hunting alone. No girl does. I mean..."

She leans towards me, and I have to blink to try to steady my heart rate, smooth out the intense insistence of my nervousness around her—it doesn't work, and she hears it, the unromantic and uncertain thud-thud-thud, because she smiles at me, a little too kindly, the kind of smile I might give somebody before killing them.

"You can just kill people and enjoy it," she tells me. "That's not something I've had the privilege of doing for *years* now, because of my job and my beliefs and my parents' beliefs—and carrying the dreams of the dead with you like that, carrying just the whisper of so many wishes and wants...it's a beautiful thing that keeps me grateful and humble, but it's...also somewhat of a burden. My parents might be disgusted with me if they were here, but I'd like to believe, with my rose-colored glasses on, that they just might understand, especially if I'm taking the lives of people they would've been even *more* disgusted with."

I narrow my light eyes at her and I try not to make it too obvious how beautifully she's wrapping me around her finger with words I empathize with all too well. "You...envy me?" She nods, her dreamy and dark eyes a destiny I could so easily lose myself in. "But I..." I swallow my pride and tell her something so honest that I can feel myself turning even more pink as I do. "But *I* envy *you*."

She laughs at me. The way she stares at me, it sinks into my soul like fangs in skin, the glow of the moon radiating off her body so sweetly it reminds me of whipped cream, of snow, of sugar. I feel like I could burn and melt and turn to nothing more than bone marrow under her black, moonlit eyes. "Yeah, well, having super speed and super strength can be pretty handy sometimes, especially when you dream of your hobby including nightly murders and—"

"No, it's not your vampirism that I envy." She leans away and frowns, and I explain: "It's the fact that you are...constantly surrounded by people. You said you were a nurse when you were human, and you're still a nurse, so you have a...stable job, and I'm sure you've befriended your co-workers over the years, and, honestly, compared to me, so far, you don't seem to be socially challenged, and you...seem like someone who behaves in whatever way you need to behave so that you don't...get caught, or don't get found out. You're not even human, and yet, from what I've seen and gathered, you seem to do a better job of acting human than I do."

"Well, you're awfully observant—and so am I, but, well, look, I *was* human, once. That part has...stuck with me."

"I can say the same about my inhumanity. It's always there. Even when I want company."

She pauses. *Understands* me. "Look, just because I'm constantly surrounded by people—it doesn't mean that I'm not..."

"Alone?"

She shrugs. "Sure. Alone. Bored. Sad. Tired. The way you were...probably feeling when we met a few hours ago. All of that."

"So, you're a...vampire with...feelings."

"And you're a serial killer with feelings," she points out. "You seem...shy, for a serial killer. Hence the poster."

"You seem shy about being what you are."

"I have to be, you know," she replies defensively. "To keep up appearances and to seem to be something *other* than what and who I really am."

"Well, so do I."

We smile at each other, two absurd strangers, wanting to be less of a stranger to one another and wanting to be stranger together. Stranger and stronger.

I'd like to shudder at my hope, because my hope has always seemed to be quite untimely in the past, but I really do want to believe that somehow, a vampire and a serial killer *can* go hunting together at night.

"It's going to sound like the stupidest, silliest thing I've ever said," she tells me, "though maybe you're the only one who'd really get it, but...I guess I was waiting for someone like you who could inspire me to...be what I am without any shame or without a doubt or worry in the world."

"Couldn't you have just...turned someone into...a vampire? Made someone like you?"

"Yeah, but...that'd be against their will. You said it yourself—or, well, you heavily implied, at least, that...no one wants this life, 'no offense' and all that. But, maybe, out there, someone could—someone could come to embrace it, just like I did." I look away briefly, afraid—unable—to look her in the eye when she sounds so sure. "But, so far, the kinds of people I've met and have never revealed myself to—even if they think they want me, want this…they don't. And to do that without someone's permission—it'd have to be…a very special, desperate kind of situation, for me to do something like that and be even more of a monster than I already am. I grappled a lot with my own inner desires, sometimes, and I really did consider doing that, turning someone and having them just be who they are with me, but…it would've been too much to handle, I think, too much to deal with, and the kind of people I'd come across, whether they were dying or not—they didn't seem like the kind of people who'd have it in them, to go killing with me, and even if they *did* seem to have it in them, they only seemed…"

"Overconfident. Proud. Cocky," I finish for her. "I know. I've been there, too—regarding simply…picking someone."

She smiles wide enough for those nice teeth of hers to show again. She looks around the room, thinking, and then, she says, "Y'know…not that you asked or anything, but…" And, whatever it is she's about to say, I'm sure no one's ever asked before, but she's been longing to tell someone, anyone: "This room…is actually shaped like a hospital room, or is meant to mimic some of the functions of one—with all the hooked-up fluids and, well, just about *everything*—and it's this way because…I actually once tried to avoid killing people by…just going after *one* person instead of many. One guy. And when I went after him…I kidnapped him and I used him, locked him up and hooked him up in here, to have and to keep as my own little personal human blood bag. But I had to keep him alive for days and days and *days* and then even *more* days and…eventually, I got tired of that, of having to feed him and take care of him just to have access to fresher and tastier blood."

"You mean you got…lazy." I smirk.

She spits out an adorable mix of both a scoff and a laugh. "Well, hospital blood bags were, indeed, a *whole* lot easier to handle, even if they did not taste the same. I got bored. I'm still bored, with blood bags, but…it gets the job done, I guess. It gets every job done except…the most important one: making me feel…alive, even as dead as I am and all. Making me feel the way any magnificent monster is meant to feel."

"You *are* a…magnificent monster, but…you're not…planning on making *me* your new personal human blood bag, are you?"

Now, only the laugh comes out, and remains all around us in the air like freedom, *real* freedom. "No. No, I'm not. I promise."

And again, those words—her promise—bring back an almost uncomfortable edge into the air, and yet, it's the most familiar and soothing discomfort there ever could be, for me. I relax my eyes as I stare into hers and do my best to relax my mind and my heart as I make my decision about her. About us. "Okay, I'll try to be killing partners with you, try to give *this* a shot, on one condition."

"Yes?" She blinks, waiting. *So patient, so pretty.*

"Do *not* try to make me your next human blood bag. Please. Seriously."

She doesn't break eye contact with me as she says, solemnly, "I won't. I promise." Then, she adds, lightheartedly, "I won't make you my dinner— just as long as *you* don't try to murder me for sport. Deal?"

A half-grin *almost* forms fully across my face, though I feel a twitch at the corner of the right side of my lips as I say, "What makes you think I could even have enough power, as a human, to *do* that?" I try to keep to myself the many ways I'm aware a vampire could go weak under a mere human thumb, if all the myths are true, if garlic and stakes and silver, all along with the sun that burns her, ought to be simple enough to do the trick, here in the real world.

She smiles at this. Perhaps she can sense my silent and snakelike consideration, my sly intellect; perhaps she can't—no matter. Choosing to trust a vampire, to make a vampire my partner, sounds like the best path I could take right now. Vampires never existed before I bumped into her, and all I can see now, before my eyes, is my future, if only till I grow wrinkly and withered—a fine, foreseeable future filled with the falling, flailing, frail, failing bodies of fools. Like she said—or claimed, rather—she is a nurse first, and those who look after people's lives for a living should also put that first, and so she should put *me*, her partner, first. I would only know about half a thorny thing or two about that, about putting others before me—I do, after all, kill people to ensure other people's peace and safety the way mine is ensured when my blade or gloved fists meet the skin of a bad seed.

"I promise I won't try to murder you for sport," I officially vow, and her smile widens.

Does she really believe me? Do I really believe what I'm saying? *So many broken promises. And so many broken bodies to go with them.*

I *should* believe. Dare to hope, dare to dream a little bigger—a little *darker*. Dream. Wish. Believe. She is effortlessly ethereal, elegant, and she must be an embrace from the ebony night sky, and I deserve nothing less. I have never deserved anything less than perfection. My dream could really come true. My dream could really envelop my reality. My dream doesn't have to be just a dream or a fantasy anymore. *Finally. After everything, all my longing. After all these nights.*

"The sun's going to come up soon," she informs me, nodding once towards the window of the room. The softest lavender light looms through the closed curtains. "A key to the front door, for the house, is in this...little black bowl right at the front entrance. If you exit the room and turn to your right, you'll see a little hallway, and there'll be the entrance, and a small table right by it with the little black bowl right on top."

"You're giving me...the keys to your house? What, you can't lock the door on your own, now that you've got a partner?" I tease.

She beams at me. "I want you to feel at home. And feel free to take a tour on your own while I'm sleeping, by the way."

I shake my head. "I've been in this...stinky motel. Actually, I changed motels after...what you did to those officers, after they were...arresting me."

I'll thank her for that, someday, officially. I'm still feeling a little too proud for that right now. I feel like a hypocrite, killing others for their pride, while I bask in mine, even if it is to a more tolerable degree within me. Hypocrisy—the thing that no real god except for the killer can get away with. I'd let Lynnette get away with it, too. She really is a goddess, the moon soaking up all the dying night-light in this little room, the moon fearing nothing but the coming of the sun—and I, fearing nothing but the going of the moon...her, leaving, having to sleep while I sweep the streets for the unworthy. But everything is different now. I will only be without her for several hours of the day...and then sunset will arrive. And I will fall into the black abyss of her stunning, soul-sucking eyes again.

"But, really," I go on, "my whole life consists of...stinky hotel and motel rooms, one after the other. So, right, sure. Thanks. '*Mi casa es su casa,*' and all that, right? But, hey…just because we're partners…doesn't mean you have to…give me permission to invade your privacy like this, y'know."

She takes a deep, shaky breath. "I've been waiting *years* for someone to invade my privacy like this," she confesses, the words heavy and hungry on her tongue. I know that hunger for company so well, for privacy to be…simply *shared*, actually, rather than a thing as intense as *invaded*. She *is* an intense creature. Then again, so am I.

"Me, too." It comes out in a whisper.

"I've been waiting…" She sighs. "All the time." A sound so silent and soft, yet so full of loud want.

"All the time," I echo. A sound so full of *need*.

We stare at each other for a moment, then, both of our smiles relaxed, her ebony eyes sparkling with the slightest reflection from the coming sunrise gleaming through the curtains, her eyes holding me down and here like an anchor till she breaks our sweet silence, rising from the bed she's set me on: "I should go to sleep."

I start rising from the mattress. "Want me to see you to bed?" I can tell that she's blushing, actually blushing, from the way the pink powder on her cheeks appears darker now.

"Sure, you can walk me downstairs, if you want. And then you can stay here for a while, look around, make yourself at home, maybe scout the outside world for a good—or *bad* victim…and the day will be yours, and…"

"And then the night will be ours."

It's so beautifully bizarre to me, that she should look at me now as if she's discovered paradise. Whereas maybe, a little while ago, it was difficult for me to breathe or for my heart to comfortably, slowly beat near her…now, some time later during this range of a few hours, both my breath and my heart grow steady, and the world around me grows steady, and the creature could very well turn the sad storm, the sad story, of my solitary life into a serenade, a well-rested and serene sea.

Without thinking, I take her hand in mine, and stand, step towards the door of the room. "After you, partner."

She gives my hand a polite squeeze, her fingers so thin and tiny and her whole hand almost barely half the size of mine, and she steps in front of me and leads the way. "Yes. Partner."

It's now, as we're standing, that I realize how short she is, how small, petite, how almost fairylike. She really is a whole foot shorter than me, and I'm about five feet and eleven inches tall, which would put her at about four feet and eleven inches. How...cute.

As we walk, she talks to me. She talks about us and our future killing sprees: "I know you don't take any personal kills. So I won't bother recommending anyone from the hospital." She gives me a sly smile of knowing—but there's some regret in that smile, some wicked and hidden and heartless wish, and I try to seem like I don't, *can't*, notice, like observing people constantly hasn't made me sensitive to the smallest microexpressions.

I stop at the foot of the cinnamon-colored stairs that lead to the second floor, and she stops with me, as if to analyze my reaction, my expression. "You really have been following me." I grin a little, not at all bothered or creeped out—she's just like me—and then...I pause and say something that surprises even me. "Anyone you *would* recommend? From the hospital."

"Why are you asking? If we do go after them, we'd only draw attention to ourselves."

She's smart. Funny. I like these traits in her. *I like her*. So far. And so I tell her nothing but the complete truth: "I'm just curious." And I'd like to see the sad and subtle regret fade from her face.

Her house is one of those townhomes like the one the rapist occupied. It looks...normal, common, like the other ones. Everything is a light brown or a dark brown or dull brown or bright brown, everything wooden, everything lacquer and like the inside of a modern cabin. It looks like a nice, simple enough place to call home—but not for me, not yet.

I'd feel a little strange staying the night, or during the day, when she and I barely know each other—maybe, if this does work out, I'll stay some other time, but it's just too soon. I trust that she won't get up in the middle of the day and interrupt her own sleep and walk through the frustrating shine of sun coming in through little openings in between all the curtained windows just to kill me or drink from me. I think I trust her. But it's myself I don't trust. I, someone who's killed people for such a long time—would I really try to kill a vampire, catch it off guard, just to prove a point to myself? Just to say that I can and that I did. I'm more of a monster than she is, and she shouldn't trust me so easily just yet.

The walnut cabinets, greenery and brown-golden flowers coming out of oak-colored and cedar-colored vases, the wash of tawny and umber and chocolate all over the place...it matches nothing about her—except for, maybe, the warmth of her heart that she has shown me so far—and it is nothing close to what I'd expect of the living space of a creature like her. It isn't dark or depressing or dirty. The interior design is a mix of modern and traditional and everything is clean beyond reason and everything seems to sparkle like her eyes, and then I realize that, given her speed, she can get cleaning done a whole lot faster than the rest of us when she gets home before sunrise—even cleaning the dishes.

She leans against the stair railing, staring up at me. I take in her stare, take in some new dark and rich and seductive coffee-like perfume subtly, and, yet, as if it is everything the world could offer me to help me fulfill my dream, everything in this human-shaped inhumanity. "Okay. Well...other nurses at the hospital do bother me, sometimes, or at least, the little shit-talk they do and drama they stir up *does* give me a hard time. It...gets *annoying*."

"They think you're a freak—I heard you and your...friend. Nurse-coworker-friend?"

"Ah. Right. Janie."

"The 'good person.'"

"Yeah, well...the other colleagues I'm surrounded by every night aren't all good—keep in mind that just because you live to save lives doesn't make you an inherently good person. They can sense that I'm different somehow, and they don't like that about me, or maybe they're jealous because I look a little too young for my age, but I've learned not to really mind, honestly. Once you're out of high school, you think that 'cliques' are no longer a thing in the adult world, but you'd be surprised how, once in a blue moon, society proves you wrong. But, again, it doesn't really matter to me. They'll be dead long before me, anyway. They'll be nothing more than the smallest of faraway memories and the smallest of footprints in my very long life. It's not worth it—holding a grudge."

"I hope I'm not too forward in saying this now, Lynnette, but..." I take a breath and try to be brave. Bold. "I do hope I'm not meant to be the smallest of faraway memories and the smallest of footprints in your life. And, yes, I don't approve of personal kills, but...if you wanted to kill me, personally...I don't think I'd mind. Just as long as it was for an appropriate reason I could understand, and I wasn't being made your food." Sarcastically, I add, "I think any human would agree that getting killed by something inhuman wouldn't be so bad."

"I don't think any normal human would agree with that. And, you'd be okay with dying by my hand, so long as I didn't drink you to death and so long as I...didn't turn you into a vampire, either. So long as I just...let you die."

"Right."

"Well, even if you did die...human and all...you..." She takes a shuddery breath—an odd, interesting thing for the undead to do. "I can tell you, right here, right now, that you..."

"Yeah?"

"You wouldn't be the smallest of faraway memories or the smallest of footprints in my life. You'd be...very relevant to me. Very relevant in my mind."

"*Very* relevant?"

"Very." She sounds so sure of herself. So sure of *me*. A stranger. With many similarities and with the same lack of soul, sure, but still a stranger nonetheless. Unless soulmates exist and we knew each other in another life and this is all just...fate. I shudder, thinking of the word. I am disgusted with myself, but I can't help it—can't help the way she makes me feel...so *human*, so delightfully human. I am torn in half, smitten with glee, and smitten suspiciously. This is all so strange. And I ought to be nothing but grateful for it. She's here. She'll be my partner tomorrow night. And I will take everything with a grain of salt, while also hoping for the best. I really hope everything works out tomorrow night. *She* can't disappoint me. Can't. Simply *can't* the way all the others have, the way the *humans* have. If she does, we will both be dead, and my dream will die, too, and it will stay dead, just like me.

I frown, taken aback. "Really?"

She nods. "All the time."

"Even after my death?"

"All the time," she reinforces.

We continue walking, then. Walking through the halls of her home, which she's opened up so willingly to a human not to be trusted, a human she trusts against all odds, against the little time we've met and spoken, against everyone and everything else.

We turn a corner, come to a dead end, and stop at a door at the right of the tiny hall that has the dead end. I realize we must be behind the staircase. This door must lead...below the staircase. She opens the door, and it gives a creak, and...there are more stairs—leading down, down, down.

"Basement?" I ask her.

She nods. "Also known as...my bedroom." She takes a step inside—a step down the stairs. "Would you like to...come in?"

All I can see beyond her and beyond the first few steps is pure darkness. "Sure, I can...see you inside." I hope I don't trip down the stairs. "And then you'll...get into bed, and I'll leave, and I'll...see you when it...becomes night again. Do you wanna meet somewhere, at a specific time?"

"I can meet you here, at home." *She doesn't say "my home." Not "my place." Not "the house." She says "at home." Just at home. At home. Home. Hers and mine now. Ours. Our home. Home.* "Just come right in when you're ready. After about three-thirty. The sun should start coming up at around six, so that gives us about three hours together. To stalk, hunt, kill, and clean up together." *Together.* I'm burning each time she says the word.

She starts walking down the stairs, and I follow her. The light from the open door disappears as it swings shut behind us with a curt creak, and then I have to use the railing to find my way after her, have to feel the surrounding spaces in order to make sure I don't bump into anything. It is almost completely dark, except for the small light still shining from the top of the stairs, from the cracks under the closed door. I can't really see anything, and even when my eyes adjust to the dark, it's still difficult for me to make out what her bedroom might be like, what parts of her personality might be reflected here, in this most private place, her own little space so full of potential secrets and poisons. It occurs to me that she must be able to see in the dark like a nocturnal animal, that she must be able to see the world without light as well as she could with light, that her inhuman sight serves her in ways that normal human sight never could. I suddenly feel very self-conscious. She must see and feel and sense everything in an absurdly clear manner, just as well as a bloodhound smells its prey from miles away.

"I'll leave my shift at around three in the morning," she informs me. "I can do this for...a bit, I think."

She really, truly thinks everything will be okay between us? That we'll work well together, kill well together, that I can help her embody the beast she is and that she can help me feel a little less lonely? That we can do what we have already done, since she killed those officers and my last attacker, that potential-partner-turned-poison, like a gorgeously gruesome monster, and since she's kept me company these past few hours?

"I think I can...leave work about an hour or two early every night I get the chance, and I'll make a promise every night to make it up at some point...and then, maybe after about a week or so, I'll start leaving earlier and earlier in the early morning, and I'll tell them, Janie and Doc, that my friend, who was all beat up, is living with me and that he needs my help and care, that he needs my personal attention. Janie will remember, at least, and you should heal and look normal again in a few weeks, so, until then, I don't think she'll—"

"Your friend. Right. Me. 'Friend.'"

"Well, I'm hoping you won't just be my partner," she admits. "Inevitably, if we're both lucky, you might just be more than that. Wouldn't a friendship be even nicer than a partnership?" Her hope sends an unexpected rush through me. I try to swallow my anxiety, how awake and intrigued she has me feeling.

"Well, both the...friendship and partnership...might be short-lived. Given that I'm mortal, and you're...not."

"Nothing between the two of us will be short-lived. Not in my mind. Even if you're...fully intent on dying human and staying dead...it's like I said: you'll always be living in my head forever, renting a room in there until the day I, too, somehow cease to exist. You'll live in my mind a long time, killer."

I don't know how to respond to this. So I say nothing. I am delighted by her honesty, the way she'd come on too strong if I were a normal person—except that I'm not, and so I soak up everything she says like an abandoned sponge now surrounded by a sea of life and starlight.

"Anyway, I think that I've acted human enough to get away with that, to make my colleagues and the doctor I work with and the chief nursing officer allow me to leave early more and more every night or every other night or however often we're going to do this—and, I mean, I've worked at this new hospital for many, many years now, so...I *will* manipulate them into being okay with it, not having me around as much, having someone else take up the last few hours of my five-night shifts until, eventually, maybe I can take more time off, even use my vacation hours, which I've *never* used, by the way. Maybe, then, I can even spend...entire nights with you."

"You want to—you'd be okay with...spending *entire nights* with me?"

"Yes, I would."

"But...you don't even really *know* me." She can see me frowning through the dark, can't she?

"I think I know you a little better than all the other partners you tried to have, tried to make yours." There's a smile in her voice. Does she know how suffocatingly curious I am about what it'd be like to have her, to try to make this vampire nurse mine? She's right—a creature such as herself, intelligent yet isolated and somehow even insecure, does know me better than the other people I've only pretended to wholly bare myself to. "Besides, I *will* get to know you even better night after night after night."

"And...I'll get to know you better, too."

"Yes. You will. I hope I won't...disappoint you. Once you get to know me better."

"I hope you won't, either. The police will be going after whoever they think killed...their kind. *Human beings* will be going after whoever they think killed their kind. So we'll have to be careful, discreet, and I'd say that...it'd be okay, for you to...play with your food and all, so long as you *do* clean up after yourself. I'll play with my...disappointments, and I'll clean up after myself, too. Like you said, we'll do more than just help each other kill. We'll help each other clean. Anyway. I'm beginning to think you *can* read minds."

"I can't, I promise." *There it is again: I promise.* My own words, mocking me. It's...sort of hot, honestly. And I'm crazy for feeling this way, thinking this way, aren't I? *Already crazy, feeling crazier.* "But I *can* read into voice tones. And I *can* read...body language." *Is that the slightest bit of slick, sweet suggestiveness that I detect in her own voice tone?*

I chuckle nervously. "And what does...my tone of voice say?"

"Your...*body language*...tells me..." I can feel her stepping towards me. I look down, barely able to make out the lines of her lovely face in all the darkness. "You won't kill me. *You* won't disappoint *me*."

"Only if *you* don't try to kill *me*."

"Drain you, you mean." There's a smile in her voice, and the way she says these words makes me turn red.

"Sure. Either-or."

"I won't. I promise." I can't help but tighten with tranquility when, again, I hear my favorite words coming out of her mouth. It's so bewildering, to hear something that makes me want to be cautious but then also makes me want to go crazy and do something as chaotic as cupping her face ever so gently in between my hands, the hands of a killer who rarely seeks or finds tenderness. She makes me want to live my whole life immediately, until, suddenly, I no longer can. She has the kind of voice I'd be more than happy to hear day after day after day—*night after night after night.*

"Okay. I promise, too." And, with that, I start stepping away from the creature, start trying to feel my way back towards the steps to find my way back up—if I stay here a moment longer, I think my heart will leap out of my chest. "So, at around three-thirty a.m., I'll come inside."

She chuckles, and I blush harder. "I'll be waiting," she vows. "Partner."

I smile at her in the dark and then leave without another word. I leave her to rest, leave the basement, leave the hallway...pick up the small key to the front door from the black bowl on the brown table at the entrance...and, locking the door behind me, I leave the home, leave her home, leave *home*, holding that key tightly in my hand and stuffing it into the pocket of my blood-splattered jeans like a brand-new promise.

# CHAPTER FIVE

# PARTNER FOUND

The day opens up before me like a red river full of radiant possibilities. Radiant *promises*.

I have never been so excited to scout or stalk or select before. I am wholeheartedly a match that can stay lit, and—against the very paranoid and very *human*, emotional part of me that's been panicking and sweating with fear—I feel like a spark has been set off under my feet and in my mind and in my heart, and I feel as though everything around me must also be set off as powerfully as that spark so that I can find even more of what I want, need, what I've searched so long for: the comfort of killing at someone else's side, killing with the one who sent that spark soaring within my mortal body in the first place.

I have never before been so fully fascinated by what the day has to offer me—and what the night finally, *finally* has to offer me. I have also simultaneously never hated the day so much—for taking so fucking long, for being so insufferably drawn out like some sadistic disease, a slow sting, softly delivering scorching death hour after hour after hour.

I'd felt anxious about finding a partner, someone who read my poster and responded, someone perfect and loyal and reflective of myself in at least more than just one way. Now, I only hope that the one I've finally found, and found so recently, is the kind I'll really be happy to keep till death—*my* death—do us part.

I know I'm speaking of the partnership as if it is a marriage. *Too soon, too soon.* But I can't help it. It *is* like a marriage—it *will* be, if luscious Lynnette proves herself to me tonight, and if I can find it in me to prove myself to her.

A serial killer and a vampire—proving themselves to each other before the sun comes back up again to steal the hours away from us. An unemployed citizen and a helpful nurse. This is certainly not the pairing I dreamed of ever since my first few years of growing lonelier and lonelier, but it is the one the universe has given me, for now, and so I will accept it with gratitude and a gulp of curiosity in my throat, with it consuming my every thought like the concept of undiscovered gold.

I have to find a victim so unworthy, so disgusting, that they are worthy of dying tonight, terrible enough to be killed by both our hands.

*Like picking out what kind of chocolate to bring on a first date. Hazelnut-powdered chocolate? Dark chocolate? Caramel-drizzled? Vanilla-infused? Mint chocolate or milk chocolate?*

I shake my head as I leave the motel room—the key to her home in the pocket of my new, clean jeans—and I try to dismiss the unexpected thought as I start making my way towards exactly the kind of place unlikeable people ought to be found: another poorly rated bar, near the motel, since I won't be going back to the other bar close to the hospital, the one now surrounded by police officers with eyes peered not just for justice, but for revenge.

*Unexpected thoughts from an unpredictable mind.*

Unexpected words from an unpredictable creature, answering, "Your partner, I hope," to my "Who are you?"

*I'm not picking out chocolate for a first date. This isn't a date. This is a partnership that will bring us both peace, and I ought to treat the whole thing as...professionally as possible, even though it is actually a very personal thing. I am picking out blood for tonight. Fresh, warm blood for my partner. For her to feast on with her fangs, and for me to feast on with fascination dripping from my eyes like tears of joy.*

I wonder just how unexpectedly—maybe even expectedly—alike the mindset of a serial killer and a vampire could be. A human who kills, and a vampire who killed so long ago that she doesn't want to do it alone—wants the strength and unyielding confidence of a mere *person* by her side.

I feel like a fool for grinning cheek to cheek as I walk on under the sun. I feel like a fool for grinning cheek to cheek as I try so hard to imagine the unimaginable: my first time killing with a partner, and not just any partner, but a nurse who is also a fucking vampire.

She could sink her teeth into any part of me she wanted, and my life would be lost, and, using a silver knife or a stake or stuffing powdered garlic down her throat, I could drag her sleeping body under the sun, and her life would be lost. And yet, we will meet at night—or, in the morning when the world is still mostly asleep and all our prey are unsuspecting and the sun isn't ready to rise just yet—and we will promise not to harm each other, not to lay a single finger on each other—unless she plans on holding my hand like she already has, giving it another soft and sweet squeeze—and we will watch other people draw their last breaths together.

*Not all fools are bad. But all bad people are fools.*

I am not bad. I am as gray as Lynnette in a world so full of nothing but black-and-white. But to be a fool...

It frightens me, to think of myself in this way, even for just a moment. But Lynnette and I—we will *not* be the blind following the blind. We will not be fools. We will be strong together and we will stay that way for as long as we can. Her presence in my life for only the past several hours has been so surprising that it has stuck to me like black tar, unyielding and shining like blood under the dark sky last night and under the stupid sunlight now, too.

I will not be a fool for trying to find solace in something so different from the world, so different from what society has painfully pierced me with, someone so unique that she ought to, really *could*, find solace in me, too. Fools are fragile. Fruitless. Forever famished. Bidding farewells all too soon.

*Especially those so immediately smitten with the uncanny, the inhumane.*

·  ·  ·

I have found our fool for the night, the dark and early morning. It's almost sunset now, as I sit by her like an innocent stranger focusing on his own little berry cocktail.

I've ordered the garlic parmesan fries here—they're not too shitty, to my surprise, and I can't help but half-smile as I chew on a single fry, thinking of how Lynnette might judge me for it. Shit—she might even avoid the mere smell of it on my breath if I end up not brushing my teeth tonight before bed. I'll follow this female fool to her home, make note of where she lives, and then I'll go back to my own motel room and I'll sleep early enough to try to wake up at around three in the morning. And I'll brush my teeth again.

I really do hope that the female fool will find her way out of this bar and make her way to her house soon. If not, I may have to find another fool—or I may just unfortunately show up on Lynnette's doorstep without any fools in mind, without any fools to offer her.

*Except for myself.*

I need to stop thinking that way—first, thinking of myself as a fool, which is such a loathsome thought, and second, thinking of offering myself up to her like some piece of meat, some piece of meat craving care and kindness and genuine company, unsure of whether to be ashamed of myself or curious and excited beyond belief.

But what if I did meet her without any prey? What would she do or say? What would she think of me? Would I face the wrath of a thirsty vampire, or would I face the understanding and forgiveness of a nurse, and...well, what would we do with our time, then, if not hunt? What would we do for the remaining hours of the early morning, before sunrise? Talk? Actually get to know each other?

How the fuck am I supposed to talk to a vampire or have meaningful conversations with someone who doesn't seem to have any social problems, especially when I can barely talk to people without sounding like a complete creep? She doesn't seem to mind at all, what I am, just as I don't really mind at all what she is—I admire and respect what she is, though I'd never want to get that way myself, since I see meaning in the concept of living only one short life and all, meaning I take away from morons whenever I can. If she minded my lack of social skills or sympathy—things that have already seemed to improve within the last several hours around her—she wouldn't have sought me out. So, will we actually get to know each other, if we don't hunt the whole time, or hunt at all? Will I be capable of speaking to her as naturally as I feel like I have ever since we first spoke to each other? Will this partnership of ours *really* work?

*I guess I'm terrified of finding out, and, more than anything, I can't wait to find out.*

The fool ends her night early. I'm more than grateful for this, to see where she lives so soon, to prepare to take Lynnette there, feeling as though the moon has already come up to watch over me.

The thought of pretending that I couldn't find a victim just to spend more time getting to know Lynnette instead of hunting with her—it's so strange, I've always preferred killing over conversation...

I'll just have to save that plot for another night.

Now, the fool is leaving—Lynnette's *food* is leaving—and I must leave, too. Find out where her place of stay is before I sleep for just a few hours. I must quickly walk after her. *Follow.* Follow the path of the late night and then the early morning to Lynnette.

•   •   •

I try to steady my heartbeat as I stand right outside her townhouse with my glove-filled and knife-filled backpack in hand, but it's hard—the harmony of it is completely broken, bursting like the heartbeat of an infatuated freak. I let out a sigh and a groan and try my best to take deep and steady breaths, to stabilize my very unstable self.

Can she hear my breathing from inside the house, my heart racing? Can she tell that I'm already here, a few minutes early, before it's exactly three in the morning?

Without doing any more overbearing overthinking, I march up the stairs to her front door, take out the keys from my new clean jeans, and, with them, I unlock the front door—I don't knock or ring the doorbell first; she said that her home was open to me, gave me the key, called her home my own, too, giving me permission to step right in without having to ask her first.

I walk in, and I am met with silence.

I call out for her. "Lynnette?"

No answer.

I walk further into the house, step towards where the hallway moves forward alongside the staircase that leads to the second floor. "Lynnette?"

Nothing.

I crane my neck, let my voice echo up into the second floor and not just throughout the first. "Lynnette, I'm here."

The suspicious silence persists. But I persist, too.

Is she in the basement? I walk in the hall, shout towards that area: "I know I'm, like, a few minutes early, but I...thought I'd just...come inside, anyway."

Still, nothing.

Maybe I'm not being loud enough. An impossible thought, since she has heightened hearing, but, still, I shout, louder, "Lynnette?" And, still, no response.

She's not here, is she? I'm too early, aren't I? Only calling out to the walls in her house, summoning nothing more than the air passing from room to room.

I place my backpack down and awkwardly stroll into the living room, which is just as brown and just as much of an equal mix of traditional and modern as everything else, every other part of the house I've seen so far. There are deer antlers mounted on the wall above the wide-screen TV and the fireplace below the TV—the antlers remind me of dominance, protection and simultaneously a cause for concern, potential danger, the sharp points sticking out like elongated, enlarged poisonous thorns. The fireplace is brick, a brownish burgundy color. There's a ticking old dirt-brown clock on the modern glass table with oak-brown legs. The glossy, orb-like modern chandelier with many more, multiple glass foggy orbs sticking out from it stands out as it hangs high from the living room ceiling, contrasted against the very old and traditional soil-soft rug running beneath everything, the table and surrounding tawny brown couches, like a muddy lake.

There's so much of her here, I conclude, who she was and who she became and who she is now. Her personality. Molded by a life that's grown up with traditional beliefs and expectations and hopes, traditional truths and tastes, and has grown even more through modern designs and decor and dreams.

Twenty-nine years as a human, a daughter with two parents, two nurses, and then thirty more years as a vampire, daughter of recently dead parents, a nurse with years of experience herself. Surrounded during night shifts, but alone inside. Alone, like me. So much like me.

I wonder what aspects of my own personality might be reflected here, in a home that she would so comfortably and kindly and coolly dare to share with me.

I sit down on one of the couches, the one parallel to the fireplace, which is a chestnut color and leather, while the other couch, against the wall and perpendicular to the fireplace, is more of a mousy brown shade and seems to have a softer and more comfortable velvet-like texture. As the minutes pass, my foot begins to tap, and I grow unavoidably, undeniably tense. It is well past three a.m. now. And as more and more minutes go by, I shake my head and bite my lip and I'm on the edge of the couch and I start to believe that I have been stood up.

And then, when it has almost been half an hour, all kinds of poisonous possibilities pass through my head. Lynnette, somehow being killed by suspicious and clever people. Lynnette, somehow being arrested by police who've found out about her existence, silver handcuffs around her tiny wrists and garlic smeared on her tiny, full lips. My found partner, lost.

It's simple.

If she has really stood me up, then I'll wait for her to come indoors before the sun rises. I'll hear her out. Maybe this is an accident, a misunderstanding. Somehow, I feel like that'll lead to disappointment on my end, anyway. For a vampire to leave me feeling disappointed—I'll have hit a new low then. Still, I'll listen to whatever explanation she offers me. If her explanation sounds valid enough to my ears...I don't know what I'd do, how I'd live the rest of my life knowing that a magical creature exists out there and that even they do not want anything to do with me. I think I'd just let her drink me up at that point.

But if her explanation sounds like complete nonsense or just an excuse to get rid of me—if no hint of honesty taints her hot tongue—then I'll shrug, pretend to be understanding, pretend that she's brainwashed me into buying into her bullshit, and wait for her to fall asleep to do whatever the hell it is I have to do to kill her before she finds the energy to wake up and kill me instead.

But if none of this is the case—if something terrible has really happened to her, then I'll find whoever inflicted that something terrible upon her, and I'll kill them.

So it's actually not that simple.

I promised myself no personal kills—I got so close to getting caught when my blade first touched my cheating girlfriend and her choice of sexual pawn years ago. Whether I kill Lynnette for offending me or kill people who may or may not have done something offensive to her, it'll be personal.

*Oh-so-very personal.*

I take a deep sigh.

*What to do, what to do...?*

I guess I should just do the...*normal* thing and...*wait.*

*But that's* so *disgusting.*

But what else am I supposed to do? I've waited this long, haven't I? For a partner, for the other part of my nightbound soul. I can wait a little longer, if only to figure out what the fuck is going on and what, if anything, I can do about it.

I look around the room, try to focus on...anything but the time. And there's so much to focus on—paintings of the woods, photos of trees, the strangest decor everywhere, from those little miniature Christmas-decorated house figurines sold during the holidays to modern little creations of clay that don't even look like much of anything. There's *too* much to focus on.

My head cranes behind me, towards the stairs that lead to the second floor...

Should I go exploring? What else of her thoughts and hobbies and likes will I find in the other rooms and hallways and walls?

My head cranes towards where the hallway leads to the basement behind the staircase...

Her basement-slash-bedroom would surely contain so much of who she is, what she's like when no one is watching—not even when her partner is watching. I wonder if I can get in and out without leaving a scratch or unsettling any dust, if she'd notice whether I was there, if the smell of my humanity might linger in the air like the heat of freshly squeezed blood.

I am about to stand, to take my chances, to give up on all this waiting around without doing anything—

She flies in through the front door, sending a gust of wind my way, the curtains of the living room swaying a little. An embarrassed smile lights up her face, and an explanation flees from her voice quicker than I can question her.

"I'm sorry, I-I got caught up with...trying to explain things to my...superiors. Trying to explain to them that I just...*had* to go and that someone else *had* to come in and cover for me. Cover 'the graveyard shift,' not knowing they'd be covering the graveyard shift for someone who'll never be in a grave, for the sake of...our own little graveyard shift of sorts, yours and mine. Ignoring getting the bloodwork of so many worried, waiting patients done—for the sake of *our* own...bloodwork..."

I don't know what to say. This *is* a misunderstanding. I've always been so quick to get disappointed, to doubt, to see the darkest and dullest in people. But she is not "people." I feel like I've just been slapped in the face. I simply can't speak.

"Are you...okay?" She can hear my heartbeat quickening the more I try to absorb all the wrong "what if's" my mind had been rustling through like the pages of a book full of nothing but misery and evil.

I still can't say anything. When I do open my mouth, I can only stammer: "I-I...I—I..."

She squints her eyes at me—at my racing heartbeat. "Is...something wrong?"

I take a deep breath, try to calm myself. I swallow my pride. "I thought you...stood me up."

She laughs at this like it's the most ridiculous thing in the world. "You thought I—" Her face softens then and turns serious save for her sweet smile. "I could never stand you up, Timothy. You're my partner now. Hell, I gave you the *keys to my house*."

And then, she's out of sight, as quickly as she arrived and I can barely see her shadow zoom upstairs.

She appears before me several seconds later. "Changed into different scrubs," she explains. "'Killing scrubs.'"

I narrow my eyes at what she's wearing. "Different scrubs?"

"Well, yeah—my work ones are a light teal color, but these scrubs are slightly darker by *just* a shade."

I feel like scratching my head. "I can't...really tell the difference."

She grins. "You're such a guy. With time, your eyes will adjust." *And so will my heart, I hope.*

She makes her way back to the unlocked front door, walking normally this time, and when she turns around, she reaches out with her hand towards me, offering it to me, offering the darkness, what is left of the night-like and moonless morning.

"Come on, now. Show me the fool you've found."

• • •

"She's a husband-beater," I clarify in a hushed voice as Lynnette and I watch through the living room windows of the house like two squatting children waiting to pull off some stupid prank like ringing the doorbell and then running off. "She was drunk at the bar, leaving voice message after voice message for her husband after, I'm assuming, he threw her out of the house. She was sitting close enough for me—and for other people in the bar, too, I'm sure—to hear everything."

Lynnette raises her eyebrows at me in the dark. "Husband-beater?"

In a low voice, I explain: "She was saying shit like: 'All you are is bruised and used and, oh, you'll tell everyone I abused you, but you won't tell them what you did to deserve it, you annoying, weak, good-for-nothing little bastard.' Something along those lines, anyway. That's what got my attention. And the more I listened...the more I thought that she'd be exactly the kind of person we'd enjoy ending tonight."

"You're exactly right. I'll take any kind of spouse-beater any night. Starting with this particular husband-beater, tonight."

"Well, then. You can be the wife-eater. Save him from this cycle of abuse if his insecurity, stubbornness, or pride won't let him save himself." It hits me then, how widely I've been smiling at Lynnette on our way to the husband-beater's home and as we've looked inside from the side of the house.

"So, how will this work, our first kill together?"

"Well, I was thinking that...I'd go in first. I'd break in—or if you think it'd be easier for *you* to break in—"

"What, with all my wonderful vampire lock picking skills?"

"With all the years you've lived and the many more different kinds of skills you might make use of tonight."

"It's been too many years since I've made use of those kinds of skills." There's a warm, darkly sweet, licorice-like quality to her voice that makes me attracted to her right now in an absurd and almost animalistic way, but I have to make myself look away, distract myself, stare back into the lightless house.

"I'd like it if *you* broke in." This is all I say to her.

"And then, what? I...kill her, right there in the master bedroom, wake her husband up to the small piece of heaven he might've missed out on ever since the two of them first met?"

I almost smile. "No. You're not going to kill her anywhere in the house, or anywhere close to the house, either. If you do kill her in the house, it has to be in the backyard, where you can hide her body behind bushes or underneath the dirt if you're patient enough—even then, it won't really matter how careful or clean you are because the police will eventually find the body by then, and hopefully you won't find yourself still lingering in the area by the time they do. Regardless, I've always preferred to kill in alleyways or abandoned warehouses or other empty buildings—places people won't even think to search till way later. Less *personal* places. As for us, cleaning up after ourselves, after one another, together...well, cleaning up might be a little easier, considering that you'll be...draining and licking up all the leftover blood."

I swallow the awkward fear that follows the image in my head, my little vampire partner lapping up blood from skin as if it is water amidst an unnaturally hot evening—and along with it I swallow my untimely arousal.

"So you'll drag her out of the house," I decide. "Maybe you can even gently...pick her up while she's still asleep...run off to an alley somewhere, and..."

"The pressure with which I run might...wake her mid-run. It'll feel like strong winds are blowing in her face. When there's no wind outside at all. Even if she wakes up, I'll just kill her as soon as possible. In an alley somewhere, like you said."

"We should find the alley first. You can leave me there, and then come back for her in the house, and then bring her back to where you dropped me off."

"Because you want to watch me."

I give her a tender look, a tender nod. "I've never...watched before. It's strange for me, even talking about it, *thinking* about it. I'm curious, what it'd be like. Not to do the killing, for once, but to watch it happening right in front of me instead—and watch it happening by a *vampire's* hand. So, yes, I'd like to watch you—if you don't mind."

She returns the look. "Not at all. I'd like to watch you, too—maybe next time, on the next night or early morning."

I can feel warmth spreading throughout my entire face. "I trust that you'll be able to...take care of dragging her out on your own. Picking her up and...getting out of the area. Without waking the husband up or startling him."

"I can't promise that."

"Well, there's no house alarm. At least, not right now. Maybe they recently moved in or something, I don't know. But...no house alarm. She was drunk enough to break into her own house earlier—or maybe the house belongs to the husband. Maybe she didn't have the keys, maybe he took them away from her...I didn't hear anything from her muttering and shouting into the phone indicating that anything like that happened."

"No house alarm. Wonderful." She turns to me, straightens herself. I give my legs a stretch and straighten myself, too. I take my backpack off the ground before me and put my arms through the straps, ready for whatever happens next. "Hop into my arms." *Never mind. I'm not ready for that.*

"What?"

"Well, I've got to run you to our killing place for the morning, don't I? And get back here as soon as possible to bring the husband-beater over there, too."

"Our killing place for the morning." I love the sound of that. "Right. Well. I honestly thought that we were just going to…run off to that…killing place. Run together. To a place that you'd spot and choose and label as…*fitting* for our…activities. You know Chicago better than I do. I haven't been here for too long."

"Yeah, I figured, since you put up your poster where you did. I'll have to introduce you to all the beauties of Chicago some other time—it seems you've only been exposed, unfortunately, to all its blandness. You won't have to stay blind for long—not with me by your side once it gets dark. Look, running together, side by side—that'd take up too much time right now. No offense. Even if you were a world-class athlete, an Olympic track runner, it'd still take up more time than necessary, and we'd lose too many minutes from the rest of our time together, before sunrise. It's easier if I'm the only one doing the running."

It makes me smile, how much she's willing to spend so much time with me—still just a stranger, fresh out of the day and plucked anew from the dark I grew accustomed to plucking from. As much time as she can, given her quarrel with the sun.

She wants to run quickly enough, away from me for only a few moments, so that she can make her way back to me with our murder and her meal and so that we can spend what is left of our hours on this early morning bathed in blood and what normal people would call a burden—so that we can do more than wait for a bloodbath, so that we can do more than clean up and bask in the aftermath of our little adventure. So that we can…understand each other more. Spend real time with each other…maybe even speaking, instead of slaughtering, or sipping on the subject of our slaughter, in her case.

For a moment, I wonder whether she has abandonment issues, whether she's already growing too attached to me in such an unbelievably short amount of time—but I could ask the same thing of myself, since what I do next is throw away all of my pride in exchange for something totally new, something that could just be much more pleasurable and fascinating if I let it.

"C'mon, Timothy. Wrap all that toxic masculinity up and put it in the back of your mind and hop into the arms of a vampire—sorry, a *woman*. 'Cause it'll be now or never—I promise."

"Okay," I tell her hesitantly, with a sigh.

She holds her arms out, and I stand sideways and step near her—and then it's like the world has been flipped sideways and I'm laying down on a bed, a bed only as soft and as fragile-feeling as the smallest two arms and hands an adult woman could have, and the world is moving by me in large gusts of wind that didn't exist seconds earlier, a blurry breeze only her speed could create and keep, capable of being conjured only by a creature like her.

In just a few moments, several seconds, we are somewhere else, and she stops running, comes to a staggering halt, but as she places me on the cold cement ground, the world doesn't stop running for me.

I bury my face in my hands. Even then, with my eyes closed against the skin of my palms, I see the wind buzzing by like so many breathtaking, beautiful, blood-red stars.

"I feel...dizzy," I groan.

She doesn't let go of my hand, and it makes my dizziness worse—makes the blush blooming throughout my skin *blossom*. "Oh, sorry. It's your first time. I think I should've moved a little more slowly."

"You moved just fine. Spectacular. I'm only human—and I feel a little woozy...I feel a little like throwing up...just a bit..."

"Here, just put your head between your legs, or just put your head down, towards the ground." *I'd rather just put my head on your shoulder.* I can tell that she's probably trying not to laugh at me. I obey her instructions, and, already, I feel maybe the tiniest bit more relieved. "I'll be right back."

The sound of her departure leaves another gust of wind filling the air near me, and then, she's back in only several more seconds, and, when I look up from the ground, I see that she's holding the husband-beater in her skinny arms. It's then that the husband-beater's eyes widen and she suddenly starts to struggle, as if her dreams have dipped themselves into her reality until her reality has drowned and now the dream *is* her reality—she's been carried at a vicious speed, and only to arrive at nothing more than extra viciousness, a violence that she may not even be self-aware enough to see as the very deserved kind. She topples to the ground near me and starts gasping for air, for answers.

"What the fuck is happening?" she whimpers. She looks at Lynnette, then at me. "Who the fuck are you people? What's—what the fuck is—?" She holds the voice of someone who never expected to be this anxious or afraid in her life, someone who feels entitled to everything, including not having any harm come to herself. I almost snicker at her vulnerability—does she even know, right now, exactly *how* vulnerable she is?

I look at Lynnette as I stand, the world a little less fuzzy now, and I tell her to "Go on."

Lynnette smiles at me, and as she does, her canine teeth elongate to become fangs.

And then, in just another flash—before the husband-beater can come up with any lies to defend herself or before she can even question what she is here for or once again question who or what we are—Lynnette is atop the woman, her fangs sunken deep into the screaming husband-beater's neck. The suddenness of the impact, the icy irresistibility with which Lynnette attacks the human, causes an artery to explode, blood streaming and splashing out at Lynnette—Lynnette, who, with her focused face, tries to suck in and contain all the pouring blood from the choking husband-beater and who tries to hold the human down at the chest and shoulder with her ridiculously small but ridiculously strong hands.

The husband-beater stops her incessant struggling after a few seconds of Lynnette's constant slurping, and then, as the husband-beater takes her last breath, all that is left now is for Lynnette to continue drinking away into the still-dark morning, and for me to watch with my widened and hope-filled and completely fascinated eyes, and for us to clean up, to make sure the husband-beater is put away somewhere safe and maybe even, with Lynnette's help, somewhere unsearchable.

As I watch Lynnette hunched over her dinner in her killing scrubs, it really sinks in, deep beneath my bones and dancing across the ballroom floor of my bewildered brain, that she isn't a psychopathic person, not a lawyer or a cocky policeman like the ones who almost arrested me or a CEO or a surgeon or a journalist—she is a kind, yet crazy, blood-craving vampire and she is one freak-of-a-nurse and she is nothing I asked for and yet everything I could've possibly wanted and dreamed of having in a fellow killer. She is magical in ways no human partner could ever be for me. Every human could try, but no human could come close to being her.

Just because I like being human doesn't mean I dislike her; just because I can no longer think of a human being as a viable partner doesn't mean I dislike myself.

I have always really liked who I am. I've just never really liked who other people are before. The last time I even tried, with my cheating girlfriend years ago, that person wound up being, of course, completely detestable. This is my first time really, truly liking someone, solely based off the first impressions she's given me so far, saving me from myself twice and opening up her home to me and sharing this secret side of herself with me and—

*The past twenty-four hours.*

It's just too soon, isn't it, to like her as much as I do right now, watching her tear through flesh to get to blood? Though, maybe not. It's perfectly understandable, actually. It is, after all, my first time—my first time witnessing and going through *any* of this. She must like me, too, enough to share all of this with me and want to share more, so many more nights or early mornings or both. I feel a thrill of luck as I feast my eyes on her radiant body, the blood splashed across her face and her hands, across that desperate, dangerous and yet delicate mouth.

She looks up at me. "I'm full."

I smile at her. "For now, sure. You wanna get started on cleaning up, then?" I can't believe it—she just killed someone, and I watched in awe, and now we're going to clean up together, and then, some other time, I'm going to kill someone, and she will watch me in awe, and then we'll clean up together again, and again and again and again until we are smack-dab in the middle of her sweet, little *All the time.* We will be eating together and washing the dishes together. We will be *living the dream*. A human serial killer and a vampire nurse will be making their dream a reality.

"I've never really...'cleaned up' before. It's just that I—well, I clean up so much at work, you know? Clean up people that have to get stitched and all that, clean up in every way I could think possible—I mean, in the ER, we had this guy who came in thinking he was gonna die, and then he just...let out a big ol' wet fart and he had diarrhea, right there on one of the hospital beds. I've *always* had to clean up. I mean...it's a *hospital*. When all is said and done, everything and everyone must stay sanitary. So, outside of that—outside of the hospital...and outside of my home, too, of course...I've just never really felt the need to *clean up*..."

I sigh. "I'm sorry, Lynnette, but when you're killing either with me or around me...you're going to have to start feeling the need." I give her a kind smile.

"But even when I first became a vampire, I left a trail of bodies for a few years—"

"And?"

"Well, yeah, people noticed, but...it's not like they noticed that it was *me*! Or a *vampire*, for that matter. Vampires aren't supposed to exist! According to society, according to the whole wide *world*, I'm not here."

"Lynnette, you killed people thirty years ago. For a few years. And then, there was this wide gap, a gap that continued since...before you saw my poster, before you saved me. You haven't killed people for a very long time, but if you start killing now, after all these years, and if people start to notice again—especially if you kill in the same city, in Chicago—"

"Which is also what I did before!" She shrugged.

I pointed my finger at her. "*Exactly*. Then everyone might start noticing a pattern, especially police officers and detectives who never got any answers thirty years ago. It's *safer* to clean up."

"But even if they *do* notice a pattern, the same drained blood and the weird torn flesh and everything—"

"Torn flesh? What, they don't notice two fang marks?"

"I use my fangs to tear the flesh when I'm almost full, so that the fang marks aren't noticeable, unless some fancy forensics team looks deeper than they should. What, didn't you see me do that with my mouth just now?"

*I was busy trying oh-so-very-hard not to imagine where else I'd want your mouth with my safety guaranteed and my limbs intact, you fucking asshole.* "So you *do* get what I mean about being safe and careful and you're just being stubborn."

"Timothy. Even if they notice something, anything...they'll be looking for, I don't know, a fifty-nine-year-old man, at most! Serial killers are more likely to be men! It's not sexism, it's just statistics."

"Your trail of bodies might change the statistics," I mumble.

"If they know what or who they're looking for—they don't. Look, we're spending too much time talking about this."

I blush—she doesn't want us to spend our time arguing. "You're right, we are." I kneel before her, kneel in front of the backpack I've brought with me. I unzip it, take my black gloves out, and snap them on my hands. "Listen, we both work with gloves, you and I. You do your work with your gloves on, the same as I do. You, in the hospital, and me, out here."

"You forgot, once." She half-smiles, teasing me.

"So that *was* you. You moved the body. The evidence."

"Yes—and *drank up* the evidence. Drank up a lot of what you left behind. *A lot.* That one girl, one you didn't forget to put your gloves on for—what was her name? Angie? Gosh, she tasted as good as she looked. Her assaulter, on the other hand..." She made a disgusted face.

"You moved the evidence. Drank up the evidence. You cleaned up." I take an extra pair of black gloves out and hand it to her. "That's all I'm asking you to do right now."

She doesn't take my gloves. Instead, she reaches into the front pockets of her scrubs and pulls out...two blue gloves that are of different quality—hospital gloves. "I came prepared."

"So then what's all the fuss about? And why didn't you have your gloves on *before* you killed the woman?"

"I forgot."

"Just this once?"

She shrugs. I am...subtly furious now. "It's not like they ever found my DNA."

"You can't read minds, but you can...make it so that you're never found out?"

"There's just never been any need before. I'm not being hunted."

I bite my lip to keep from yelling at her. I can't yell at something, someone, like this—someone who is so strange and different and adorable and admirable that every little word coming out of her mouth, even the ones I very much disagree with, is a word I want to shut out or interrupt with a very human kiss. "There'll be a need now." She groans quietly and waits for my inevitable instructions. "Look, I know that, deep down inside, you're like those middle-aged people who are way too stubborn to change their ways or try something new, something that doesn't exactly match the things you've learned and kept inside ever since your youth—"

"*You're* not fifty-nine years old, and you're *already* too stubborn."

"Just...humor me. Put your gloves on and help me move the body."

She puts her hospital gloves on. "I don't see the point in putting my gloves on now when they weren't on before." I'm about to give her a look, but then, she declares, "I'll be moving the body, you know. I can do it in seconds."

"Stop trying to show off. I'll pick the spot."

"I'm not trying to show off," she says in a small, enchanting, defensive voice. Her eyes soften, then, as she explains: "I'm trying to impress you. It's *not* the *same*."

I blush again. "Well, stop." I turn towards the dead husband-beater—and then I pause and turn around to face Lynnette again. "What're you doing, trying to impress a human serial killer, anyway?"

She shrugs. "I don't know. I can't really explain that myself."

I shake my head and look across the empty, dark streets in front of us, thinking about where we should leave the husband-beater. "You can't or you won't?"

She looks down, awfully shy as she confesses: "Can't. Won't. It's not really the kind of thing that can be explained with words."

I'm beet-red now. Is she telling me that she's...attracted to me? That she really, actually likes me? How would I even begin to tell her I feel the same way and that, when we're talking and even bickering like we were just now, it feels like I've known her my whole life?

I must be dreaming, hoping too hard, reading into things.

I shake my head at myself and swallow whatever salvia is left in my dry mouth and I simply say, "We can drown her." It is a declaration, and yet, I don't know Chicago as well as she does, so I ask her for reassurance, for permission—and I've *never* asked anyone other than myself for reassurance or permission. "Can't we?" I wonder aloud, knowing that it is more, that it really *is* reassurance and permission and that only *she* has the power to grant me it.

"At the ports by the heart of the city." My own heart is drumming. She can hear it. She's still trying so hard, maybe even too hard, not to look up at me.

"The heart of the city," I repeat, and only then does she look me in the eye again, her black eyes sparkling and so full of dreams that may very well be reflecting my own—I hope, at least, that this is what I see in her warm eyes.

From then on, it's nothing but plain work between the nurse and I—at least, that is what I wish I could say, think, believe. Even as she picks up what is left of her food and as we slowly walk together towards the area where she says the abandoned ports are—even then, when there is silence between us, there is nothing uncomfortable or ugly about that silence. It is lovely. *She* is lovely. We are lovely together.

We arrive at the abandoned ports, and the coolness of the water almost reaches us with a breeze. Lynnette sets the dead husband-beater down.

"We need something heavy to place on her so that she'll stay drowned," she muses, looking around, and then...she spots something that shines under the sky as it grows less and less dark with time. Time, our enemy and our friend. The vampire nurse, potentially my enemy and potentially my friend and my partner and my brand-new *everything*.

She places long pieces of heavy metal atop the husband-beater and drags her out into the water. It stuns me, how quickly she does it all—before I know it, she's swimming out into the middle of the water with the dead body in her grasp, and then she's going down, below the surface, way out of my sight. And then, she comes back up, at the edge of the place where the dock meets Lake Michigan. I flinch, startled, and she grins at my reaction as she climbs up a ladder leading down into the water, below where I stand. I offer her my hand and, grinning harder, she doesn't take it.

She stands in front of me, stunning, with the grand lake behind her and with the wetness of it having drenched her short black hair and her scrubs and having removed most of the fresh bloodstains on her skin. I stare down into her eyes, stare so deeply that it feels more intimate than even the temptation of glancing down at the body beneath her soaked scrubs.

She stares back into my eyes, holding our quiet intimacy for a moment longer, until it is as loud as my heartbeat.

"Will it be my turn...to watch you tomorrow night-slash-early-morning?" she asks me. "Well, actually, I can—I *will*...take...the whole night off. Just one whole night. Maybe more nights off, in the future, but, for now...just one, in all its entirety. From sunset at around seven p.m., till sunrise in the early morning."

*All night and then the early morning.* It sounds like such a delicious dream. I've never had anyone watch me do my justifiably wicked work before. But that is all it is, for now: a delicious dream, cascaded by a reality that can only be called...romantic, with its necessity to be slow and with its demand for patience, its room for peace and simultaneous lack of peace, as with all other romantic, rose-colored, rich things.

I hesitate before I respond. I give the kind of answer I don't want to give, but the kind that I *must* give if we two sickos are to survive each other so soon...

"Maybe it's best if you...don't try and take tomorrow night off," I try to suggest kindly, though it sounds more like a demand in my head before I say it. "I mean, you can do that some other time, maybe every now and then, but...don't...tarnish your relationship with your job, your career, your colleagues, so soon—at least, not for me, not for a serial killer."

She laughs. "Ha! My relationship over there is *already* tarnished. I'm a nurse who's secretly a vampire, for fuck's sake! And I'm a nurse who is only social when I absolutely have to be. I'm *good* at it, being social at work—doesn't mean I *love* it. But I *do* love my *job*. I belong there, I do, I love being a nurse and helping people. It's all I've dreamed of ever since I was a kid, doe-eyed as I stared and smiled at my hardworking parents—even when they struggled, they did it together, hand-in-hand. They were partners. And you know what I've always dreamed of, even more than being a nurse? Having a *partner*. Now, it doesn't have to be a romantic partner—it could be a friend, a work partner, but all that is easier said than done when almost everyone back during your human years didn't have the nicest impact on you, and when almost everyone you meet nowadays is either envious of you in one way or another, or calls you weird, or just stays away from you because they simply sense that there is, at the very least, something wrong with you, if not something inhuman about you."

"I...know exactly what that feels like. To want...a partner. To crave...company for the longest time."

"Alright. Then don't tell me not to take the night off."

I sigh. "I'm sorry, but I have to. I really do think that it'll be best if we...well, maybe we hunted again the night after tomorrow. Maybe even a few nights later."

"Ugh. You sound like you should be my parent instead of my partner."

"*I* don't have a job. *You* do. I don't want to be...*that* much of a bad influence on you."

"You're not a bad influence at all. If anything, *I* might be a bad influence on *you*." She is. And that is what makes her perfect for me. And that is what petrifies me. "What are you afraid of, that seeing too much of each other is going to be...?" She can't say it: *A bad thing.* It's too simple, and it's too heavy, and it's wrong.

*I'm traumatized, and I'm terrified, lovely Lynnette. The last time I trusted a girl and was absolutely taken by her mere presence, she disappointed me. I am scared shitless of whatever it is we've got going on between each other, this thing that will continue between us until...well, hopefully until the years pass and I grow old and stinky. But what if you disappoint me before then? What will I do with you, with that disappointment? What if I disappoint you before then? You'd kill me, wouldn't you? You'd kill a disappointment, too.*

It's too strong and savory of a confession. I need something simpler, sweeter. Light like all the reflected shine of blood in her black eyes.

But she sees me, sees right through me. She knows me without knowing me. She understands me without having to listen to what life has been like for me, a very important chunk of my whole life so far, these past several years of solitary slaughter. "You're afraid we're going to kill each other," she deduces.

I gulp. "Yeah." The sound is a whimper. I feel brave, to bare my humanity before her now, the thing that makes me proud to kill the way I do, to be the way I am. I am human, and I am vulnerable before her, and she is a vampire, and she is vulnerable before me, and we are vulnerable together, and we could be very weak together, but we could be very strong together, too.

She takes a step towards me, causing me to step back towards the port, the city, the world. "You're afraid that we're going to get like those married couples"—*Am I dreaming, or did she just say* married couples?—"who see so much of each other that they start to annoy the shit out of each other. You're afraid that...the more we see of each other, the more prone we'll be to disappointing each other, and the possibility of us wanting to kill each other will simply be..."

She says, "Higher," and, at the same exact time, I say, "More."

She steps towards me again and, this time, I don't step back. We're very close now, maybe too close. I am looking down at her, and she is craning her neck gently to look up at me. The way she's looked up at me ever since we met yesterday morning kills me. For the past twenty-four hours, even if I closed my eyes out in the sun and dreamt of her. *All the time.*

She does the unthinkable, the impossible, and simply reaches up to place her palm on my cheek, her skin a neutral temperature against the fevered warmth of mine. It makes breathing the tiniest bit more difficult. For someone who is antisocial and socially awkward when they have to be social, someone who can only breathe the easiest when their knife is slicing fresh skin and muscle, breathing—living—is already hard. It is when she speaks that I realize that, at the same time, the only thing other than killing that can make breathing easier for me is *her*.

"You're a serial killer," she says with a deep and meaningful breath, looking deeply into my eyes as if I'm some icon, the perfect role model. *Hers.* "I am so certain that there are many monsters like you out there, both here in Chicago and out there in the world. I can't be certain whether there are many more monsters like *me* out there. But, Timothy, for at least the past day, here is what I *have* been certain of." She stares at me, and I wait. Finally, she says, with deep sincerity in her big black eyes: "I am not going to hurt you. If you don't hurt me. You still have a copy of my front door key, y'know."

"Wait. Just a *copy*, huh? So, not the actual key. Not that it makes a difference, of course. Thank you for trusting me that much already—even though you very well know it *could* be a mistake." I smile, but then I gulp again. "Still. I think it'd be better if we...did this again the early morning after tomorrow. Maybe even a few...early mornings after that. Let's say *just a few* early mornings later. Tomorrow, the next one, and the one after that. And then, on the fourth early morning, maybe..."

*And then, maybe, just maybe, All the time. Someday, some night, some early morning, it'll be the beginning of "All the time" for the two of us, until I simply get too old. Just like you said, Lynnette. All the time, the two of us. I promise. All the time.*

And then, in response, she does something even *more* unthinkable and impossible. She stretches herself up on top of her tippy toes, and her lips barely reach the outline of my bony collarbone. She places a kiss there, barely a peck, before retreating. My heartbeat quickens, slows, and I feel like a rush of blood should burst out from my neck at her touch, taken aback by it. As she lowers herself and her feet go back to being flat in her shoes on the ground, her eyes darken so much that I can't spot any reflected light in them anymore.

*She's thirsty. Is she still thirsty? Didn't she feel full, or was that a lie? Can she even feel full? She must, if blood is her food. And yet...that look in her eyes...*

I can't let myself think that she could be thirsty for anything other than my blood; it'd drive me crazy to think about such *human* things after we've done something so very inhuman together. And how would she feel? Would she feel...human about me, too, in a way? She has certainly proved that being a vampire doesn't mean you can't feel emotion. How is she feeling right now? About this, about me, about us? It's already driving me crazy, wanting to know and not deserving to know yet. *It's too soon, too soon.*

The blood that runs with such pressure throughout my veins, underneath the skin of my collarbone area and my neck—the blood must make her thirsty as soon as she gives me that peck. Is this a threat, a promise of pain...or a promise of loyalty? Is this promise...breakable or unbreakable? Would she ever break a promise she made to me, if we are alike? What kind of promises would I be capable of breaking out of any I'd ever make to her, a fellow creature of the night who is simply not human like I am? Would I ever dare...?

My eyes instinctively drift down from her tense eyes and down past her lips and down to her own collarbone. I wonder how she'd react if I kissed her there, too. If I made only a very human promise against her porcelain, perfect skin...

The thought makes me look away from her immediately, as if I've already suddenly looked too hard, too long, too much. The invisible intimacy of it makes my ears hot, the warmth colliding with the icy feeling of the freezing Chicago morning, and it makes my blood boil, makes my heartbeat quicken again, makes me full of a different kind of want and need that I haven't genuinely experienced, that another person hasn't inspired in me, in a very long time.

By the time I can muster the courage to look back at her without thinking about all the other different places I'd kiss her if only she'd let me, so many echoed promises splattered across so many of her body parts like a river of doom and desire, drawn blood from spots I'd dare to bite with my very capable human teeth and all the places I'd leave a teasing tickle or bruise with a hot pinch or bury my tongue in and across, too many promises to break and too many to keep—she's gone, chasing the last bit of darkness away, along with every last bit of my comfort and peace till I next see her. Till I next give myself the bravery to see her despite all the emotional and physical damage it may promise to do both of us monsters and murderers in the end.

·  ·  ·

The early mornings and the days and the nights and then the early mornings again—it's all torture. All of it. Just about every second and minute and hour.

I was always meant to be alone, because I had to be, because my hobby and the hunt required it of me. Now, I don't have to be alone, and I'm not meant to be alone anymore, because I believe that I have found someone who is very much the same as me, despite the degree of her inhumanity.

And, still, I *do* have to be alone. Because I am still not entirely sure who, or what, it is that I have found—or, rather, who or what has found me. I know her like I've known her forever, and, still, I don't know her at all, and I certainly still don't know her as well as I'd like to know her. And I would like to continue getting to know her. This new, and possibly very permanent, partner of mine. But I *have* to be alone. For now, at least. She makes me feel too nervous, and, at the same time, she makes me feel too alive, so much prouder to be the way I am than anyone else ever has, maybe even myself.

I listen to the days drag themselves out like the slowing notes of a depressing song on the piano, the terrible ticking of clock after clock after clock, the musical and clicking call of cockroaches, the scorching rays of the sun reaching out like a warning. When I get bored or impatient or tired enough, I take out the copy of her front door key from the pocket of my jeans one day and take it out from the motel room drawer on another day and I stare at it and fiddle with it, my fingers scraping and sweeping across the small piece of metal like the promise it is, deeply, with thought and care and wonder.

I can't stop thinking about her, and I wonder whether she can't stop thinking about me, either. *The serial killer who can't stop thinking about the vampire nurse.* Isn't it possible that the vampire nurse can't stop thinking about the serial killer in return? That I am only human, but she admires me as I am, appreciates what I do and the deaths I can bring forth, bring her not on a silver platter, but a gold one, harmless and luxurious and stolen from some store somewhere. It is possible, it *has* to be, otherwise she wouldn't have answered my summons—and it's bothering me a little, just how much I care about this.

I can't wait to see her again. To speak to her again. I can't wait to kill, of course—to find a fool and make even more of a fool out of them. I can't wait to kill in front of her—it makes me feel animalistic with excitement and empty with anxiety at the same time, like it's supposed to be some sort of sick mating call, dance, ritual.

But, more than anything, I just can't wait to be in her presence again.

But I am also craving a cheeseburger dipped in garlic sauce, and this could be a sign of how wrong this all is. I won't crave the sun or silver, but if my breath could smell like garlic all day, I'd let it, happy and full.

I've really got to ask Lynnette some questions about what her weaknesses, other than sunlight, actually are.

•  •  •

"It's your turn," she announces as she approaches me on her doorstep. "Your night."

"My turn. My night." And it *is* my night. It's not even midnight yet. We're still somewhere between eleven and then.

"You really managed to convince them to let you go early, then?"

We start walking away from her house, down the street. "Well, I told them: 'He's actually not just a friend. He's my partner. He's my found family.'" I catch the corner of her lip twitching shyly as she says this.

I honestly really can't stop blushing around her. "It's a little early to be calling me all of that, isn't it? Saying such things about me."

She shrugs. "No, not really. You're interesting enough."

"So far," I warn her.

"So far. Anyway, yeah, they agreed to let me go early just for the night, but I figure that if I just use all my *vampire charm* on them again, maybe every now and then till we get to every night, or till we get to *All the time*, well, it won't be a problem at all. They'll find someone to cover for me, anyway. Lots of desperate, young ER nurses, ready to make a great impression any time of day or night. 'Fresh meat,' some doctors call 'em. In one way or another, they all sort of remind me of the way I used to be, back when I was a *human* nurse. I was desperate and willing and eager and excited and stressed out and foolish and...well, there were *a lot* of feelings. After I turned, there were only a few feelings, and then, when I decided to become a *vampire* nurse, well, the feelings had still faded, though not as much as when I first became reminiscent of nothing more than a bloodthirsty monster."

"*Vampire charm.* You haven't been...using any of that on me, have you?" I ask nervously.

She laughs. "Oh, no, it's not, like, an actual power or anything. Told you, the only power I've got is simply being an outcast."

"And being super fast and super strong. Having super-heightened senses."

"Well, yeah, but nothing special other than that. I don't have the power to charm anyone or manipulate them any more than humans have the power to charm and manipulate each other, through fake empathy or falsified sympathy or flirtation, and so on and so forth."

"With all your beauty, though, and everything you've learned your whole life so far, you've gotta be doing it better than any other human, of course, even the older ones."

"You think I'm beautiful?"

I can't help but grin. I only say, "So, flirtation. You flirted with your superiors, then? Your colleagues and whoever you had to convince—"

"No. None of those people are who I've been flirting with."

I keep my eyes on the ground as we walk on and try my best not to sound too interested. "So who *have* you been flirting with?"

"What, my little peck a few days ago didn't give that away?" I feel her tense up when she lets the quiet wash over us momentarily. "Have *you* been flirting with anyone?" Her sweet voice suggests an unspoken question, an extension of the question already boldly spoken: *With me, for instance?*

She's very forward. She is this inexplicably interesting mix of introverted and extroverted, it seems, shy about some things and outspoken about others. I'd find such forwardness from a woman intriguing, and I have, before, but my intrigue didn't last long, not before irritation took its place.

But everything is different with her. I welcome her forwardness as I welcome the night—welcome *her* and everything about her as I welcome the night.

I can't respond. I can't tell her that, yes, I *am* calling her beautiful, and it would be such a fascinating thing, for me to flirt with a vampire, and that, no matter how hard I try not to, I am currently feeling the way I do around a vampire, feeling the way I do *for* a vampire, and it is all already very fascinating, indeed. I tighten my grin, make an effort to make it go away, but it doesn't, and I focus on the ground until she says something again. Something new and different, I hope, something that doesn't draw attention to how she makes me feel. "Have you chosen anyone for tonight?"

I nod. "You know that's my job."

"Your part of our bloodwork, now that we're each half of one whole."

I'm failing to ignore how much I love the sound of that. *We're each half of one whole.* That's the kind of thing I've always thought about, always wanted. *All I've ever wanted.*

She has made me the sweetest suggestion, the darkest deal, and each time she's called me her partner, her words have deafened my ears like the most magnificent melody and have drenched all my energy and my heart with such a dainty touch. Her words are delicious, like garlic-covered fries or chocolate-syrup-covered strawberries or, in her case, blood-covered skin and muscle and bone. It's incredible, still surreal to me that we are here, side by side, killer and creature, nomad and nurse, violence and the vampire, a cold-hearted man and his cute curse. *She* is incredible.

"I picked him out during the day," I simply inform her. "I've picked the spot where we'll kill him, too."

"An alley somewhere?"

"An alley somewhere. Nearby."

"So, what's his problem, our kill for the night?"

"Oh, he has more than *one* problem."

"Don't they all. All these humans," she mutters. "Except for you, of course."

I pause. "I have quite a few problems."

She pauses, too. "Yes, but you're...different. And so are your problems."

"And the degree of my difference and all my different problems are...acceptable to you?"

"Just as mine are acceptable to you."

I simper and try to focus on the thrill of the plan, the kill, the aftermath, now that I can finally extend that high with Lynnette by my side—Lynnette, who already sends a rush through me without looking at me or touching me, who already makes me feel more alive than I've already been by simply being there. "A few hours ago, at about five in the afternoon, he caused a ruckus in one of the nearby bars. He wasn't even drunk, but he acted like the kind of person who would be. He picked a fight with the bartender, who was just trying to do his job and didn't even deserve to be harassed like that. The guy just...caused a lot of unnecessary commotion that clearly even the seemingly strangest people in that bar were put off by. He was such a bother that someone even threatened to call the police *at least* a few times before he finally left. Which would definitely *not* have been good for me."

"A nasty little troublemaker," she muses.

"*Our* nasty little troublemaker."

# CHAPTER SIX

# PARTNERS IN CRIME

"So, this one *does* have a house alarm?" Lynnette squints at the dark house through what looks like the laundry room window. I can only look at her through the dark.

"Yes, this one does. So we won't be breaking in." She looks back at me, the cutest question on her calm and calming face. "We'll be drawing him out," I explain.

"Drawing him out. Akin to...dragging him out?"

"You dragged someone out last time. But that was...very assertive and physical."

"Well, actually, I didn't. I called out and the husband-beater came outside on her own, and then I dragged her from there." She didn't actually go inside the husband-beater's house?

"Oh. Okay. Well, anyway, this time, we'll be ringing his doorbell. Knocking on his door."

"Acting like we're...Mormons? Or house cleaners?"

I shrug. "Just going from door to door this early in the morning."

"Will I be the one to talk him into dragging himself out?"

"Peacefully." The word sits on my lips like a hiss. "Till I take away his peace in the darkness of an alley, and then—"

"And then I'll preserve what is left of his peace in my belly."

I grin. "Ready?"

"Wait—he doesn't have any cameras, does he?" She squints at the sides of the house, upwards near beneath the roof, able to spot things I never could, not in the dark or in general.

"No cameras."

"Okay. I'm ready."

And, with that, she moves, almost like a careful doe, towards the front porch of the single-story house. I crouch behind a bush at the corner of the side of the house and crane my head ever so slightly to watch her put into motion the very start of our work. She approaches the front steps of the porch with open grace and the overconfidence of an ominous, omen-bringing goddess.

And, then, as she steps right before the closed front door, her entire demeanor changes. The attitude with which she holds her body completely shifts. Her confidence seems to crumble, her coldness seems to collapse, and all the coolness that she carries with her contorts until I realize that she is about to seem *very* human. She's hunched now, like someone who is shy and *only* shy, someone who seems insecure, and even though she is short, she somehow looks even shorter now, her fingers intertwined in front of her as if she's some lost intern, her top lip biting down on her bottom one. She's going to be *acting*, and I wonder if she'll be any good—or at least good enough for the purpose that the night presents us with and promises us.

With the single press of the man's doorbell, a low-pitched noise that her pretty fingertip brings forth, our night begins. Our work begins, and she's up first. She'll be up last, too, to collect all that blood from him with her pretty mouth.

*Everything starts here. And then...All the time...until I'm gone. Six feet under, with her as the only person who'd mourn me above ground. Maybe she'll wear black scrubs to my funeral as a nice inside joke. I'd be too dead to laugh, but perhaps we'll practice before. Maybe I won't be able to walk anymore, and she'll move me around in a wheelchair at night, or maybe I'll start forgetting everything, including her—that would be the worst sign of all, a sign that I'm about to go. And we can practice, and she can order black scrubs online and then wear them and read me the eulogy she's prepared for the end of my days. We can't do it in a church—maybe just a nice cemetery somewhere.*

I've never looked forward to my old days before. Now, somehow, I can, and I do. I will be wiser and I will be killing more wisely with her head resting on my shoulder, and we will grow old together while she never ages a day past twenty-nine, and I will be a happy old man.

The front door opens with the kind of hesitation a killer hungers for.

"Um, hello?" The man steps out in front of the safe walls of his house. He sees a short, innocent-looking, slim young woman in scrubs. It reminds me of how often I have been underestimated, too, for one reason or another—it sends a warmth through me as I keep watching, my eyes glued to the two of them, unyielding predator and unaware prey, as if I'm watching a play that's been put on just for me. All for me. Maybe even, truly, very possibly...*All the time.*

"Hello, sir, um...I'm sorry to bother you at this time, but I'm actually...a little lost. A *lot* lost, actually..." She sounds...phenomenal. Exactly like a young intern, a human being, someone who makes mistakes and needs guidance from her fellow neighbor. The man briefly looks her up and down and yawns into the palm of his hand. "It's my first time in Chicago, and I don't know where I am and—and it's my first day at work, and...I mean, they didn't even hold the interview at the hospital or anything, and—"

The middle-aged man rubs his eyes, like he's been napping all his anger away. "What, you don't have Waze or even a map or anything? Aren't you young'uns always figurin' shit out with all your new technology?"

"I'm older than I look, sir." She cocks her head to the side as she says this in the smallest of voices, as if to signal to me the loveliness of the inside joke. I smile and try not to laugh at that from my hiding place. "No map, no...applications on my phone. Nothing. If you could please just point me the right way—"

"Oh, well, I could help you download an application or two, y'know. Download Uber or Lyft or—I'm not a fan of any o' those myself, though I can help you—"

"Oh, no, sir, that's alright. I'm not a big fan of those, either. Or of technology in general."

"Not a fan, either, huh? Alright, then."

"Yeah, I just...if you could just point me the right way—"

"The local hospital's really just a few blocks—" The man sighs and shakes his head, as she expects him to—as *we* expect him to. "You know, it's late and it's dark out. Why don't I walk you over there?" His kindness is a lie, a disgusting contrast to his true colors that were painted all over the insides of the bar he left earlier today, and Lynnette and I both know it—or, at least, *I* know it, because I was there. But the middle-aged man doesn't know himself, doesn't see himself. *Fool.* He must be single, all alone and without a family in this house, since he doesn't seem to give a second thought about whether anyone else in the house might question his exit or be concerned about it. *Good.*

"Oh, thank you so much, I'd really appreciate that," Lynnette says in such an upbeat way that it reminds me of the first few times I heard her voice not too long ago.

And then, they're walking away, and I'm following them.

Moments later, when Lynnette is moving towards empty streets, the man slowly starts to see that it is not him leading her, but that she is the one who is leading him.

"Uh," he starts, "kid, what're you—"

"Ah, sorry, I just remembered that someone told me about a shortcut back here."

"Um, well...I don't know about any shortcuts, and it looks like you're getting mighty far from the hospital. It's not this way, it's actually—"

"Well, according to my friend, the shortcut will lead us to—"

"Hey, now, if your *friend* is so helpful, why didn't you just ask this friend for help on how to get there, and why'd you—why're you—?"

But it's too late. They've reached the alley, the smell of trash ripe and rude. And I am walking up right behind them.

"Hey, c'mon, now, I'm telling you that you're going the wrong—"

I've set my backpack down and my gloved hands are around the man's neck before he can finish. But I don't snap his neck. I simply hold him by the throat from behind and throw him against the wall at his side. He gives out a surprised grunt, tries to ask what the fuck is going on—oh, and he'll find out soon enough.

His head hits the wall and he holds it in pain, squinting at me with betrayed eyes, looking at me and then at Lynnette, his eyes darting between us, back and forth and back and forth like he's afraid that I'm going to hurt her, too, after I'm done with him or maybe even before. I almost smile at how little of a clue he has about what she could do to him if she wanted, what she *will* do to him after I've spilled all his blood out just for her.

I could never hurt her. Not unless she hurts me first, I don't think. At least, I don't think I *ought* to hurt her, certainly not anytime soon, because everything's going just fine so far—more than just fine, even. *Perfectly,* I could dare to think. Would she and I hurt each other and would we be okay with that because of our little pact? A pact that I hope really will be ongoing. I think of this new dream—of our little *All the time.*

"Hey, now," he moans, sounding comically offended, "I wasn't gonna do anything to hurt her, I promise!"

The promise rings in my ears like a poem. *I wasn't gonna do anything to hurt her.* I promise. I promise. *I promise.* His true intentions sit on his voice with the pretense of innocence, while my intentions now sit on my hands with ice-cold ire.

He thinks that I think that he was going to hurt her, and that I am somehow her protector, maybe a friend or significant other or *partner*—and I *am* her protector and she is mine and already I'd be absolutely anything she needed me to be...anything, of course, except what she is: immortal, infinite, nothing but limitless imagination to drive you, endless years later, so far from where you started and the kind of human being you thought you'd be and stay as and die as. He thinks this because hurting her is what he could've done, out here in the darkness, if he wanted, because he thought himself capable against what he thought to be a petite young lady.

I punch him in the face, and he gives out a yelp and holds onto his freshly bleeding nose. My knuckles will be very bruised, but this is not a new thing for me. The new, beautiful thing that moves me forward is the fact that this is a demonstration of my best—arguably worst, in society's opinion— behavior, my strength, the essence of my humanity, all its heartfelt hellishness. The new, beautiful thing that moves me to punch the idiot before me more and more and more is the fact that this demonstration is all for her, for Lynnette.

Is she enjoying it? Watching me? I'm enjoying it, knowing that she's watching my every move. I'm especially enjoying the fact that she isn't jumping in at every other moment to offer help. She must be enjoying it. Seeing all this blood spilt, growing thirstier by the second.

I won't look behind me, won't look back at her while I do my best to destroy the man, won't let the single, sweet line of her smile break my attention, distract me like the freeing crush of a skull, but, still, I can almost feel her smiling that soft smile as she watches from the shadows of the alley, and it makes me feel like a wild animal, a rush running through me like bloodied red river after river after river, all as I punch and kick and scratch at the man who now wails and whimpers and writhes beneath me on the ground.

The man looks up with me with eyes that are afraid and upset. He doesn't have anger, though he does have uncertainty. He should be uncertain enough to get angry—but he is too fearful now, because my anger and liveliness outweigh his, outweigh any he could feel at this moment. He had enough anger today, anyway—enough to make so many already-uncertain and already-uneasy and already-strange people feel even more uncertain and uneasy and strange.

*Uncomfortable—the thing I do not feel while killing. Uneasy—the thing I do not feel while killing with Lynnette. Strange—the thing I love to feel alongside her.*

The anger of this man will follow him his whole life if Lynnette and I let it. That anger will ruin the world around him, unless she and I ruin him for good first.

Isn't indirectly saving other people the same as directly freeing monsters whose monstrosity isn't even in their full control, freeing them from themselves, their own breaths? If the man wanted anger management classes or therapy or any kind of help, he would've sought it out by now. He's too set in his ways to ask for such help now, too much of *who he is*—Lynnette and I might relate to that, in one way or another, but only for a second, an inch, so far from *All the time*—and he's too far gone for any kind of redemption arc.

*One less fool.*

"You're playing with him, aren't you?" Lynnette asks at my back, not too far from where I stand above him now.

Her ethereal voice makes it hard to focus, but I still try, and I *do* have an answer for her: "*You* could be the one playing with your food." *Could be, should be, would be...*

"Maybe some other time. Some other night, or early morning. Maybe three more nights from now," she teases.

"Maybe." *Three more nights from now. Soon. Very soon. Yes, please, Lynnette. Lynnette and the night. The winking, wide-smiled moon. Please, please, please. Promise me, promise me, promise me.*

I take out my knife now from my back pocket and unfold it. It's silver and it shines awfully bright under the moonlight and under the spread-out glow of the streetlights at the entrance of the alley.

It reminds me about asking Lynnette what exactly it is that could harm her. I'm unsure whether I'm curious about this because I want to protect her or because I want to be prepared just in case I have no choice but to poison her. I like her, I really do, so much, so soon—and that itself is a dangerous thing that could throw me off the course of who I am and who I've been and who I want to be and who I need to be in this small human life of mine. Or it could throw me right on course, like the deliciousness of destiny I am oh-so ready to dance with. It could be bad or it could be good. It could be wrong or it could be right, imperfect or perfect. I want it to be good, right, and perfect—*need* it to be. I don't want to hurt her. I can't. I *won't*. I promised, didn't I? *I promised.* And she promised, too—promised me she wouldn't hurt me.

And, still, sickly enough, the pleasure I feel around her doesn't make the killer in me any less curious about what it'd be like to try to hurt such a magnificent beast such as her. That is a curiosity that will have to be put away for now. The curiosity I have about us, about our *All the time*, the new dream of simply being partners, is at the very forefront of my mind. My very insane mind.

*I am very much insane. I wonder how insane she is. Whether she could even be as insane as...a human being. I wonder whether she was insane at all back when she was a human being.*

I plunge my silver knife down into the man and watch him squeal like a pig under every slice. He tries to put his hands up, either surrender or engage in some kind of unnecessary self-defense or escape, but nothing stops the knife from meeting his skin each time—meeting the palms of his hands, his forearms, his shoulders, his face, his chest. And it's when the knife deeply enters his chest that he finally stops struggling and wheezes out his last breaths atop the darkness of the streets and under the darkness of the alley and all its shadows, including myself and Lynnette—Lynnette, who I finally turn to and nod at, signaling that she can now drink from this man, that she successfully led the man to my work and that my work is now done and that her work can begin.

•  •  •

When she's done drinking from him, her mouth having covered all the spots where I sliced him, she turns to me with thankful eyes, blood once again staining her face and mostly her mouth.

"Y'know," she starts, "if you're going to be staying in Chicago for a while, and if we really are going to keep doing this…" She really has decided, then, that I am worthy of an *All the time* beside her. The scary thing is, I've decided, too. She is my partner and she will be. *All the time.* Unless one of us betrays the other before I, a human, can complete my lifetime and can go through a whole *All the time.*

"You're about to tell me that I might consider getting myself a job," I guess.

"Yeah. I just think it'll—"

"I'll consider it." I don't. I won't. "I promise."

"Okay. Great. I just think that…it might help you…fit in more."

I nod. But then, I can't help but say: "Well, even then, I might not fit in very much. My poster made that clear enough."

She rises from the dead man. "I saw your poster as what it was."

"A desperate call for company?"

"Well, sure, but not just that." She steps towards me with sincerity and a deep sympathy in her expression, a funny contrast to all the blood there. "A cry for help, Timothy."

"It was not—"

"There's no need to hide it or feel weird about it. I was doing the same thing, too. I just wasn't as obvious or vocal about it—about my own cry for help."

"Your own cry for help?"

"Well, yeah. I'm…a vampire who needs help with…well, properly being a vampire."

I look her up and down and try not to turn rosy as I do. "Well. You're doing it now, aren't you? Better late than never."

She gives a happy, content, full sigh. "Yeah. I am."

"You don't have to…chain yourself to the idea of what your parents would've wanted for you. There was no way for any of you to know that you'd…wake up one day craving human blood. They were good people, I'm sure. But, generally speaking, of course…sometimes…being a good person doesn't help anybody. Sometimes, being good just lets more bad into the world. You and I recognize that. That's why we're here. That's why you were such a good and very human nurse for so long. And it's why, now…you can use that inhuman part of you, the vampire you are, to…cleanse the world of bad people. Do good by doing one supposedly morally bad thing at night."

"A very human nurse for so long." She smiles, looks down, looks at the dead body that we'll have to move soon, and hide well. When she looks back up at me, there's a sparkle in her eyes. "*Human*. You know…it feels like I'm honestly more human than you are."

Are my eyes sparkling, too? Sparkling with…raw euphoria. "And I'm more inhuman than you are."

She turns back to the body she's drained. "Are you gonna move him?"

"Yep."

I move to the body, and start dragging the dead man away. The high has still stuck with me, and my heart is pounding delightfully. There's no blood that I have to clean or wash away or erase, because she has taken care of all of it—or, at least, most of it, enough of it to make me feel at ease. I am not killing alone or cleaning up all by myself. I finally have company, and I could almost cry.

•  •  •

"Want me to walk you home?" I ask her when I'm done hiding my destruction and her dinner. I feel like an idiot—she doesn't *need* to be walked home. But she nods—she wants to spend even more time with me tonight, even though our official work is finished.

We start walking, and, after some time, she turns to me as we walk on. It's nice that we can walk together now, not currently in a rush to get our bloodwork done. We are at even more peace now, enjoying the night. The aftermath. Side by side. "Oh, before I forget," she starts.

This makes me grin—she almost really does sound like a fifty-nine-year-old woman who's got so much on her mind and too much on her plate...maybe even a mid-life crisis like the quarter-and-a-half-one I was suffering through before she popped into my life mid-attack. *Before I forget.* She's the only twenty-nine-year-old-looking fifty-nine-year-old that could make my heart palpitate like this—and palpitate peacefully, strangely enough. I am at ease with her, and it both frightens me and fuels within me the finest tranquility I've ever known.

"Your results came back, by the way. Your blood test results."

"Right. The bloodwork I got done without knowing it. The blood you drew from me." I shake my head. "And?"

"You're a perfectly healthy human being. Your iron levels are just a *little* low—you might want to get some supplements at the local pharmacy. Maybe even the one at the hospital—I could get you some."

"*Steal* some for me, you mean."

She chuckles. "I *am* your partner in crime. Red little tablets to swallow with water—unless you want the organic kind."

"What you're saying is...I have low iron levels in my blood, and..."

"Your red blood cells don't carry enough oxygen. You're not deficient *yet*, but if you carry on like this, without any supplementation or any changes to your diet, well, you will be."

"What you're saying is I need more blood?"

We laugh together. It just *sounds* right, laughing with her. "It's funny, when you put it that way," she says. "If your low iron levels happen to transfer to another state, say...a new body, a new life...then you might just turn out to be the thirstiest vampire there ever was. The hungriest one out there. Not that I'd know, of course. But, if at all possible, you'd certainly be a *much* more impatient and thirsty vampire than I ever was thirty years ago when I was first turned."

I shrug. I don't want to think about that. I don't like even the mere possibility of it, even the thought, the dream in the palms of her hands, the chance, whatever it is that she calls it in her head. I don't like the fact that she's thought about it enough to bring it up, even if it is brief and part of this conversation about my blood test results and even if she doesn't mean anything by it. I *hope* she doesn't mean anything by it. The smile on my face grows sterile and static before it completely dies. "You're not going to turn me," I tell her. Demand of her.

"I won't. But, it's just that I honestly...don't really see the big deal. I would've, thirty years ago. But, now, I...don't."

"I do. It's not the kind of life I'd want for myself. I like being this way."

"You like being a human serial killer. You like having weaknesses, but not being too affected in any way by those weaknesses. You like being a person with all this power in the palm of your hand"—*Can* she read minds, or do we really think very much in the same way, and what does that say about us and our abnormal souls?—"and I feel like, maybe, knowing that someone stronger than you, someone human, *can* take away that power if they wanted to, gives that power more meaning."

"You're right. And I don't want you to take the meaning behind my power away."

She nods. "Okay. I won't turn you, then."

I try to make my smile come back. "Try not to sound or feel offended. It doesn't have anything to do with you, with the way you are, the way you live, with who or what you are. I promise you that."

She shrugs. "Don't worry. I get it. It's just your preference. Besides...it might be hard. At first, of course. But the weaknesses...can be limiting, of course."

I realize then that my question on her weaknesses might just be answered now without me even having to ask anything like even more of a creep.

"When I sleep during the day, I sleep like any other person does." I still haven't really seen her basement-slash-bedroom. I hope to, at some point. But, still, not anytime soon. *Too soon, too soon...* "But if I didn't sleep—if I appeared before the sun, it would burn me to death. So would silver and garlic and a stake to the chest. Just really those four traditional things that have always injured and killed vampires. If I only get struck by sunlight for a second, on just one part of my body, or if silver or garlic or a stake doesn't get pierced into me or only makes contact with a bit of my skin, like my hand instead of my heart—I'd be scarred forever, and it would hurt very much, and I wouldn't heal from any of it the way I can heal from everything else. But if I swallow garlic instead of just touching it, for example—well, I'd be dead.

"So there are, of course, *cons* to being what I am; I won't deny that or argue against it. But, in my opinion, the pros always outweigh the cons. Maybe I'm just used to it by now. Maybe I've accepted it to the point of self-love—because *that* is what I feel: self-love. Appreciation for what I became all those years ago. But, again, I get it. Again, you just have your own...preference."

I nod. "A preference. *My* preference. Yes." I say nothing about her list of weaknesses. I'd like to keep her away from the things that would dare make her weak. And, at the same time, I'm humanly—*psychotically*—curious about what would happen if I pushed her against all of those terrible and dangerous and power-sucking things.

"I respect that," she declares, a sense of duty dwelling on her velvety voice and in her velvet-dark eyes. "I can respect that."

"Thank you. Just as *I* can respect *you*. Just as I *do* respect you."

"Thank you."

I turn to see that we've arrived at her townhouse.

"Do you...want to come inside? Maybe...spend the night?" she asks, blinking slowly, blood drying even more slowly under those mesmerizing dark eyes of hers.

I clear my throat and try to do the right thing—the human thing that not even some humans would do. *Be a gentleman.* "No. I don't think I should. Not tonight, anyway. Maybe—"

"Maybe three late nights or three early mornings later?" She sounds so optimistic. Just as she did when I first asked her what she was, and she responded that she hoped she was my partner, the night she saved me.

"Maybe." And that's all I tell her with a blush all across my face before I walk away from her and from the night.

.   .   .

It hits me, the next day, in the morning when I wake up, that I don't even have her phone number or her email address. I only have her house address. I have no way of contacting her except to show up on her doorstep a few nights or early mornings later. I could write her a letter, but by the time I mail it to her, it'll be too late, and by the time I simply slip it under her door and she responds with another letter—well, that'll be too stupid of a thing to do, because by the time we get past the line of "How are you doing?" and the potential promise of "I'm fine, thank you, how are you?" it'll, again, be too late and just won't matter, anyway. That just won't make any sense— and I'm starting to like how we make sense together, how we do things that make sense to us.

There's something very intimate and personal about the fact that we don't have each other's phone numbers or emails the way so many other *partners* in the world must. I like it. It feels like what we have—whatever that is—and what we'll grow to have—whatever that turns out to be—is real. Even if she could give me a quick call or text in between breaks at work in the middle of the night—what difference would that make and what kind of bland, surface-level, replied-to-every-other-hour conversations would we have that would make our in-person walks and talks and kills much less interesting?

I am as far away from her and as close to her as I need to be.

And, still, I feel butterflies in my stomach as I wait for the days to pass, so that I can see her again and again and again under the gleaming moonlight and streetlights.

.   .   .

The next time we meet, three nights after our second night killing and cleaning, I do the luring. She does the killing and the cleaning, and I clean up whatever is left of the blood she's sucked and licked—and watching her do all that sucking and licking makes me so shy and so desperately in need of being even closer to her that I have to turn away from the scene a few times, only hearing the cute little noises she makes when she's slurping up the life from our victim—and I drag our kill away, hide it away. A woman this time, middle-aged and cruel and seemingly mentally unwell somehow—perhaps we've freed her, or perhaps we've shown her that mental illness doesn't exactly make being cruel an okay or acceptable or excusable thing. We surpassed her cruelty with our own as the light faded from her eyes.

When Lynnette is done, she starts licking the leftover blood of the woman that has splattered all over her arms, fingers, and legs. Watching her do this arouses me even more, and again I have to turn away. But as soon as I turn away, she walks up next to me and says, "We can head on home now."

But I can't move—I can only stare at her beautiful face and stand still in the presence of her strangely beautiful spirit, so full of energy and so enigmatic. "You missed a spot," I let her know. The spot is really a few different spots across her face. The blood of the woman still lingers upon her like yet another promise that neither of us can decipher the meaning or purpose of.

"Oh." She licks her thumb and smears it across her cheek, picking up only a fragment of the blood that is all over her face—can't she feel the stickiness or persistent wetness or slowly forming dryness, or has the high of the kill and the aftermath of it consumed her, too? "Did I get it?" It's adorable, how she asks me this.

"Actually...you missed a *few* spots."

"Oh. I should...go home and take a shower, then."

"Yeah. That'd be a good idea."

"And I'm assuming you don't want to come in tonight, either?"

I shake my head. "Maybe three nights or early mornings later."

She smiles at this. "Maybe."

. . .

Three nights later, I find myself on her doorstep again. Three nights later, she's lucky enough to have the night off again, and she does the luring again, and I do the killing, and we do the cleaning-up together again. And when it's all said and done and I try my best not to gawk at her like she's the most fascinating woman I've ever met—and she *is*, and she is more than a woman, too—she starts licking the leftover blood on herself again and I have to look away again.

She's stunning and adorable at once, and I never really knew—or *saw*, at least—that it could be possible for someone to be both of those things simultaneously, without effort. It drives me a little crazy—I want to give her the biggest of hugs, squeeze her like she's some little bunny, and, at the same time, I want to give her pleasure and I want her to scream my name till her two canines turn into fangs. It bothers me, what I want—it isn't normal. But we are not normal. It bothers me to wonder whether she feels the same about me—again, given the little time we've spent together. I can only hope to continue spending more and more and more time with her.

"Did I get everything?" Again, she looks up at me with those sinister yet sweet black doe eyes.

I shake my head. I can't speak, because, this time, as she starts to lick her finger and tries wiping away the blood on her face, I can't help but picture myself...licking all that blood off of her skin with my bare tongue, listening to her moan happily as I do. I wonder if she'd sound just as cute and precious, moaning—how *human* she'd sound. I shudder at the image of licking our dead human kill's blood off her face—it's such a *vampiric* thing to do, and it's the last sort of thing I'd do. I am disgusted and intrigued, turned on and off at once, and it pains me, this odd and new mixture of feelings.

I have to end the night now, before my strange feelings take over and show themselves, and all of them, combined, might either offend her or open her up for me like a flower and I have no interest in finding out how that might end on this night. But, as I open my mouth to speak, she's already spoken: "Don't say 'Maybe' this time. Tell me you'll come inside next time."

I feel myself turning red again. "Three nights from now, you'll come inside my house and—"

"And, what? After your shower, you'll...turn on the TV? Make me some tea or coffee?" Would she really do such human things for me?

"Sure, to be hospitable. Yeah, if you wanted me to. But, really, I'd just spend time with you. I'd focus on you, and you'd focus on me. We'd be in each other's presence even more than we already have been, even more than we already are." I don't know what that means, what such a thing would truly include, and why she'd want this—she really must be as alone and lonely as I am, then. And I want, *need*, to know what it means and what it'd comprise. It'd be what I want, anyway—spending more time with her. I'm glad to hear that she wants the same thing, for now. "So don't say 'Maybe.' Tell me you'll spend more of the night with me next time. Promise me."

I hesitate. And then, I take a deep breath, and speak: "Okay."

"Say it. Promise." Her black eyes are pleading.

Those eyes are pools of promise after promise after promise—and I still can't begin to really understand what kinds of promises, unbreakable or breakable, the normal or my abnormal kind. I'd like to understand. I'd love to understand *her* more and more and more. Understand *us*. This almost paradise-like, pretty partnership.

So, I obey her. I give her what she wants—for the time being—and try to forget my fear and simultaneous fascination for the moment:

"Okay. I promise."

It's as I start walking away from her without so much as a farewell or goodnight—too tense and too confused and too captivated to say anything more through my dry throat and mouth—that I start to hear her softly, soothingly humming something behind me while she watches me leave...a song. I recognize the melody immediately—it's "Put Your Head On My Shoulder." The song that was playing in the bar on the night she first saved me, and as nothing more than a shadow, from the arrest of those police officers. She was there the whole time, waiting and watching and making sure to follow me and protect me and rescue me like my own personal guardian angel. The song—a cover of which was playing on the hospital TV screen when I woke up in the hospital room.

*Such a romantic song that just so happened to play the night she first made her presence very clear without clearly showing herself to me, and followed me to the hospital room, where she began her night of treating me and healing me. Such a romantic song. Could it mean something? Does it? I shiver inside once more as I think about...fate. Destiny. That concept of "meant to be." Soulmates...*

It makes me want to throw up a little, but for the first time in years, since my very first murders, I find myself...*oh-so-very curious*. I crave a cure for that curiosity, and she may very well be it. *It. The one...*

What I do give her while she continues humming, what I *can* give her, is a small smile as I look back at her before disappearing into the night, leaving her lovely humming voice behind me, leaving without her by my side and without her lovely little head on my patient shoulder, or mine on hers.

. . .

I feel everything again over the next three days and nights. I am everything from impatient to at peace again.

The second night of waiting, when I return to the motel room I'm staying at, the moment I only make it several steps into the lobby...something stops me dead in my tracks in the middle of that empty lobby.

A song. Playing ever-so-softly from the speakers of the lobby. It sounds static and almost subtly spooky.

But one thing is for certain.

It's yet another cover of "Put Your Head On My Shoulder." I find myself staring wide-eyed at the speakers, like I've found myself in a dream I either don't want to get out of or in a nightmare I need to get the fuck out of if only to protect myself—if only to protect my quickly growing feelings, my quickly beating heart. I need to rid myself of my...confusion. My *curiosity*. At least, for the night—the night, during which only more waiting awaits.

I stride over to the bald, mouse-looking motel owner, who sits behind the register, minding his own business, his egg-shaped head and round eyeglasses buried in his cellphone. "Could you...change the song, please?" I ask him softly, trying not to sound rude, or at least not *weird*, about it.

He looks up at me and frowns, the whites of his drowsy or drug-affected eyes overcome by red. "Oh, what, you don't like Franklaay or Melodyz Town?"

"Please, if you don't mind—I'd just really appreciate it if you could change the song."

He shrugs. "Okay, well—how about this, then?" He turns around, presses a few things, and then turns back to me, the music having changed...and, from the lobby speakers, there plays another cover of "Put Your Head On My Shoulder." "This version is a little more *modern*, I guess you could say." He sounds so proud of his "new" choice, it makes me sick. "By vict molina, creamy, 11:11 Music Group—"

"No, change the—"

"Okay, fine, how about this one, huh, this nice-voiced fella, Harrison Craig?" He turns around again, presses a few things again, and another version of the same fucking song starts playing again.

"No, no, change the—"

"Alright, then how about—?"

"Change the *song*, please."

"Okay—"

"The. Fucking. *Song*. *Please*," I say so darkly and lowly it almost sounds like the growl of something, someone, inhuman. The kind of growl Lynnette would make if I ever pissed her off, I'm sure.

He holds his hands up, as if to surrender. "Alright, man. Relax. Changing it. Changing the *song*."

He turns around, presses things again, and, thank goodness—the song changes, and a song I don't recognize at all starts playing.

I sigh and make my way up the stairs—there's access to the second floor outside from inside the second floor of the lobby, which only includes restrooms.

When I get inside my room, I throw myself on my bed, groaning.

Another thing is for certain, too, and remains certain, remains *All the time*.

Again, I can't wait to see Lynnette. And I honestly would like to hang out with her in whatever way she'd like us to hang out after we are done with all our glorious bloodwork.

I am simply that curious. Curious enough. I've stayed curious and I will stay curious. She's sparked something new and nectar-sweet and nocturnally nerve-racking in me. It's a delicious and dangerous feeling I can't shake off even when time spent without her passes by.

•  •  •

"You're coming in this time." She wipes her red mouth from her dinner and gives me a very playful look. "You promised. You promised me." I wonder if I could ever be a late-night snack for her—and not be killed or bled and tasted to death in the meantime.

"You really wanna spend time with me that badly? *More* time."

"Why wouldn't I? You're my partner in crime. Why shouldn't I want to spend time with you outside of just our bloodwork?"

I shrug. She has a good point. I feel the same way. I *do* want to spend time with her that badly. More time. Outside of just our bloodwork. *Partner in crime.* I'm still not too used to how much I love it when she says things like that. "I'm keeping my promise. I promise."

She laughs. "*I'm* the vampire, and *you're* forcing me to invite *you*, the human, inside my home."

I frown, but the smile on my face stays. "I'm not forcing you."

"Oh, but you are." She cocks her head at me in this suggestive and flirtatious way with a sensual smirk, and I have to keep my head down. Regardless of what my voice or expression or body gives away during this conversation and has given away during previous conversations, she is completely correct, and I would love nothing more than to be invited inside her home and to be in her presence in a place where all her loveliness isn't shrouded by the darkness of the night and where the wholeness of her personality isn't veiled by the enthusiasm of the moon.

"If you say so," I mutter.

"I *am* saying so."

"Speaking of being invited in—*do* you actually have to be invited into someone's home to really make it inside?"

"I actually have no idea. I've only ever been invited someplace, or I've...pursued my meals outside of...the walls of any kind of building. For example, when I got my interview to work at this hospital, I was technically basically invited into the hospital because, yes, I actually did have to have my interview at the hospital. So they told me to come to the hospital, via email and then over the phone, and...well, I made an appointment with them and I went in a week later. I've never exactly tried breaking in someplace, just to check.

"As for everything else that'd normally require an appointment or would typically require entering a building—maybe going to the bank, getting groceries...well, just about everything can be done online these days, so that solves a lot of things for me, and, anyway, it's not like I could just walk out in the middle of the day and deposit a check or something. So I typically get all that stuff done either early on when sunset's ending, or right before sunrise begins—and, again, typically, it all gets done online, anyway. Anything, everything. I'm very lucky to be what I am in a time such as this, when technology is just...super helpful and just a great way of avoiding human beings in general."

"I see. Well, I totally get what you mean. I feel that way, too, and I'm not even a vampire."

She beams at me with her eyes in such a sincerely caring way that it makes me want to retreat into myself, my shell of avoidance, that it makes me feel like she's about to say "*Yet*," which I don't like. But I do like the smile in her eyes, even if it scares me a little—even if so much about her, of course, is bound to scare me a little.

She walks ahead of me—and reaches the foot of her house, uses her own key to unlock the front door, and swings it wide open for me like a gentlewoman. I smile at her with tight lips as I pass by her and I try to breathe evenly as I find myself back in her lair.

"Do you want anything?" she asks me, closing and locking the front door behind her. "Water, beer, wine, a cocktail, coffee, tea...?"

"No, thanks. I usually like berry cocktails, but...no, thanks."

"You're not thirsty or hungry? I've got some veggies and snacks in the fridge. *And* berries. To keep up appearances and all, just in case. They haven't gone bad yet."

*I'm hungry for your flesh pressed warm and tight against mine, thirsty for the soft wetness of your lips on mine.* "No. I'm really not thirsty or hungry. Thank you. Are...you...?"

"Oh, no, no." She pats her flat stomach. "Our kill for tonight was...more than enough for me." She walks towards me. Walks closer and closer and closer until she's inches away from me in her living room. She looks up at me with her dark and dreamy eyes, the darkest and most delightful of smiles. "Though, I would like to...know what *you* taste like, just one time..."

I chuckle uncomfortably at the vagueness of her words. She'd like to know what I *taste* like. Surely, she means my blood, and not the mere, human taste of my sweat-salty, lust-scented skin. "Hey, now, you promised me you wouldn't make me your dinner, Lynnette."

"I know. But I didn't say anything about dessert. I didn't make any promises about that," she teases me, her eyes wild and playful.

I cross my arms. "Still. You promised me you wouldn't drink from me."

She puts her small hands on top of my crossed arms, and I inhale through my nostrils at the gentle grace of her touch. "I promised you that I wouldn't drain you. That I wouldn't *kill* you. And you promised me you wouldn't kill me."

I uncross my arms and our hands fall at our sides together. "So...what, then, you've got the whole self-control thing figured out? You're going to taste me, once, and then you're going to...let go?"

"I can't promise that I'll have enough self-control around you or that I'll let you go." These words of hers—are they about my blood, or is she simply...*obsessed* with me? "But you won't die. You won't even...come *near* death. That, I can promise."

"Okay. If you promise..." I can't believe that the words, so nonchalant and as nice as the cruel and cold night could be, are coming out of my mouth, just like that. Am *I* obsessed with *her*?

She inches closer to me and stretches up on her toes in order to reach the place she'd pecked me once before: my collarbone...but I can feel her breath, light as a feather across my skin, as she places her small hands on my chest and pulls herself even more upwards so that her mouth might just barely reach the base of my neck, within which my blood pumps so fast and so hard that I feel like my jugular vein might burst and I might die right here and right now, anyway, without even so much as a neck bite or a broken promise from her.

My breath hitches within my exposed throat—I feel too much...and it's all just so overwhelming, and she's just so overwhelming, and it's all just still...*Too soon, too soon*—and I gently put a hand on her little shoulder, keeping her in place, not quite able to press her mouth against my neck yet, and I give the smallest push on her shoulder, signaling for her to get back down, flat on her feet. She does, and her hungry eyes move from my neck up to my also-very-hungry eyes. I wonder if part of the hunger she feels for me is the same as my very own human hunger. That very basic yet beautiful hunger for lips on skin, a hunger that had been distant from me till I spent time with her.

"Not tonight?" she asks, ever-so-sweetly, ever-so-innocently.

"Not tonight," I manage with a rough, dark voice.

"Tomorrow, then," she decides for the both of us. "In the early morning. After our kill."

"Tomorrow?" *Too soon, too soon...*

"Tomorrow. I'll work at night, but I'll let them know that I've got to end my shift earlier. And I'll meet you here, in the early morning, at around three. And we'll kill someone together, and I'll drink from them, and then we'll come back here. And I'll have...*one* drink from you."

"Just one. Just a sip."

"Just a taste. Not nearly enough to kill you, I promise."

I nod. "Okay. Good."

She cocks her head at me and looks at me with those wickedly wondrous eyes. Eyes that seem to hold the whole world, and me, inside them. She holds *me* inside her, and she looks like she can tell. My breath is uneven and so is my heartbeat, and my hands are clammy and my throat is dry and only holding her in my arms and finding myself, raw and thick and truly inside her, might help me find the peace that not even having just a partner in crime could bring. Would she even like it, if we were together, if I told her how much I genuinely liked her, killer-to-killer? Would it feel the same, for a human to make love to a vampire? I need to stop thinking about these things, because she looks at me like she knows how I feel, if not what I'm thinking, but emotions and thoughts are connected and *of course* she, with the reach of all her inhumanly powerful senses, knows how I feel, or at least how my body reacts the more that I'm around her, with everything burning from the inside out, everything stiff and soaking sloppily and sun-dry at once and steadily unsteady. "I make you very nervous, don't I?" she asks.

*Fuck, how am I supposed to answer that?* I take a deep inhale and exhale just as deeply and I gulp and lick my lips, because there's just absolutely no use in hiding my very clear nervousness. "Well. You *are* a vampire. That's enough to make any normal person nervous." It's not a lie. It *is* part of why her being my partner in crime makes me nervous.

"But you're not normal," she counters.

"No. I'm not." *And you make me nervous in an abnormal way, Lynnette. I am not nervous for normal reasons around you, not entirely.*

She makes a confession that sounds unbelievable to me. "You make me nervous, too, you know. *Very.*"

I frown at her. "Really? I do?"

"You do." She says it like it's the most matter-of-fact thing, and I have to take a minute to digest this, absorb it the way I'd absorb every other thing she could ever explain to me in the dark.

"How?" I finally ask.

She looks down at her small sneakers, so black you couldn't tell if they were bloodstained. "Well. You *are* a serial killer. That's enough to make any normal person nervous."

I walk back till I feel the back of my leg touch one of the couches in the living room. I sit back on the arm of the couch—almost instinctively thinking about how much easier it would be now for her lips to reach my neck and my face and my mouth—and I smile at how she parallels my words. "But you're not normal," I tell her, "and you're not a person, either."

"No. I'm not either of those things. And, yet..."

There's nothing but silence between us, then. My struggle to breathe through my nose, and her unwavering, pale-as-moon and black-as-night gaze. I'm the one who has to look away first—because I'm human. "I'm sure all my nervousness is very obvious to you, since you've got super-hearing, but…it's not exactly obvious to me, you know. *Your*…nervousness," I tell her.

"Well, my body functions like anyone else's, you know. Except for a few things."

"Like…?"

"Well, my lungs *do* function, and my heart *does* beat, and I do breathe and sigh like a normal human being, and I get full when I drink too much blood, and I even hiccup every once in a while, and I do use the restroom, though, because all I like digesting and *can* digest is blood, everything comes out all—like…red liquid, and I'm not just talking about…pee," she says in the most adorably awkward way.

"Oh, jeez. Well, it's a good thing that it's…normal for you. A human would definitely have to go see a doctor about that."

"Right, well. Sorry for the disturbing image. Anyway, other not-so-normal—or not-so-typically *human*—bodily functions include…the fact that I don't get my period anymore and I'm one-hundred percent sure I can't get pregnant. I don't exactly have a manual or any kind of guideline lying around for me to pick up and read and follow, and I can't really ask doctors about this without revealing myself, but I'm not human and I don't get my period anymore and so I must not be capable of getting knocked up, either. This isn't the kind of life I'd want to bring a kid into, anyway."

*Yeah. Even if we adopted a kid, it'd have two killers as parents and that obviously isn't very healthy.* It's too late—*too soon*—and I've already thought what I've thought, and I'm just glad that I'm not stupid enough to have said this out loud—and I *do* feel like quite the fool around Lynnette. Lynnette and I, parents to a child, the impossibility of it—if I'm not obsessed with her already, then I'm having the weirdest and strongest crush on her, the kind I've never really had on anyone before, because I've never met a vampire before—I've never met *her* before. It pleases me in the most untimely manner to understand that, if she ever wanted us to be engulfed in the other's naked embrace even once during what is left of my human lifetime, I could release myself in her all I wanted without a worry.

"What I'm saying is," she continues, stepping towards me again, though, this time, I can only press myself harder into my sitting spot on the arm of the couch and I can't move backwards unless I want to find myself falling to the side and on the body of the couch—and give her all the room in the world to fall with me and atop my body—"that it *is* obvious to *me*, how nervous you make me. I can show you—the obviousness of it." All her rambling—similar to the other kinds of ramblings she's showcased ever since we first met, though this one has a difference in tone to it, an almost more tense tone, that I can barely detect with my very human hearing—has made it only somewhat obvious now. But I *am* curious about how she's going to *show* me.

My hand is in hers before I can even blink or gather my thoughts or respond to her or tell her the truth, how I feel, that I am more than okay with being shown the obviousness of her humanity. She puts my hand against her chest, and I can feel it—warmth, and beneath it, her beating heart. It beats...irregularly. With uncertainty and excitement. Like mine. Just like mine.

"See?"

I can only nod and hope for this small moment to never really end, for the sun to never really come back up. I didn't mean for her to feel like she had to show me how nervous she could be—how nervous she *is*—when I told her that it wasn't obvious to me.

"You can *feel* how nervous I am. Beneath your touch resides my humanity." Her words stun me a bit—mesmerize me, make me feel magnificent, magnificent like her, both of us lonely and awkward and odd nighttime creatures, both of us blessed by the moon and gray with our questionable actions and morals under the grayer clouds. I try to keep my hand still against her chest, right atop her bloodied teal scrubs. "If you could touch me anywhere else...it'd be even more obvious to you."

I close my eyes and shiver, delighting not-so-subtly in her words.

And then she starts moving my hand down her body, in between her small breasts—and touching her scrubs rather than her skin doesn't make the gesture any less unfamiliar to me...touching the very human body of a thing that isn't human. I pull away immediately, before she can take my hand any further.

"We have to stay partners," I say in one breath—my voice intense—more to myself than to her as I stand and, turning my back on her, walk to the other side of the living room, near the second couch.

"We *are* partners." She sounds oh-so-innocent again, even though she was guiding me quite slyly only mere seconds ago with her bold, small, sensual hands. "But can't partners be friends, too?"

I sigh and turn around to face her. "We can be friends. We are." Her eyes light up, and I emphasize: "*Friends.*" The light in her eyes doesn't dim.

"I'm sorry," she says, and her eyes move back down to her sneakers. "It's just that...I've avoided forming emotional attachments with normal people for a very long time. You see, whereas you may be passionate, the other person might feel passive. Where you seek paradise, someone else might seek poison. And where you'd like to be playful with them, they'd like to see you in pain." Her eyes move back up and find mine. "So I've just...avoided forming emotional attachments with normal people for a very long time," she simply repeats with a sigh, unsure of what else to say.

"Normal people," I say with a nod.

She nods, too. "But you're not normal," she says again.

"No. I'm not," I say again, smiling. It's my turn to look down shyly at my own night sneakers now as I ask her: "So, have you...developed some sort of...emotional attachment? Do you feel...emotionally attached to...anyone?" *To me?*

"Yeah. I do."

"Mm-hmm." I keep staring at the rug of her living room, tracing all the brown patterns as if they, too, like Lynnette, could save me from myself.

"To *you.*"

*Holy shit. Thank goodness, but...holy shit.* I freeze. "Hmm."

"Do you?"

Then I have to look up at her and I have to attempt to be on my best behavior, try to see right through her as if one simple facial expression from her wouldn't break me down or build me up. "Do I...what?"

"Do you...feel emotionally attached to me?"

I suck my lips in. "Mm-hmm." I cross my arms again. "A bit. Yep. Yeah." I'm trying, and most likely failing, to hide how exposed to her I feel and how unnatural that has been for me my whole life when interacting with anybody—but how she makes it all so eerily *easy*. "I suppose it's perfectly natural for...partners in crime, and for friends, to grow to be somewhat emotionally attached to each other," I casually add.

"I suppose," she echoes, taking a step towards me. "We sort of *have* to feel emotionally attached to each other, don't we? No one else...*gets* me the way you do. Your strangeness and mine—they fit well, don't they? *We*...fit well...partner. *Friend*."

I can only nod. Agree, while wanting to scream "Yes! Yes!" but having to keep my mouth shut—because of my past trauma with feeling something for a girl, because I can't actually act on any of what I feel for her until I am certain, and to the point of no return, that what I feel is more than surface-level lust, more than just human fascination...that what I feel is *irreversible*. She seems to want to be close to me, to almost *yearn* for it, even—I yearn for it, too, but, again, I simply don't feel ready enough to act on any of my emotional attachment just yet. It's funny: she can live forever if none of her weaknesses or limits bother her, but she's eager to lean in to her most human desires, while I—a human who will most likely be dead in at least fifty or sixty years, if not sooner—am perfectly fine trying to set boundaries and taking my time with the kinds of emotions that most people would greedily take advantage of feeling very quickly. She has forever, but she wants to be quick with her wishes. My time is limited, but I'd like to stretch my wishes out patiently, if only to test myself and the breadth of my humanity.

"So, then, *friend*, you're not nervous enough not to hang out with a vampire in her basement-slash-bedroom, are you?"

I uncross my arms again, and I start moving around her, around the first couch she's by, towards the front door, already getting my copy of her house key out of the pocket of my pants and taking my backpack off her clean floor. "Actually, I should...probably get going. But—"

"Tomorrow, then."

"Tomorrow?" So much has been moved to tomorrow, it seems. So much could, might, *will* happen.

"Tomorrow." She moves with me towards her own front door. "You know...that doesn't necessarily answer my question of whether you're nervous enough not to hang out with me in my basement-slash-bedroom."

I feel the corners of my mouth lifting in a small smile. It's all I can give her right now—I can only give her so little, these nights and early mornings, not because I'm human, but because I'm a *proud* human and still just trying to invite the other aspects of being a person in: socializing, caring, wanting, needing more than usual, more than just the companionship of the night, more than just any good well-deserved kill that a serial killer could appreciate.

I don't know what to say to Lynnette, how to answer her or appropriately respond—I have every right to be nervous, but my nervousness is perfectly balanced with an indescribable need to be alone with her, to see the most intimate parts of both her and this place she lives in, to have the kind of privacy with her that not even the ridiculously loud crickets outside could ruin.

All I can finally get out is a flat: "Goodnight, Lynnette."

She tries and tests me one last time. "You really won't stay a little longer? Stay till the night turns into tomorrow morning, at least? I didn't give you that key for nothing, you know."

I shake my head apologetically.

She nods, understanding. "Goodnight, Timothy." Her voice indicates a freeness, flexibility, and self-respect and simultaneous respect towards others that most humans can only dream of embracing both within and outside of themselves.

The only thing I can dream of now that I have her, my partner, my *friend*—the only thing I can dream of, the only thing I *will* dream of tonight and every night I don't see her, is her and her black eyes and her black hair and her berry-blotted lips and the blush she sends across my skin whenever she's near, the boldness of her personality and the brightness of her voice, the rose-colored glasses she seems to see our black-and-white world through, the kind I used to wear before everything turned blood-red for me years ago under the shadow of charcoal, clouded sky.

It'll be the first time I take the moon with me well into my sleep.

•  •  •

The next day doesn't come quickly enough. And then it's night. And then it's the early morning, and there aren't nearly enough mixed-berry cocktails or garlic fries or garlic-flavored anything in the world to keep my own personal thirst or hunger for Lynnette's presence from consuming me almost entirely.

The way I felt so reserved before feeling open enough to type out and print and hang my paper poster, before Lynnette decided to answer my call and I met her—the closer I get to her townhouse, the more such feelings fade.

"Thank you for helping me." Her words catch me off guard. She doesn't even say "Good morning"—she just dives right into *thanking me. She* catches me off guard, already standing in front of her door this early morning, coming out from the shadows and already brighter than the inevitable sunrise that will separate us hours later. Brighter even than the moon.

"Helping you?" I raise my eyebrows at her as I approach her.

"I feel...stronger already. Like the bloodsucking demon I was always meant to be." She laughs as she says this, and it makes me beam at her. "The beast I was before I calmed down a little and stayed loyal to my parents' hopes and dreams for me...balanced with the human I still am deep down— the humanity I still hold inside."

She starts walking away from the house and away from me, eager to start our hunt. She's almost...*skipping*, like a child content with everything around her. She *is* skipping—and then she halts and watches me walk over to her. And then we walk forward together.

"I don't think I would've found the courage or openness to wholly embrace myself like this if it weren't for you," she explains. "I was so stubborn, you know. But, yes, I see now that my parents would've wanted what's best for me...and I thought, for so long, that pursuing nothing but my career and sticking to hospital blood bags, was best for me. But reading your poster, right by the place I'm employed, made me realize that...there's more to life than work. And there's more to me than keeping the dead alive—*trying* to keep the dead alive—through who I am and what I do. My parents would've wanted me to be *happy*, and to stay that way for the rest of my life—especially if that means forever now. So—what if killing bad people makes me happy? What if drinking blood from them, and doing all of it with the coolest serial killer at my side, makes me the happiest girl I could ever be?"

I swallow what she says. It gets me thinking about something I've never thought about before, something I never thought I *could* think about before...

Maybe there could be more to life for me than work, too. *My* work. I don't have a job or career that I've been pursuing. Not since my old girlfriend cheated and then I just had to kill her and her side piece and then my family died and I dropped out of college and could only think about living my life day-to-day—or, rather, night-to-night, killing more and more and more. So killing has, in essence, been my work, my everything.

But maybe...there could be more to life than this. Could there be? More to life than my bloodwork—and hers, in the streets as well as in the hospital? What if...there could be more to my life than what I've grown so accustomed to doing, and *enjoying* doing? I could enjoy more than just this, if I tried, if I let myself, if I stopped being so stubborn, the way Lynnette has gotten herself to stop, found the strength to find her way out of the maze of her comfort zone—and for her own good, too. What if there could be more to the night and the moon than just a signal of blood, more to *my* nights? What if there could be more to *me* than just the killing I've made my whole purpose, my whole life?

It scares me to think about it. At the same time, I find myself...almost relieved. Like a sick man who has been chained to disease for so long that he doesn't understand a cure when he sees it, much less when he swallows it.

But my desires are not a disease. Society would have me think of it that way, never knowing or understanding that I am simply saving everyone else a whole lot of trouble by picking out a few rotten seeds and scattering them across the streets, fertilizing ground and grass with necessary red.

Still, there could be more to life than curing the world of walking illnesses while other people point at you—the same people you indirectly protect—and, unaware, call you the problem itself, just one more walking sickness. There could be more to my tiny human life than the draw of death.

I break the calming quiet between us with the musing of a simple and reflective "What if."

She grins and takes my hand in hers. "What. If." With the other hand, she gestures towards the emptiness beyond the both of us and beyond this neighborhood, towards the waiting darkness. "Shall we?"

•  •  •

She licks the blood dripping from her lips, but, this time, her eyes don't leave mine as she does. I'd look away uncomfortably, awkwardly, a great lake of lust looming in my overwhelmed heart and a load of it lingering hard right below my hips, but by the time I look back, she'd still be staring me down while feasting rabidly and rapidly on the rude fool we've chosen for the early morning.

The luring, the killing, the aftermath...it all results in a hot chill that leaves me feeling like I'm having some kind of amazing out-of-body experience. *It can't be matched*—that's what I always thought, back when I first started killing and then when killing became the norm for me, when it became and stayed such a pretty part of my everyday life...

But, ever since Lynnette bit her way into my nights, the high has been...even more breathtaking than I ever thought possible. The high leaves when she isn't there, though a fragment of it does remain, sometimes, when I think of her. But when she's right in front of me—even then, without the need for either of us to kill, some form of the honey-sweet high still exists.

It takes me back to the time I believed that any kind of lonely so-called villain in this world ought to stop wishing for someone capable of being just as vile to fly into his life like some chaos-seeking hero—because, in the real world, the monster is isolated and must stay that way in order to keep playing the monster, keep playing the role it loves being in, and monsters don't get partners.

I'd thought: *Besides, don't partners usually do some betraying, too? Engage in some kind of sabotage? Which, in turn, becomes self-sabotage, in one way or another. Partners are too much to take care of, so hard to keep in check, right? Wouldn't having someone here also threaten to destroy me the exact same way it would claim to complete me? Even the most supposedly trustworthy ones could turn on you and are just as worthy of suspicion if they're committing crime just like you all the time—All the time—whenever they want, whenever they can.*

But here I am, a monster, and here is my monstrous, magnetic, mesmerizing partner, my killing-muse, my chaos-seeking lady-hero, someone I trust and someone who is easy to care for and understand and take care of because of how similar we are, someone who is easy to keep in check and who threatens to destroy me only by claiming to complete me so much more than I could've possibly imagined...and neither has betrayed the other.

*Yet.*

Lynnette was beautiful this early morning. She chose the fool this time and she was the bait, the lure for my hook, which in turn became the lure for the hook of her eventual fangs, piercing him as he died from my silver knife. She'd chosen a boy in his early twenties, young and fresh and careless and as stupid as they come, the kind that she'd overheard a while ago, bragging over the phone to his gang of jock guy friends about how he'd assaulted some poor girl after he'd gotten her drunk. It probably hit a nerve with her, hearing that—since she'd gotten turned when she was drunk, against her will. She watched his house for a few nights, on her way to work. Stopped dead in her tracks and looked at the house she'd stalked him to and wondered when, if ever, she might get a chance to drink the blood of someone so dirty, so undeserving of life. She told me this morning that I could give her this chance—and I did.

She acted like a foolish, human, drunk girl to get his attention, a cute and little and helpless nurse in scrubs enjoying her early morning off. He was taking a stroll—supposedly enjoying the absurdly early morning, or looking for someone just like her to take advantage of. She lured him, and I followed the two of them, and then it started:

In an alley somewhere, he started tearing at her, trying to get through her scrubs, and she started screaming against him. "No, please, don't. Please stop! Get away from me! Get off! Help! Someone help!" The way she imagined so many victims of his must have screamed into his ignorant ears.

I slid into the alley and watched them from the shadows, right behind him. He was so eager to just get what he wanted without a second thought, and he looked up at her while trying to force her scrubs off, and I could see the corner of his lips turning up in an evil smile—only to see that she was smiling wide back, smiling with just as much evil intent, which he wasn't expecting and which had caused him to freeze.

And then, as she kept her smile on, her fangs appeared, and she gave him a dark chuckle as he stumbled backwards, scared and confused...right into me.

I tapped him on the shoulder, and when he turned around, I, too, gave him a dark smile, right before sticking my knife deep into his abdomen area. I repeatedly struck that knife of mine into him till he stopped struggling and began his slow process of death and he fell down to the ground, fell against the alley wall Lynnette had been cornered against only seconds ago.

When I looked up at her and stood up, stood away from the young terrible man to let her start her bloodwork—her own unique part of *our* bloodwork—she leaned down and started licking and sucking away at him at all the knife-made entryways I'd opened up for her. And then she started...*grinding* on top of his dead body, saying things like: "Oh, do you like that? You like that, don't you?" She started really getting into character, panting and groaning against the corpse, her own dinner. "Oh, c'mon, now...don't be that way, don't tell me you don't want me. C'mon...don't say 'No,' you don't really mean it...they *never* mean it..." Before she could drink him dry, she was mocking the sexual assaulter, even in death, for being even the kind of monster the two of us could never be.

It was the scariest and simultaneously the most stunning thing I'd ever seen.

I have to say something to her, anything, everything—now. Our comfortable and stark silence is beautiful, but my words could outweigh that beauty, and I could say something meaningful and powerful and give way to even more comfort if I just open my mouth, so I do: "Thank you. For saving my life, twice. For...saving me from myself, really."

She wipes more blood from her mouth with the back of her thankfully gloved hand, and those intense eyes seem to smile. "So, I thank you, and, *now*, you thank me."

"I *am* thankful. Very. I'm very...grateful to have met you."

"Me, too. And you...will express your gratitude—"

"By keeping my promise and spending more time with you today, yes."

"If you really *want* to, yes." Sadness enters those eyes—subtly, but strongly enough for me to notice. "I'd never force you into something you didn't want—promise."

"I *do* want to. I promise." And it's true. This promise is a real one. I really don't want to leave her side—the days spent without her are becoming days spent full of defeat, the kind of darkness even a serial killer dreads. She and I are the same, born from different worlds and yet thrust into similar circumstances, surrounded constantly by the sting of our secrets, our innermost cries for comfort, our sweet sickness, the stunning thrill of the kill, and the sourness of having to do it all alone for me, and the sourness of not feeling capable of doing it at all for her...before we met each other.

"Thank you." She visibly relaxes. Relieved.

She's so alone. So, so alone. All those people at work, all those human beings to laugh with and emotionally invest in—and, yet, no one who could really understand her, no one for her to confide in, almost everyone cruel and cold towards her from a distance. I could kill all of them over the span of several nights, free her from their cocky gestures and judgmental eyes, the white noise that leaves a shit-talking jerk's mouth. But it would be personal, so I couldn't kill all of them, really. It would be way too suspicious and, despite all the power we have together, we'd be just a fraction closer to possibly being found out—and, for me, a small fraction is significant enough.

*And, yet, if she wanted me to...if she asked it of me...if she only, simply wished it...*

I remember how she'd told me she knew I didn't take any personal kills and that she wouldn't recommend anyone from the hospital, and how her face had held only a shade of regret, a shade shiny enough for me to spot, enough for me to feel the tiniest bit heartbroken over, a shade of regret that got me thinking of ways I could make her feel better.

I shudder. It would be revenge on her behalf. Would I really break one of my rules for her sake? A rule I've kept with me ever since my killing became more frequent years ago, a rule that I kept to myself and that I promised I'd keep forever because of the very first two times I engaged in killing two people for my own personal benefit, for *revenge*, and almost destroyed what could remain of my unchained life because of it. Could I really do such a thing, risk such a thing again, if only to see those black eyes shine, to see that soft, petal-pink mouth smile? Do I really care for her this much already?

*Yes. So, maybe. Someday, maybe. Maybe even...All the time...with promise after promise after promise...*

· · ·

She takes me by the hand again and leads me towards her basement-slash-bedroom as soon as we're inside her home. Sunrise is close outside now, the sky caught in an indigo bloom, between the coming gold of the morning from the horizon and the dark navy sky frozen from last night.

As we walk down the stairs to her basement-slash-bedroom, she turns to me and gives my hand one of her kind signature squeezes. "You know...you're not nervous because you think I could kill you at any given moment. I mean, you are, but that's not all there is to it."

She flips on a switch, and the room comes to life—and I shouldn't be surprised, but I am. I don't know what I was expecting to see of her most private lived-in space—so much more decor than the living room holds, framed photos of her throughout the years, never aging past twenty-nine, and framed photos of her and her parents, sentimental objects lying around or placed neatly on a brown bedside table...

But there's close to nothing here. Only the brown bedside table, two framed photos, a few modern decor pieces, a small twin-sized bed, three drawers set against the wall of the left side of the basement across from the bed at the right side of the basement, probably all containing clothes and extra scrubs...

"Your room is...," I start, with no idea on how to politely finish.

"Empty," she finishes for me. "Everything I've collected over the years has either been scattered throughout the house or is upstairs."

"Upstairs?"

"Sentimental stuff, you know. Stuff my parents liked, stuff I've liked and held onto over the years. This and that. I didn't want to crowd my own...bedspace."

I nod, looking around at nothing. "So, you have the house of a fifty-nine-year-old woman, one room with a hospital bed and IV fluids and other medical things that could be described as the room of a nurse, and—"

"And I have the basement-slash-bedroom of a vampire. Every part of this house...describes me and reflects who I am quite accurately, I think."

"It does. It's all..."

"Messed up like me?"

"I was going to say 'Very nice.'" But it's not very nice at all. It's clear to me now—this most private part of her entire living space is basically empty because she is lonely, alone, because nothing recently worthwhile has found its way here...except for, maybe, if she could see me that way, *me*. My living space is whichever motel room I find myself in depending on the current town or city or state I've found myself in, always passionless and empty, always alone and lonely, *All the time*—and I'm always moving, moving, *moving*...and now I'm simply still here, still in Chicago, Illinois, still sleeping at the same motel room I've chosen to be in ever since almost getting arrested...still at Lynnette's side, solid and steady and unmoving...and I think that says something about who I've become since I met her, *means* something...

She beams at me and walks over to her bed and sits down on it—it's cream-colored and it looks like the kind of bed you might find in a mental asylum and it's just as bland as the rest of the room. The motel room beds I've slept on within the past several years have at least been more *colorful.* "Anyway...I feel the same way you do, you know. I mean, I *am* nervous around you, as we've established, but it's *also* not because I think you could kill me at any given moment—you could, simply by using my weaknesses against me." I sit next to her on the bed, my hands clamming up again. "But our nervousness...isn't simply confined to a fear of dying at the other's very capable hand. It's a more...complicated nervousness that requires more than an open mind...isn't it?"

Strangely enough, bringing up the matter of our nervousness so casually does make me feel a little less nervous now. I'm still turned on by her, still fascinated by her, still feeling the slightest rush at the slightest movement she makes...but I feel my untouched peace returning to me—it is always there, around her, even when it seems to be hiding from me for only a moment. "It's the kind of nervousness that would take an open *heart* to understand it."

"And is your heart open, then?"

"To *you*?" She nods at my question. "All the time," I answer her.

And then she leans towards me on her bed, leans forward like she's going to try to kiss me, either on the neck or on my lips or some other easily accessible part of me, and my heart starts pounding—if we're ever going to have a moment such as that, it needs to be a moment that can be thoroughly savored, a moment that I can really promise to keep and a moment that I can really keep with me *All the time* and the kind of moment that really could be sacred and could really mean something. A moment engulfed by pure and deep and irresistible feeling—and I still don't know what to even call what I feel for her. I should wait, at least, until that moment, out of respect for her. She must be terribly certain about her own feelings and what she wants, having lived for longer than I have.

I lean away from her and gently put my hands on both of her shoulders, stopping her from coming my way any more, from inching her way up to my face. "You are, after all, my partner," I tell her. "And you're my *friend.*"

She stops when I say this and, with a sad understanding in her dark eyes, she nods. I already know why she is nervous around me, and why I am nervous around her—besides the fact that we can so easily tear each other apart if we wanted. It's also because...we could so easily tear *into* each other, too, if we wanted—her, with her long nails and her fangs and her delicious-looking lips, and me, with all my hardness and my fingers and the softness of my tongue.

"I know why I'm nervous around you," I declare. "And I know why you're nervous around me." She raises her eyebrows at me, questioning me, waiting. "It's because...we're..."

But it's so *hard* to get the words out, the proper words. It's like telling her I'm attracted to her and that I'm crushing on her would cause me to crack and crumble—still such a small confession compared to how I really feel, because, deep down, I know I am more than just attracted to her and more than just crushing on her, though I wouldn't have any idea of how to convey that to her, what with my last romantic social experience ending *badly*, for lack of a better word, and with that relationship being the final one I ever had before I embarked on a relationship with only the moon once I became the night.

And, now...the moon is here, made real. I wish I could have her straight away. But I am human, and not a very normal one, and I need time.

"It's because we're attracted to each other," she finishes. She can probably smell it on me, the desire I have for her, feel it, hear the blood rushing through me, through every *inch* of me.

"I *am* attracted to you," I admit. "I won't deny that."

"But you will deny the both of us any chance of acting—very *humanly*—upon that attraction."

"I've never...been through this before," I try. "This is all still very...new to me."

"It's new for me, too. It's funny, isn't it? How our struggles and nightly needs seem to be pretty much the same, how we have so much in common, but how we're dealing with this and with those conflicts in different ways—how we deal with this newness so differently. You've allowed me to adjust to my inner demon, and I can feel myself growing and glowing with every kill you allow me, every bite you accompany me on. So, now, I feel like if I want something, *really* want something…I really shouldn't be ashamed to go after it, no matter what—or *who*—it is. *That* would've made my parents very happy for me—I see that now. You, on the other hand—you seem like you won't allow yourself to adjust to *me*. Or maybe you have and you just don't know how to show it, how to express the…"

"The peace your presence…truly gives me," I acknowledge, playing with my fingers, intertwining them and stroking them awkwardly and looking down at my lap.

"I don't mind. I can wait. I've always…admired celibacy, in people." She puts her head on my shoulder, and it brings the song into my head, and I sigh, feeling quite at home here in this little space she's created for herself—the contact between us is such a tiny but tasteful thing.

"Have you…?"

She lifts her head from my shoulder and cocks her head to the side. "Have I been…celibate? Yes. Being a vampire…well, it doesn't exactly make much room for any intimate relationships. And that includes genuine friendship—I only have Janie from work, and there are days when I honestly think of her as more of an acquaintance than a friend."

"It's the same with being a serial killer." *Though I have zero friends, zero acquaintances. I had nothing besides the night and the moon. Now, I have no one besides you, Lynnette.*

She gives me the sweetest look. "Another thing we have in common. Just like our unique…nervousness." She looks up at me…and then, as her face moves closer, as if to nuzzle my neck, she whispers adorably against my skin, "Don't get too nervous, now, okay? A promise is a promise."

*Oh, shit.*

Her mouth is at my neck, and I try to sit perfectly still as her fangs pierce me only about an inch or so below my jawline. There's a sting, deep yet delicate somehow, and I wince—and then I shudder and my eyes roll to the back of my head and close as her small, soft, sweet mouth covers her bite marks and she starts to slowly draw my blood from the two tiny openings. She moves her hand to the back of my head—at first, I think it's for support as she drinks, but then, her fingers are at the nape of my neck and she's gently grabbing a fistful of my hair there, pulling me closer to her, and it feels so good to have her fingers in my hair like that, I find myself leaning into her lips, her tongue, her body. I feel intoxicated—*she's* intoxicating—and I try very hard not to moan or sigh in complete ecstasy against her.

After just a few perfect seconds of this, she pulls away from me, and I open my eyes and see her shyly looking up at me from underneath her thick, long eyelashes. My eyes linger on her lips, so pretty, so lovely, red with my blood like her canine fangs, now retracted to be normal bloodied teeth.

"Sorry," she breathes. "Just a taste, I know—I promised."

I don't know if I'll be able to speak at all, at first. Finally, after a few seconds of surprise and silence, I inhale, exhale, take in the stain of the moon and the scent of the night radiating from all over her, and I'm able to say, "It *was* just a taste. I promised I'd...let you have just a taste. It's like you said...'A promise is a promise.'" I'm grateful that my voice doesn't sound weak—but she has me weak on the inside, and it's an imperfectly perfect thing that makes looking back into her eyes a difficulty.

"You're sweet—for defending me from myself. You taste...nice. Very nice. You *are* sweet."

Without thinking, I lift my finger and gently scoop up some blood from her bottom lip and suck on my red-stained fingertip. My blood tastes metallic. *Interesting.* Not bad at all. "Thank you. You're right. I *do* taste...'very nice.'" She laughs at this, but I immediately wipe the smile off my face and point a stern finger at her, my expression suddenly very serious. "But, remember, no turning me. Just because I think I taste nice doesn't mean I want to go around tasting other people."

"What about me?"

I freeze. "What?"

"How would you like to...taste *me* someday?"

I frown. "Your blood?"

She looks away, biting down on her bottom lip. *Like a silly little college schoolgirl.* "Any part of me you wanted." *And a very horny one at that.*

I take a deep breath and the hand with my blood still on my finger involuntarily twitches at her invigorating words, her incredible voice. "You've *got* to stop that, Lynnette."

"Stop what?"

"Stop *flirting* with me like that." I try not to smile or turn red.

"Why not? It's not like you'd do anything about it, anyway."

"Anything to stop all your flirting?"

She half-smiles, looking back at me, her eyes dark and daring. "Anything to *make me* stop all my flirting."

"Oh, you want me to *make* you, do you?" She chuckles, and I shake my head at her with a half-smile that mimics hers. "What long years of celibacy will do to a vampire, if not to a human," I murmur.

"Will you...cuddle with me, then, at least?" And then she stands, and she starts undressing, peeling away her scrubs, and I immediately turn away from her and freeze myself in place, staring at the stairs of the basement until every single fucking step has been burned into my already-burning mind.

"W-what?" I can't get my heartbeat to slow the fuck down, hearing her clothes fall to the floor.

"You can turn around now," she says several seconds later. When I do, I see that she's put on a nice, white, sleeveless pajama dress that ends in ocean-like waves right at her knees, and she's taken her killing shoes off, too, her small feet pale against the cold ground. I can't help but catch a peek of what she's pulled off herself—the scrubs, but also...her bra, and her underwear. I gulp as she moves back onto her bed and scoots over, scoots up against the wall, making as much room as possible for my tall, lean, big frame. "Will you...cuddle me to sleep?"

It sounds like a trap, at first, like she's going to fuck me right then and there as soon as I'm with her on her bed, which I certainly wouldn't mind but which would leave me feeling like it happened too soon and too hastily and which, in turn, might make Lynnette feel like she's been used rather than made love to, which wouldn't be my intention at all—but then I realize that, for her, the morning is like the night for most normal humans, a time in which sleep is inevitable and required of the body. She is simply tired, and she'd like to go to sleep so that she can wake up at night feeling energetic for, most likely, our next hunt, or a shift at work, or both, one kind of bloodwork after the other—and she would simply like to be joined as she falls asleep, even if I don't fall asleep with her.

She really is so much like me—so deprived of human touch, by choice and without choice, so without human understanding, so without the privileges that being normal comes with. For a fraction of her years as probably quite a normal person, and for a fraction of my years as normal before I embraced the abnormalities that hid, and hid well, within me, we were both doing just fine—and then a human fucked me over and a vampire fucked her over and then we were never quite the same. I became a serial killer, and she became a vampire. But she stopped her killing after her first few years of turning, whereas I never took a break after my initial becoming.

Maybe that is what she presents me with: a break. I never thought I needed one. I never considered it. I never thought I'd need to stop doing what brought me the greatest rush and joy and peace. Now, though, there is something that is as equally great as all that rush and joy and peace, as the feeling of killing, and it is simply being in her company. It's a privilege, to kill with someone as fascinating as her, to have the rush emphasized and the high exaggerated just because she is always there with me.

I do something that seems very dreamlike, something that is very much out of my comfort zone, and yet, something that would actually make me feel very comfortable, the way killing with her does:

I say, "Okay."

And I turn around, find the light switch, turn the lights of the basement-slash-bedroom off, and then I turn back towards her.

"You don't...have any pajamas for me, do you?"

"No. Nothing that'd fit you." I really hope she won't ask me to cuddle naked with her, but then, she says, "I don't mind getting blood or anything on this bed. I'm going to wash it and my killing scrubs when I wake up, anyway."

I nod at her answer, and then, I start crawling my way onto her bed and onto the room she's left for me in the dark.

She turns around to lay down on her bed, to pull the covers over herself, to make sure there's room for me...and, honestly, there's barely enough room for me—both she and the bed are so small—but I can tolerate it and behave myself, and if I press myself up against her, spoon her and cocoon her small body with mine, I'll be fine and I won't fall off or slip down the edge of the bed. I slide under her cream-colored covers, which are as soft and silky as the mattress beneath us, and, at first, I feel awkward, *agonizingly* awkward, as I move close to her and then closer and closer until the entire back of her body, her knees folded up to her chest, fits perfectly within the confines of the front of mine.

And then, I feel her...*warmth*. Her softness. How *human* she feels. How human she *is*, how perfectly small she is and how I can *feel* her breathing against me, how *alive* she is, in her own unique way, her shoulders moving up and down a bit with every deep and loosened breath, her little hands wrapping tightly around just a fraction of my forearm as it curls around her body, around the space right beneath her breasts. And I begin to relax against her, begin matching her calm breathing, feeling like I'm floating on clouds, like she's right there floating with me, like I'd love to mold my body with hers and I'd love for this moment to never end...feeling like I could stay just like this with her and on this bed for the rest of my little life...

"What's *that*?"

And, just like that, the moment is over. She scoots playfully up against the hard thing that's poked her in her ass through my jeans, and I am sweating with nervousness, but I am absolutely relieved to know that it is not what I think it is—I've made sure to leave just a few inches of space between us so nothing awkward happens, so she can't physically feel how into her I am even if she can hear it or smell it or sense it. "Shit, it's my pocket knife, sorry." I could almost wipe a bead of sweat or two from my forehead.

I reach down into the front pocket of my jeans and pull out my pocket knife and move it to the back pocket of my jeans instead. It feels like I'm...putting away a promise.

And then...after a few minutes of readjusting...the moment comes back, continues...

And, before I rest my eyes completely, I catch myself savoring the feeling of her body touching mine, how she's wearing nothing under this pajama dress, how, if she wanted me to, I'd reach up and play with her nipples through her pajama dress, feel how hard they might be, or I'd reach down and lift the skirt of her dress up and finger her till the sun became as bright as the night for her. I wouldn't even care about feeling good myself. I *really* do care about her.

And it's killing me, wanting her this much, caring for her this much.

The minutes pass by, and maybe they become hours, but I still can't sleep. I wonder whether I could slice that part of myself out, the part that has grown to be so absurdly human ever since I first laid eyes on her, my savior, my burning, sunlit moon. I bring my hand next to her ear, and I softly snap my fingers. Her ear doesn't twitch and her breathing doesn't get uneven. She really is totally asleep.

And then I take my pocket knife out...and get the blade out...and I look at how the sharp, silver blade shines a little in all this darkness, like it's trying to bring the rays of the sun inside, like that tiny white glint of light on the metal could turn red...and not even with the blood of a normal human being or a human being at all...

I hold the blade near her neck. I could do it right now. The silver would leave her helpless, and I'd slice and slice till not even her speed nor her strength could help her struggle against me. I could kill her right here, right now—before she could have even the sliver of a thought of killing me, for whatever reason, one reason or another, maybe many reasons...

And then, with the blade frozen in the air near her soft and sweet and pale skin, I think of the time I bravely told her, not too long ago: *"I do hope I'm not meant to be the smallest of faraway memories and the smallest of footprints in your life."* And I think of how she told me, without any doubt in her words, that I'd never be a memory or a footprint like that. That I'd be very relevant to her, during our bloodwork together and even after my death. *"All the time."*

We'd barely met, barely known each other, and she still had enough confidence in me and enough belief in our combined capabilities, both mentally and physically, to label me as someone, something, important to her. Now, I know her enough to believe that I feel the same way and that she'll always be important and relevant to me, because I'm already thinking of her when she's not around and even when she *is* around I'm already thinking about how much closer to her I'd like to be—feeling her teeth and her mouth against my neck and cuddling with her now is more than I could've ever hoped for mere days and nights ago, *dreamed* for—and when she's around I'm also already dreading the time we'll have to say goodbye to each other.

I put the pocket knife—the poison promise—back into the back pocket of my jeans, and inhale her perfect perfume before falling asleep, with no dream to dream of or dwell on as soon as I shut my eyes, because my dream's right here, half-alive, though I hope not half-asleep—not awake, not aware of the thought that just ran through me like yolk through a cracked egg.

Just in case, I whisper to myself in the dark, so lowly that I hope it wouldn't cause even her super sensitive ears to twitch: "I was just testing myself. I see now that I could never hurt you, Lynnette—my little, loyal, loving, lust-filled, light-filled Lynnette. I promise." And, with that, I leave her, leave the basement-slash-bedroom, leave her home, the brightness of the world outside catching me off guard.

# CHAPTER SEVEN

# NEW NIGHTS

She doesn't meet me the next night. I wait outside her house, on her doorstep, just like a guy waiting for his babe, and she never comes, not from the street nor from inside. It leaves my mouth dry, leaves my heart even more dry, and I do *not* have any good feelings when I am left waiting all night—once again, I feel like I've been stood up. It scares me—maybe she knows what I considered doing last night. Maybe I've ruined everything—my desire, my dream...

The night after that, I'm on her doorstep again, waiting again. As the minutes escape me, I start biting my nails, almost...terrified—and not even for myself, but for her, wherever she is, whatever she's doing. Is she alright? Has she been found out? Has she been...*killed*, someway, somehow? The way I was about to kill her last night. Do the authorities—do *people* know about her now, about *us*? Did we slip up, make a mistake? And is *she* paying the price right now?

"Sorry!" Her voice calls out to me from the shadows of the street, and I take a deep breath of overwhelming solace. "I got held up at work yesterday, and they made me stay longer tonight," she says, walking towards me. "I'm starting to think that we might have to stretch out our bloodwork nights and early mornings—"

I stride to her and pick her up in my arms. She's extremely light and I barely feel the weight of her against me as I hold her, her arms around my neck. I breathe in deeply against her, overcome by how glad I am to see her, alright and alive—as alive as she can be, anyway.

"Hey! You okay?"

I put her down and a big sigh leaves me. "I thought—I-I—thought—I don't know, I thought something—I thought maybe something—something happened—I thought…"

"You thought…something happened to me?"

It takes me a second to look away from the ominous darkness of the streets, back at her playful, flattered face. "I don't know. Maybe. Maybe the police found out, maybe they…I don't know. Forget it—it's stupid. You're okay, and you're here now."

That beaming look of hers fades almost instantly. "I might not have been so okay the morning we cuddled." I frown at her, and the only part of her that the playfulness comes back to is her slightly upturned lips. "I know. I know what you tried to do. You considered killing me."

*Fuck.* "I…I-I—I—"

"You don't need to explain anything to me." She puts her hand on my chest, looks up at me like I haven't even done anything wrong. "You're a serial killer—it's what you *do*. And I'm a vampire—it's what *I* do, too. What you've encouraged me to do after such a long time." Have I also encouraged her to consider actually killing me now?

"You were awake. You heard."

She shrugs. "I'm a light sleeper."

"You're a *vampire*, and you have super hearing."

She shrugs again. "Tomato, tom-a-to. You made the tiniest bit of noise—the kind of noise that wouldn't wake a human up, but…"

I shake my head. "Are you…angry with me?"

She smiles, and that flattered expression returns. "Does it look like I'm angry with you?"

"…No…"

Her hand leaves my chest. "Well, that's because…I'm not." She seems very sincere, very genuine.

I frown, totally taken aback. "I don't underst—"

"I knew what I signed up for when I decided to take on a serial killer as a partner—just as I'm sure that you knew what you signed up for when you agreed to take on a vampire as a partner. And, as a friend, now. I bit you and drank from you"—she reaches up and her fingers trail lightly across the marks she left at my neck, and I shiver, delighted, at her fleeting, flower-petal-soft touch—"but I didn't kill you, and you took your knife out while you thought I was still asleep, and you held it close to me, but you didn't kill me, either. We were…testing each other, weren't we? And it looks like we passed, didn't we?"

I still seem to be in shock, still seem to have a lot of trouble absorbing what she's saying, how much she seems to mean it—and she really *does* seem to mean it. I feel incredibly lucky to be alive, to be by her side, to call her my partner and my friend, all the while dreaming of, maybe, someday, having the courage to call her more…*All the time.* "Mm-hmm."

"So. I'm your…'little, loyal, loving, lust-filled, light-filled Lynnette,' am I?" She grins as she says this, and I go pink.

"Mm-hm…you really are."

"You *really* thought something happened to me?" She's flattered that she means that much to me, and she doesn't even know the half of it—or, actually, she does, and she's just teasing me for it, because she can sense it on me, the drumming of my heart, the blood that rushes through all of me when she's there and even when mere thoughts of her possess my peace and even prolong it at the same time…

"You had me worried sick, you know," I say openly.

"You know, even if the police somehow *do* manage to deduce that this is the work of a thing that isn't even human, and that vampires do exist, it's not going to matter. I mean, what can they do?"

"Oh, I don't know—use garlic, silver, a stake, and sunlight against you?"

"What are they gonna do, grab the sun and hold onto it, stuff it somewhere, and then pull it out of their asses just to blind me with it? They're human."

"Okay, and *I'm* human, and I almost killed you while you were sleeping during the very start of the day, so—"

"*Almost.* But you *didn't.* You considered it and you tried, but you didn't. Because you *like* me too much."

"Well, you can't make police officers like you, trust me—I'm human, and I don't have your 'angelic charm' or whatever, but what I am absolutely sure of is that you can't make police officers like you, especially not when you've killed quite a few of their coworkers and friends."

"Okay, no, I can't make them like me. But they can't kill me. I'm way too fast for them, anyway. What are they, against me, when they can't be as sly or as cunning as a killer such as yourself? What are they against the both of us, together?" Her words are so wonderful I don't know how to respond to them, to her—perhaps no response at all would be perfect. She gives me a thoughtful look and says, "I don't feel like hunting tonight, honestly. I mean...I love it, don't get me wrong. It's...my favorite thing to do, I admit. And...you're—"

"Don't tell me I'm, like...your favorite person or something." My ears grow hot.

"You're well on your way to becoming that. You really could be." My cheeks grow hot, then, too. *I feel the same way about you, Lynnette.* "Anyway, I...was thinking that we could keep doing this every three or four days or so...maybe even once a week, so that I can at least keep up appearances at work and have extra time to myself, too..."

That doesn't sound like her, especially that bullshit "extra time to myself" bit. She didn't give a shit about that before. She was so eager to spend so much time with me—*All the time.* She was willing to take whole nights off work, sacrificing her duty of saving people to slaughter them beside me instead. "Are you sure you're not mad at me?" My voice rains with regret.

She gives me a soft smile. "I'm not mad at you at all." She could promise me that she means what she says, but I'd be conflicted, confused as to how to believe her when I've made so many promises of my own and have broken almost all of them in the end. "And I still do think that there's more to life than the bloodwork I conduct within those hospital walls. But I feel like I should..."

"Lie low. Stretch out our bloodwork days and nights, like you said."

"It doesn't have anything to do with you, I swear." *"I swear"—just another way of saying "I promise."* But she sounds genuine enough, and she steps forward, reaches up towards me and puts her hand on my cheek. I find myself leaning into her touch, her warmth, her honesty. "It has *everything* to do with...me. I feel...indescribably attached to you, Timothy. There will be days and nights when I will have to...survive being separated from you, if only to understand what it is I need from you, what it is I desire with you, what it is I want for you. Spending a decreased amount of time without you isn't what I want—but, for the time being, it is simply necessary."

"I feel...the exact same way, Lynnette." Is it possible for two people to feel things to such a similar extent? If they're close...then, maybe, right? I catch myself thinking of the ridiculous but righteously romantic phrase *Meant to be* again, and, again, I don't know whether to feel foolish or fascinated. We've taken risks with each other, considered killing each other very recently, all *too* recently, and, somehow, it's brought us even closer, so close that one of us has to force some space between us—there is something seriously wrong with the two of us, and it's so beautiful I could almost scream with joy, almost smile so wide my lips hurt or go numb.

"So...can we just...cuddle again tonight instead? Just for...one night."

*We can do more than one night if that's what you want, Lynnette. If you want, three nights from now, we can snuggle up in bed again. No blood—just you, me, and the bed in your basement-slash-bedroom.* I smile so wide, I feel like an idiot for it, but I can't help myself. The only thing I could crave as much as the kill is cuddling with her. "I thought you'd never ask." And if this is another test, this time, I'll pass even more than before, by not considering hurting her at all. We'll both pass. That's a promise.

•   •   •

When we cuddle that night, I am, once again, nonchalantly at rest with the soothing wash of what almost seems to be normalcy. We cuddle again three nights later, after killing a local pedophile, because it's what she wants, and then again three nights after that without doing any killing before or after, because I decide that even more bloodshed can wait a few nights more. And, again, I grow so used to it, to *her*, that I can't think of our partnership being any other way, can't imagine having to be apart from her day after day after night even if it *is* necessary, can't picture the rest of my human life without this creative and calming montage of killing and cuddling and cuddling and killing.

Three nights after that, we forget about hunting and we find ourselves within the small home we've made of her basement-slash-bedroom—mostly just her bed—instead. Our positions have changed. I feel as held by her as the night must feel by the moon.

Three nights after our first cuddling session, I was still spooning her and we were cuddling on our sides. Three nights ago, on that second night without a kill, she wanted to try spooning me instead—it was quite an impossibly adorable thing, with her tiny body trying to stretch out and envelope the largeness of my own compared to hers, and it was so cute I had to turn around and start spooning her again instead, and she laughed so loud as I tickled her into submitting to my turn to spoon her that she let out a snort while turning her back on me, and it was such an innocent, sweet, silly, playful moment. It was the kind of thing that made me feel like I'd missed out on so much of what was supposed to be a normal youth full of girlfriends who liked cuddling and partners who had the same mindset as me in high school or college—not that Lynnette is my girlfriend. She's my partner and she's my friend and that's all she'll be until...

*Until the time is right. Until I'm ready to promise the rest of my small, human* All the time *to her and our endeavors.*

Now, she's laying right on top of me in her pajama dress, and I'm staring at the ceiling like the dumbest, happiest serial killer there ever was as she breathes in the bloodstains on my street clothes and as her body molds like clay against mine, her nipples hard and pointy against my chest under her pajama dress.

I keep my pocket knife in my backpack by the bed now instead of the back pocket of my jeans, and she keeps her fangs in her mouth, though I'm starting to see that neither of us would really mind if the other did something deadly or tried something risky again—if anything, having her fangs dip into my skin again would turn me on, and I wonder whether she's enough of a masochist like me for some silver-caused scars to turn her on, too, and that's just how much we trust each other now, I suppose.

We're talking about our initial impressions of each other, the night she revealed herself to me about more than two weeks ago now. She's giggling on top of me, and I'm giggling below her, my body rumbling with amusement as I squeeze her tightly against myself, teasing her for her silly, funny confession:

"Timothy, I honestly thought you were a vampire first, for just the *tiniest* second." I groan and chuckle at the same time. "Seriously, I'm not joking!" She slaps my side playfully, her head still resting on my chest. "Saw your poster and thought: Well, holy shit, this guy must've been lonely for centuries if he really went ahead and made a poster as a last resort for company! And then I saw you, and I thought: Wow, this guy really has the face of...someone who belongs in the Victorian era."

"I have the face of *what*?"

"You literally look like you crawled out of another era and wound up in the present. I mean, you do look lost, here, locating nothing but bars that used to be taverns back in the day."

"Okay, how? How do I look like a Victorian guy? Or someone who's from another era?"

"Y'know, the...typical features, I guess. I'm not that old, of course, but, still, you see all the memes on the Internet, and you look like someone should draw an old Renaissance-style portrait of your face."

"I...don't know whether I'm supposed to take that as a compliment."

She breaks free of my tight, playful hold, and props herself up on one elbow on my chest, staring at me almost blissfully as she says, "You should. You look...timeless, that's what I'm saying—or, well, *trying* to say. You look more like a vampire than *I* do."

I roll my eyes. "Okay. Thanks, I guess. So, my...features?"

Her fingers are on my face, tracing my nose, my lips, as if to find an accurate way to describe her interpretation of what I look like. Thankfully, the bruises on my face have gotten much better, healed much more nicely than the ones across my abs and my back. "Well...your entire face is...very angular. Your nose is sharp, and so is your jawline, and even your eyebrows are sharp, and...your lips are pointy, and...you're...simply very handsome, in this 1850s or early 1900s kind of way. You're exactly the kind of person who deserves to have their portrait done."

"You think I look good, then?" *Handsome. Simply very handsome.*

"I think you look *very* good, yes. So, what did you think of *me* when we first met?"

"Well. I was terrified and fascinated at the same time, and…I still am. If I didn't know that vampires were a thing, I would've thought that, maybe, you were some kind of angel, or a goddess."

"A goddess, huh?"

"Yeah. Do you believe in that kind of stuff? Angels and gods and goddesses, or just the one God, or…?"

Her shoulders bob up and down once in a casual shrug. "I've been through enough to believe in nothing and everything and anything, all at the same time. How about you? What do *you* believe in? Well, *yourself*—that much I know. But, aside from that…what *else* do you believe in?"

A nice moment passes as I look at her like she's part of all that matters to me—and she *is*…a *part*, but a very significant one. I give her the only answer I can: "You. I believe in *you*."

•   •   •

Five nights pass before we meet again. Five long, lightless, lackluster nights. I could stalk her, watch her go to work at night, even make an excuse to go see her in the ER, get myself irresponsibly injured…but maybe that would be such a creepy thing that I'm not sure whether even *she*—with all her shameless personal creepiness and her admission of it back when we first met—would approve of that kind of boundaryless invasion of space, especially *work* space, and especially in the kind of hectic place that might distract me from focusing on her alone and might distract her from focusing on taking the blood of patients and giving them the full attention of any kind and dedicated hospital nurse.

She skips over to me in her scrubs like some magical human-looking creature straight out of a fantasy story as I wait on her doorstep. "You know, I've been thinking—and I'm pretty sure that, even if I hadn't seen your poster, I still would've found you. I still would've made my way to you, somehow."

I smile as she takes me by the hand. "What are you saying, that you think we're soulmates?" The more I think about things like this regarding her and us and our partnership and unique relationship, the less I cringe the way I used to when such topics suddenly confiscated themselves in my chaos-driven, chaos-seeking mind.

"Well, soulmates *do* exist in *every* kind of relationship, I think—friendships, found family...it doesn't necessarily have to be *romantic*." It's nice to see that she's catching on, that she understands how unprepared I am for my feelings—for *all* of this. Even though I've grown used to most of it, there are still other things that I am most definitely *not* used to yet, like the profound, passionate impact she has on me some nights and the peaceful effect she has other times.

"Wait, what are you doing?" I ask her when I see that she's leading us into her house. It seems that we will not be seeking out chaos tonight—and, unlike before I met her, I'm oddly okay with that, if it's what she requires of the night.

We head inside and the coziness of her home, as always, hits me with a great and golden comfort. "Work was *bloody* tonight—bloody *lately*, and...it was *so* bloody that I couldn't handle it anymore and I decided to have some blood bags on my 'bathroom break.' Having so much fresh blood lately has sort of been killing my habit of self-control. So, honestly, I'm full, and I've basically had my dinner—in fact, I'm *so* full right now that I don't even really need the *fun* of killing tonight. But, if *you* do, then we can—"

"No, it's alright. We can..."

"Head over to my—"

"Your basement-slash-bedroom. Yep. Though, I *will* tell you, Lynnette, that you're really pushing it, with all this *not*-killing every now and then. I *am* a serial killer, you know—it's what I *do*."

"Well, maybe it's not all you have to do. Maybe you can *do* something else, too, *be* a serial something-else." She gives an excited gasp as we head down the stairs to her room. "You can be a serial foodie with me!"

"A serial foodie?"

"Well, it *is* your first time in Chicago—and *has* been, so...really, the first thing you've got to do when you get somewhere new is check out all the great food. At least, that was *my* opinion back when I was a human."

I plop down on her bed and stare at the floor while she starts to undress. "Okay, but...*with you*? You're not exactly a 'foodie' anymore, are you? I mean, all you want is...blood....right? And I know that's your food, but...it's not really the same, is it?"

She slides into bed, and I follow. This time, I'm on top of her—and it's nice that she doesn't complain about my weight or anything, not that I weigh too much at all for a lean five-foot-eleven man. I rest my head on her chest, and she puts her arms around me, rests them on my back. It's a weird situation we have, something we understand and yet still have so much to understand about.

Whatever this partnership or friendship or slow consideration of a relationship is, I wouldn't trade it for the world nor moonlight, not for a hundred deserved kills.

"You're right," she says. "Actually, once I became a vampire, since, all I wanted to digest was blood, even when I tried anything else, any 'human food,' well, everything else automatically tasted like shit. So, even if I could somehow still digest human food, I really wouldn't like it or want to like it or have any of it."

"That...really sucks."

"It's one of the only things I miss about being human. But...well, cheese pizza tastes different from pepperoni pizza, but they're both pizza—human blood's very similar to me, to my taste buds, fresh blood versus blood-bag blood. I just *really* prefer fresh blood...I guess, the way some people prefer pepperoni pizza over cheese. One just tastes...staler and plainer than the other. So I really don't mind anymore—but I would *love* to take you, poor human, on a journey of Chicago food-tasting that you badly need."

"So you'll just be watching me eat."

"I'll get full with red beforehand so I don't get jealous or anything, I promise. The inner human foodie in me...would be more than happy to watch you eat. I'll take you to all my favorite restaurants that I went to back when I was human—it'll be a blast! What kind of food *are* you into, anyway?"

"Oh, you're gonna kill me," I groan.

"Why? What is it?"

I sigh. "Garlic. Garlic-flavored anything...is what I'm into."

"You fucking like *garlic*?" I can hear the disgust in the groan of her voice. The betrayal.

Now that I'm being honest, I have to continue to be honest—but all the way: "I fucking *love* it, but the bars I'd inhabited didn't exactly have an expansive menu. Even places with garlic fries—well, let's just say the food is extremely subpar. Anyway, I just kept...ordering drinks instead of the bland food that's expected to be served at any bar—especially a bar with *that* many low reviews on Yelp. Anyway, you haven't been able to see me have lunch during the day. But, then again, the menus I've come across during the day aren't exactly expansive, either. Very limited menus with tasteless hotdogs and flat chunks of dough and tomato paste trying to pass as pizza."

"Well. As I've mentioned to you before, if I swallow garlic, I'll die. But...if I'm around it, or if I smell it, it's like...having a deadly allergy. If I touch it, it'll burn me and leave either a burn mark or a scar or both, like the sun and silver and a stake to the skin on the chest area. So...this is going to be tricky. If you're going to consume any garlic at the restaurants I take you to—and there *will* be garlic at the restaurants I take you to, I couldn't exactly resist it myself back when I was human—then you'll just have to be careful and try not to get any of it near *me*."

"Okay. I'll be careful, I promise. *Super* careful."

"Okay. So, first stop, an absolute must in Chicago, of course: a great deep-dish pizza place. Not too far from here, actually. About...six hunts from now?"

"*Six* hunts from now?"

"Okay, *four*."

"Lynnette..."

"Okay, *three*. Sorry. Just—"

"Trying to...let me take my time. I know. Thanks. I'll figure things out with or without spending time with you, you know."

"All the time."

"All the time. It's better if I...figure things out while I *am* spending time with you. Just so you know."

She pauses. I can hear the fear in her silence, the way her hands tighten at my back. "Do you like me?"

"You know I do."

We both know what is unspoken: we don't know whether I am capable of the *other* "l" word, and we don't know whether even that would be enough to keep us from destroying, or actually killing, each other. People who spend a lot of time together in one space, such as her townhouse, eventually might end up either being perfect for each other or might end up wanting to murder each other—"those married couples," she'd said, and we haven't exactly been doing this long enough to know how things will turn out for the two of us if we keep spending all this time together. What we do know is that only time can help us both.

I am a killer, and the scariest and simultaneously somehow most seductive thing in the world would be for me to suddenly no longer be who I am, who I've been for so long so far. It's not like understanding or admitting any of my deep affection for Lynnette would stop me from continuing to be myself—it's that it would open up a whole new set of possibilities that may outweigh the part of myself that I enjoy so much. Would it mean I have a soul, feeling love? Would it mean that I could go, say, six whole months without a single life taken and spend that time vacationing and only watching Lynnette hunt and drink all across the country, or even the world? Would it be so wrong for me to enjoy making love more than creating loss?

*Whatever this partnership or friendship or slow consideration of a relationship is, I wouldn't trade it for the world nor moonlight, not for a hundred deserved kills.*

What's happening to me? Is it *okay*, or am I too stubborn to let it be, or will it actually end up being something that is *wrong*, or unhealthy, for the both of us? The humanity she's inspiring in me, a killer human, and the inhumanity I'm inspiring in her, a kind vampire.

So much to think about.

I have at least half of my whole human life left to think about it, and the other half of it to act on any decision I make regarding my feelings for her, if she'll have me, mortal and murderous me.

I know what I need to do. I need to let go of the trauma I suffered at the hands of the first significant romantic partner I ever had. That proud, narcissistic bitch broke the promise she made to me—the promise to love me, to never hurt me—and I've been breaking promises ever since, just to protect myself, to break bad people before they can break me and other potential victims, too.

Lynnette isn't the same as someone who didn't care about me, someone who cheated on me, someone who took advantage of my humanity. Lynnette is just like me, and I have to keep repeating that in my head.

As I rest on top of her, I can see that we are both still just children at heart. Still just a part of the silly little youth—her, someone who didn't have the most normal time in her late twenties, and, me, someone who didn't have the most normal time in my early twenties. Socially strange and physically repressed and incapable of letting words do too much of what mere action can.

• • •

The nights pass us by like a swarm of migrating black birds. And every night is more beautiful and more bloodstained than the one before it.

We've got to be about a month into our bloodwork now, right? Maybe more. The bruises from when I was almost beat up to death have healed completely, and I'm back to looking normal, or, well, back to looking "very nice," according to Lynnette. Time has passed quickly, and we've gone on our three hunts, and I've grabbed onto every single minute with her as tightly as I can, kept all the moments we've shared within myself like warm, gently held secrets—secrets of my growing devotion to her, the kind of thing I could only ever share with her when I feel absolutely sure about how to call my emotions whatever it is that they are.

Maybe I have never felt such a thing before—not even with my cunt-of-an-ex-girlfriend. Maybe that's why this is so hard to process for me. I am, after all, a serial killer who *chooses* where to place his empathy or sympathy, and kills people he interprets as bad, kills people he interprets as undeserving of that empathy or sympathy. I am someone who kills people without any bad feelings, so long as I see those people as nothing more than bad. And she isn't even a human being—she is a creature that I never even knew could have a place in this world before I met her.

*Of course* it's hard for me to process this—it's my very first time feeling anything *this* deeply, and for long enough for normal humans to call each other their significant other. And that's what I want, isn't it, what I desire, deep inside? For Lynnette to be not just my partner in all our bloodwork, but for her to be my *romantic* partner, too. What *isn't* hard for me to process is that I care about her beyond reason and I would destroy so many more people, take them away from their friends and their families and their lives, if it made her feel good about things, about *everything*. The hard part is trying to understand how to...deal with these feelings, how to manage them, how to eventually, possibly act upon them, if at all.

I have to keep reminding myself of all the time I have, all the time she's giving me, even with how impatient her immortal heart must be with me deep down. And I have to keep reminding myself that being with her is, and could continue to be, a charming change compared to what happened the last time I felt something for a girl. But that girl was just a broken, bitter, biased, bitch-of-a-girl, and Lynnette is the moon. Perfect for the night.

· · ·

It's a Thursday night right after sunset—about two hours before some restaurants close while others barely start to close now—and she steps out her door and comes down her front doorstep wearing dark blue jeans and short brown leather boots and a cozy-looking brown sweater that exposes her shoulders before the sleeves run down all the way to her little hands, almost covering at least half of them with their length. I never thought she could've possibly gotten cuter or prettier than she already was, and I thought wrong. I've barely seen her in anything but scrubs and pajamas till now. She's done her makeup a different way—her big eyes somehow seem even bigger and her lovely lips are even lovelier and her short, sleek hair seems even shorter now that it's been curled for the night.

Something was missing in my life, before, a social aspect that I'd kept down for very long, too long, a craving other than the sight of spilt blood that could be satisfied just as much with some searching. And I searched, and I screamed out from my poster, and here she is.

She really is a goddess.

I wouldn't necessarily worship her for eternity—I can't, anyway, being mortal and all. I wouldn't dedicate all I am to her—there are things I would do for her, things I normally wouldn't do for anyone and not even myself, but she and I both know about the importance of the night, about how, even when there *are* more important things to life than murder, victims still wait at least once a week every now and then, still wait at the end of the sun. And I *would* kill for her, so much, as much as she wanted me to, kill and kill and kill, night after night after night and promise after promise after promise, again and again and again.

And it's now that I realize that I wouldn't be able to let go of who I really am, how inhuman I am. I know it's not the kind of thing she, also a killer, would ask of me at this point, anyway, or ever during my limited lifetime— but it was a nice and brief mental exercise, anyway, a hard but interesting one, thinking about what I *would* give up for someone so special like Lynnette. And I would not give up the inhumanity I hold within my humanity for anyone or anything.

"You ready to try some deep-dish pizza? And if they've got anything with garlic on the menu—which, if my memory serves me, they *do*—please do me the biggest favor you've ever done anybody and *resist* ordering it." She'd asked me to simply be careful before—now, she's asking me to fucking resist. *Oh, what more will you ask of me, Lynnette?*

Trying to figure out whether I'd give up garlic for her is harder than trying to figure out whether I'd give up killing.

Giving up killing was theoretical—and highly unlikely, I now see—but this is *real* and this is *now* and this is *happening* and it's fucking terrifying.

I clear my throat and say: "I'm going to need to take a look at the menu first."

• • •

We're going to be having dinner in a restaurant together for the first time—
or, the way I've watched her have dinner in alleyways, she'll now be watching
me across a wooden table—and I'm fucking losing my mind.

They've got a basket of warm garlic and melted cheese bread rolls for six
bucks as an appetizer—and I haven't had a decent meal in several months
now since I live my life thinking that my inheritance will vanish into thin
air at any second if I'm not careful—and I don't know how to tell Lynnette
that I need to have those rolls before the night ends, so I do what any guy
does and I try to distract her from that inevitability, that fact:

"You know…on the night we met, the night you saved me from that guy,
Ollie, when I kept sort of fading in and out of consciousness—well, I guess
I was wondering what happened with your friend, Janie, and Stevie C., I
mean, did they actually—?"

"Oh, that didn't end up going well, actually." She puts her hands in her
lap. "It turns out Stevie C. is actually 'madly in love with someone else,'
though he won't tell me, or anyone, who that is."

"Oh. Sorry to hear that."

"It's okay. Janie's a strong gal—she'll be okay. She's a catch, she'll start
crushing on someone else in no time. Maybe a doctor or new receptionist
this time. And Stevie C.—I don't know, from what I heard and saw and
smelled and all that, it seems like he doesn't hang around that good of a
crowd. Men who are nurses who unfortunately happen to be…actual
psychos. Coming from me to you, I mean, that's really saying something,
isn't it? I told her as much, too, but…when you're into someone, you're into
someone, I guess."

"Well, it's good that Janie's…strong and all."

"Well, you've *got* to be, in healthcare. And I'm not even just talking
about people who work there like me. I'm talking about the people who walk
in and need *any* kind of health-related help, too. I mean, I actually *do* have
an idea of who Stevie C. *might* be—"

"Are we ready to order some drinks?" Our waiter walks over to our table and stares us down with a strained smile and bored beetle eyes. Not a single feature on his face matches his upbeat tone of voice.

"Yeah, actually, I'll have the berry vodka cocktail."

"Alright, sir, you've got it, and you, ma'am?"

"Nothing for me, thank you."

"Alright, I'll be back soon to take your order," he promises, leaving.

I hope he comes back later. I'm starving, and the thought of getting those garlic rolls won't leave me. I have to nudge Lynnette to continue—I have to distract myself, too. "So, you were saying...?"

"Right—so, I have an idea of who Stevie C. might actually like at work. See, Janie's the kind of girl who's nice to everyone. Everyone likes her. It's like she walks between worlds—the world of coworkers who think I'm weird, and the world of...well, really just my world, in which I don't really have anybody. She's so nice that she *can*. But people like Stevie—people who seem nice on the outside but really aren't deep down—will always be attracted to equal fakeness. We attract what we are, right? Janie sees the surface-level goodness in Stevie, and she likes that. But Stevie sees the shameless bitchiness in the nurse I'm sure he actually likes, and he likes that. It's the kind of shit that reminds me that some people out there never really stopped being a high schooler or college student, all dramatic roamers and lost or even found—all those certain people ever did was simply have several more birthdays."

*You and I see the good and the bad in each other and we like that.*

"Anyway, this nurse who's caught his eye—well, actually, let me back up real quick. There was a girl, a young woman, who came in with her parents— this was in Urgent Care, not the Emergency Room. She'd been sick before, and she was doing better, but she'd had trauma that she didn't know how to deal with. If someone who's never had anxiety or depression before all of a sudden starts getting anxious and depressed, it might be very hard for them to accept it, understand it, or know how to feel better. And she was getting all the *physical* side effects of feeling all that stress: gastrointestinal pain, abdominal pain...she'd mentioned that it felt like her insides were being torn apart. The problem is she mentioned this stuff to the wrong nurse. And I—

someone who could've actually helped her feel better, before the doctor came in to do his job of actually making her feel better, something he actually did a great job of, bless him—was in the next room and I was able to hear everything.

"The girl told this nurse how she was feeling. Her middle-aged parents added some info, their theories, how the mother thought it was similar to stress she's gone through when she was trying to finish up her master's degree while the father feared that it could've been something more dangerous. The girl worried it might've been a tumor—*that's* how much of an impact mental stress can have...to the point of physical pain. The nurse in that room...laughed. And emphasized that the girl was twenty-two...and told her to grow up. 'C'mon, you're twenty-two. And you're here with your parents. C'mon!' Of course, it was probably meant in a way to poke fun, and the girl and her parents all awkwardly laughed back, and that was the end of that exchange before that nurse walked out and the very sweet doctor came in. But it doesn't matter how it was meant. What the nurse said was...very belittling. And you should never, *ever*, under *any* circumstances...belittle a patient. Not even if they actually deserve it, not even if they're belittling you, the nurse or doctor, first."

I'm starting to forget all about garlic now. Her story, her passionate voice, draws me in as the moon and hopes for our bloodwork do every night. The waiter comes back, asking us for our order: "Have you decided on anything yet?"

I look at Lynnette and smile. "We'll have one Chicago-style cheese pizza," I tell him. "We're going to share it together," I lie.

"Alright, you got it."

After the waiter leaves, Lynnette continues, as if we weren't interrupted at all: "Anyway, *I* was...very close with my own parents. If I'd ever felt bad about anything, I could just tell them. So, to see two middle-aged parents accompany their worried daughter—I mean, she literally looked like she'd had a panic attack before she walked into the Urgent Care waiting room—well, I didn't think anything of it. Her parents reminded me of my own a bit. I don't think it matters who you are, a friend or a family member or a significant other—when you accompany someone to Urgent Care or the ER of all places, someone who feels fucked enough to find themselves amidst all that chaos, it's a sign of care. Even if that someone is needlessly worried about their situation and their own health, it doesn't matter—to me, it's a sign of love. For that nurse to react to such a simple act such as that...says a whole lot more about that nurse than it did that girl.

"I think that anyone who could be judgmental like that probably felt a lot of coldness and distance from their own family—wouldn't know how to respond to love if they saw it displayed right in front of them. Sometimes, 'independence' can be synonymous with 'lonely.' Sometimes, caring is mistaken for codependency by someone who's never been shown love and doesn't—*can't*—know what that looks like. But, regardless of what you personally can or can't comprehend, being a nurse—and one who takes shifts in Urgent Care or the ER, at that—means *not* being judgy or rude when it comes to the people who walk in through those doors. That nurse had no feelings, no empathy, no emotional intelligence—only prejudice and the ability to get degrees and study hard. As someone who majored in STEM—well, my parents actually called it: Smile, Talk, Empathize, Mind those around you—I think majoring in a field that *isn't* under the Humanities means that sometimes you have to be the most human of all. And that nurse, that inhuman, rude nurse...was not meant to be a nurse."

I could listen to her forever. I don't want her to stop talking, for my own deep voice to ruin things. All I can manage is: "You...*really* don't like her."

She laughs. "Well, it's not just because my friend's crush likes this good-for-nothing."

"Oh? Not just because of that, huh?"

"Nope. The nurse's name is Sunny, by the way—such a stupid name for someone whose heart has no light—"

"But a perfect name for someone as harmful as the sun," I murmured. *Harmful to you, Lynnette, and harmful to my heart when we're separated by that sickening star.*

She smiled. "Well, *Sunny* is the same young lady who mocks me the most at work behind my back. I know she's just jealous of me because I'm a fifty-nine-year-old who still looks and sounds twenty-nine, but...still. She'd be my one personal kill, if I had one. I'd sort of be getting revenge for Janie, too, not just for myself. And I know you don't do personal kills. I saw what happened the last time you met someone who wanted you to..."

The silence that comes from her next is enough to drive me insane.

I briefly think about the time I was thinking about looking for a partner, looking up the careers fellow psychopaths might pursue, coming across a list, thinking about how some of the most genuine, kindest people pursue these same careers, and how, among them, hide the demons, trying their hardest to blend in so seamlessly in with the angels. This nurse *Sunny* sounds like too much of a hiding human demon, a pretender, exactly the kind of person I'd never want as a partner, hiding behind angelic smiles, stealing serenity from real angels like Lynnette, whom the serendipity of meeting has brought so much sweet serenity into my own life.

Lynnette seems to be struggling so much to tell me the truth, how she really feels, the fact that she'd really appreciate this personal kill, if we made this kill happen together and cleaned up real good together afterwards, so good that no one could catch on even though it was so purely personal. It is worse than the consequences of risk and revenge—we take risks together every time we're in each other's orbit, anyway. Consequences swarm us, surround us.

"But I want you to know that...," she struggles, "well, I'm not going to ask, but..."

"You just did. And the answer's 'yes.'"

And, just like that, I'm breaking one of my own rules, and I broke my garlic-wanting tongue's heart tonight, and everything's changing, and I wonder what other parts of myself I'd break for Lynnette. So many parts.

Because it's clear to me now, tonight, as clear as the blood-soaked and simmering night, the brightly shimmering moon.

I'm in love with her.

*Love—that's* what I've been feeling. That's what I feel for her, how I feel about her. I've been flooded with fire, the warmth of a granted peace so golden and so giving it pierces me like the light gold, heavy moon—no, like the lightness and heaviness of all the stars, no, the whole galaxy itself, all of it, all at once, *All the time*, everything, anything, all replacing my loneliness with love.

*Love.*

The cute, killer quiet between us is interrupted by the next song that comes on in the restaurant. I involuntarily frown at the way the melody progresses, and then I have to pretend like I didn't tense up all of a sudden as the singing starts, even though Lynnette can probably hear, see, or sense every clenched muscle across my body.

I point up, trying to seem casual, even if it's pointless and useless. "It's 'Put Your Head On My Shoulder.' A cover by Michael Bublé."

"Hmm. I prefer the Nancy Sinatra version." So that's the version I hear in my head for the rest of the night.

. . .

"You were right. Chicago-style pizza...right here in Chicago...I mean, wow. That was some *good* food." I stretch under the black sky as we walk through the streets, fulfilled. Satisfied. "I can't thank you enough. For everything. You...really didn't have to pay."

"I did. I watched you long enough after reading your poster to see that. And speaking of watching someone long enough, about Sunny—I've stalked her, of course. I know where she lives. I knew I could tear her apart if I wanted but I just hadn't done any tearing or drinking in so long that...it seemed somehow impossible. And, more than that, I couldn't, because..."

"Because you didn't want to do it alone. Because you wanted to be...accompanied by someone. And that...would be a sign of care. A sign of love." Does she understand? No, she can't. She shouldn't. Not yet. Before she can interpret my words in any way, I speak again. "You wanna come to my motel room sometime? It's just...we've spent a lot of time at your place. I'm saying it'd be more than okay if we wanted to spend some time at *my* place, too, even if it isn't exactly the most dependent of settings."

"Oh, shit." She kicks the ground with her shoe. "Well, now you've invited me, so now I *can* come inside."

"Oh. Were you going to try to see if—?"

"Again, I haven't broken in anywhere to make sure about whether the whole 'having to be invited' part of being a vampire applies to me or not."

"You really are..."

"Way too innocent to be a vampire?"

"You've killed and drained too many people now to still be the kind and innocent nurse you once were—or managed to be after your first few years of fully embracing vampirism. But, no, I was actually just going to say 'good.' You really are...a good person..."

She hears the glint of guilt in my voice, in my eyes. "Now, don't go and feel like you've been a bad influence on me. I mean, you *have* been a bad influence on me, but, again, it's exactly what I needed and asked for—for someone to help me embrace all that makes me what I am. You're sort of the best thing that's ever happened to me, you know." The words are out of her mouth before she can stop them, like so many other things she says and beautifully babbles on about, rambling and ranting and ruminating, soft as roses to my ears whereas anyone else might've thought it—thought her—to be ridiculous.

"You're...sort of the best thing that's ever happened to me, too."

"We've been the best and worst influence on each other. It's been...beautiful."

*And I never want it to end. But I'll have to get arthritis someday. Even then, I'll get behind a walker or, again, get on a wheelchair and still join her at night. Just one old-looking elderly man and his young-looking old lady, murdering morons.* "So, the motel I'm staying at. My motel room. I've invited you. Maybe next week, on Friday, you can come over. And...I only invited you to *my* motel room. We can always...try to break into some other person's room. See what happens."

"I'd like that."

"Oh, you'd feel safe doing something that *dangerous* with me?"

"Very safe. I feel safe with you all the time, Timothy."

"It's funny. Weird in such a nice way, Lynnette, that you feel that way. That I tried to kill you in your sleep, and you—"

"You were testing me, just as I had tested myself with you when I drank from you. I think about your blood, sometimes, Timothy, how delicious you tasted." I blush. "Tell me, Timothy: how would you kill me, if you could, if you wanted to?"

I stiffen before her. "I can't. I wouldn't. I don't want to."

"Relax. It's only hypothetical. Killer-to-killer—tell me."

I take a deep breath. It's not an uncomfortable one—it's lovely, to entrust someone so much with all your strangeness, slivers of your sick self, your slyness, and even slices of your stupidity. "Okay. I...wouldn't use garlic. Or the sun. Too boring. I'd use my silver knife. The way I use it on everyone else. Don't think I'd find a stake anywhere. But I've got my knife with me. All the time."

"And I'm not everyone else."

"No. You're not."

She beams like the moon she is, the moon she represents. "We're going to go hunting next Friday. I'm going to take you to one of my favorite ramen places the Thursday after that. And then, maybe, the Friday after that...I can come over to the motel you're staying at." I love this, how she's already making little lovely plans for the coming weeks, still just the start of our *All the time*, assuming I'll have a long and peaceful human life.

"One of your favorite ramen places?"

She raises her eyebrows at me and laughs in a way that says, *"Of course that's the only thing you're focusing on."* "Yes," she says. "You know, I...used to not like going to any of these places after my parents passed away. They were restaurants they loved and that I also loved when I was human. When we'd spend time together, at night—and I'd always make any excuse I could to make sure I could see them at night, if at all, barely. And, well, I'd always make sure I was full beforehand and I'd always feel terrible, honestly, haunting places I used to love eating at but could no longer eat at, like a ghost. My parents even asked me if I had any eating disorders I should tell them about after I kept refusing to eat for a while, whenever we did meet up at a restaurant that the human me loved.

"Anyway...I've never gone back to these places, these restaurants, ever since my parents passed away. I've had no reason to. But, now, Timothy...I feel like that can change for me, especially now since I have the time to go out while pretending to *absolutely* have to get time off work every now and then, and now, with you...tonight...going back to that pizza place wasn't so bad for me. I thought of my parents, of course, but I also...thought of how going back to the places we loved together could be another way of keeping their memory alive with me. With your help. Your...company. Besides...I have forever left to try new blood from new bodies, but *you* only have this one life, and I want you to experience new, different things, including new food."

All I can do is scoff and swallow the fact that I'd slaughter entire civilizations for her, as powerful as I, a powerless human compared to her, could be. "You think I haven't tried ramen before?"

She rolls her eyes. "You hadn't tried Chicago-style pizza before tonight. Maybe you've tried ramen, but you haven't tried ramen at the place *I'll* be taking you to."

"As long as it's as special as you." And the words are out of my mouth before I can stop them, too. Around Lynnette, I seem to lose myself, and my mouth seems to lose itself, too. My tongue runs wild, my mind clear, everything...as fine as the chains of freedom I gave myself years ago when I began to kill.

"Oh, don't you worry, it is," she teases, flashing those all-too-nice teeth at me. "We'll hunt next Friday, then—we'll save Sunny for later, though, I'll figure out what we ought to do with her—and then, the following week, we'll get some ramen in your tummy."

"I can't wait to have you feed me. Again." I feel my cheeks warm up, a deliciously dirty joke stirring in my head somewhere, though I don't, and can't, say anything more.

She grins, wide, catching onto my thudding heartbeat, loud in the noiseless night. "Well, *you've* been feeding *me* this whole time. It's only fair."

*But life isn't very fair, is it?* I shoo the sad thought away. "You really did save me, you know. Twice. Back when we met. I was just—"

"Too proud to admit it when we met."

I nod. "And you really were...a symbol of hope for me."

She's smiling so wide now her cheeks would hurt, if she was a human being. *Fuck. So cute.* And hope asks, so hopeful: "And I still am?"

"All the time," I tell her. "You've made my dream of finding a killing partner come true."

*Maybe you'll make so many more dreams of mine come true, Lynnette, my love.*

. . .

The way she hunts, as opposed to the way I hunt, takes my breath away every time. The way she bites into her food, plays with it, teases it—she's so small and soft against almost every person we come across, all underestimating her when she's the one who does the luring while they just look at me funny or weird when I'm the one trying to be the bait.

I could watch her hunt and kill and drink night after night after night.

I wonder whether she could watch me kill night after night after night—whether she really does feel as at peace as she claims, just watching me eat human things, the way I feel when I'm just watching her, taking in everything she says and does.

The Thursday the week after our next hunt finally arrives—a night for her to watch me eat human food. I guess most people would call this a date, but we're not most people, and I'd like it if we could call all our nights and early mornings of bloodwork "dates," anyway. If *she* could.

She's waiting for me this time, on this nice Thursday night. She's already standing in front of her doorstep. She's dressed in a short, tight black dress that makes her look even paler somehow, black high heels, with fake silver jewelry adorning her neck and her fingers, her short hair curled again. *Gorgeous.* "I took the whole night off," she tells me happily as I approach her. "I won't have to leave later like I have to sometimes." *We've got the whole night to spend together.*

"That's nice."

She rolls her eyes at me. "It's more than nice."

"If you say so. Now, then." I gesture to the darkness ahead of her neighborhood street. "Go ahead, lead the way to...the best ramen in town, apparently."

"It *is*! You'll see." She struts off in her high heels, and, slowly, I follow.

And the restaurant isn't really too far away at all. Still, I wonder whether walking in high heels turns her vampire feet stiff and sore and sleepy the way it does a human's—whether she'd want me to carry her on her way back home. But maybe she'd prefer to speed back over instead—carry me instead. I certainly wouldn't mind.

We're at the restaurant, and I can't keep my eyes off a beef garlic-flavored broth with garlic noodles. She sees. She knows. From the corner of my eye, I can see that she watches my eyes soften before the menu I'm trying and failing to cover my face with.

"You're looking at something garlic-flavored, aren't you?" She crosses her arms.

I sigh. "You know me so well. I'm sorry. I'll order something else."

"Don't. Just...order the garlic ramen."

My eyebrows come together. "What?"

She takes a deep breath. "Order. The garlic. Ramen."

"Are you...sure...?"

She uncrosses her arms. "Just as long as you're careful...I'm sure." I gulp. "Now, when the waiter comes, order it." But, first, I order my drink: a sparkling alcoholic jelly drink in a berry-mix flavor.

The interesting, complex, comfortable and simultaneously cold quiet between us is, yet again, interrupted by a song change in this new restaurant, though the song certainly isn't new. "You've got to be fucking kidding me."

"It's 'Put Your Head On My Shoulder' again," Lynnette comments curiously, looking up and around at the ceiling of the restaurant, as if to find the speakers. She smiles at how anxious I suddenly seem.

I try to smile back. "This song just keeps making its way to us, doesn't it?" The waiter returns, and wants to take my order. "The garlic beef ramen," I tell him. "Nothing for the lady. And, by the way—what's the...artist of this song? Do you know, by any chance?"

"Oh, yes. The Macarons Project. We play their music here all the time. Good, aren't they?"

"Ah. I see. Yes, very good. Thanks."

After he leaves, Lynnette says, "So. This song keeps making its way to us." She gives me a playful look, her eyes wide, her smile wider. "What are you saying, that you think we're soulmates?" I'd asked her that, once. "You think it's a sign? That we're meant to be?"

I now throw her own old words back at her: "Well, soulmates *do* exist in *every* kind of relationship, I think—friendships, found family...it doesn't necessarily have to be *romantic*."

She smiles at how I tease her. "We can't necessarily be much of *anything* for long if you're so intent on staying human and dying."

"I'll live a long, human life, and leave you and your nights fulfilled by then, I promise." She doesn't say anything for a bit after that, and the sadness that is now swallowing up her face and soaring across her big, beady, beautiful eyes doesn't go away. It makes her look away from me, look into her lap as if she'll find some solace there, some solution to my stubbornness. But we both know that she won't, and that my stubbornness will survive even till I show her my newly written will many years later, an old man, and dedicate whatever I have left on this earth to her. I sigh, and I reach out for her hands across the table. "Lynnette..."

A bowl of hot garlic ramen and my berry drink comes between us. "Here you go, sir."

"Oh, wow, that was fast, thank you." I hungrily pull the bowl in front of me, the smell of garlic already filling my happy nostrils.

The waiter turns to Lynnette. "Miss, are you sure you won't have anything?"

She smiles uncomfortably at him. "Oh, no, thank you, I'm full."

After he leaves, I try to make her smile, make her laugh, anything to make her look and feel a little less upset, if I can. I blow on my bowl of ramen and point at it playfully. "You sure you don't want some?"

"Oh, shut up and eat." It kind of works. The smallest smile plays at the corners of her lips—but she eyes the bowl almost worriedly, like she's scared the garlic is going to jump out and get her.

So I take up a spoon of the garlic beef and garlic ramen, making sure to get actual pieces of garlic in the spoonful, and I start shaking dramatically, inching the spoonful towards her across the table, my tone of voice exaggerated in its concern: "Oh, shit—oh, shit, it's gonna get you—careful, it's gonna spill!"

She immediately starts recoiling in her seat, starts to lean away from the table and my quivering hand with the spoonful, her eyes big with fear. "No-

no-no—" I can't tell whether she was exaggerating about garlic causing her the symptoms of a deadly allergy or not, but I can see her inhaling and exhaling through her nostrils in a sudden panic, can barely see the tip of her nose growing slightly pink, a striking difference against all her unchanging paleness. "*No*, don't-you-fucking-dare-Timothy-no—"

"I'm just fucking with you," I say, shaking my head at her, taking the spoon back towards myself.

She sighs, relieved. The pink of her nose seems to go away, and she breathes normally now through her nostrils. "The consequences of partnering up with a human, right?" I like the way she says that, and with a genuinely amused grin before a playful pout, *partnering up*.

"*Befriending* a human." I sigh. "Seriously, again, no offense, but I really don't want you turning me or anything. Lynnette...I like you, but I'd rather just...stay the way I am. Human."

She looks down at the table between us. "I'm still having a hard time getting why, to be honest."

"Maybe it's the only thing about me that'll puzzle you and escape your understanding *All the time*. Well...I like a good cheeseburger. I love my steak *cooked*—well-done—and I love *garlic*, again, garlic-flavored *anything*." I point passionately at the bowl in front of me, and then my drink. "And a good cocktail, preferably fruity and berry-flavored. Berry-flavored wines and other mixed drinks, good whiskey. I'm not giving the taste of any of that up for...blood. Just to crave *blood*, like, c'mon."

"It just sounds like you're being a little too simple and a little too stubborn," she grumbles. "How can you like me and like who and what I am and not want to be a part of that?"

She's right, but... "I *am* a part of you, a part of who you are. We're partners, and we're friends, and we're *close*, and we will always spend nights together—right up until I'm simply just too old to...do it anymore. This is who I am. This is what I want—or what I don't want, rather."

I *would* love to see the world from behind the eyes of this creature. But I'd love to stay myself, stay human, stay who I am and who I've always been and who I always will be. I'd love to see the world from behind *her* eyes—and not from behind the eyes of a vampire. I'd love to see the world through her without actually becoming what she is, an impossible wish, and yet another beautiful dream, another bold but faint fantasy.

I suppose I could just watch her for my short forever and that would be more than enough. She is more than enough. She is everything. She is a promise. She is my little *All the time.*

She leans forward on the table and eyes me curiously, her voice careful and quiet and...cut. Like a reopened wound. "And you really don't think that's ever going to change?"

"Not for me."

She shakes her head, confused. "But people change all the time. That's part of being human, the thing you love so much. Even me, something inhuman—I change all the time, too, over the years. I learn something new every now and then, and then I improve myself and who I am and what I want accordingly." She thinks changing my mind would be an *improvement*? She looks away again, unable to look me in the eye as she makes the following confession: "It's just that...any form of inspiration I ever had to actually do something new and different and exciting with my life—none of it ever made a difference till I met you."

"I feel the same way about you, but this is the one thing about me that won't change, Lynnette, I promise. Seriously...if anything ever happens to me while we're out hunting, you have to promise me that you won't turn me. Okay?"

"Okay. I promise."

• • •

She keeps her distance from me after I finish my ramen and we leave the restaurant and we stroll under the moonlight, and I can already tell that, even though she took the whole night off, we won't be spending all of that time together. I don't know whether it's because my breath smells like garlic or because I've pretty much told her that she's going to have to watch me slowly strive towards death the older I get and watch me really die someday if we really choose to do this *All the time.* It's *my* choice, though—even if it sounds sick to her ears and breaks her heart, she should at least just respect it.

I'd taken my first spoonful of ramen—and she'd been right, it really was inexplicably tasty. She'd asked me to describe the taste to her since, of course, a part of her missed that part of being human. I only moaned with pleasure and commented that I wouldn't trade my life for, no offense, anything like the kind in which I couldn't have garlic. She rolled my eyes at me, commenting back that she's accepted herself and she appreciates herself and she wouldn't trade being a vampire for any other kind of life, either.

I don't know whether that simultaneous similarity and difference in us brought us closer or farther apart.

Now, I try to bring a lighthearted air between us again, hoping to get as close to her as possible without breaking any of her boundaries or mine. "So, my motel room next week. Do you plan on staying over...the way I do at your place sometimes?"

"Yeah, I'd like that. I'll stay for as long as I can, and before sunrise, I'll zoom my way back home."

"That sounds good. And, before you spend the bulk of your night in my room" —I clear my throat and try not to blush at my own words, the images they bring to mind—"we'll break into someone else's room, see how you do when you're not invited inside. We'll break a few rules, maybe even...break a few people..."

It works again. Yet another tiny grin is tugging away at her lips. "Well, now you're just breaking my heart, saying that. You know better than to tease me like that. We won't be breaking anybody—we can't do that where you're staying, because it'd be too personal."

"Well. I agreed to kill Sunny with you for your very personal reasons, didn't I?" She squints at me. She really does know me so well, because, then, I say: "You're right. No personal kills at the place I'm staying at. Now, that's *way* too risky. But I'll see who's been signed out of the motel for the night, who's left their room—I'll be extra careful and I'll make extra sure that the room we choose to break into isn't one that's occupied at the moment you come to the motel."

She nods.

She doesn't give me her usual tight, adorable, warm hug that night before leaving, and I feel empty without her arms around my waist and her head right at my chest, empty as I watch her speed off in the most abrupt flash.

• • •

*Let go. Let go of what she did to you. That cunt. That human, promise-breaking cunt. It's time to let go once and for all, killer.*

But if I let go of the thing that inspired and brought out the hidden murderer in me, will killing still be the same? Would I still relish in the feeling of making it rain red with Lynnette?

*Friday.*

If I tell Lynnette how I feel about her, would she be a little less sad about me not wanting to turn into a vampire, not wanting to live for eternity with her? Or would that confession make everything worse?

*Saturday.*

These are the questions that plague me throughout the next week.

*Sunday.*

It's funny. Once, I'd waited week after week, day after day, for my possible partner. Now, I wait week after week and day after day for my partner to turn into my potential forever, the small human forever I've got. I wasn't even looking for anything besides a partner to kill with, didn't even care who they'd be or what they'd be like so long as we understood each other and thought and believed in the same things—but I certainly wouldn't have minded having more than just that if the partnership naturally progressed in a positive way. And, now, maybe, just maybe…this—Lynnette at my side—isn't exactly what I was looking for, but is what I so badly needed, deep down…

*Monday.*

The feeling is the same—instead of waiting in a bar, I'm waiting wherever, whenever, still drowning in the dark, anxious and excited at the same time. My nights were numb, once, and now, they are new. They've been new for weeks and weeks and weeks and weeks and weeks now. So new—and new *All the time*—that things never feel numb and *I* never feel numb when I'm with Lynnette.

*Tuesday.*

Is she waiting, too? Waiting for one of us to make the first move?

*Wednesday.*

Would everything be alright between us, if we decided to take our partnership and our friendship to yet another level?

*Thursday.*

Would that be yet another dream coming true? Would it be real and perfect and everything I'd imagined up until the end? Would we vow to love each other till I passed away? Would *she* promise to love me till then, and love me still, even when I followed after her in the dark on an electric wheelchair, even after I was put six feet underground?

*Friday.*

The questions haunt me, and even when I see Lynnette walking towards the motel from my room window as the night and the moon comes, they don't disappear. I leave my room and move down the stairs and saunter towards her and all the questions follow. She's staring at the open door of the lobby, staring with a funny frown and funny smile, and then I hear it.

"I'm starting to think that this might be our song." Lynnette chuckles, partially in shock and partially fascinated. "Wherever we go, it seems to follow."

"Put Your Head On My Shoulder," and, this time, it's the original, the version that was playing in the bar the night I got arrested, the one by Paul Anka.

Even when it's just a melody in our heads, it follows. And, wherever we go, the dark of the night and the early morning follows, too. Wherever we go, images of the moon in the sky or behind our eyes follow. *All the time.*

"Our song." I nod. "You know, the song made me nervous, when I was getting arrested from the bar and when I woke up in the hospital room and when I heard it again afterwards, right here in this motel lobby, because *you* made me nervous, and the song just kept bringing to light what I already knew subconsciously." I pause. "The fact that...I'm never going to find anyone else like you."

"I'm never going to find anyone else like you, either. Not in a hundred years. Not in a thousand." Her voice is bittersweet. Because, someday, I'll be gone, and she'll have to. She'll have to try to be social, normal, till someone comes along and gives her an excuse, the right, to be exactly as amazingly abnormal as she is. "Does the song still make you nervous?"

"Only as much as you still do. More than anything...after we heard it...quite a few times, while we were spending time together...I felt happy, hearing it. You're right. It's our song." I start walking towards the stairs that lead up to the rooms on the second floor, and, as a silent invitation, I gesture for her to follow me, which she abruptly does, the music echoing in the background as we leave it and the office-slash-lobby behind. "So, you've never really tried to break in anywhere or get through any doors without having to be invited inside, directly or indirectly?"

"It didn't occur to me."

"It didn't *occur* to you? Really?"

"A lot of things didn't occur to me before I met you."

We arrive at my room. "You're..."

"Really a good person?"

I step a few doors down and reach the room I know will be empty tonight—and empty for two more nights, according to the small note the motel owner left next to the room owner's name in the sign-in sheet of the lobby-slash-office, which I stole the room owner's room key from earlier today. "'Ridiculous.' I was going to say 'ridiculous.' In the cutest way possible, of course."

"You think I'm cute?" she chirps with a chuckle.

"Oh, *constantly* cute. I'd be an idiot if I didn't."

I unlock the stranger's door and gesture for Lynnette to wait outside. I walk into the room, and turn around to face her while she stands right beyond the open door.

"Okay." I don't say anything else or make any other gestures or anything, afraid that any one of them might be interpreted as an invitation and ruin our little experiment.

She tries to step in—but she stops, like there's something invisible in her way. "I can't—" She bangs on the invisible barrier, her face scrunched up in frustration, and I'm about to tell her to stop and that I can invite her in, but then, within seconds, a wide, wicked smile crawls takes over her face and she steps inside without a problem. "Just kidding. I guess I don't need to be invited in, then, huh? One thing that doesn't apply to a vampire like me."

I shake my head at her and grit my teeth to keep from grinning like a fool. "You're so fucking—"

"Funny?"

"Silly."

She walks in and out of the door like a child, and then, she squeals with joy, and when she next comes in through the open door, she closes it shut and then she skips right up to me and gives me a tight squeeze, a hug that's so tight I feel like I'm going to break in her little arms, her head at my chest. I'd trade in my small acid soul to feel this *All the time* till the end of my time—again, if I even have what other people would call a "soul," though I'm certain now that Lynnette would certainly think I've got one the way I think she, the living dead, does. "We're more than partners," she murmurs against my chest. "We're friends. But we're more than friends, too, aren't we?"

I swallow. And I try...I really do: "We've been at this for longer than about two months now. I know you well enough to know you in my dreams when my eyes are closed and in my sunlit days when the world is closed to you. And that's saying something, considering that I don't have any friends—or anyone else, for that matter—and considering that the last time I cared about anybody was when I was still just a young and stupid college student. Yes, Lynnette. We *are* more than friends."

She looks up at me, and I look down at her, and again I think of how much I like the words: Sin. Soul. Blood sacrifice—the thing that no real god except the killer requires. I think of all the time we have left together—how we have all that time left to get as horribly inhuman as humanly possible and to actually piss each other off or betray each other. I say something dangerous, something that'll take us both in the right direction, something that is as meaningful and powerful as simply telling her I love her:

"We're *best* friends."

"Best friends," she agrees, content and glad, her black eyes softening as she stares into my eyes, and we *are* partners and friends and even best friends, except that killing partners and best friends don't look at each other the way we're looking at each other right now.

"We've been best friends for a bit now," I say with a smile.

She smiles, too, and takes my hand, and leads me to the bed of the stranger. It's then that I understand that we were never meant to make it into my room—that she was never meant to make it there, to a place so empty and so soulless and so temporary that it would reveal nothing about myself to her, anyway, except how much I need her, something that she must already know, already understand.

She plops down onto the bed and I plop down beside her and curl around her as I always do. Never once has she said anything about this kind of contact being too much for her or the sound of boiling blood behind my skin being too much for her.

"You know, Sunny's got such...an attitude," she groans. "Working with someone like that all night long is...just plain torture. There are some other nurses, you know, who are actually kind enough to respond to Sunny, behind my back—though I can always hear them when I'm working and when they're on break, of course—and they say they actually want to be like me when *they're* in their late fifties, that they'd give anything to look as young as I do when they're older. That's nice of them. Though, all that hope and subtle jealousy makes them ultimately agree with Sunny, in the end, someone who has no respect for her elders. You know...it doesn't matter how old you are, fifteen or forty or fifty-nine. It doesn't matter how much forgiveness you can give or what you learn or experience. I believe that, deep down, revenge will always be such a pretty thing."

"Well. We're going to get her one night, Lynnette, I promise. A night of your choosing. Whichever night you deem fit."

We sigh together, looking forward to the night she'll pick, and that's how we stay for a while, for a few hours, before my eyes open, because I hear an upset sniffle coming from her, her head tucked under my chin.

She's crying. "Lynnette? Lynnette, what's wrong?" I prop myself up on my elbow on the stranger's bed and wipe a tear away from Lynnette's cheek.

She wipes her wet eyes. "Oh, it's nothing. I was just thinking about...this quote I'd read a while back..."

I frown. "A quote? Well, what'd it say?"

"Oh, nothing, just...'Don't depend on a man; he'll die. Don't step on a snake; it'll bite.'"

I try to understand what the quote might mean, why it has her so upset.

She isn't a man, but I am—does she not depend on humans, or a man like me, to make her happy because she's immortal, and they aren't? Has our codependency when we go out to kill confused her as much as it has confused and simultaneously calmed me? Has our partnership both surprised her and given her solace, the way it has for me? If she is depending on me, a serial-killing human, to have fun in the dark and have company and understanding, does it upset her to do the opposite of what this quote in her memory warns her of, because I will be gone and returned to dust one day? Has she been reluctant to trust a human being, not just because they also treat her like she's nothing more than a fellow gullible person, but also because of the inevitability of their—my—mortality?

Has love made me blind to my own previous thoughts, beliefs, and rules...and has it blinded her in some way, too? Does she really...*love* me, as more than just a partner and a best friend? Against my better judgment, I leaned into my humanity and my emotions and I found someone to depend on and have a good time with in the dark because I was lonely and desperate—but she is a vampire who will not die, and she is not a human, so she can be trusted, from my perspective, can't she?

But that's just the problem, isn't it? We are both killers. We could be perfect together, so perfect, a match made in the hell I don't believe in—and, just as much, we can cause each other a whole lot of pain instead of peace or pleasure, if we dare.

"Am I...the man in this quote?" I ask her.

She nods. "And I'm the snake." Sobs are stuck in her throat. "Timothy, you're the bestest friend I've ever had, and I don't want you to die, ever," she cries.

"Hey, hey, hey..." I stop trying to wipe her tears and start running my hand through her short, soft strands of black-as-night hair. "Like I said, that could be anywhere between about thirty to, oh, I don't know, sixty more years from now. We have loads of time to be together—I mean, to spend time together." But I realize it might not seem like a very long time at all to a vampire—or to a busy nurse who has other life-altering, life-*saving*, life-changing things to do for people almost every hour of most nights and early mornings. "Now, just sleep, and we'll go hunting next week when we see each other again."

"I can't sleep unless it's daytime," she grumbles in a whisper, her voice stuffy.

I hold onto her tightly. "Then just rest. You're going to be okay, aren't you? You'll be okay." *Okay without me by your side so many years from now. But enjoy our now, Lynnette. Please.*

"Yes, I'll be okay."

"Alright. Then rest, and we'll kill someone next week, and it'll make you feel much better, I promise."

•  •  •

My eyes open in the early morning while it's still dark outside. I'm relaxed against Lynnette, but I can feel her go stiff when I look down at her head on my chest—her eyes are wide open already, too, and she's staring at the ceiling, lost in thought.

"Did you...rest at all?" I try not to sound too worried.

She doesn't respond for a minute. And then, she says: "Timothy, how long have we been doing this? Hunting together every now and then? Not necessarily every night we can, every night we get the chance, but...enough. How long has it been, do you think?"

I don't have to think at all. I know *exactly* how long it's been. We'll have so many anniversaries in the future, celebrating the Thursday night we first met. "I think it's been...oh, I don't know...about three months."

"And do you know how long...it takes, on average, for a normal human being to fall in love with someone?"

I pause. Why is she asking me that? "No. I don't."

She pauses, too, before answering: "About three months."

"Oh. Um. Okay. Cool." My heartbeat quickens. She must sense, *know*, how I feel.

After another minute, she says, "You know, I'm starting to think I might quit my job."

I frown. "But, Lynnette...you *love* being a nurse. You're kind first, and a killer second. A nurse first, and a vampire second, remember?"

"Yeah, but...well, I *am* a vampire. Honestly, I can try out something new, go back to school, maybe get a different career, learn a bunch of languages, travel the world making sure to catch night flights...there's *so* much to do, so much I can try, and I have forever to do it. I do love being a nurse, but I don't have to do it all the time, for the rest of my life. And...I feel like the surrounding environment, wherever I go and whatever I do, will always be a little toxic, full of people who ignore me or stay away from me or say stupid things behind my back or think I'm strange because they don't get me or because they aren't willing to understand me. So there's no harm in trying new things, I guess..."

She doesn't sound very sincere. I tuck two fingers under her chin and tilt her head up at me. "These are all just excuses, aren't they?"

She sighs and nods at me sadly. "I want to spend as much time with you as I possibly can, before...before..." *Before I die either from old age or other very human reasons.* She's thinking about the future too soon and too much, *our* future, but I can't blame her for it—when you care about someone, that's just what you do and you just can't help it. "You know, I've been telling my superiors that my beat-up friend, who I consider to be my found family, is extremely sick, that he has an infection. I've been convincing and charming enough, at least to my superiors, but still. I think I've broken enough promises, when it comes to that."

"Well, it's not like you *lied* to them," I joke. "I *am* sick—sick in the head, at least. And I *do* have an infection."

"And what infection do you have?"

I blush. *I'm in love with you, that's what. I—a sicko, a serial killer, previously lonesome and lost with a lackluster life—have been bitten by the love bug. I've been bitten by you, Lynnette.* "Oh, well...I like killing bad people, and I like doing it with a vampire—killing. That's an *infectious* enough thing, isn't it?"

"I suppose so." In such a quiet and weak voice, she adds, "I...have an infection, too."

"Is it the same thing, that you like killing bad people with a serial killer?"

"No." Her voice is soft and...striking, too, startlingly emotional. She sits up, turns away from me, and stands, facing the closed door. "An infection is an...all-consuming thing, when you've got it. It just...doesn't let you go." She turns around to face me, and she takes a deep breath, her starry eyes wide and wonderful, holding a black sea in them now that they're all teary. "I'm in love with you, Timothy." The confession comes out in a big, beautiful breath. It takes my breath away, too. Her confession is exactly what I couldn't say.

I stand from the bed, collecting my thoughts, my feelings, my own confession. "That's why you asked me how long it takes for a normal human being to fall in love with someone just now. You want to know whether I've fallen for you."

She nods, shy, scared, desperate, lonely, loving, everything I am and more.

"But you're forgetting one very important thing, Lynnette." I slowly approach her in the middle of the room, inches away from her, the smell of the moon radiating off her as always. "I'm not normal. And I did not fall in love with you during these past three months." She looks away, clearly disappointed, but I cup her face and bring her eyes back into mine. "In a way...I think I fell in love with you the moment I saw you, met you, the very first time I got to know you, the moment I first spoke to you."

Tears well up in her eyes again and she smiles between the palms of my hands against her cheeks as she clutches to the fabric on the collar of my shirt and says, "The same thing happened to me. Because of how long I've lived. Because of so many things. So much about you. So much about me. Because of the disappointments I've faced, in the past. Because I've never met anyone like you before. Because...Because—"

"Because we're not normal."

And, with her face still between my hands, I lean forward as much as I can, hunching over her, and I feel her stretching on her feet and then on her toes below me so that our faces can reach, and I give her a kiss that starts out sweet and soft, but before I know it, her fangs are out and she's bitten down on my bottom lip—it stings briefly in such a hot, perfect way—and the taste of my coppery blood lingers between both our tongues and her hands are reaching all the way up, up, up the nape of my neck and into my hair, tugging at the strands there, pulling me down to her as if we are giving each other breath just as much as we've been taking it away together. Swiftly, I pick her up in my arms, and her legs wrap around my waist, and she is weightless as I hold her up in the air. We are weightless.

We are weightless together.

"We're more than best friends, too, then, aren't we?" she breathes against my lips.

"We're everything." Our foreheads touch tenderly. It feels incredible, to touch someone like this and for it to mean something after so long.

"Everything. I like that. Everything to each other." *So creepy and cute. So complete.*

"Let's get out of here." I rub the tip of my nose against hers. "Let's go kill someone."

I put her down and she smiles excitedly, walking to the closed door with me closely behind. Never before has killing someone sounded so romantic, but here we are, she and I, about to go on a date—that's what this is, now. Ferocity for me and fun for us and food for her.

I'm not afraid of death or getting caught. I'm afraid of living without her. But I'm also terrified of living forever, of becoming what she is and losing all the things I love about being able to kill as a mere human being, holding power without power, holding power without the beautiful breadth of *her* power. So this will be temporary, at least for her. But, for me, it'll last until I die—hopefully. She will watch me grow old, watch me smile at her, toothless and tired, and watch me fade with nothing but gratitude for the partnership she gave me during my temporary human life. She will be the one to carry our mesmerizing, melodic memories with her into years of infinity. And, whenever I die, I won't have to live without her anymore. *She* will have to live without *me*. But she'll survive and she'll be alright in the night and under the moon, this aggressive and assertive angel of mine.

And, as I hold her hand in mine and we casually prowl towards our potential prey in the dark, I think to myself that...

*I've never been happier.*

*I promise.*

CHAPTER EIGHT

# THE NURSE IN THE NIGHT

About a week later, her door is open, and music is playing faintly from inside, and I walk into her townhouse to find her waiting for me, standing in the middle of her living room. She has the biggest grin on her face, and the music is loud now, and I listen, enchanted. "Put Your Head On My Shoulder." Our song. Our love melody and our killing melody at once. An instrumental version. She reaches out and takes me by the hand, and we start dancing, her head against my chest one second and then her body twirling under my arm the next.

The spontaneity of it, how stunning she looks in a casual black sweatshirt and tight, black, sporty leggings, her small hand eaten up in the big palm of mine, and how the song surrounds us yet again as if to drown us in our sweet solitude and our simmering desire for each other and her dreams and my daydreams of us, just the two of us and the waiting darkness and winking moon outside—it all cascades me with the coolest feeling of contentedness and comfort, one that only she and the night and the moon can cause, one that only she and I can cause alongside each other.

"Hey, hey, hey, what's going on?" I say with a smile, pulling her close to me.

"It's a piano cover this time," she comments, "by Riyandi Kusuma."

"Okay. Our song. Yes. Nice. So…what's the occasion?" We spin around and around to the softness of the piano.

"Tonight's the night," she declares, delighted. "We're going to kill Sunny."

"Oh, great—then it sounds like it'll be a *very* nice night." I'm happy for her. I'm hesitant, but, still, somehow...so proud of her. "Who's doing the luring? Are we attacking her at the same time? And you'll drink from her afterwards, surely?"

"No need to lure her. I'm going to kill her at her door."

"Oh." This sends a twitch of uncertainty through me. But I have to ignore it for her, don't I? Sacrifices—other than blood sacrifice—have to be made for the one you love. I'm allowing her this personal kill, anyway—allowing myself this already perilous step out of my comfort zone. The phrase *Love is blind* and the thought of her having called herself a snake—sly, slippery, soulless, slick and sick, and smart as sin—sends yet another frightening twitch of uncertainty through me. "Well, Lynnette, don't you think there could be any...consequences to that?"

She shakes her head, very matter-of-fact. "No. She lives alone, and her house is up on a hill, away from the rest of the neighborhood, so no witnesses—no extra, unnecessary blood. And we'll clean up after ourselves. And I'll drink from her, before we clean. I just want you to watch tonight."

I sway back and forth with her. "You're really pushing it again, you know. You know just how much I love joining you in the process and the buildup, before you get your fill in the aftermath."

"But you'd do this for me and you'd let me have this one because you love me. Just this *once*, just this one night...*perhaps* you'll consider loving me *more* than the process and the buildup and the kill..." *More than even the night and the moon, our equals, such great parts of us?*

Despite the confusion still corrupting me, churning around in my belly like a stubborn sickness, I nod, anyway, and tell her, "You're right. Tonight's kill is all yours. And I *do* love you."

"I love you, too," she says as she tries, adorably, to take the lead, twirling me around, straining since I'm so much taller than her. I've never let anyone take the lead before, not in a dance and not in a kill and not in much of anything in my life, but I'd let her take anything from me, now and forever—except for my human life, of course, the day forever goes frigid like a fossil, so many of my own. "I love watching you kill. It's *sexy*."

"And I love watching you eat—watching you *drink*. It's the cutest thing there is."

She giggles, and I lean down and kiss her. I was so worried before, so nervous a couple of weeks ago, letting my trauma and my experiences get in the way of letting things be this easy and this wonderful and this loving and this simple with her.

And it really *is* simple, with her.

In fact, it's so simple and perfect, in such a way that I'd underestimated before, that, when we get to stupid Sunny's place, Lynnette doesn't even have some villain-monologue or proud speech or words of revenge prepared, not even a smug smile, the vengeful victim in her not wanting to prolong what she deserves by a second. It's just another thing that I love so much about her—how, especially now, she isn't cocky the way so many of the people I'd met in the past were, so many people who could never be my partner or my everything the way she's become. All daringly gloveless Lynnette does is ring Sunny's annoying high-pitched doorbell while I stay behind to watch like she's putting on some little performance for me—a performance that won't require any words, only action, a dark dance, a ballet of brutality, with only the beautiful expression of her very subtly enraged and vengeful body, the rosy and ravenous expression on her face.

And then, as soon as Sunny frowns at Lynnette—and it's this bitchy frown, the kind that would ask, without a sentence or even a single sound, what the fuck Lynnette is doing here, but before Sunny can even open her crooked mouth or frown her crinkled forehead any more, it's over. And, now that it's absolutely clear that Lynnette doesn't actually need to be invited anywhere to get inside...

In a flash, Lynnette has taken Sunny through the living room and out into the backyard—a better place to clean up more easily, I'm assuming. I close the front door, then the backyard door as I follow the slight trail of blood across the carpet of the home through to the dark outside. They're on the grass together: Lynnette, biting into Sunny with great greed, and Sunny, choking, screaming, bleeding out, dying.

Lynnette moans against Sunny's collarbone, her eyes closed in total ecstasy, warm blood moving down her throat, splaying blood unforced and unfocused across her moonlit skin. Lynnette's moans grow louder, longer in her blood-gurgled throat, high-pitched and musical and mesmerizing to my ears. I squat before her on the grass of the backyard and watch her continue to drink, lost in the meaning of Sunny's life flowing in her veins and down into her tummy, lost in the beauty of not just a life taken, but a *bad* life, a very bad one indeed. Sunny didn't make Lynnette's life at work easy, either directly or indirectly, by simply existing, being a nuisance, still just a child trapped in an adult's body, as so many of us are, though those like Sunny have it worse, a lacking mind, a lacking heart, lazy development, something to loosen a terrible tongue with terrible intentions and to laugh at tranquility lost—but here Lynnette is, now, not making things any easier for Sunny, making sure Sunny would continue to choke and scream and bleed out slowly till she could simply no longer have enough blood to keep herself awake and in pain.

*Breathtaking. Extraordinary. Absolutely divine, the way Lynnette always works and drinks, the way she thinks and moves and simply exists.*

Lynnette starts to grind against Sunny's dead body, her hips eager and excited from the thrill of just having killed someone who can't be described as anything other than a big bully, her hips moving back and forth and back and forth, her liveliness such a wonderful contrast against the lifeless corpse, romantic red against bruises of blue, the hue of her pale skin still paler than that of her kill's.

She takes Sunny's limp wrist up against her fangs and bites down on the inside, hard, and sucks, deeply, moaning still, grinding still with her tight leggings...and then her eyes open, wide and hungry, and she stares at me, her black eyes begging, her voice whimpering in between moans as she continues moving against the body, and I lean towards her, tender but just as eager at the same time, understanding exactly just what more she could still be hungry for.

Quickly, as if in just a flash myself, I pull myself over the dead body and onto Lynnette, and she rolls over, away from Sunny, to the grass, and, aggressively, she pulls me by the collar of her shirt down to her, and kisses me, deeply, with a ferocious and animal and bloodlust-driven intensity that was simply not there quite as much during our first kiss. I push my tongue into her mouth with a reflected need just as unavoidable, a touch just as tenacious while her sharp fingernails dig into my shirt and she starts to tear and tear away at everything that covers me and keeps me just an inch more, just a barrier's worth more, away from all her softness, her skin, the sweet smell of death and darkness enveloping the two of us as we begin to envelop each other.

She moans and whimpers against me, the notes of her voice a magical embrace, a call to taste me head to toe and for my tongue and my lips and my hard fingers to do the same across all of her, every moon-soaked, murder-and-musk-smelling meadow of her skin. She succumbs to me like a siren, starved. We have both been starved of something as simple and strong as company, and that starvation has given way to other, more invisible starvations, the kind that don't make themselves known—so completely— till you meet someone worth craving—completely.

She completely undoes my shirt—I can feel how torn up it is by the time she's succeeded in pulling it over my head, and I start tearing back, my hands greedy as they grab at her sweatshirt and pull it off her and then her thin, fabric, black-laced bralette, and then her tight leggings. Everything is ripped, gone, and I can't wait to rip into her, for her to rip into me with her fangs— we're basking in the start of a kaleidoscope of killing and courtship, cutting and coming, and the cold hits my bare skin as the Chicago night wind briefly makes itself known across this neighborhood, but Lynnette is as warm as the living and she runs both her hands through my hair, fists forming there and holding me close to her, my mouth on hers, always, forever, *All the time.*

"What's *that*?" she asks, bringing me back to the time she felt my pocket knife behind my jeans, almost the way she does now.

Except, now, her voice is this crooked, crazy mixture of playful and pleading, teasing and untamed as she runs her fingers down, below the belt loops of my jeans, curious in this dirty, almost deliciously cunty way that she's never expressed to me so clearly before.

She really *is* a monster on the inside, and I love her for it, love her so fully as she is. She *is* insane—I wondered, once, whether she was as insane as I am, and, now, I have my answer, and I am wild with glee, ready for her to consume me and ready for my body to clash with hers till we both collapse, burning like coal, crashing crimson waves, immersed together in the wildfire of our desire and love and understanding and acceptance.

"My pocket knife, sorry," I whisper heavily against her, an amused laugh escaping me.

I reach into the front pocket of my jeans, take the knife out, prepare to toss it away from us and onto the grass—but Lynnette's hand clutches onto my forearm, stopping me. I turn to stare at her with the retracted pocket knife still in my hand. "Don't toss it," she whispers gently. I relax my grip on the pocket knife, relax my forearm, and let her lead me. She brings my hand over, the one with the pocket knife in it, and...

She holds the knife against her throat and, with her fingers on mine, guides me to pull the silver blade out while I use the elbow of that knife-bearing hand to support myself above her, my elbow steady on the ground. The blade is so close to her skin it could burn her if I'm not careful, if she makes any sudden movements and lets it. I suppose that this is what being kinky looks like for a vampire and a killer who are together, and the dangerous excitement bleeding from her black eyes sends chills down my spine.

"Don't be afraid," she whispers seductively.

I've tasted the blood of Lynnette's victim tonight across her tongue and lips, tasted her mouth, tasted her skin. I can taste more, and it's alright, and that's what she seems to be saying to me. I am overcome with more want than ever before. It's been years since I last merely kissed a woman in my early twenties—and no one within the last decade has made me feel the way Lynnette has. When I touch her, it's like I am equally the most fragile and most powerful being on earth. Imagine that, just the thing of my dreams all along, for someone besides myself to see me as I *am* instead of what I could be—a human serial killer, the most fragile and most powerful being on earth. Everything I am, ever was, and ever will be. *That* is what I believe in and *that* is what it is to be the living and a killer at once: a human god. She sees that, now, surely, as I hold the silver knife so close to the skin of her neck, capable of causing her so much pain, and, with the fingers of my other hand, diving into her black laced underwear to tear through it and bunch it up and throw it on the grass, capable of causing her so much pleasure at the same time.

I play with her, with two of my bloodstained fingers, teasing the soft flaps of her skin, admiring how wet she is for me, how wet and sticky with fresh and drying blood from the kill and how wet with pure need. She whimpers, and then, when my two hard fingers enter her, her head falls back, she moans—and then I hear a sizzling noise, and I look up to see the silver of the blade burning Lynnette's skin, replaced with what looks like crackling ash and flame.

I pull my fingers out and take the hand with the knife in it away from her skin immediately, panicking. "Oh, shit. Shit, shit, I'm so sorry, I'm so—"

"Don't be." Her voice is soft and sweet. I'm about to try to toss the knife on the grass again, but, again, her hand comes down on mine, stopping me, and she shakes her head.

She sits up, and, in one swift motion, she tears away most of my jeans and my boxers. I stare at her in amazement as she takes no time scooting onto my lap, and then, bringing back the knife in my hand back near the burnt slice at her neck, she adjusts herself and settles down...right on top of me. We both moan as I fully enter her, and start pounding into her like it could be sunrise again at any moment, though we both know better and the sun is hours and hours and hours away and cannot take any more from us today than we let it. Her hands are in my hair, at my back, on my shoulders, at my chest, and my one hand is supporting her by her waist, while the other still holds the knife against her neck. My eyes don't leave her as she breathes heavily and squeals and cries out every time I fill her up. She's heavenly, the only thing outside of myself that I really do believe in, have faith in, would keep so many promises to, oaths, vows. Even prayers.

Almost instinctively, I let the silver blade of the knife drift against her skin, as light as a feather, across her collarbone, down her shoulders, watching the sparks the weapon leaves behind, watching as lines of her flawless skin here and there turn, forever now, red and black like coal and fire, day and night, sun and moon, flecks of ash and dead flesh. She hisses and moans even more loudly, the honey-sweet combination of fascination and fear spreading across her like melted ice and devouring her completely.

I can feel her shivering—I've just made her come, and I love watching the way her face looks so at peace, and I need to do it again, make it happen again and again and again, *All the time*. We are full of romance, and yet, this seems so raw and rigid and romanceless at the same time—only what killers can achieve. We are hard and we are soft. We are everything, *All the time*. Everything to each other. Partners, friends, best friends, lovers. I don't slip out of her, because I'm not done yet, still hard inside all her tightness and wetness, and I start to pound into her again, signaling to her that she's really not done, yet, either.

"Harder," she squeals. "Harder," she begs in a voice so quiet it's almost airy. She's breathless and broken against me, her eyes shut tight, her entire body shaking like a leaf against the relentless firmness of my own, so impacted by every move I make, so...human. So human with me—and I, so inhuman with her, as I listen and I pound more deeply into her, and, at the same time, dig the silver blade deeply into her skin, seeing drops of blood spill and seeing burn marks follow. "Yes," she gasps. "Yes, yes, yes!"

I come inside her with a deep moan of my own, shaking against her, and, as I exit from her body, limp and worn out, she leans forward and rests her head on my shoulder. And then, within seconds, she looks at me and leans towards me, towards my neck...and I hear her fangs come out with a noise that sounds like clicking, and I gasp as she bites down on the side of my neck, the side she hadn't bitten before, when she first tasted me. I close my eyes and moan as she drinks from me a little. She pulls away from me, then, and, just like that—I'm hard again, stiff as can be, and I don't know whether it's because I'm in love with her and I know that she loves me too or because we're not normal and we make sense together and we're as crazy and strange as the other or because we're *everything*, but this has never happened to me before, and when she brings me to life again just by drinking from me and looking at me with those cozy, coal-black eyes, I don't let the moment pass, and I adjust myself under her and ram myself back up into her again.

I continue to move the blade down between her small, cute breasts, down her pointy, tiny nipples, down her abs, down to only about an inch from where I thrust into her with everything I have and everything I am. I look down, watching as the slightest, string-thin burn forms right where she needs to be touched and teased and played with on the outside. She screams, delighted, unable to bear the bittersweet sensations I force across her body, coming again. "You feel so good inside me," she tells me in a shaky breath, almost afraid of how good I feel, her voice coming out in a deliciously spent wheeze, a wild whimper, terrified and tranquilized. "I told you once that I see myself inside you," she whispers.

And, without another word, she brings her own wrist up to her mouth, bites down, and then brings her wrist over to my mouth. I open and drink from her bleeding, bitten wrist without a care or a thought in the world. She lets out a nice, little sound of pleasure as I drink from her.

And, just like that, with her wrist at my mouth and her other hand at my chest, and one of my hands holding the blade and moving it like a swirl of fire across the most sensitive parts of her while my other hand grips her hip, I start moving inside her again on the ground, her legs wrapped around me, my force hard and quick and only as heartless as we monsters both need it to be—just like that, we make the night all ours.

.  .  .

We stare at the stars and the moon, laying down on the grass of the backyard, naked, still only mere feet away from Sunny's rotting flesh. Lynnette's head is on my shoulder. Everything is perfect. We cuddle just as we did back when we were partners and friends and when we, like the silliest and loneliest and strangest young adults—fifty-nine is still quite young for a vampire, I imagine—snuggled up against each other without a word about what it might have meant or how strangers or friends or killing partners, or professional partners of any kind, do not usually embrace each other the way we did, wrapped up in each other's warmth, the mold of the other person's outline, their figure, their breath and blood. It's what we do now, but now we have a word and a feeling for it, and now our awkwardness has subsided to make room for home: *Love.*

"You know," Lynnette starts, "I'm always licking blood off the ground like some dog, and I don't mind, but, still—what if, just one night, we didn't? Clean up. What if we just...left everything as it was?"

I frown. "But it's...protocol. It's what...any serial killer out there knows to do: bring the appropriate cleanup material from the store, bleach, everything, and it's why my big backpack's always stuffed"—I point to my backpack nearby on the grass—"and it's...it's *protocol*, Lynnette. We *always* clean up—you with your super speed and strength and your sweet tongue"—I tilt her face up towards mine, lean forward, and give her a kiss, briefly darting my tongue in her warm, blood-breathed mouth—"and me with all my cleanup stuff. It's what we do." *We eat at the table first and then we wash the dishes together.* "Besides, I thought you dragged and killed Sunny out here, outside, so it'd be easier to clean up for us."

"I just thought that...everything would be nicer under the moonlight."

"More...romantic?"

She moves her shoulders up and down in response. *Adorable.* "Beautiful. Everything. The night."

"Mmm. It's incredible."

"What is? The night?"

"Yes. And us. The fact that...we're here, and we're..." I laugh. "I mean, killing people together is our love language, for fuck's sake."

She laughs. "And I wouldn't trade it for the world."

I laugh back, unable to tell her that I, too, wouldn't trade it for the world, or anything else—not even a vampire's life. I turn her wrist and look at the place where her own bite marks were minutes ago. "Thank you for not draining me, by the way, when you drank from me again, but...when I drank from you in return, well...nothing happened, right? I mean...nothing *will* happen, right? There won't be any...consequences? No problems that might arise from a human drinking vampire blood?" I was so overcome with being inside her and feeling every inch of her against every inch of me that it hadn't occurred to me what she'd done, what I'd done, what we'd done, till afterwards, when we lay side by side and stared at each other and at the night, all bare and beautiful and full of bliss.

She shrugs. "No, I don't think so."

"You don't *think* so?" I hear myself panic slightly.

"No, no, no. There isn't. There aren't any consequences. You're gonna be fine!"

"You sure?"

"I promise," she huffs. "Are you afraid of...?"

"Turning into a vampire?" I stiffen. "Yes."

She shrugs. "It's...okay. Again, that's just still...your preference." But I can hear the sadness in her voice, even if it's subtle. "I promised not to turn you, Timothy, no matter what. And a promise is a promise, isn't it? Nothing's going to happen to you. You...really do have OCD about it, don't you? Wanting to...die human..."

I sigh, shrug. "OCD, stubbornness, trauma—whatever it is, I've got it, and that's that. I wouldn't change any of it for anyone or anything."

The sadness in her eyes says: *Not even me?* And, in my head, I say: *Oh, Lynnette...it really has nothing to do with you. But every second I grow closer to my own limited lifetime, I also grow closer to loving you more and more for this one lifetime. Maybe you will find someone like me again, maybe you won't, but I will die knowing that I could never find someone like you again even if I was crazy enough to live for another hundred or thousand years. I will die, and you will remain special, and I will rest, serene, in having known and loved you for as long or as little as I humanly did. I know myself too well to choose an immortal life, you see, because, with enough of a routine, I might grow tired or bored again, and, with enough time in our endless* All the time, *you might start to see the absolute worst in me, the things that have caused some other people to stay away from me while those things currently draw you in, and you might even begin to despise me, and the moon, while I have eyes to see it and human breath to bask in its presence, should forbid that I ever live on this planet long enough to despise a stunning siren such as you.*

But all I say in response to her sad silence is: "Well...speaking of promises...sometimes, a promise that's made...ends up being the worst when it isn't kept, because a promise is *made* to be kept—but, sometimes, once in a blue moon...a promise ends up being perfect *exactly* when it isn't kept. And, Lynnette, I promised myself...that I wouldn't engage in any personal kills, and I'd always clean up after myself. And, here you are, and you've successfully managed to...get me to break my own rules. The promises I've made to myself."

"And this is...a bad thing?" She cranes her neck and looks at me with her wide, worried eyes, afraid that she's caused me to betray myself.

I shrug. "I don't know yet." I do have a bad feeling, but I don't know how to tell her that—maybe it's because I've done things a certain way for myself for so long and I never expected anyone, not a partner or anything else, to come along and change that so drastically for me. "For now...what I do know...is that everything is perfect. Promise or no promise. Broken promises or kept ones."

"You know...a promise is a thing you should keep no matter what, Tim."

I beam at how she calls me "Tim." I cup her cheek with my hand. "I am your promise, Lynn." *Tim and Lynn. How perfect.* I lean forward till our foreheads touch. "And you're mine."

She beams at me, but her eyes stay blank, black. "But you always break your promises."

Her reply is unexpected. I can't tell whether she's teasing me or if there is some terror that dwells within her. I don't even know where such fear might be directed—towards the fear of losing me, or towards...*me.* Unpredictable me. I simply give her a quizzical look—maybe she's just pointing out the hypocrisy here, that she should be as allowed to break her own promises since I break my own, too, whatever kinds of promises they may be—but before I can figure out an appropriate way to respond, she's already standing up and reaching out for me with her hand.

"C'mon," she offers, "I can get you back to your room."

"What about all our stuff? Our clothes?"

She puts her hands on her hips. "Our clothes aren't really *clothes* anymore, are they?"

I look at the ground, seeing that she's right and all our clothes really are a torn-up mess. "So, we're...really not going to clean up?"

"Well. If you were a vampire, like me, you'd clean up the way I do—by drinking and slurping and licking everything up. But you're not. You need to get out of your own head, Timothy. No, we're not going to clean up tonight. If you're worried about us being seen or even found out later—we won't be." *She could almost add: "I promise."*

And then I pick up my backpack and pocket knife, and she picks me up in her arms, both of us naked, and, with her super speed, we fly through the streets, unbothered and unparalleled by a single thing.

CHAPTER NINE

# NURSED TO LIFE

We don't wait to see each other after that. We can't. Only the kept promise of *All the time* would be more than enough for us. She gets off work early to see me in the early morning. She *can*, because she is magical, and no human on earth except for me could make her listen to what they said or demanded, and she is effortlessly effervescent when she skips up to me in front of her townhouse in the dark.

"How was work?" I ask her.

"Well. Sunny's missing. And everyone cares *so* much. Yadda-yadda-yadda. Blah-blah-blah." She rolls her eyes. "Janie is content—though, of course, she's too kind to show it, to show how little she actually cares about what happens to someone as soulless as Sunny. Stevie C.'s heartbroken. But it's okay—that's to be expected from a moron like him. I mean, what can you do, right? Bitches are always also into other bitches. But I think I might've managed to make him feel better today at work." Her voice is strange, like she's hiding some sort of sick secret. I don't like the way she sounds. It sends the kind of chill through me that is so far from the kind of nice, perfect chill she'd sent through my body last night.

"Why'd you do that, if he's such a bitch and all?"

"It was the human in me, I guess."

*Or was it the monster in you?* I shake the eerie echo away. "*How* did you manage to do that, to make him feel better?"

She shrugs like she did last night—as if she doesn't know a damn thing, and as if, even if she did, she wouldn't tell me or show me. "I don't know. I just spoke to him, I guess. Tried to behave...as humanly possible. Said all the usual things empathetic people are supposed to say to each other—that he'll move past this, that everything will get better with time."

I try to ignore the knot in my throat and I walk on with her, towards our kill for the time being. Not a personal one this time, thank goodness.

The nights and early mornings pass like this, and the interesting, fun, new thing is that she starts to kill more and more like a human rather than a vampire. She drinks, sometimes, but she doesn't really use her super speed or strength as much for the next few nights—not as obviously, anyway. She seems to be trying to match my tempo, trying to see what things are like from my eyes the way I've always wondered about her perspective—without either of us becoming what the other is. It's all so beyond anything I could've ever imagined, so flawless.

But I can't shake the feeling, as time passes, that, somehow, we are being followed, being stalked the way we stalk so many others. Followed like a promise. It makes me feel empty and numb and all sorts of *wrong*—but Lynnette is here, and she can hear everything and feel everything and see everything that I can't. She can protect us both, if something that I can't see coming just so happens to occur. I can trust her to do that, because we love each other and we'll keep loving each other, *All the time*. Because partners and friends and best friends and lovers—they keep their promises to each other, against all odds, even if they're killers and killers are inherently untrustworthy.

•   •   •

It's Friday night. Lovely out. Lovely Lynnette with her hand in mine. We stroll through the streets, eyes searching, always secretly seeking out more struggles and screams.

I can't help but stare at her, sometimes, even as we just walk side by side. I can't believe that I finally did it, that it finally happened for me—I got my Bonnie, my Clarice-slash-Will, my hunter at heart, my animalistic aggressor in arms, a cute little fellow killer right by me for the rest of my little life.

She leads me in the dark, and then I see that she's led us both to a dead end. "Oh, whoops," she says innocently. "Sorry, I thought I saw some—

never mind, let's just turn back." And she leads me back towards the opening of the alley we've entered—

Three young men stand there. Two of them are holding onto knives. The last has a pistol in his hand.

*Has the universe turned on us, then?* This is all I can think the second I see the three strangers. *Is there religion and is there a God and have Lynnette and I failed in being as justice-bringing as we'd like to believe we are, and is this karma, the world's revenge on the two of us?*

Lynnette doesn't move. "Stevie?" she says.

The man she's addressing speaks. The one with a gun—the kind of weapon I'd never be caught dead using as a serial killer, the kind that lacks intimacy and takes the high of the moment away, the kind someone would use if they wanted to get the job done and nothing more than that.

Stevie. Stevie C. from work? Janie's crush. The guy with enough brains to work in a hospital but not much more than that. The one...dumb enough to be grieving Sunny.

"It was you," he growls.

*What are you? Your partner, I hope.*

"You said as much," he barks, his voice full of rage and regret. "We've been following you enough. A few nights now. We *know*."

Lynnette steps forward. "If you know...then you must have a death wish." It frightens me a little, what she says. *She* frightens me. She always frightened me, *All the time*—but, now, there is no fascination to go hand-in-hand with that fear. There is only uncertainty and terror stuck in my gut, sticking to the insides of my chest like an awful ache, an awful ache all over me, like my own body's warning me of something. "What do you *think* you know, anyway, Stevie?" This is clearly a standoff. A standoff, in an alley, in the kind of place where nothing felt like much of a standoff before because we were the victors every single time—how poetic. I feel like vomiting— why don't I feel good? Why does this feel different than every other time that we've been in the dark together like this? Why don't I feel confident or powerful right here, right now?

"Everything." The two young men at his side stay silent like obedient dogs.

"Like...?" Is Lynnette toying with him? Does she know that we're going to be okay? We'll be okay, won't we? They're just three guys. She can take them all out in a second. I can make sure she doesn't get hurt, too, watch her back.

"You're freaks. Killers!" Stevie shouts angrily. I can barely make out what he or the other guys look like in the dark, but they're all bigger than me, bulky and broad-shouldered.

He doesn't say anything about her being a vampire. And then I remember how, for the past few nights, Lynnette really wasn't doing anything vampire-like. Did she know we were being followed by them? Did she say something to him in the hospital to lead him to us? Was that her plan, to make sure he would find out about us, only to meet his own end idiotically at our hands? Will we kill the three of them tonight, too, and will she act like more of a vampire tonight when she drinks from them?

"You killed Sunny," Stevie spits.

Lynnette takes another bold step forward. "She deserved it," she spits back.

I frown at her response. What is she *doing*? Does she *know* what she's doing? She sounds like a part of her that's been hidden away from me this whole time—hidden away from herself, too—is coming out now. Cocky. Proud. Arrogant. An unstable disaster—more than the kind that even a vigilante-like serial killer could be. Someone I don't recognize. The kind of partner I never wanted or needed...

"She. Deserved. It," Lynnette threatens, her teeth clenched. And all I know is that I don't feel good. *I don't feel good, I don't feel good.* I don't feel the way I always do when we're about to end someone's life. I don't feel the high coming for me. Tonight, in this alley, I have not become a killer or a coward—I have simply become...confused. That is how Lynnette is making me feel right now, with her strange words and her strange demeanor, behavior that I'd find to be incredibly sexy if not for the knot still stuck in my throat and my gut and my chest.

Stevie yells out, "Fucking get 'em!" through his teeth.

And then, in an instant, bullets fly from the gun in his hand and the other two men are running at Lynnette and at me and I don't think I'm shot but Lynnette is screaming, "Run, Timothy!" but I don't know where the fuck I'm supposed to be going because it's dark and there's nothing but a dead end up ahead.

When I turn around, I can see Lynnette moving in quick, blurry, whip-like movements—biting into one of the other men, sucking deeply from a burst vein of his, and then all I can see is the other man trying to attack Lynnette, too.

But Stevie—Stevie's coming right at me with his gun, an eye for an eye, and it doesn't matter if I move and it doesn't matter if I lunge forward and stick my blade in him. This is why I've never used guns and this is why I never went after people who might've had guns on them—nothing with recognizable or traceable bullets and nothing that'd make noises louder than human screams, noises loud enough to attract attention. Stevie's not interested in intimacy tonight, not even the intimacy that should come with taking revenge—he just wants to be done with it, done with everything, done with what he set out to do. He doesn't want to take any more time not being able to deal with the grief he holds over Sunny's murder.

I don't know what I'm doing anymore—I *always* knew, but it seems that Lynnette has now compromised even that, even my knowledge. There is a gun facing me—again, the kind of thing, the kind of confrontation I never wanted, not as a human being or as a serial killer. Guns are disappointments. Guns are lazy. Guns are offensive. Even the moon scowls down at them, the quickness and impatience with which they defeat and destroy and deafen.

I reach for my pocket knife. For once in my life, I am sure it will do nothing, and even so, this is the other half of what it means to be human, and this is the other powerless half of what it means to always mostly hold power—and the last time someone held a gun at me was when those police officers from the bar at least gave a damn about surrender whereas Stevie won't care now even if I do hold my hands up—and I've already spent a decade killing without being successfully killed or captured, and...if it's time for me now, then, I'll go as politely as a promise.

Stevie shoots, and I feel the bullet hit me right in the shoulder. He shoots again, and pain like no other I've ever experienced pierces me right in the chest.

"Timothy!" I hear Lynnette scream as I fall to my knees with a groan, hear my pocket knife fall to the ground. I can barely see, with muddy vision, what seems to be Lynnette snapping Stevie's neck in a flash. She's beside me on the ground now. She's whimpering. She's crying. She's shaking. She's calling for me. "Timothy?" She shakes me gently. "Timothy! No-no-no—"

But doesn't she see? Can't she see the blossoming, bittersweet understanding in my eyes? The acceptance with which my face relaxes as the flush from my skin starts to fade? Can't she see that it is simply my time now, and it is time for me to go, for her to let me go?

"It's okay," I wheeze as she puts my head in her lap. I have very little breath left, but I will use it to tell her that I love her and that this is just a part of life, *my* life—one that I always expected, whether it was now or many years later, one that was bound to find me sooner or later, one that would come for me just as I caused so many others to see this part of life, so many times, so soon, so late, but always, *All the time*. "Lynnette...I love you," I breathe. "It's okay. It's just..."

"Sh-sh-sh, I'm here, I'm here." Her cries stiffen, stifle, like she understands something, if not me. But I hope it's me she understands.

"Just my time," I manage, agony continuing to rocket through me as everything around me, as the night, grows even colder than before. "It's okay...promise..."

*Promise...*

I can feel her shaking her head above me and can barely see it as tears fill up my blurred eyes.

But it really is fine. I wish I could offer so many words of soothing and surrender, but I can't speak—it hurts too much and I feel like I'm drowning or floating or both and I can feel the wetness of all my own blood pooling out under me—and all I can do is look up at her with my emptying eyes, wondering if she understands, pleading with her to understand and wipe her own tears away. Everything's alright.

*Everything is as perfect as it will ever be when you, Lynnette, living and dead, are right beside me, living or dead. Lynnette, my love, can't you see? Can't you understand? We had months together, a few wonderful months. It could be said that, perhaps, we lived a whole lifetime during those few months, those several weeks. It was the kind of life I'd always wanted. And only when I was brave enough to seek it out did I find it—find you. It was my lifetime, and I lived it as I saw fit, and now I guess I just have to be done living it, and that is more than okay. This is the natural order of things—a killer, sooner or later, always gets killed, in one way or another. I would have much preferred to die this way than to have died doing something other than what I loved—even if I just tried tonight and failed. Trying to do something you love and failing in doing it—that's still just a part of loving it.*

*And I loved every second I spent with you, Lynnette. I don't regret a single moment of it. I don't believe in much. But I believed in myself and I believed in you and I believed in us. I believed in the moon and the night and the hunt and our bloodwork and the warmth all of it brought me—the warmth you brought me, Lynnette.*

*Most humans worry about their legacy, what they'll leave behind when they die. I never worried about that, though, because I knew my legacy—I knew that it was a beautiful thing to take rotten seed and rotting life during the small span of my own life, to do something only humanly limitless only during such a humanly limited frame of time. And, besides, Lynnette—now, you will carry my legacy with you. You will do what we once did together. You will haunt alleys and bars and abandoned, acidic places, keeping an eye out for abandoned, acidic people, monsters under human skin, more monstrous than I, a serial killer, or you, a vampire, could ever even dream of being. Pure evil—and you will drink from pure evil, and you will continue to shine under the moon, and you will carry my torch with you. You will carry our bloodwork with you, Lynnette, and keep memories of us alive that way, the same way you'd continue being a kind nurse even in the face of cruelty and you'd haunt old restaurants you can no longer eat at to keep memories of your human parents and all their nursing alive. Because the ones we love always stay alive within us. And I will always be found in the blood-bag breaks you continue to take at work, in the bad blood you continue to spill, Lynnette.*

*I understood the breadth of what I did and what I could do. There is nothing more powerful, nothing more capable of divine and delicate design and simultaneously capable of destruction, than the human being. Even after they are buried six feet below, some humans still manage to leave so much design and destruction in their wake—husbands who left their pregnant wives too soon, children who left their parents too soon, abusers who left their victims too late.*

*And everyone who has ever done a terrible thing or has been a terrible person will still be mourned by someone out there. Even the countless assholes and bitches I've gotten rid of over the years—I did the world a favor and secretly blessed it, but someone out there, maybe another asshole or bitch, found a reason to cry. Even thieves and corrupt politicians and pedophiles and rapists are mourned. Even I will be mourned—me, the serial killer, wolf under black sheep's fur, someone who kills for justified and good reasons in my mind, someone who will be mourned by a partner, a friend, a best friend, a significant other who is a vampire nurse.*

*This was all there was to my life, Lynnette, and it was such a lovely one while it lasted. And getting to know you and knowing you and knowing how much I love you—that was great while it lasted. Everything and everyone comes to an end—even me. Maybe even bloodwork—all our love and the simplest of human things, like cuddling or eating out, overtook our bloodwork every now and then, and conquered our most primal and basic killer desires. And, perhaps, maybe even you, someday, long-lasting, limitlessly living Lynnette.*

*It's okay. I promise. This is one of the most sincere promises I've ever made, and I'm making it to you, Lynnette, on my deathbed in the middle of a cold and dark street. It is the last promise I'll ever make—and, so, I can't break it. And you—you are going to be okay without me, Lynnette. I promise.*

She looks so much like the moon as the world around me grows as black as her eyes.

•   •   •

"Keep him breathing!"

I remember the time Lynnette carried me to the hospital after I was attacked.

"He's still in PEA."

I remember the night she and I first met.

"Entry wounds. Right shoulder. Left chest."

I'm not being carried by anyone now—I'm laying down on something with small, squeaky wheels and there's an oxygen mask on me and I see bloodied teal-gloved hands and more teal and blue and green fabric on me and all around me. This much I can tell.

"Bullets still inside."

Unrecognizable voices are all around me. And so much teal. Light blue. Light green. Turquoise. So much light...

"Pressure on the wound. Keep him stabilized."

"Oh, shit, Lynnette, is that your friend?"

"They've got to save him, Janie," I hear Lynnette sob deeply.

•  •  •

"We're gonna lose him!"

Lynnette moans loudly from far away. "No-no-no-no-no-no—"

•  •  •

No one is nearby. I'm still laying down. White light is still shining brightly from above.

In a blur as I fade in and then out again, I can see everyone, dead, vague figures and outlines of people, still and bleeding on the floor of the room they've taken me, the room they've tried to operate on me in. Doctors, nurses. Other patients. Everyone.

Lynnette, at the center of it all, standing, drenched in blood.

•  •  •

I don't know how to feel. Because I feel everything. When I wake up, I feel everything, like a newborn baby. I am scared, soothed, startled. I am suffocating, summoned, set free. I am a hundred stars, longing to be near the moon. I am everything—everything but lonely. I feel everything, but I don't feel alone.

I can't pin myself against one feeling. I wake to a wave, a myriad, a constellation. I wake to the vampire nurse, the moon, at my side again. I do not feel terrified of her. And, yet, when I wake, my bottom lip is trembling ever so slightly, and my eyes are twitching as I try to absorb her in her entirety.

"Hey, sleepyhead."

Her voice—such a dreamy and delicate voice. The voice of the moon.

I blink. Open my eyes.

And the world comes at me with so much full force that I flinch. The world is...loud. And everything is clear. Bright. We are in the room in Lynnette's house that's like a hospital room, and every shade and shape and shine of every lightbulb in the room is too vivid, too violent in the way it all presents itself to me, every piece of decor, every piece of furniture, even the absurdly soft hospital mattress I'm on.

"Sorry, you'll get used to it," she says. I must've been so unconscious, so *dead*, that everyone's efforts to bring me back to life caused me to come back to life feeling the way I do now: overwhelmed.

I grasp at my throat and wheeze. "Thirsty," I manage.

She already has something in her hand, something like a bag of energy juice that she brings up to my mouth. I can't see it—it's still so hard to focus on any one thing—but it smells absolutely divine. "Go on, take a few sips. Drink."

I do, and it's delicious. It's all there is. Coppery. Sweet and somehow salty at the same time. It tastes like the stars and the moon, like the dark, delectable night. It's *everything*.

*And I've tasted it before. As a human.*

My eyes go wide in realization and I flinch away from...*the blood bag*. I start panicking, and start breathing heavily. "Lynnette, what did you do?" But Lynnette won't meet my eyes. "Lynnette, what happened?" I start screaming: "What fucking *happened*? What did you fucking *do*, huh, Lynnette? What the fuck did you do?!" Louder: "What did you fucking do to me?!"

Her voice is not dreamy or delicate now. It is dark. Dangerous. The moon and all its promises have no place here. "I'm sorry, Timothy. I know I made you a promise. But I'm so sorry."

## CHAPTER TEN

# THE NURSE AND THE NIGHT

"I did what I had to do. I'm sorry. I needed to be sure that if something happened—"

"Shut up." There are no bullet holes, no wounds, not even any fang marks on me. It's like nothing ever happened to me at all.

She doesn't shut up. "I wanted you to live forever. Like me. When I fed you my blood—it stuck to the human blood in your system like glue till you died and then it took over like—"

"Like poison. Bleach. Acid."

"Like water. All I had to do was bite you after you drank, and you'd turn. You just died first. I told you there'd be no consequences to drinking from me. I lied. *Had* to. I had to be sure that you'd survive anything that could happen to you. To us. That you'd survive with me. Like me."

"Shut up."

But she keeps going. "You said once that I saved you, twice. That I saved you from yourself both times, before we even met. I was like an angel who saved you. So why can't you just see this as the same thing? Me, your angel, saving you once more."

"Shut. Up."

But she just keeps talking. "I told you once that nothing between the two of us would be short-lived. It's what I believed. It's what I still believe, what I'll continue to believe—*All the time*. And it's what I'd like for you to believe, too."

"Shut. Up. Lynnette."

She hands my pocket knife to me—she surely picked it up after I dropped it and started dying—as if it's supposed to be a gesture of good faith. I grab it from her roughly. "I know I also told you once that I'd never force you into something you didn't want. I promised."

"Shut up!" I lunge, and my speed unfurls, and I'm across the room in a flash. I wobble, steady myself. I punch the walls of her house again and again. "Shut up, shut up, shut up!" My fists move through the walls like the house is made from nothing.

"But I tried to save you the normal way. The human way. But nothing worked. They couldn't keep you alive—keep you breathing." I can hear her trying to hold back tears, her voice making a choking noise as she speaks. "Nothing else was going to work."

"Just shut the fuck up!" I speed over to her and hold her against an unbroken wall, my silver knife at her throat. "Shut the fucking fuck up!"

But she still keeps trying to explain and justify what she did to me, her neck stiff and her chin up with the silver under it. "This was a desperate, special situation, Timothy!"

"All your talk," I gasp, sobbing, helpless. "About how you'd never turn someone against their will. About how you were turned without consent, and yet, how you'd never change a thing about being what you are—what is that, some kind of metaphor for surviving abuse? What, you're stronger now because something happened to you, something you couldn't control or stop?"

She has forever now—she won't need to stop anytime soon. She can take all her time now. Now, she has her *All the fucking time*. Her fucking little *All the time*. "I nursed you to life the way no other doctor or nurse could. The way no *human being* could."

I take my knife away from her throat and step away from her, thinking, my brain rattling, a million things and a million sensations fleeting through every part of me at once. "You said something at work, didn't you? You said something to Stevie C.—wasn't he supposed to be such an idiot, the kind that would never catch on to anything at all, a fake and brainless son of a bitch, like yet another kind of nurse who isn't meant to be a nurse? You did something at work, said something to him to lead him onto us, to get him to catch on to us, or else he would've never have figured it out and he would've never known—because who the fuck on earth could ever figure out that it was you and me, huh? Serial killer and vampire, nobody, nothing—anybody, anything, everything to each other, *everything*. You said something. You wanted me to be killed. You wanted me to die. You wanted me to become like you, wanted to turn me, wanted to have me forever—and you would've done anything to have it all set in stone. Have *me* set in stone. And you *did*. Didn't you? Didn't you?!"

She says nothing, and I scoff. Love really is this unwinnable game. And I, the fool, have rushed into everything with Lynnette, and we did fall in love and we kissed each other goodnight, but now this is all just a big mess I don't know how to get myself out of—and I almost always figure out how to get myself out of a mess. But those were mundane messes, the kind that only someone mortal could cause—this is so much more than that now, and I'm fucked.

"It was all just an excuse, wasn't it? I got killed...then everyone failed to save me at the hospital, and you killed them all, too. Maybe that's why you even chose to get rid of *Sunny*—so that Stevie would have a reason to come after us, to come after *me*. Oh, was *that* your mastermind plan? Fuck. You wanted to do something different, for once in your life. Something other than playing pretend and being nothing more than just a human nurse. Which isn't even something to take for granted, by the way! I'm sure your parents told you, time and time again, just how many people out there would die—no, kill—to be in your position! I'm not an academic, I'm not employed—and even *I'm* aware of how fucking difficult nursing school must be!"

She doesn't confirm nor deny anything. All she says is: "I loved being a nurse, seeming normal. I just loved myself more, what and who I really am beneath that, *beyond* that, who I could be if I only *let* myself, the way you taught me. And, more than that...I just loved *you* more. So much more."

"Big mistake. Or didn't your parents ever tell you, ever warn you, back when you were human? Never give up your career or your passion for someone you love. If they don't last, at least the work will."

"I didn't give anything up. You...are someone I can perform bloodwork with. You are someone I am passionate about."

"You thought, once, that maybe work was all you had, all there was to your life, human or not—now, you figure, maybe you were wrong. Well, once, I thought that maybe trying to find a partner, to be less alone in the world was all I had—and, now, I figure maybe I was wrong."

"I gave you life, Timothy. I've given you a *new life*."

"You took my life away from me!" I choke, my throat burning from all the screaming and still from my remaining thirst—the new bloodlust she's forced onto me. "You knew what I wanted, how I felt about living the way you do! How I wouldn't trade anything for being, and *dying*, human! I mean, you knew, Lynnette, you *knew*. You knew me better than anyone else, because I never *let* anyone else know me the way you did. You were my partner, Lynnette. My friend. My best friend! You were the love of my life!"

"I *am* your partner, your friend, your best friend. The love of your life. I *am*—"

"And now—and now you've fucking betrayed me, too. You've gone behind my back, too, and you've stabbed me there. And you think you're better than a human being? You're fucking worse, Lynnette. Fuck you."

"I am the love of your life and I always will be. *All the time*, Timothy."

"You were. You're not anymore."

"You're just in a bad mood about all of this. Time will pass, and things will get better. For you. For *us*."

I shake my head. "Life is meaningful and special because one life is all we get."

"So you're saying my life isn't special?"

"Your life didn't seem all too special till I came into it!" I yell. "You wanted a partner as much as I did. You're a magnificent beast, and yet, you still wanted something more from your non-human life. That's the worst part—the longer you live, the more you want, the greedier you get, the more grotesque the world around you gets, till you've gone from being a serial killer to being godlike to becoming the fucking devil!"

"You don't believe in religion. There is no afterlife. There is no devil."

"But the thought counts! The idea, the *concept*, of it! Nothing is a sin when all you believe in is yourself and the one you love—until you fucking devour and destroy, not just an unlucky few, but *everything* around you! *Including* the one you love." She jokingly said we might get like one of those married couples who want to kill each other over time, once. And here we are now, screaming bloody murder at each other.

She scoffs. "What, so I've *destroyed* you? You thought I was a god, once, an angel, and now I'm the devil?"

I nod furiously. "Yeah. And, *now*...if it's what I wanted...I could destroy you, too. And I don't just mean with silver, sunlight, garlic, whatever the fuck. I mean...I could *destroy* you," I spit at her, waving the silver knife her way.

"You don't make any fucking sense, Timothy. You *love* me."

I shake my head sadly. "I love you. I love who you are. I admire you. I appreciate you. But I don't *worship* you. I don't worship what you are, even if you're more powerful than I am on a physical scale."

"Oh, because you're too *proud*?"

"Because there is *nothing* I worship more than the hunt, more than the night. As a *human*."

"But you also worship nothing more than having company. There is *also* nothing you dread more than being all by yourself. And now you won't have to be. *Ever*. We can be proud *together*. We can have fun at night *together*, because the day won't have us, anyway. We can worship this idea of killing bad people together—and drinking from them. Everything, we can do *everything* together. Always. I know...that this is new. Different. You're probably...very scared. It'll take you some time to get used to it. But you'll adapt. You'll see. If only you could let go of your stubbornness for a second."

I sit down on the hospital bed and sigh. "I'm not scared. I'm angry. Disappointed. Upset."

She sits down with me. I want nothing more than to be far away from her right now. "Okay. You're angry. Disappointed. Upset. But you'll get over it. You know why? Because I did. And we think about many things the same way, so I know you'll get over it, too. You'll understand."

"And what if I never do? What if I stay like this...forever? Angry. Disappointed. Upset."

"If you never forgive me...then..."

"You won't let me go, will you? You won't let us go our separate ways. You'll try to make me forgive you."

"Maybe...we can take some time apart. And we can meet again in a few hundred years or however long it takes for you to feel better about this and about me and about the fact that I fucking did this because I can't imagine a life without you."

"If we take some time apart, we'll never meet again."

"Then we won't take time apart. And you'll forgive me. Someday, you'll have to."

*Someday. All the time.*

I had a dream, once, to have a partner I could kill with. To have a friend. To have someone I could depend on by my side at night. *To have someone.*

*My dream will be real as long as I am alive.*

I'm not alive anymore. I am dead, so is my dream dead now, too? Did my dream die the second Lynnette found me? Did *she*, then, become my dream? If she was...then she isn't anymore. She can't be. Not with this betrayal. She has killed me. She has killed her promise, killed any potential future so full of more promises, a future that could be enjoyed *All the time.*

"You speak and behave and think like a god already, like a thing above the people you kill. You did, back when you were human. Why not embrace having become one now? Having become godlike."

"There was beauty to doing what I did and saying what I said and behaving the way I did without actually being a god, or being godlike."

"And there will be even more beauty to it now. To you. To us—we will be together. Forever. I will always keep you company. You've marked me already," she says, gesturing to the burn marks from the night we made love. "I'm yours, and you're mine. *All the time.*"

"Garlic," I sob hysterically, cradling my face in my hands, moaning into the palms of my hands. "I won't be able to taste *garlic* anymore. Or berry-flavored alcohol! No, instead of loving the taste of garlic—I'll *die* if I have any! You've fucking taken garlic and berries and alcohol away from me, you fucking cunt! *Garlic*! Fucking damn you! You fucking bitch!"

She hums "Put Your Head On My Shoulder" tearfully to me in response.

•   •   •

I try to kill myself over the next few days.

Using my own silver knife, trying to keep my tired eyes open when the sun comes up so that I can step outside. Holding garlic to my mouth and wanting to cry from the pain of it and also from the fact that I can't *love* the taste or smell anymore, and now instinctively loathe it instead.

I almost succeed a few times, but Lynnette saves me every time. She watches me, making sure the love of her life doesn't succumb to suicidal thoughts.

She finally has someone to eat with, and I finally have someone to wash the dishes with.

She keeps telling me I need time. Once she starts saying that, she doesn't stop. And once she doesn't stop, I have to think about cutting my own throat. And once I start thinking about that, I can't stop. And, so, since I can't stop, I have to think of ways to turn my deafening little dreams into relentless realities during the ongoing days and nights. But she just won't let me. She just won't let me go. She hides the silver knife away somewhere I'll never find it, says she wishes she could do the same with the sun.

*It's a shame you never really know who you're speaking with, who you're involving yourself with, till it's too late. That goes both ways, for both the predator and the prey.*

She tells me that I have all the time in the world to adjust to things now, to leave my human stubbornness behind me. She should have accepted me as I was and she should have left me unchanged—but love is all about change, little or drastic, or so she says. But I can try to kill myself or try to kill her if only to prove to her and to myself that love is actually all about basking in sameness, in sweet cycles. It's this thought that was part of what made me fall for her.

A few weeks later, she says I should stop drinking from blood bags, and she takes me on my first hunt at night. We choose a drunk misogynist. Our bloodwork is just as messy and beautiful as it has always been.

I look up at the moon. It seems to be singing down to me, yet another cover of "Put Your Head On My Shoulder" filling my head—one by the band The Lettermen. I can't tell whether the moon is mocking me or mourning for me or if it's just happy for me. After all this time, after all our *All the time*, I still can't tell.

I look at Lynnette, my flawless future, my flawless forever, my everything, my *All the time*, doing my best to ignore the little voice in the back of my head that tells me we are embarking on another routine together, she and I. A sinister cycle—sweet to her, still sick to me, sad like the cycle of loneliness I'd trapped myself in before. Bittersweet. A routine that will last longer than any normal routine should last. A routine that will go on and on and on for more than just one lifetime. *All the time*.

When she looks back at me with the loveliest of smiles on her face, the blood of our victim dripping from her fanged mouth like a pool of all the red berry-flavored alcohol I once tasted and sipped on and swallowed and loved in one local bar and then the next—all that taste that I can never have again—I can imagine that little night voice vanishing a bit more. I imagine myself replacing the voice with my own, sooner or later, across the suffocating span of our *All the time*:

*I love her and I'll always love her and she really is the perfect company to keep and I'd never do anything to hurt her.*

*I promise.*

ACKNOWLEDGMENTS

Thank you, first and foremost, to my family, friends, and family friends for all your support. Thank you for pouring your love into me so that I could pour my love into my work. To my mother: Mom, I'm not so sure I kept my promise to give you a romance with a happy ending, but, perhaps, with your rose-colored glasses on, you'll beg to differ.

Thank you to everyone at Black Rose Writing for seeing the potential in this story. *BLOODWORK* was a book I tried to write with a light hand. I had quite a bit of twisted fun writing this novel, trying not to take myself too seriously, trying not to ache over every single word the way the obsessive poet in me would.

And, to all my teachers, professors, classmates, colleagues, and, of course, my students: thank you for nourishing my need to learn and grow. To every English teacher and professor I've ever had: thank you for believing in my writing, for encouraging me to push myself further than I could've ever thought possible, and for helping me improve as a writer, as an artist, and, ultimately, as a person.

# ABOUT THE AUTHOR

Melissa Demirel is an author and screenwriter with a love for deliciously dark movies and novels. She received both her Bachelor's and Master's Degrees in English with an emphasis on Creative Writing from California State University, Northridge. At CSUN, she has also worked as a Writing Center Tutor in the Learning Resource Center, as a Supplemental Instructor for Freshman Writing classes, and as the Writing Consultant for Graduate Master of Professional Accountancy Program students in the David Nazarian College of Business and Economics. She lives in Los Angeles, California.

# NOTE FROM MELISSA DEMIREL

Word-of-mouth is crucial for any author to succeed. If you enjoyed *Bloodwork*, please leave a review online—anywhere you are able. Even if it's just a sentence or two. It would make all the difference and would be very much appreciated.

Thanks!
Melissa Demirel

We hope you enjoyed reading this title from:

www.blackrosewriting.com

Subscribe to our mailing list – *The Rosevine* – and receive **FREE** books, daily deals, and stay current with news about upcoming releases and our hottest authors.
Scan the QR code below to sign up.

Already a subscriber? Please accept a sincere thank you for being a fan of Black Rose Writing authors.

View other Black Rose Writing titles at www.blackrosewriting.com/books and use promo code **PRINT** to receive a **20% discount** when purchasing.

9 781685 133757